BOOK ONE OF THE LOST TRILOGY

LOST GIRL

ANNE FRANCIS SCOTT

For David,
Thanks for making life fun!
~

Love you to the stars and back...

"Plans can change in a heartbeat.
The wind shifts and the clouds rush in.
The air sparks and hums, and before you can even think
about running, you're standing in the middle of a storm."

— *Allison Weathers, LOST GIRL*

CHAPTER 1

The Treadwell Farmhouse
June – 2004

*I*T'S *MINE.*

A grand, old Victorian farmhouse. Allison Weathers hopped out of her Explorer and walked across the front lawn. The summer sun warmed her face as she gazed up at the turret that framed the first-floor library and upstairs master bedroom. Her friends back in Nashville hadn't believed she'd do it—make the move to a small town like Dawson Mills. Barely a speck on the map, one of them had told her.

Yeah. Just a peaceful little patch of the world tucked away from the bustle of the city. The town her mother had headed for all those years ago when she'd simply walked out the door without a word and—what?

Vanished. At least, according to the private investigator Allison had hired a few months back. Beverly Kincaid might have started for this small Tennessee town, but it didn't appear as though she'd ever made it.

Allison had been so young then. She hardly remembered the woman.

She could be dead for all you know, her dad had warned with a bitter edge in his voice as sharp as honed steel.

That was the point, though, wasn't it. She would *know.*

A warm breeze stirred the tree leaves, snatching a few unruly curls that had sprung loose from her ponytail. Allison brushed them back and closed her eyes, breathed in the fresh country air.

A tap on her shoulder had her whirling around.

"Jesus, Steve."

"Sorry, Sis." Her brother's deep-brown eyes sparked. "Little jumpy, aren't you?"

She glanced over at his van. He'd parked on the lawn, behind her Explorer, to make way for the movers' truck. "I didn't hear you pull up."

"Guess you were zoning."

Allison smiled. "Maybe." She watched the two recruits Steve had snagged—Tammy Bishop and Jeff Parker—hop out of the van and just stand there for a moment, gazing off to the north, where the foothills sloped into the Smoky Mountains. Her mouth curved in another smile. She had it all here: solitude, and a view to die for.

Steve took a few steps back, then surveyed the house. "So, this is it."

"Yep. What do you think?"

"It's huge." He shook his head. "Hell of a lot bigger than it seemed in the pictures you pulled off the Internet."

"I guess it is." Allison scanned the multitude of windows, moving her gaze up to where the metal roof took a steep pitch along interesting angles. Nearly 4200 square feet of living space. Much more than she needed, and the interior required some work. But, my God, the place was gorgeous. And she loved the idea of owning twenty sprawling, wooded acres to jog on.

The real bonus, though, was the wraparound, covered porch. Like many of the verandas on the Southern homes built in the early 1900s, it invited you to kick off your shoes and stay awhile.

She intended to do just that.

Steve glanced up at the mountains and eyed the dense tree line, frowning. "Not a lot out here, is there?" He held up a hand when

Allison shot him a look. "Okay, okay. We've already been over this. You're happy, I'm happy. But I gotta say it: I think you'd've been better off to stay put for a while." He shook his head again. "Christ, Sis, your career's just getting back on track."

So they were going to talk about this. Again. Allison sighed. "I realize that I need to focus on my sculpting, which I intend to do. But staying in Nashville for another six months or a year just wasn't an option. You know that."

It was called *a life*, dammit. Any woman within spitting distance of thirty-five had a right to make her own choices. And sure, she would probably make a few mistakes along the way.

It was what she needed.

Those heavy-lidded eyes of his latched onto her as the silence dropped, like a curtain, between them. Allison took a second to rein in her short temper—something she had supposedly inherited from her mother. Once Steve got an idea into his head, there was no giving it up. He was stubborn, just like their dad.

He had his own mother's smile, though, she thought, catching the flash of it—quick, warm. Contagious.

"I love you for caring. But."

"But," Steve echoed.

"End of discussion." Or not. A shadow flitted across his face. Steve, along with most of Allison's friends, had thought she had lost her frigging mind.

If only they knew the half of it.

The low rumble of a big engine coming from somewhere down the street had them both turning. "That would be the movers." Steve motioned for Tammy and Jeff. "Unload the kilns first, right?"

She nodded. "Have them back up to the garage."

He tapped a finger to his forehead in a small salute, and she hurried over to the detached garage, hoisted up the door.

Okay. Allison rubbed her palms together. *Here we go.*

The rumble turned to a dull roar when the movers' truck pulled around the last curve in her driveway. Grinning, she stepped off to the side, out of the way.

It happened fast—that all-too-familiar feeling of sick dread; it slammed through her, snatched the breath from her lungs and had her heart pounding. Eyes on her—cold, wicked. She whipped around, scanned the dense row of pines and underbrush along the western edge of her property.

No. No, just her imagination, that's all. The lunatic who had made her life a living hell was locked behind bars, where he damned well belonged.

Allison shuddered. His filthy hands on her, groping, and the cold, sharp steel pressed against her throat wasn't something she would likely forget anytime soon. But the nagging fear of some pervert trailing her, waiting. Watching...

She thought she had managed to shake it.

Airbrakes hissed as the big truck backed in and rolled to a stop. Focus narrowed on his sister, Steve walked over to her. "Hey." He kept his voice low. "You okay?"

"Fine." She summoned a weak smile.

He held her gaze with his. "Why don't I believe you?"

"Because you have a suspicious nature." Allison nudged his arm with hers. "I'm good. Really."

Steve shrugged. "Okay, then. Let's get this party rolling."

Twilight shadows had settled over the living room. Allison skirted around one of the unopened boxes and began switching on lamps. From out on the back porch, Steve's laughter drifted in through the open kitchen door, followed by a hearty burst of the same from Jeff.

Men. They were like children, only bigger.

"Those two are having way too much fun out there."

Tammy grinned. "Sounds like it." She gathered up empty boxes, began stacking them in the corner. Under the lamplight, Allison studied the clean, angular line of her jaw, those incredible high cheekbones. Oval eyes, dark green, like polished, nephrite jade. A flawless olive complexion.

She'd like the chance to sculpt that face from clay.

And she would just about kill to have Tammy's long, silky black hair instead of the fiery-red curls she had been born with.

Tammy wadded the last of the tissue paper Allison had used for packing her art-glass collectables and stuffed it into a trash bag. "Think I'll crash the party. You coming?"

Allison glanced around the room. It'd be nice to look at something other than boxes for a while, get some air. But she needed a few minutes alone. "I want to stay inside and relax. You go ahead."

Nodding, Tammy held up a hand, wiggled her fingers.

Alone now, Allison ventured over to a window and peered out. There were no city lights, no cars rambling by, just the vague, slightly beveled shapes of trees through the leaded glass, dark and colorless in the deepening shadows. Her gaze shifted to the far side of her property, where the thick row of pines had already faded into a wall of blackness.

A good place to hide.

She shuddered and moved away from the window. Much as she hated to admit it, her dad, as usual, had hit the mark when he had warned her: *Fine. Go wherever the hell you like. Your mind will tag right along.*

Allison sank down onto the sofa. Just once, she'd like to have a conversation with her dad without it erupting into a war of words. Just once. That didn't seem like a whole heck of a lot to ask.

And starting down that dead-end road was no way to spend what was left of her Saturday night.

She flicked a stubborn curl back from her face, then turned her focus to the spacious room, taking in the massive, gas-log fireplace with its stone hearth, the built-in oak shelving along one wall.

Time to think about something pleasant, like getting herself settled into this house.

What a job that had turned out to be.

Her gaze followed the glow of lamplight down to where it warmed the knotty pinewood floor, scratch marks and all. Unpacking was just the beginning. The hardwood floors needed refinishing—she glanced up at a corner of the ceiling where the plaster had peeled away—and there was a fair amount of patchwork and painting to do. But the real challenge would be the kitchen, with its ugly, chipped linoleum and stark fluorescent lighting—please; she didn't even want to go there right now.

All of those things were cosmetic, though. The house was sound. It had good bones.

Maybe that was the reason for the kinship she'd felt toward this rambling old place the minute she'd set eyes on it. Beneath the fading paint and peeling plaster, a strong structure waited for a little hard work and loving care to make it shine again.

A new life. For her and the house.

Allison closed her eyes for a second and breathed in the pleasant scent of aged wood and hearthstone. Then nearly choked on it when the soft shuffle of footsteps snuck up behind her. She whipped her head around, frowned at the open pocket door where she had expected to see Steve or one of the others.

Glancing over at the empty boxes stacked in the corner, she frowned again. One of them had probably just shifted. Or she was hearing things.

No. No more voices or strange, unexplained noises in the night. She was better now. She intended to stay that way.

Laughter erupted in the foyer. She pulled her mind back to where it needed to be, grateful for the distraction. Steve and Tammy bounded into the room. Jeff popped in behind them, his blond ponytail slung over the front of his shoulder, pale blue eyes lit up as he plopped down into the cushy chair angled next to the fireplace. "This place rocks!"

Allison grinned. "Couldn't have put it better myself."

Tammy eased onto the loveseat. Steve plunked down beside her and shoved a hand through sandy-brown hair that tended to fall whichever way it wanted. "Anything to eat around here?"

Food. Allison hadn't even thought about it.

A quick mental inventory of what she had in the fridge that they could throw together didn't pull up much. Cold cuts, cheese. The makings for a salad—maybe.

None of it sounded good.

"If you can hold off a bit, there's a small market up the road that delivers pizza."

Steve's jaw dropped. "They have *pizza* out here?"

Tammy rolled her eyes. "This is Dawson Mills, Steve-O. Not the moon."

He shot her a look, and Allison bit back a grin. It was good, for a change, to see someone pulling his chain.

They settled on pepperoni, the men compromising on mushrooms, and Allison grabbed her cell phone, checked for a signal, then scrolled through the contacts, found the number she had punched in for the Hilltop Market. While she ordered their pizza, Steve dragged over one of the boxes and dug out an old photo album, thumbed through the pages.

Tammy leaned closer, pointing at one of the photos. "Is that your parents?"

"Yeah. About twenty years ago." His gaze drifted over to Allison and settled there, unblinking.

It took about two seconds for her to interpret that brooding look.

He wouldn't.

"So, Sis, you going to give in and call Dad after you get settled?"

He did.

Heat rushed to her head. He was just like their dad—couldn't accept that she would work through things in her own time, her own way.

And she couldn't believe he had popped open this can of worms in front of Jeff and Tammy.

Damn his hide.

Eyes narrowed, Allison took a slow breath. "Listen up, little brother. If you know what's good for you, you'll change the subject."

Tammy and Jeff exchanged a quick look. Steve flashed a sheepish grin. "She's pissed."

No one laughed.

Trying to tamp down her irritation, Allison snatched the remote and switched the television on. Steve meant well, she knew that. And, yes, eventually, she'd have to pick up the phone, make peace with their dad, or at least make the effort.

An effort that would most likely be one-sided. Jack Kincaid wasn't the kind of man to change direction midstream.

She flipped through the channels, found an old mystery movie that had just started. After a few minutes, Tammy broke the silence. "I love this movie."

Jeff cleared his throat. "Yeah. It's a good one."

Allison glanced sideways at Steve. He gave her the innocent-little-boy look he always used to get her to crack a smile. It was working, too. She had to bite back the grin. But no way would she cave. It was just such a kick to see him grovel.

She ignored him, kept her eyes fixed to the images and motion on-screen, until the knock at her front door reminded her she hadn't eaten since breakfast. Her stomach was way past empty.

"That's the pizza." Steve got to his feet, reached for his wallet. "I'll get it."

Yeah, groveling was good. She liked him this way.

Her gaze trailing him through the open pocket door, Allison gave Jeff and Tammy a wry smile, then grabbed the remote, lowered the volume. "You guys want beer with your pizza?"

Jeff perked up at the offer. "Wouldn't turn down a cold brew."

"I'll second that." Tammy hopped up from the loveseat. "Need some help?"

"Sure." Now that she thought about it, an ice-cold Heineken would have gone down good a half-hour ago.

They skirted around the sofa. To get to the kitchen from here, they would normally take the open area behind the staircase, rather than crossing through the foyer and weaving back down the narrow hall. Less footwork. But the least Allison could do was to help Steve with the tip.

She dug into the front pocket of her jeans. And jolted.

Paintings—those she had stacked against one wall—seemed abandoned in the hollow stillness.

The front door was wide open.

CHAPTER 2

"STEVE?" WITH TAMMY AT HER heels, Allison ventured onto the front porch. Two red squares of taillights flashed then vanished around a curve in the driveway. Off to the side, pizza boxes sat on the shadowy section of porch, abandoned.

She called his name again.

A cricket chirped from somewhere out on the lawn.

Where did he go?

Allison cupped a hand above her eyes to block the glare from the porch light, and scanned the vast darkness, trying to shake off the disquiet that churned in her belly.

"Maybe he went out to the van for something," Tammy suggested.

Uh-uh. The cargo light would be on.

They both whirled around when something rustled along the side of the house. Steve popped out from the darkness, and Allison slapped a palm to her chest. "*Jesus!* You scared the devil out of me."

"*And me.*" Tammy glared at him.

"Sorry." He took the steps two at a time, scooped up the pizza boxes. "I heard voices around back, went to check it out."

Voices? Allison froze.

Under her brother's weighty gaze, she wanted to shrink right down through the floorboards.

"It was nothing," Steve said, still eyeing her. "Just a couple of kids."

Allison breathed a small sigh.

"They probably live next door, but…"

"What?" Tammy demanded.

He shrugged. "Not sure. It's just, well, one minute they were there, then"—he glanced at Allison—"you called me, I turned my head for a second. When I looked back, they were gone.

"Guess I scared them off."

Tammy grinned. "I can see how that would happen."

Lips curving, Steve narrowed his eyes. "Little girls with smart mouths don't get pizza."

She shot him a smug smile. "And bullies don't get beer."

With a half laugh, he started back into the house. Tammy was right behind him.

Was it just Allison's imagination, or had she suddenly become invisible?

She followed them inside, wondering what kind of parents would let their kids roam around after dark. Allison shut the door, turned the deadbolt. This wasn't the city. Most people probably knew their neighbors. Still…

Steve made some offhand comment that had Tammy rolling her eyes, then zipped back into the living room. Shaking her head, Tammy started for the kitchen.

Allison caught up with her. "I'll get the beer. You grab the napkins and—*Jeez.*" She shivered, rubbed her palms briskly over her arms.

"What's wrong?" Tammy flipped the light switch and the overhead fixture flickered on. Under the harsh fluorescent light, her complexion had an eerie grayish tint.

Allison tried to shake off the ungodly cold that had just blasted right through her. "It's like a freezer in here. Can't you feel it?"

Lips pursed, Tammy slanted her eyes. "No. But Jeff mentioned something about the kitchen being chilly when we came in from the back porch." She picked up the package of paper napkins and some Dixie plates off the counter. A frown shadowed her face.

"What?" Allison asked.

There was a blip of silence—less than a heartbeat—and Tammy grinned, her expression doing a one-eighty. "Honestly? I wouldn't notice the cold unless I had icicles hanging off my nose. I've been told I keep my apartment like the inside of a meat locker.

"Maybe there's a problem with the AC—the airflow or something."

Allison shivered. "I guess." But the inspector she'd paid to look at the house hadn't mentioned any problems. Could be that the unit just needed a routine servicing.

She put it out of her mind for now and grabbed the beer from the fridge. When they walked back into the living room, Steve was already wolfing down a last bite of pizza, and plucked up another slice. Allison passed him a beer. "Save some for the rest of us."

"Got two here," he managed through a mouthful. "Help yourselves."

She handed Jeff and Tammy a beer, then settled onto the sofa. The old movie was still on, black and white images moving across the screen, the volume muted. Allison scooped up a slice of pizza and bit in. *Man, it was good.*

"So, Sis,"—Steve raised a finger, swallowed—"you still planning to build a studio out here?"

Allison took a quick sip of beer, imagining herself lugging pieces from the middle bedroom upstairs down to the garage whenever she was ready to fire-up the kilns. Not her idea of working smart. "I really don't have a choice. I've got to get everything in a central location."

Jeff let out a low whistle. "That's going to cost some bucks."

"Really," Tammy echoed.

"I know." Just thinking about it made her cringe. "I've done the math. It's scary."

Steve nodded. "You remember how freaked I was when I moved my recording studio."

Allison just smiled. Steve had known darned well that it was one long stretch for a dollar, making the jump from the older part of downtown Nashville to the pricey Music Row location. He had done it anyway. And the change had paid off.

Something else he had inherited from their dad—business savvy, and good old-fashioned Irishman's luck.

While she ate, Allison listened to him ramble about the big-money deal he had brewing with one of the record labels. She supposed she'd get her chance soon enough. The August 1 opening at Maison's Gallery in Atlanta would be here before she could blink.

Her first exclusive showing in over two years.

She tried not to think about what would happen if it flopped. Buying this property had stretched her finances thin. She'd had to grit her teeth when she got the electrician's bill for running 220-volt service into the garage for the kilns. Twelve-hundred dollars and change.

God help her if the AC needed any major repairs.

Allison sipped the last of her beer. She noticed Tammy had slumped back in the chair, her eyelids drooping. "We're all beat. Why don't we turn in?"

Tammy yawned. "Sounds good to me."

"Hope we're all keeping close quarters tonight." Lust peeked through the smile Steve flashed Tammy, and Allison arched a brow. His gaze zipped over to Jeff. "Old house like this, out in the middle of nowhere,"—he lowered his voice, put on a stone-face for effect— "got to be home to at least one ghost. Wouldn't you say?"

Jeff nodded. He had the same serious-as-death expression pasted on his face.

"The old guy who lived here—didn't he die in one of the bedrooms?" Steve's gaze slid back to Tammy, his mouth curving. Her eyes went wide.

For a few crazy seconds, Allison struggled to keep her pulse from racing. She managed to shove back the raw panic that had spiked through her and took the remark for what it was—Steve just being Steve.

You little shit. She narrowed her eyes at him.

He ignored her.

"Tammy's bunking with me tonight." Allison bit back a grin when Jeff snorted. "You boys are sleeping in Mr. Treadwell's old room."

Jeff nearly choked on his pizza. With wicked satisfaction, Allison noticed her brother's slick smile, along with his summer tan, had just faded.

CHAPTER 3

ALLISON STEPPED OUT ONTO HER back porch, and took in the crisp, mountain air. She gazed at the brilliant blue sky, scanned acres of rolling green that edged up to lush woods. Listened to the absolute quiet.

Sunday. The only day of the week when the entire world seemed to stop and take a breath.

The panic attack she'd had yesterday—imagining someone watching her. It seemed foolish now. What was it Mae Davis with Mountain Realty had said?

Nothing much ever happens in this town.

And nothing, she thought, smiling, had gone *bump* in the night. So much for Steve's ghost theory.

She went through the routine of stretching thigh and calve muscles, checked the hair tie around her long mass of curls, then zipped her nylon jacket. The screen door opened and Steve poked his head out, yawning. He raked a hand through his tousled hair. "You going running?"

"Yep." Allison strapped on her mileage counter. "You guys help yourselves to breakfast while I'm gone."

His mouth stretching open in another wide yawn, Steve nodded and stuck a hand out to wave her off.

Allison jogged along the eastern edge of her property. In the distance, squirrels fussed and chattered in an agitated barking as she passed through patches of shade cast by oak and walnut trees.

The smile she'd felt tugging at the corners of her mouth began to fade. She had left her own... ghosts, for lack of a better word, behind. But why had her mother chosen this small mountain town? For the solitude? Or was it something else?

What had she been running from?

I hired a private investigator to look for Mother. That simple admission from Allison had leached the color from her dad's face. In less than a heartbeat, he shut down. Went rigid. But that hadn't stopped her from saying what she needed to say.

I overheard your conversation with Gran. She remembered shaking from the anger, the warm sting of tears. *All those years... Would it have been so difficult just to tell me where Mother had gone?*

I was trying to protect you.

Protect me. From what?

A straightforward question that deserved an answer. But he had only glared at her, grim, and tight-lipped.

Jack Kincaid was a stern businessman who ran his personal life with the same staunch discipline as with his many corporations. He knew how to get what he wanted, when he wanted it.

He was capable of a lot.

Not murder, though. Never murder.

Allison zipped around a clump of bushes, shoving the questions out of her mind. For now. Whatever had kept him silent for so many years would eventually come out. Secrets had a way of doing that.

The smooth, grassy terrain turned rocky. Allison adjusted her pace, her footing, and zigzagged around trees bunched close together, her lungs really starting to work. Up ahead the land took a downward slope. If she kept her direction, she'd come up on the creek Mae had mentioned that flowed along the back edge of her property.

Not today, though. She'd have to save it for tomorrow, after everyone had gone. Then she'd take her sweet time meandering down to the water, and get a good feel for the lay of her land.

Allison cut to the left, her breath coming in short bursts as she headed into a grove of Black Walnut trees, and the air began to stir. For just a second, she could have sworn she heard voices, distant and airy.

She slowed her pace, tilting her head to listen. Caught the faint echo.

Movement flashed in the corner of her eye. She stopped, breathing heavy, and scanned the edge of the woods.

There. Standing just this side of the tree line, sunlight bouncing off his bright gold hair. A young boy. He didn't look much older than eight or nine.

Even from this distance, she could feel the pull of his piercing stare.

Behind him, a small head of coppery red hair popped out from the woods and darted back in before she could get a good look. Then the boy was gone. Just—gone.

They were quick. She had barely blinked.

Allison stood there for a moment, getting her wind back. Her gaze shifted to a Monarch butterfly that flitted past the trees, where a patch of Black-eyed Susans painted the open hillside bright yellow. Kids roaming the woods alone. Did their parents know?

Wouldn't be easy, she supposed, keeping track of children with an entire summer ahead of them and nothing to do with it but explore. And it was none of her business, really, but if she caught them out here alone again, she intended to have a talk with them, at least find out where they lived.

Allison started back for the house. When it stretched into view, she paused, taking in the intricate angles that blended seamlessly with smooth curves, the country porch where she could lean back in one of her padded wicker chairs, with her feet propped up, a chilled glass of tea and a good book in hand. Looking out over acres of yard and beyond.

Home. This was home now. She was going to be happy here.

Steve popped into the kitchen just as Allison stepped in through the back door. She spotted the plate covered with aluminum foil on the table and inhaled the aroma of fried sausage, her mouth watering.

"Hey, Sis. We saved you some breakfast."

"Thanks." She waited while he pulled two cans of Coke from the fridge, then grabbed a bottle of water and gulped it down, aware of his eyes on her.

"Listen, what happened last night—sorry I brought up the thing with Dad, but he's worried about you. You've got to know that."

"Yeah, I do. And it's not something I want to talk about right now." Or tomorrow, or the next day, she thought. "Let's just forget it, okay?"

"Sure."

She grabbed a glass, filled it with orange juice. "What are you guys up to?"

"Hooking up your surround sound and the rest of the stuff—DVD player, stereo. It'll be a while before we're done."

Nodding, Allison eased into the chair that faced the large bay window. She peeled the foil away from her plate: sausage and scrambled eggs—still warm. Her stomach rumbled.

She grabbed her fork and dug in.

Steve popped the pull-tab on one of the cans and took a long swig. "So,"—he put a fist to his chest, belched—"sorry"—Allison waved it off—"what do you want to do with the empty boxes?"

The plan had been to keep them for storage, but they wouldn't last long in the cellar. It was too damp down there. She took a quick drink of juice. "Let's just haul them up to the attic for now. Thanks."

As he turned to leave, sunlight glinted off one of the panes in the bay window and caught her eye. "Hey, Steve."

"Yeah?"

"Those two kids you saw last night—what did they look like?"

He paused for a second. "I didn't get a good look at the little girl. She stayed back in the shadows. Guess she was shy. But the boy was kind of a country-looking kid—wore overalls, had blond hair, I think. Why?"

"Just curious."

Steve shrugged. Barely aware that he had left the room, Allison went back to her plate. Her gaze drifted past the shimmering windowpane out onto the back lawn. What were those kids doing out in the woods alone? There was a creek down there somewhere. Who knew how deep it was.

When kids got to playing, their little minds tended to wander. Anything could happen.

Anything.

For a while, she sat there, imagining the worst, until laughter drifted in from the living room. Allison gave her head a shake, glanced at her watch, and groaned. She gulped down the last of her juice, then whisked the dishes over to the sink, and ran upstairs for a quick shower.

"It'll be great in the winter, having this gas fireplace in your bedroom." Tammy ran a hand over the mantel. "I love the green marble."

"I fell in love with it too." Allison finished towel drying her hair, tossed the damp towel into the hamper. "Thanks for unpacking the big suitcase, by the way."

"No problem."

They both glanced over when Steve rapped on the door and poked his head in. "Hey."

The look Tammy gave him was something between a scowl and half-hidden amusement. "Can't you boys play by yourselves for a while?"

"Yeah, yeah," Steve shot back. "You girls come up to the attic as soon as you can. Think we found something."

He was gone before Allison could ask what. She hated when

he did that—made her crazy with curiosity. "Wonder what they stumbled onto."

"I don't have a clue." Tammy grinned. "But I'm dying to find out."

Allison slipped into some comfortable flats and they hurried down the hall, starting up the narrow wooden staircase that led to the attic. The stairs creaked and groaned beneath their feet. "Well, these are fun," Tammy muttered.

"Yeah. Loads." Allison hadn't even stuck her head up here, and she had forgotten the inspector had warned her about these stairs. Replacing the loose treads had just hit the top of her to-do list.

A single, bare bulb hung from a fixture in the center of the attic, casting a dim circle of light onto the plywood floor. The air was stale, heavy with dust. Allison wrinkled her nose.

Tammy squinted. "I can't see a thing."

"Me neither." They stepped deeper into the shadows, and Allison swatted back a thin, silky cobweb, cringing. She hated spiders. And she wasn't overly fond of dark, musty attics. Peering past the faint light, all she could make out were two vague silhouettes that seemed to shift. "Guys? Where are you?"

"Back here." Steve and Jeff popped out from a dark corner. "I brought this." Steve switched on the flashlight he was holding, ran the beam along the exposed rafters. "You've got more fixtures up there, but we couldn't find any bulbs downstairs."

He lowered the flashlight, the beam arcing over the large window that someone had boarded up. Allison wondered why anyone would cover it to begin with. The inspector had told her the window was fine. "What did you two find that's so interesting?"

"Over here." Steve swept the light across several pieces of dust-covered furniture stacked along the back wall. Most of the pieces had seen better days. Some were broken; others had simply outlasted the style of the times. And all of it, Allison thought, looked lonely.

Tammy rolled her eyes. "You two clowns dragged us up here to look at some old furniture?"

Allison shot Steve a look. "Well?"

"Yeah—no—I mean—"

Jeff's hand shot up. "It's like this: we hauled up the empty boxes, found that stuff"—he pointed to the furniture—"scattered all over the place. Right, dude?" Steve nodded. "We had to move it all out of the way and—"

"That's when we found this." Steve handed Jeff the flashlight, then walked over and turned one of the upholstered chairs on its side. Jeff held the light steady while Steve bent over to show them where part of the black mesh fabric on the chair's underside hung loose. "Material's been cut."

"Cut," Allison repeated.

He pointed out the large safety pins dangling from the fabric. "Came unpinned when we moved the chair."

It took her just a second. "What did you find?"

Grinning, Steve motioned to Jeff, and they headed back into the corner. "Follow us, ladies."

With the hodgepodge of furniture stored up here, Allison wasn't much surprised to see the worn, old writing desk. But when Jeff brought the light in closer, casting a spotlight on the marred surface, her breath hitched.

"Wow," Tammy whispered. "Is that what I think it is?"

"I believe so." Allison stretched a hand out, gently lifted the object off the desk. Smooth, supple leather the deep black of a moonless night. A solid brass latch, with a tiny keyhole in the center.

She brushed her fingers over the embossed, gold script on the front cover of the diary. *Bobbie Jean.*

"Hang on a second." Steve pulled a Swiss Army knife from the front pocket of his jeans, selected the tiny screwdriver. "We can try using this to pick the lock."

He held out a hand. Allison clutched the diary to her chest.

"I'm not sure we want to do that." A look of utter disbelief passed between Steve and Jeff. Tammy's rapt expression sank.

She didn't blame them. She was itching to read the thing herself. "Bobbie Jean was Jay Treadwell's wife."

"Treadwell," Steve broke in, "the old guy who owned this place."

Allison nodded. "The real estate agent told me that Mrs. Treadwell died suddenly—a heart attack. It was a long time ago. She was young, in her early thirties, I think."

She absently traced the elegant gold script with her finger. "They had two kids. The son lives with his family in Chattanooga now, and I think the daughter and her husband are in Memphis."

She looked up at her brother. "With both parents gone, I imagine they would love to have this."

"I disagree." Steve went on before she could argue. "The lady went to a lot of trouble to stash that book up here. Got to be something she wanted to keep to herself." He glanced over at Jeff, cocked a brow. "Wouldn't you say?"

"That'd be my guess."

Good point. Still...

Allison gazed down at the journal in her hands. Not everyone was lucky enough to have a piece of family history left behind. "I need to think about this for a while." Over their groans, she added, "For now, could we please just get back to work?"

By late afternoon they had unpacked most of the boxes, had worked themselves half-ragged hanging the new rods and curtains Allison had purchased for the windows. She'd left only two uncovered—the big bay window in the kitchen, along with the arched window in the middle bedroom.

Jesus, what a job. It had hit her after she'd climbed the stepladder so many times that her feet ached: she'd eventually have to clean every window in the house.

Not a project she was looking forward to.

Now, since she had insisted on feeding Steve and his friends before they started back to Nashville, they were all sitting at the picnic table out on the back lawn, munching on grilled burgers. It felt good to get off her feet, relax for a while under the warm sun.

Steve took a long pull from his Coke can, and gave her a thousand-watt smile. "Sure you don't want me to crack open that diary before we leave?"

Jeff and Tammy stopped chewing, their brows on the rise.

She sighed. She'd put the diary in her nightstand drawer, had almost forgotten about it. Almost.

"Maybe it was meant for you all along," Tammy suggested. "To read, I mean."

Allison frowned. It seemed a stretch to believe that some odd twist of fate had brought the journal to her—or her to it—just so she could pore over the secrets of a dead woman. "I haven't decided what I'm going to do with it."

They just stared at her. No one but Allison seemed to notice that the sun had just ducked behind a patch of clouds.

Finally, Steve shrugged. "Suit yourself. You might want to think about installing an alarm system, though."

"Why? You plan on sneaking back here with your little screwdriver?"

"Now there's an idea." His mouth curved. "But I was thinking of Old Man Treadwell—he might come looking for his wife's diary."

Steve being Steve again. Allison snorted, and wadded her paper napkin into a ball, tossed it at him. He snatched it in midair.

"Don't say I didn't warn you." Grinning, he tossed the napkin right back at her. "Just watch out for cold spots."

Cold spots. She shared a glance with Tammy, shuddering as her mind tumbled back to the desolate place where she'd sworn she would never go again.

"Hey." Tammy put a hand on her arm. "Are you okay?"

Allison took a breath to steady, and nodded. "I'm just tired. Guess the move finally caught up with me."

Eyeing her, Steve frowned. "You sure?"

"I'm fine." Allison glanced up at the dark clouds that had rolled in. "I think you'd better hit the road before the weather turns bad."

"You're changing the subject," Steve said, his tone flat.

True, but she didn't want him driving the long distance to Nashville in rough weather and told him so.

They hurried to finish eating, then scrambled to clear the table before the sky opened up. Allison helped load their overnight bags into the van. She thanked them for all their hard work.

Jeff climbed into the back and rolled the window down, gave her a thumbs-up. "You've got a really great place here."

Allison couldn't help but grin.

Before she hopped into the van, Tammy pressed a scrap of folded paper into Allison's palm and whispered, "Call me when you open up that diary."

With a half nod, she stuffed the paper into the pocket of her jeans, then felt the hard stare of her brother's deep-brown eyes as he walked up to her.

"I want you to think about calling Dad."

Allison opened her mouth, and he held a hand up. "I know you think Dad tries to run your life. I'll be the first to admit that he morphed into one big pain in the ass back in December, after that creep attacked you. But he was just trying to make sure you kept it together."

His gaze softened. "Hell, Sis, you were a wreck after you lost Ken."

Yeah, she was. One dreary January afternoon, and icy roads, had turned her life upside down. Over two years now, but it seemed like only yesterday when she had walked through their living room, answered the doorbell, and they had told her Ken was dead.

They had been married for five years, six months, and three days.

The memory still tore at her heart. But that didn't mean she would shatter every time a crisis happened in her life.

Steve was still searching her face for an answer. She wondered what he'd say if he knew the truth, why their dad had dragged her to all those doctors after Ken died.

"Dammit, Steve. This isn't about Dad. It's about me. I'm pissed at myself for letting him get control of my life. And I'll be damned if I let it happen again."

He nodded. "I get why you felt that you needed a fresh start. But—the thing with your mother, it's been a long time. Maybe you should just let it go."

Allison narrowed her eyes. "Could you? *Would you?*"

He swore. "No. Guess I wouldn't."

Sighing, she shook her head. "I just need to give it some time."

"Okay, okay." He raked a hand through his hair. "Seriously, though. I'm worried about you living alone out here in the middle of nowhere."

"Well, don't. I can take care of myself." A strong gust of wind lifted her curls. She glanced up at the dark, angry clouds. "*Now go.*"

Allison watched his van pull down the driveway, past the big oak tree, and then disappear around the curve. She felt the stillness wrap around her, and for the first time, realized just how alone she was out here.

But hadn't that been what she had wanted, the solitude?

Thunder rolled across the sky as the first big drops of rain splattered the driveway. Allison rushed back up to the house, just as the rain began pelting the metal roof.

CHAPTER 4

F ROM INSIDE HER LIBRARY, ALLISON could hear the wind whipping around the eaves. She placed the last book on the top shelf, trying to ignore the constant, angry whooshing of air. It was making her jittery.

Although it wasn't just the stormy weather that had kept her on edge.

Watch out for cold spots.

A joke, sure, but she hadn't been able to shake the disturbing image the words had triggered in her head—Jay Treadwell's unsettled spirit shifting in the shadows. And there were plenty of shadows in this big old house, a multitude of dark corners.

Damn Steve, anyway.

But, of course, he didn't know.

Allison scanned the rows of books arranged by author, then paced over to one of the windows. The sky was nearly black, still heavy with clouds. At least the rain had finally stopped.

Steve, she realized, hadn't called. He had promised to check in once he got back to Nashville. Allison glanced at her watch. Half past seven. The weather had probably slowed him down. That and he'd have to drop off Jeff and Tammy.

Well, Jeff anyway.

She smiled. Several times today, Steve had jumped in to help Tammy with whatever box she was unpacking at the time. Once or twice, his hand had brushed over hers, lingering just long enough for Allison to notice. She wondered if the relationship was serious, hoped so. She liked Tammy. The girl had spunk. She'd have no problem keeping Steve in line.

A yawn snuck up on her as she watched another mass of thunderclouds rolling in from the west. The dreary weather made her want to crawl off to bed, snuggle into a nest of down pillows and soft, quilted covers. Allison gave her head a shake, told herself she could sleep later. It wouldn't take that much to finish up in here.

She went over to her desk, grabbed the bundle of cords there, then got busy hooking up her laptop and combination printer/fax machine. She really didn't know what she'd have done if Steve and his friends hadn't pitched in to help with the move. Although her life would've been a little less complicated right now if they hadn't found that diary.

Some secrets were better left alone.

Or were they?

I was trying to protect you.

Had Bobbie Jean attempted to do the same for her own children? Her family? If that was true, why write down what she wanted to keep hidden, and risk having the diary discovered?

Guilt, Allison thought. The conscience could hold only so much weight.

How much of her dad's silence over the years had kept him tossing and turning at night?

Probably not much, she admitted with an irritated little shove of the power cord into her laptop. Once Jack Kincaid made a decision, he put it behind him. There were no second thoughts.

And Allison saw no reason to go digging into a dead woman's past, a woman with whom she had absolutely no connection. For good or bad, the diary belonged to Bobbie Jean's children now. Just as soon as she settled in, she'd talk to Mae Davis with Mountain Realty about forwarding a package to the family.

She pulled her mind back to work, and reached down to plug

the power-strip into an outlet. Outside, the wind gave a desolate moan that shot a chill up her spine.

The lights flickered.

Her gaze darted up to the ancient ceiling fan with its single globe. "Don't do this," she murmured.

The lights flickered again.

She jumped up, swore when she nearly tripped over a box, and hurried to the kitchen for the flashlight. Allison jolted when ringing pierced the silence. She snatched the receiver from the ancient wall phone that hung next to the fridge. "Steve?"

"Sorry, sweetie. It's just plain old Jackson from Atlanta. But how is that hunky brother of yours anyway?"

A snicker tickled the back of her throat. Jackson assisted Sheila Danson, the owner of Maison's Gallery. He was the most upbeat person Allison had ever met. He never failed to coax a smile from her.

"Steve is just fine. Now, please tell me you got my shipment and everything's intact."

"We did, and all is well. I finished unpacking the last of the pieces yesterday. *And girl—your work!*"

Allison's heart stuttered. She'd warned Sheila that her style had gone through a drastic change, had even e-mailed a few pictures to lessen the shock. "So... what do you think?"

"Love it! It's all so *edgy.*"

Edgy. Well. That was as good a description as any.

"Listen, sweetie." Jackson's voice had softened. "You just keep using your work to get through all the bad stuff and everything will turn out fine. Although,"—he let out a dramatic sigh—"why you would want to hide your gorgeous self away in some one-mule town is beyond me."

Allison bit back a grin. "Solitude is good for the creative soul, Jackson."

"I suppose. Listen, if I don't talk to you again before August first, remember you promised to wear that sparkly green number to the opening—the one that lights up those stunning eyes of yours."

"I remember."

"Good. Now, Sheila wants a word."

While she listened to a recorded announcement of the gallery's upcoming events, Allison dragged a chair over and sat. "Hey, girl. You get settled in?"

"Almost." She was fidgeting with the phone cord, made herself stop. "Jackson said you got everything okay. What do you think?"

The long pause that followed had Allison holding her breath. "Honestly? Those pictures really didn't capture the half of it. Your work is, well, dark."

"Dark-good or dark-bad?"

"That depends."

"On what?"

"Don't get me wrong, the work is definitely cutting edge. It's just that your public will remember a drastically different style. We'll really have to hype the new you. I'm going for a theme show—play up the mystery, the moody angle."

Allison rolled the idea around. Yeah, the theme angle could work. She liked it. "What do I need to do on my end?"

"Well, the press will be here, and Sandra Bergman, of course. You remember Sandra."

An art critic. For *The Times*. Sandra had worked the art circle for longer than what Allison could remember. The woman could make or break a career with just a few keystrokes.

"The old girl is still damned choosy about who she takes a shine to," Sheila noted. "But she's always liked your work."

"That was before."

"And this is now. You asked what you needed to do. I'll tell you. I want two or three more pieces along the vein of your *Dead Man Walking*. Smaller, though, and subtle—followers."

"Okay." But Allison's heart had just wrenched. *Dead Man* had come from a black, empty place inside her. She wasn't sure she could go back there.

"Another thing we'll need is a focus piece, something we can display in the front entrance." Sheila paused. "And this is imperative, Allison: it's got to have substance, power. We'll need the piece to carry the theme.

"Are you up to it?"

She had—what?—six weeks. Jesus.

"I don't like the dead space I'm hearing," Sheila said, but not without empathy.

"I was just scheduling things out in my head. Don't worry. I can handle it."

"Good girl. Now keep in touch. I want you down here a day or two before the show. We'll need to set up a press conference, maybe do a lunch or dinner thing."

The press. Like Sandra Bergman, they would demand to know where Allison had been for the last two years.

"Allison?"

"Right. I'll see you then." She hung up, and just stood there under the glare of fluorescent light, her stomach twisting into a knot.

Dead Man...

Why had Sheila chosen to focus on that particular piece?

It was the eyes. Allison had worked over a week on the eyes alone. Massaging the clay, sculpting, trimming. Erasing it all with the hard swipe of her thumbs and going at it again, until what stared back at her was a pair of vacant windows.

Then—and she wasn't quite sure how she had managed it— she had carved in the faintest hint of life. A spark hiding behind the glass.

Allison grabbed a bottle of water from the fridge to wash away the dryness that had crept into her throat. To get back to that dark place, she would have to revisit some of her worst nightmares.

This time would she be able to control the path her mind took? Keep herself just outside? On the edge?

With a shudder, she went back to the library, then sank into the leather chair behind her desk, propped her elbows onto the smooth mahogany surface, and cradled her head between her hands. The spine of a small book on the top shelf drew her eye. The book she'd purchased for reference shortly after Ken had died. When she had started seeing... things.

Outside, thunder rumbled over the gusting wind. On a sigh, Allison moved her hands over her face and closed her eyes, barely aware of the phone ringing again, as a violent rain began slamming against the windows.

Thunder cracked. Allison jolted as her eyes flew open. Lightning flashed. Furniture popped out from the dark. Above her, rain ricocheted like bullets off the metal roof.

She tried getting her galloping heart under control, and struggled to work through the haze in her head brought on by an exhausted sleep.

Steve. She remembered talking to him just before going to bed. Thank God they had made it back to Nashville before the weather turned wicked.

On the heels of another angry rumble of thunder that rattled the windows, the lightning stopped, and the dark swallowed her up. A sudden banging started downstairs, the hard raps of a door slamming in succession. Allison jumped, then shook her head with a breathless laugh. Probably the screen door. She didn't recall latching it.

She fumbled for the switch on the bedside light, swore when it clicked and nothing happened. Pulse still tripping, Allison groped for the flashlight she had brought up, and switched it on. Helpless horror gripped her as the beam shrunk to a tiny circle and then vanished when the batteries conked out.

Crap. Double crap. She'd have to feel her way down that dark stairway. She'd be lucky if she didn't break her neck.

Another flash of lightning lit up the bedroom just long enough for Allison to get her sense of direction. She found her slippers, grabbed her robe, then maneuvered out into the hallway, surrounded by the muffled rumble of thunder.

She felt so small in this rambling, old house.

Relax, Ken would tell her. *This house—it's what you wanted. Just go with it, babe.*

Yes, that's exactly what she should do.

Her hand found the banister, gripped it like a lifeline. Ken had always known the right thing to say.

Allison felt the sting of tears coming on and had to blink them back. She would never feel quite right being one instead of part of a couple.

Thunder boomed, startling her, and lightning flashed. She took advantage of the sparse seconds of light that shot through the windows in the foyer and hurried down.

The minute she set foot in the kitchen, the temperature dropped.

Cold spots.

No. No, dammit. Just the AC again.

Shivering, she tugged the collar of her robe close around her neck and rushed over to the back door. The wind moaned like something possessed, sending another shiver through her, while the screen door banged relentlessly.

Allison fumbled with the deadbolt, yanked the door open. Rain rushed in against her face. She grabbed hold of the screen-door handle and jerked it toward her. When she reached for the latch, thunder cracked, spreading sheet-lightning across the sky.

In those brief, few seconds when the atmosphere turned an eerie greenish-gray, she glimpsed a small, crouching figure bolting across the back edge of her lawn.

She froze.

CHAPTER 5

To get the kinks out of calve muscles that felt as though they'd gone dormant, Allison grabbed hold of the back-porch rail and began stretching. She'd worked through two dreary days of rain putting her studio together, sketching ideas for the pieces Sheila wanted. None of what she'd drawn had seemed right. Her mind just hadn't been able to travel far enough into that dark place.

Pushing that aside for now, she turned her face up to the cloudless blue sky, and took a deep breath of fresh, morning air. The ground had soaked up the water like a sponge, so there'd be no sloshing through puddles or mud.

What more could a girl ask for?

Maybe a free overhaul on the AC. During the storm a couple of nights back, once the electricity had blinked back on, she'd been forced to run the heat. Crazy, for this time of year.

Oddly enough, the problem seemed to have worked itself out. Still, she'd have to get a repairman out here. Soon. Before the entire unit decided to crap out on her.

Arching to stretch the muscles in her lower back, Allison scanned the edge of the woods, frowning at the memory—a flash of lightning, rain bulleting the ground at a slant, the small, crouching figure darting across her lawn. Had to have been a dog. A stray. Poor thing had probably been scared to death in the storm.

The animal must have wandered off. She'd seen it just once.

In a blur of movement, a large bird—a hawk, she thought—

swooped down from the trees and soared back up to the sky. Allison watched the long span of wings circle above the distant treetops, then zipped her nylon jacket and took off down the steps.

No mileage-counter today. She was going sightseeing.

He parted the bushes, raised the camera to his eye. He hadn't been sure about the girl—still wasn't. The shitty weather had kept him holed up inside for the last couple of days, and he'd gotten only a glimpse of her when she'd moved in. Too damned many people around. That, and the minute he'd tried bringing her into closer focus through the binoculars she'd turned to stone.

She was completely unaware of him now. And she was alone.

About damned time.

He zoomed in on her with the lens, not surprised that he recognized the wild tangle of red hair, the sly, green eyes. Even the freckles.

Yeah, he remembered the freckles.

So… little girlie's back. Only she ain't so little anymore.

That no good sack of manure had lied. He pressed the button and the shutter clicked. Now. Just let him try to deny it.

He watched those long legs of hers pumping, carrying that slim, curvy body across the ground. Lord, but she was a pretty thing.

His heart skipped a beat when she darted into the woods. *Where's she going?*

Like he didn't know.

The terrain turned rocky as it took a downward slope. Lungs straining, Allison adjusted her pace and footing as she weaved around old-forest growth that, like a giant canopy, blocked out a good portion of the sun. For a second back there, when she'd zipped past the trees, she'd felt an uneasy prickling at the back of her neck.

She glanced up at the stingy bit of sunlight that managed to poke through the dense tree cover. Maybe not the best of ideas, coming out here on her own. But everything seemed fine now. Peaceful.

If a couple of kids could wander around out here, no reason why she couldn't do the same.

She kept telling herself that as the trail she followed led her toward the tranquil sound of running water. When the trees opened to a small clearing, she saw the creek—a wide ribbon of water rushing over rocks—and throttled back to a steady jog, gradually slowing to a walk, getting her wind back.

The sudden odd sensation that she had traveled this way before crept up on her. Just a glimmer of feeling, really—nothing specific. Frowning, she scanned the trees that formed an almost perfect circle around the clearing, bringing into focus a mental picture of the serene, open patch of ground she and Ken had wandered up to on a weekend hiking trip to the Smoky Mountains.

Not the same, but… close enough.

The soft chirping of birds coaxed a smile from her. Music for the soul, Allison thought, and moved down to the creek, her gaze following the bank that swept along a gentle curve. A few feet from the water's edge, a Giant Oak towered like a solitary bastion. She hurried over to get a closer look.

The tree was massive. She felt dwarfed just standing beside it. The trunk, much wider than what she could wrap her arms around, was knotted and gnarled. It was beautiful.

She looked up at the sprawling, twisted branches that stretched for the sky. Pure, simple power. Could she create the same rugged, flowing movement with clay?

Maybe.

Allison closed her eyes and placed her palms against the trunk, began feeling her way over the rough bark, memorizing the trail of jagged edges that carved out crannies, the occasional feathery bump of moss. Lost in the primal sensations, it took her a moment to register the cold creeping up on her, the familiar prickling at the back of her neck. She spun around, let out a shaky breath-of-a-laugh when she saw the dog.

And the chill in the air—typical, Allison reminded herself, this close to mountain water and deep in the woods. She took a small step forward. "Hey, there."

The dog looked up at her with soulful brown eyes and wagged its tail. A cocker spaniel mix, she thought, but hard to tell. Its thick, black fur was matted, filthy. Beneath the tangle of all that fur, she could see the animal's sunken belly.

Poor little thing.

Allison gentled her voice. "You've been lost for a while, haven't you?"

The dog whimpered, and a clump of bushes off to the side suddenly stirred. She whipped around, zoomed in on the spot where the movement had come from, and had the unsettling sensation of eyes on her. Watching her.

Jesus. How could she have been so stupid? Coming out here without her cell phone or pepper spray.

"Who's there?"

The bushes rustled again.

Shit.

Allison scanned the area for anything she might use as a weapon, spotted a large stick.

Not much, but it would have to do.

She sidestepped, crouched down, and snatched up the stick. Her gaze zipped to where the dog had been standing. Gone.

Heart thumping like crazy, she clutched the stick in a white-knuckle grip and took several steps back, her eyes aimed at the bushes.

Without considering whether it was wise to run, she whipped around and dashed back through the clearing.

When she jerked the screen door open and scrambled into the

kitchen, Allison cursed herself for not locking the back door. But, by God, she would lock the damned thing from now on.

She flipped the deadbolt, then plopped down into the nearest chair and blew out a ragged breath.

What the hell had just happened out there?

Shaking, she brushed the sweat from her eyes, taking short, shallow gulps of air over the fire in her lungs. She had never run that fast in her life.

Through the bay window, she watched a squirrel scamper across the lawn, ordering herself to get a grip. Probably some small animal moving around in those bushes—a rabbit or something.

No. No, that couldn't be right. A starving dog would have scented a meal in a heartbeat and flushed it out.

Allison stared across the long stretch of ground that met the edge of the woods, and nearly jumped out of her skin when the phone rang. Swearing softly, she shoved up from the chair to answer it. Then felt her knees go weak at the sound of a friendly voice.

Of the few people she had encountered in this town, Mae Davis with Mountain Realty was the only one Allison could put a name to. "I'm glad you called."

"What's wrong, dear? Nothing with the house, I hope. I like my clients to be happy."

"No. No, that's not it at all. I just—" Allison stopped right there. Mae would think she had lost her mind, but there was no good way to say it. "This is going to sound crazy, but I think someone is watching me."

Through the long pause, she imagined the pretty, middle-aged woman with auburn hair and hazel eyes frowning down at the receiver in her hand.

"Why don't you tell me what's going on?"

Okay, okay. Allison blew out a short breath, then told Mae about the day she'd moved in, the uneasy feeling of someone watching

"My—oh, no. These aren't for me." Toni picked through a few of the kits. "My niece, Jenna—she's spending the summer with me. Thought I'd grab a few things to keep her occupied."

Allison glanced at Toni's basket. "I'd say you've definitely got that covered."

"You'd think. But when it comes to the art stuff, I really don't have a clue." Toni shrugged. "I just closed my eyes, started grabbing things off the shelves." She gave Allison a wry smile. "Guess it's a crap shoot, huh?"

"Not necessarily."

Toni cocked a brow. "You know about these things?"

Allison bit back another grin. She liked this woman. "Let's just say I can probably help narrow your selection."

"Good. That's good." Toni's mouth curved. "And not that I'm trying to bribe you or anything, but *that* would be worth a slice of Wilma's apple pie."

Apple pie. Probably baked fresh, right there in the café. Yum. "With coffee?"

Toni nodded. "You bet."

They stepped aside when a woman leading a young girl by the hand skirted around the end of an aisle and moved past them. Mother and daughter, Allison thought as the little girl pointed at just about everything in sight, eyes wide from the want of it all, while the woman kept a firm, protective grip on her daughter's hand.

Two clasped hands. A simple bond that spoke volumes.

What would it have been like, she wondered, to have that?

She pulled her focus back to Toni. "Tell me about your niece. Does she have any hobbies?"

"Hobbies. No, not really. Jenna just turned sixteen. Guess you could say she's different from most kids her age."

"Different, how?"

Toni glanced over at a customer who had stopped to browse the display of ceramic bisque, then motioned for Allison to follow her

44

down one of the aisles. "My niece is what you would call—" She paused. "Complex."

"Most teenagers are."

"True. But with Jenna, it's more than just your average raging hormones and emotions."

Absently reaching for a miniature brass vase on one of the shelves, Allison gave her a sideways glance. "Now you've got me curious."

Toni smiled. "Sorry. Can't really go down that road until I know you better."

The gaze in those sharp brown eyes held firm. Allison put the vase back, lifting her shoulders in a slight shrug. "Guess I'll have to accept that. I haven't known *you* long enough to pry."

That got a chuckle out of Toni. "I will tell you that Jenna's quiet. Unusually quiet. Reserved. She has one or two acquaintances, no close friends. Keeps to herself for the most part."

A lonely way to be at any age, Allison knew. Growing up in a household where the mere mention of her mother's name would generate an icy wave of silence from her dad, she'd preferred just to stay invisible.

Thank God she'd found her art. Or the art had found her, she supposed.

"I noticed some sketchpads at the front of the store. Drawing, or even just doodling, sometimes helps your mind to, well, to bring out what's inside you."

Toni considered. "Might be a good idea. And I thought about picking up a journal. That, along with the other... it just might work." She beamed. "Thank you. Let me just dump this stuff and grab the other, then we can go have that pie."

While Toni put the kits back where she'd found them, Allison grabbed a few items on impulse, then pointed out the charcoals and sketchpads as they walked to the front of the store. Apple pie and some of the good, roasted coffee from Wilma's Café—she could already taste it.

Toni unloaded the contents of her basket onto the counter. "You mentioned that you're new to the area?"

Allison nodded. "I bought a house just outside of town. The old Treadwell farmhouse."

For one sparse second, Lilly stopped scanning items. A frown flitted across Toni's face. "What?" Allison's gaze darted over to the gentle, softly wrinkled face behind the register, then whipped back to Toni. "What's wrong?"

Toni opened her mouth, stopped, shook her head. "Nothing. It's nothing. I think that one just caught us off guard. Am I right, Lilly?" The older woman nodded, smiled.

"Never been out to the place myself, but I hear it's huge." Toni handed Lilly a twenty for the purchase. "Just seems like a lot of house for one person."

Okay. She'd gone a little—well, maybe a lot—over the top with the space. Not the kind of news, though, that would typically get such a reaction. "Why do I have the feeling there's something you're not telling me?"

"Because I live in a two-bedroom cracker box and you noticed the envy oozing out of me?" Toni laughed. "Seriously, though. The upkeep on a house that size is going to be a real challenge."

"I know." Allison shrugged. "But I fell in love with it the minute I saw it."

"Guess you can't fight love." Toni took the bag and change Lilly handed her, ignoring the amused blue eyes.

"That's right," Lilly agreed as she rang up Allison's purchase. "Love is a powerful thing." Slanting a look at Toni, she handed Allison her bag. "You girls hurry back."

Out on the sidewalk, Allison blinked from the bright sun and stepped back, away from the noontime bustle of activity. "Ms. Jameson really is intent on fixing you up, isn't she?"

Toni nodded as she fished through the purse strapped over her shoulder and tugged out a ring of keys. "She thinks the sun rises and sets around Ray. The sheriff," she explained when Allison lifted a brow. "According to Lilly, he's"—she held up two fingers on each hand, wiggled them to mimic quotation marks—"'the one' for me."

"The one," Allison repeated. She had told herself the same thing about Ken the very first time she'd looked into his warm, hazel eyes and felt an unexpected jolt, and then, suddenly, it was just the two of them in a room full of people.

Half smiling, Toni nodded again. "Lilly figures that I should be just as sure of a future with the good sheriff as you are about the big old house you just bought." She made a face when her cell phone rang, then grabbed it from her purse, glanced down at the call display. "I should probably take this."

Allison moved off to the side and managed to stop her mind from wandering down a melancholy road. She would always love Ken, but he was her past. This town, the house, whatever direction her art took, was her *now*. And her future.

Although she had to admit, Toni was right about the house. Too much space for one person. Didn't matter. Allison loved every inch of it. But she doubted an overabundance of square footage was what had sparked Lilly and Toni's odd reaction.

Jay Treadwell died in that house. Some people were superstitious about things like that. Allison thought she probably should be herself. Considering. But the minute she'd stepped over the threshold, she'd felt as though she belonged there.

Fate had been leading her to this small town for some time. It had finally managed to get her here.

"I'm sorry." Toni flipped the phone shut and shoved it back into her purse. "Something's come up. I need to get back to the office."

Disappointed, Allison summoned a faint smile. "We'll get to-gether another time."

"Soon, I hope. I've got a thing for Wilma's apple pie." Toni handed her a business card. "Call me when you're free."

"I'll do that." Allison glanced down at the card. "The Dawson Times. You're a reporter."

"Yep. I also answer the phones on occasion, make the coffee, and sweep up the place."

This time Allison didn't bother to hold back her grin. She gave Toni her own cell and home number, but promised to call, feeling a twinge of car envy when Toni slipped into the classy, silver Mustang convertible parked several cars down.

Well, Allison conceded, her ride wasn't glamorous or sexy, but it got the job done.

Cringing when she saw that the time on the meter had expired, she yanked out her keys, hopped in and cranked the engine. Then headed down Main Street the way she had come. When she slowed at the intersection, an exhaust system sputtered and rumbled behind her.

Her gaze flicked up to the rearview mirror.

The beat-up truck with the tinted windows. No passenger, just the driver. A man.

A strip of dark tint covered the top of the windshield, and he'd lifted his head—deliberately, it seemed—so that it angled up. All she could see was the jut of his chin.

And his arrogant slice-of-a-smile.

CHAPTER 7

OVER THE NEXT FEW BLOCKS, the old truck stayed far enough behind Allison to keep her from getting another look at the driver. She glanced into the rearview mirror again, eased up on the gas. The truck immediately fell back.

Okay. She gripped the wheel tighter and put more pressure on the gas pedal. Her stomach pitched when the truck lurched forward to match her speed. *Following me.*

Why?

Without signaling, the truck whipped onto one of the side streets. Allison let out a breath she hadn't even realized she'd been holding, and her racing heart began to settle down. She relaxed her grip on the wheel and steered past the town limits, told herself the man was just a lousy driver. That, and Dawson Mills was a small town. Wouldn't be unusual for two people out running errands to take the same route.

So why did her brain keep insisting that her eyes stay glued to the rearview mirror?

She heaved a sigh, and swore. Focus. She had to shift her focus, put her mind to work on something productive.

Keeping one hand on the wheel, Allison rubbed her neck where the muscles had knotted. As the houses gradually gave way to rolling hills and winding road, she considered how to broach the subject of her mother the next time she saw Toni. Without having to answer too many questions.

A reporter had resources, along with an inherent curiosity. Allison just wasn't comfortable dredging up that painful bit of family history to a woman she was almost positive she liked but hardly knew.

Then there was the one, miniscule part of her that had always wondered about her dad. She had never believed him capable of murder. But—what if she discovered otherwise?

What would she do?

Allison pulled to a stop and cut the engine, gazing at the rambling old house that had already begun to feel like home. She would just have to deal with the situation when and if she stumbled onto it.

The horrible possibility of her dad hiding a gruesome truth for decades stayed with her until she walked into the foyer and the loud, persistent ringing of the phone jolted her back. Allison hurried into the kitchen, dumped her purse and shopping bag on the table, then snatched the receiver off the wall phone.

The deep, male voice had her stuttering. Paul Bradford. The contractor. She'd forgotten all about him.

"Remodel work. Yes. And I really appreciate you calling, but—"

"Sorry. Could you hold for just a second?"

Well. Jesus. She leaned against the counter, listening to murmured conversation on the other end of the line. And heard another noise over the muffled words. Faint, she thought she had imagined it. But the sounds were beginning to build—footsteps, scuttling. The rattle of a knob on a locked door.

Allison's heart leapt into her throat. Her gaze skipped over to the back door, zipped to her right, settled on the door to the utility room.

A blank, quiet stillness stared back at her.

She blinked, shook her head. Must have been construction noise in the background.

"Sorry about the interruption. Things are a bit hectic around here."

"Fine," she muttered. "It's fine."

"I can juggle my schedule this afternoon. Why don't I drop by around four, do a walkthrough."

Four. Today. Irritation nipped at her. Apparently, the question of whether *she* would be available had never entered his mind. "As I was saying, I'm nowhere near ready for an estimate. I've just started making a list of things that need to be done."

"I understand. But as long as you've jotted down the basics, might be a good idea for me to go ahead and take a look. Could save you some time, maybe catch something you'd miss, spark some new ideas."

A valid point, Allison conceded. Although his pushy manner was still bugging her.

In the background, the echo of hammers banging nails into wood picked up. He paused, waited for the noise to die down. "I realize that it's not much notice, but I have to be honest with you. I've got several jobs going right now. If not today, I have no idea when I'll be able to do this."

"A bid would at least give you something to work with."

True. And maybe he could recommend someone to look at the AC. "All right. Let me give you the address."

"No need. It's the Treadwell house, right?"

"Yes."

"See you around four."

Allison hung up, and just stood there for a moment, not at all comfortable with the idea of a man she had never met knowing where she lived. Although anyone Mae recommended would be okay.

Still.

Frowning, she glanced at her watch. He wouldn't be a stranger for much longer.

Because she wanted to sketch the Giant Oak she'd come across this morning, while the image and textures were still fresh in her mind, Allison had bought some time by bolting down the small salad she'd thrown together. A poor substitute for the apple pie she'd missed out on. Then again, she admitted, all that sugar and pastry would go straight to her ass. The three slices of pizza she had devoured Saturday night had probably blown her monthly allotment of carbs and fat, anyway.

She skirted around the rectangular worktable in her studio. Sunlight streamed through the big arched window that overlooked her back lawn, bathing the room in natural light.

Perfect. The space was perfect.

And the built-in window seat, with the plush cushion upholstered in a cheery, floral fabric—she could see herself indulging in a few daydreams there.

Not today, though.

Allison popped a CD into the portable stereo—U2, one of her favorites—then grabbed a sketchpad and charcoal stick from the cabinet. She got comfortable on the cushy window seat, set the remote to the stereo beside her, then took a moment to clear her head by gazing out the window.

The sky was robin's-egg blue, like polished turquoise. And the tree leaves, summer-green, fluttered in the slight breeze. Smiling, she watched two squirrels scamper around the base of a walnut tree. Hard to believe that just this morning she had bolted out of the woods and across this same lawn as though the devil was at her heels.

From the small stereo, mellow harmonica notes floated through the room, fading, as Bono sang in the low, easy style of a musical whisper the last words of *Running to Stand Still*. Allison propped the sketchpad on her lap and closed her eyes for a moment, then slowly opened them back up, letting her mind drift along, vaguely aware of the light scratching sound made by her charcoal stick as it raced over the page.

Between the dark, jagged lines that formed the image of a centuries old trunk, she rubbed in subtle shades of gray, giving the surface dimension, creating the effect of deep, carved-out crannies. Shorter, rugged strokes added gnarled, twisted appendages that jutted out and up, groping for the sky.

Her hand came to an abrupt halt. She blinked, and with a smudged finger, traced the oval-shaped blank spot she had left in the center of the tree's trunk.

Why—?

"*Find me.*"

The slim charcoal snapped between her fingers as she froze. Trembling, Allison snatched the remote, switched off the music. And listened.

"*Find me.*"

Faint. Airy. A distant whisper of a plea.

She didn't even want to think about where that voice was coming from.

"*FIND ME.*"

"No," Allison muttered to the empty room, her insides quaking. "You're not real. I don't hear you."

Slowly, deliberately, she reached down and picked up the broken pieces of charcoal.

You're hearing things again. You should see a doctor.

Her belly twisting into a hard knot, Allison tried shoving those words out of her head, out of her memory. But they were branded there. Not just the thought of them, but the sound, the voice. The low, wary tone her dad would use when he thought she had slipped back over the edge.

Allison shook her head. "No." She set her sketch aside, stared out the window. "I'm not crazy."

What, then? What did hearing a voice that wasn't there make her?

The same old questions. God, those she'd thought she would never ask again.

Allison sat rigid, listening for the faint, small voice. All she could hear was the jerky sound of her own ragged breathing.

She couldn't stand it, the shaky helplessness of it.

She shoved herself up, paced the room. Peeked into the closet. Nothing other than what she had put there—bricks of clay, her smocks, some cloths and hand towels. Allison went out into the hall, looked both ways.

Alone. She was alone here. She knew that. But it didn't stop her from searching her own bedroom and the bathrooms, the spare bedroom at the end of the hall.

Her gaze darted over to the narrow staircase that led to the attic. No one could get to it without walking past the door to her studio, and she had left that open while she'd worked.

Allison sighed, rubbing the back of her neck as fatigue crawled through her. She had pushed too hard this last month. Scrambling to finish pieces for the Atlanta show and getting them shipped out, the constant battling with her dad over her need for independence, the last-minute sale of her home in Nashville.

Then the move. And now, well, her mind was tired. Overworked enough for her to imagine hearing things.

When her brain started to lag like this, she wasn't herself, couldn't think clearly. A lingering side effect, she knew, from all the different medications prescribed to her by well-meaning doctors.

And she was standing here, she suddenly realized, in the middle of the damned hall, having her very own pity party.

Allison shook her head in disgust. She didn't have time for this.

She squared her shoulders and went back to her studio, ignoring the troubled little whisper in her head.

There now. He believed he had everything he needed. Barbed wire, pressure-treated posts, metal spikes. Plenty of wood, an assortment of nails. A shiny new padlock.

He wondered if the girl had noticed him following her, hoped so. Nothing quite like scaring the shit out of someone to get them talking.

Smiling, he pulled the canvas back over the bed of his truck, covered it all up, nice and neat. The supplies would be safe enough, he thought, in this old building. Once dark fell, he'd get busy putting the cage together.

A frown wiped the smile away. Before he could start his little construction project, he had to snip the loose end he'd left dangling.

He walked over and inched the door open at the back of the building, took a long look to make sure it was still just him and good old Mother Nature out here. Early this morning, he'd watched the girl jogging into the woods, and imagined she'd come out clutching a nice bundle.

A bundle that belonged to him.

Couldn't be sure, though. He'd been forced to cut his stay short when the walking, breathing pain in the ass had come barreling up behind him through the underbrush like a fucking freight train.

Squinting against the harsh sun, he swore when he felt the first dull throbbing in his temples that signaled another one of his sick headaches. Soon the dizziness would hit. Then the pain would be like a jackhammer trying to split his skull wide open from the inside out. Unbearable pain that sometimes made him think it might be better just to put a gun to his head and end it all.

Eyes watering, he swore again and jerked both hands up to his temples, pressed hard with his fingers.

Damned if he'd leave this world with unfinished business.

Strong, late-afternoon sunlight slanted at an angle through the arched window. The warmth from it was comforting on her back as she sat, hunched over, on the stool at her worktable. Allison added the finishing strokes to her sketch, set the remaining nub of charcoal aside, taking a moment to stretch her neck and back, then rolled her shoulders.

She frowned down at her drawing. It was good, in a dark way. The gnarled, twisted branches were like writhing, skeletal arms that groped, searching. They were racked with pain. Not the physical kind, but an endless, torturous longing for something... lost, she supposed.

Desperate. Angry. The image tapped into her deepest center, the place where all the primitive emotions and fear twisted together. She wanted to look away, but couldn't seem to pull her gaze off it.

The sinister feel gripping her from the page was exactly what Sheila wanted.

Although the odd blank spot in the center of the trunk was still there. Waiting.

For what?

She had no idea.

A sudden hard knock on the front door downstairs made her jump. Allison checked her watch: 4:15.

The contractor.

She grabbed a towel and wiped the charcoal from her hands, slipped the sketchpad into a drawer on her worktable. Froze when she heard the whisper again: "*No. Find me.*"

"Stop it," she murmured as the cold dread slid through her like an icy premonition, giving her a glimpse of dark days to come. She knew that darkness well, had no intention of going back there.

Trembling, Allison hurried down the stairs, managing what she hoped would pass for a smile as she opened the door.

He wasn't what she had expected. He'd been harried, brusque, and even a bit rude over the phone. But now, except for his slight, visible jolt when she had opened the door—and her paranoid mind had probably just imagined that—he seemed almost serene.

He had the bluest eyes she had ever seen. Clear as a bright September sky. Piercing, Allison thought as she shifted under his unblinking gaze.

Why was he staring at her?

It took her just a second. God, he knew. He knew there was something wrong with her.

He cleared his throat. "Miss Weathers?"

Allison grappled for focus. "Yes."

"Paul Bradford." He shifted the clipboard he held and stretched out his hand.

She took it, surprised that her own hand was steady. "Please, come in."

Tall, and lean, he stepped into the foyer, taking a long, slow look around. A glint of sunlight from the windows overhead played across his face. He had a good face, Allison thought. Bronzed by the sun, with strong lines and sharp angles that melded into a sleek, muscled jawline, softened just enough by thick hair the deep, golden amber of dark honey that brushed the collar of his denim shirt.

Confident. A man who, probably in his mid to late thirties, seemed perfectly at ease in his own skin.

She'd give just about anything to be able to capture that calm strength in clay.

His gaze wandered over to the stairway and up to the second level. For a second, Allison thought she noticed his shoulders stiffen. But—no.

He shifted his attention to a corner of the foyer. "You've got some cracked plaster there."

"I'm afraid you'll find that in most of the rooms."

Paul took a pen from his shirt pocket, and jotted down a note on the pad clamped to his clipboard. "Assuming the foundation's solid, should be an easy enough fix." He scanned the floor. "Pinewood looks to be in fair shape."

Allison nodded. "I'd like to keep the original hardwood floors in all the rooms, maybe go a bit lighter on the finish." She paused, debating over which room to take on next. She hadn't spent enough time in her own house, wasn't yet familiar with it. And, dammit, she should never have let him talk her into doing this so soon.

He was already moving toward the library.

Well. Guess that settled it.

Paul stopped to look at the few remaining paintings she'd left stacked against the wall. "These are good. Really good." He peered down at the bottom right corner of one of the paintings where she had scrawled her signature. "You're an artist."

"Actually, painting's just a hobby. I sculpt for a living."

The slow, easy smile that spread across his face and lit his eyes had her stomach doing an odd little leap. "Like I said, you're an artist. And a good one."

"Thank you," she managed, and got a jolt when they stepped into the library. Confused, heart hammering, Allison rushed over to her desk, grabbed the small book that sat next to her laptop. The book she had purchased for reference after Ken died. She'd put it on the top shelf and left it there Sunday night, when she'd been working in here, unpacking things.

How—? She couldn't seem to finish the thought.

"Something wrong?"

Paul had moved next to her, close enough that she could sense the subtle, masculine scent he wore. Allison shook her head. "I'm... not sure."

She turned slightly, looked into his eyes, wanting to find an answer, some logical explanation there. "I don't remember pulling this off the shelf."

Dear God. She really was losing her mind.

He took the book from her, studied it. A frown crept over his face. "Occasionally, I do the same thing—get busy, lay something down and then forget about it."

His slow, sympathetic smile was the same cautious, consoling look all the doctors had given her each time she had insisted that what she was hearing, what she was seeing was real. During that dark, uncertain time, Allison had wanted desperately just to back into the nearest corner and vanish. She wished she could do that now.

Paul handed her the book. "Like I said, I tend to be absentminded myself. Usually happens when I've got too much going on—brain overload."

Nodding, she slipped the book back into its slot on the top shelf. Yes. Too much on her mind. That had to be it.

CHAPTER 8

TONI LEANED BACK IN THE chair behind her desk to grab a few seconds of well-deserved down time, and glanced around her tiny, cramped office. The room, in serious need of a fresh coat of paint, was about the size of a shoebox. One slit-of-a-window off to the side gave her a miserly peek at what the weather was doing.

But what the heck. It was practically home.

This old weathered-brick building had housed the *Dawson Times* for nearly a century. Her great-grandfather had started the paper, passed the business on to her grandfather. Now her dad kept the small, independent press running.

She was grateful to be a part of it, stingy workspace and all.

And speaking of work. Toni opened her Outlook calendar, began updating her schedule for the next couple of days. She glanced up when Kara Simmons, the woman who somehow managed to keep the office *and* Toni's dad organized, rapped on the door.

Kara poked her head in, her stylish, slender-framed bifocals perched on the end of her nose. Like her caramel-brown eyes, her smile was lively.

How did she do it? Toni wondered. Skating along the back edge of sixty and the woman was a tidy ball of energy.

"I'm heading out. Need anything before I go?"

Toni checked her watch. The afternoon had buzzed right by her. "I'm good. See you tomorrow."

Kara nodded. "I'll go ahead and lock up, then. You're the last one here."

"Thanks, Kara." Toni went back to typing, one part of her brain tuning in to the vague sound of keys rattling, the front door opening, closing.

After hours and alone again, she mused as her fingers flew over the keyboard. With her dad out of the office since mid-morning—something about looking into questionable funding for the new high school—she'd spent the last several hours putting out fires he'd left on this end. First on the list had been an interview with the zoning commissioner about the sudden commercial land boom that had started up just outside of town. Next, she'd followed up with a phone call to Mayor Stevens. The lengthy conversation had netted her zilch.

Toni typed the last entry, closed her calendar. "You're beat, Harper." And famished.

Her stomach rumbled in agreement.

"Yeah, yeah," she muttered and reached into her top desk drawer, rummaged through the supply of takeout menus she kept stashed there, and glanced over the selections. Anything that qualified as sustenance would be appreciated at this point, but—hold on. Today was Wednesday. Gino's had a special on pepperoni pizza. She could pick it up on the way home.

Toni gave her niece, Jenna, a quick call to let her know supper was on the way, then placed the order. Before heading out, she went through the motions of clearing her desk, and scowled when her stomach rumbled again. The piece of Wilma's apple pie she'd missed out on today would have at least curtailed the annoying hunger pains that were gnawing at her.

And the leisurely break would have given her the chance to have a nice girl-to-girl chat with Allison Weathers.

The woman was young, single. Had relocated from Nashville—a good-sized city—to live in a small, laid-back town like Dawson

Mills. Purchased a huge, old house with more than enough space for a person to get lost in.

Not a crime, that. But curious.

Interesting enough, Toni figured, to warrant looking in to.

She'd heard rumors about the old Treadwell place. Vague, though. Insubstantial snippets of hand-over-the-mouth gossip from a couple of Ray's deputies who had responded to late-night calls.

Haunted. Or so Jay Treadwell had claimed in the few months before his death.

No details there. Ray had threatened to fire anyone in his department who breathed a word about the old man's "delusions" outside the office. The good sheriff had also slammed the door shut on any story that might be there before Toni got the chance to pursue it.

She was still pissed about that.

Toni glanced down at the phone, tapped a finger on her desk. Ray was about as pigheaded as they came, and she was no stranger to standing her own ground. She'd been told she had a mile-wide stubborn streak. Toni liked to think of herself as being persistent whenever the situation called for it. Either way, her relationship with Ray had made for one volatile mix in the dating pool.

Last summer, she'd finally called it quits.

But she still had a few close sources in the Sheriff's Department who could access the files on Jay Treadwell.

Toni grabbed the phone, punched in the familiar number. Maybe she could wheedle the information from one of them.

From the library, Allison went with Paul into the living room, vaguely aware that he seemed familiar with her house. While he surveyed, measured, jotted down notes, she half consciously let her mind wander back to the small book now tucked away on the top shelf in the library where it belonged.

Ghosts and hauntings. The paranormal. She had studied those pages like the gospel for nearly a year, had come away from them even more unsettled. And confused.

Jesus, if she *had* left the book on her desk, she would remember. Wouldn't she?

"Think we're done with this room." Paul scribbled a final note and walked back over to her.

With tension squeezing the muscles in her neck and shoulders like a vice, all Allison could manage was a small nod. She led him to the half-bath tucked behind the stairway, then to the formal dining room. Gradually, while he worked, he steered her mind around to what they were supposed to be doing here by making suggestions, asking for her input. She was grateful for the change in focus. And impressed. He caught the little things, like surface scratches on the bathroom tile, hairline fractures in the plaster, nicks on some of the baseboards and window trim.

He had an artist's eye for detail. His work, as Mae had promised, would be better than good.

An open archway in the formal dining room led to the kitchen— the only room in the house that would be a major challenge. Paul suggested recessed lights, and Travertine tile for the floor. Allison liked the idea—a definite improvement over the dated fluorescent fixture and chipped linoleum.

He jotted down the note, scanned the scarred laminate counters. "Those countertops used to be tile. We could do that again, but granite would look great. I know a wholesaler who'll give us a good price.

"I'd keep the cabinets, though, refinish them." He ran a hand along their scratched, painted surface. "They're oak. Made by a local craftsman, in the late seventies, if I remember right."

So she hadn't imagined it. He knew the house, the history here. Some of it, anyway.

Glancing over his shoulder at her, Paul cocked a brow. "What do you think?"

Allison pulled her focus back. "I agree with you on the granite. Go ahead and check into that. And I definitely want to keep the cabinets." She paused while he jotted it all down. "You really are familiar with this house."

She caught the split-second's hesitation in his eyes. Then it was gone. "I grew up with Bill Treadwell, Jay's son." Paul went over to the window above the kitchen sink, and gazed out. "Spent a lot of time here."

The subtle shift in his tone to quiet, solemn, told her that at least some of his time in this house had been less than pleasant. Allison wanted to ask about that, but when he pulled his gaze back to her, the look somehow managed to scramble every thought in her head. A couple of sensations hit her at once—an uneasy wariness; for the life of her, she couldn't read what was behind those intense blue eyes. And then a slow stirring of lust. Sheer lust.

Something she hadn't felt in a long time—strong enough to make her knees wobble.

Put it away, she ordered herself as she caught the fleeting image of Ken's warm smile, felt an ugly twinge of betrayal. *Just put it away.*

Needing to wet the dryness that had crept into her throat, Allison went over to the fridge for a bottle of water. "Would you like something to drink? I have Coke, juice, water."

"I'm all right. Thanks."

Aware of his eyes still on her, she gulped down cold water. When he finally turned away and began moving around the room, scanning the walls, the ceiling, taking notes, Allison couldn't help but notice the snug fit of his jeans on slim hips, broad shoulders that looked rock solid. She took another long drink of water, forcing her eyes to travel a different direction.

Allison stepped back from the rush of cold air when the AC

kicked on—a reminder that she needed to have the unit checked. "I... wanted to ask you..."

Paul turned, brows rising.

"I've noticed the kitchen seems chilly sometimes. Drafty. Sunday night, during the storm, I lost power for a while, and..." She shivered. The icy air in this room had chilled her to the bone. "It was freezing in here. I know this is going to sound weird, but I had to cut the heat on."

A question flashed in his eyes just before they sharpened with steely reserve.

What? she wondered.

Nothing. You're on edge, that's all.

And if she intended to make a life here, on her own, she needed to stop imagining things—situations, whatever—that weren't there. "I was hoping you could recommend someone to check the central air."

"I can, yeah." He paused, blue eyes brooding. "But it could just be the airflow needs some adjustment. Why don't I have a quick look?"

"I'd appreciate that."

Paul set his clipboard on the counter. "If I remember right, they ran the main ductwork in the cellar." He gestured toward the door to the utility room. "Through there."

Nodding, Allison put the remainder of her water back in the fridge and followed him into the half-cluttered room that held her cleaning supplies, the washer and dryer, the water heater. It was easy, she thought, too easy, really, just to let him take the lead.

The stress, the worry, must have torn at her today more than what she had realized.

Paul opened the small door that led to the cellar and flipped the light switch. Behind him, Allison took it slow down the narrow, wooden staircase, shivering from the dampness that rose up to meet them. She glanced around at the brick walls and concrete floor—improvements Mae had mentioned that Mr. Treadwell had made sometime in the mid 70s. A definite plus over packed earth and rock, but with the ancient, abandoned boiler standing in the far corner, and the exposed ductwork, plumbing pipes, and wiring overhead, the space still looked half-finished.

And it was clammy. The heavy dampness seeped right through her.

Allison rubbed her palms briskly over her arms. "It's really damp down here."

"It is." Paul walked over to the large duct that ran from the air-handling unit and reached for what looked to be some sort of metal lever. "You could open the windows, let in some fresh air, but I wouldn't advise it." He pulled the lever toward him an inch or so. "Not until you get some screens."

Screens. Allison glanced up at the horizontal windows that lined the top of the west wall. Well, eventually.

"I think that should help." Paul batted at a spider web. "Ready to go back up?"

"Definitely. Thank you."

"No problem." His quick, warm smile made her feel better. About everything.

Careful with her footing, she followed him back up the narrow steps, and from the corner of her eye, glimpsed sudden movement in a shadowy corner below. Allison's breath hitched as she tightened her grip on the banister. A trick of the light. That was all. There was nothing down here.

Nothing.

When the phone in the kitchen rang, Paul gestured toward the foyer, and Allison nodded with a distracted jerk of her head. It was slight, but he caught the tremble of her hand as she reached for the receiver.

He picked up his clipboard off the counter. He hadn't managed to ease her mind about the book, after all. Apparently, the best he'd been able to do was distract her. And either that hadn't lasted long, or something else had upset her.

Paul wanted to cover her shaking hand with his, to comfort. Instead, he walked away, swearing silently to himself.

This damned house. Trouble always came back to haunt it.

He glanced around the foyer as he crossed over to the foot of the stairs. The last thing he needed right now was more work. He'd do good to keep a handle on all he had going between now and the middle of next year. But he had to admit he'd been wondering who had bought this old place. Then Mae Davis had called.

A young widow. Living alone. In this house.

Curiosity had turned to concern.

Hell, he'd practically forced his way in here today. And it had taken just one flash-of-a-second after she'd opened the door for it to register: he knew that face. Those summer-green eyes, something small and frightened there. A tumble of fiery-red curls. The spatter of freckles across her nose.

His heart had damned near stopped. But Lord, it couldn't be—

He severed the thought before it took root in his head, because the idea was impossible.

Maybe.

Probably.

"Sorry." She walked up to him, the strain in her voice carrying through to those gorgeous green eyes. "That was the owner of a gallery in Atlanta. I have a show there in August and—" She stopped. "And I'm babbling. Sorry. Again."

"It's okay." Paul tried what he hoped was a smile, then followed her up to the second level. He wasn't ready to do this, to go into that middle room. How many years had it been? Christ, how many *decades?*

The implications of that alone should have kept his mind occupied, but staring up after her… He'd have to be half dead and blind not to notice the sway of those slender hips beneath her denim capri pants.

Easy, he warned himself, and pulled his thoughts back to business. Not a simple task, with her constantly in his line of sight, but they worked through the master suite quick enough. The space was in decent repair. Large but cozy, he noted as he followed her back down the hall. A grand space that still carried all the old Southern charm.

He would enjoy bringing the shine back to it. If he could somehow manage to put the past to rest.

"I'd… like to save the middle room for last."

He heard the ragged edge in her voice, but only nodded as he felt his own tension easing.

It's a room, for Christ's sake. Just a room.

He was still telling himself that when they walked into the smaller bedroom at the end of the hall and the memories came flooding back. After his wife died, Mr. Treadwell had moved into this room. But long before that, his son, Bill, had inhabited the cozy, compact space.

Like stepping back in time, Paul thought as the part of him that remained in the here and now noticed the graceful way Allison moved about the room. The piece of him that had taken a leap back saw only the ghosts of the two boys he and Bill once were. Just a couple of lanky kids with nothing better to do on a warm summer night but gaze out the window through Bill's telescope at an endless sky, hoping to catch sight of a shooting star.

Allison stepped up beside him. The nearness of her yanked the part of his brain that had gone missing back to the present. "I think this room is—" She tilted her head. Curls spilled over her slender shoulders like an untamed waterfall, the hint of a question shadowing those sexy green eyes.

"Something wrong?"

"No, I—" Her gaze drifted up to the ceiling. "Thought I heard a noise."

"In the attic?"

"Yes. But it's gone now." She paused, working her bottom lip. "Mice, I guess."

"Yeah. Could be." Paul set his clipboard down and pulled his measuring tape from his belt, then went to work as she stood quietly next to the wall, her eyes fixed on the ceiling in a faraway stare that hitched itself to heavy thought.

Mice. She didn't believe that any more than he did.

CHAPTER 9

W HATEVER HAPPENS, DON'T LET HIM *see you panic.*
Allison held her breath, conscious of Paul's eyes on her,
and opened the door to her studio.

No disembodied voice. No movement.

She could breathe again.

Lifting her gaze for just a second to thank the heavens, she
stepped inside. Paul glanced around the room, his jaw set, eyes a
darker blue, now. She supposed some of her tension had rubbed off
on him. Stress had a way of doing that.

He set his clipboard on the end of her worktable, then walked
over to the shelves where she had placed some of her sculptures, the
last few pieces in the line before her mind had lost its way in the
dark. He reached toward her *Falcon in Flight,* ran a finger over one
of the bird's outstretched wings. "Your work?"

"Yes, just... part of a collection I wanted to keep."

"It's good."

"Thank you." She wondered if "good" would be the term he'd
use to describe her recent work.

Not likely.

Allison pulled the stool out from her worktable and sat. "I'm
going to stay out of your way while you look over the room."

Nodding, Paul strung his measuring tape along the baseboards.
"If you don't mind me asking, what brought you to Dawson Mills?"

So many layers to the answer, here. She decided just to peel them back, get down to the core. "Guess you could say I got tired of the city. I moved here from Nashville."

"Nashville. Haven't been there in a while, but I hear it's growing."

"Not fast enough," she muttered, and caught the glance he sent her just before he yanked it away. The size of the city hadn't been anywhere near large enough to keep Allison from feeling as if it were slowly closing in on her. Choking her.

Paul walked over to jot down the dimensions. "Since you're using this as a work area, anything special you want done in here? Maybe add some additional shelving?"

She considered. "I think just the basic cosmetics. I'd like to build a separate studio on the property—soon."

"You give the go-ahead on that sometime in December or January, and you'll save quite a bit." The dark edge in his blue eyes lightened when he gave her one of those easy smiles. "Wouldn't necessarily have to start construction until late spring or early summer, but the building trade tends to slack up during the winter months. We place advance orders with the local suppliers, we lock in a better price."

"I'll keep that in mind."

She watched him move about the room, running his hand along the walls, noting the cracks in the plaster. It was easy to envision him bringing this house back to life. A reality that could happen only if the Atlanta show paid off. Until now, she hadn't let herself consider the possible alternative.

A vicious panic crawled through her. She took a slow breath, tried to focus on that tiny place inside her where the calm centered. Just one short week ago, she had been sure of her path, her work. Her mind. She had believed she was on the mend.

Allison glanced down at the drawer that held her sketchpad and shuddered. *A sane person doesn't hear voices that come from nowhere.*

How many times had her dad tried drumming that into her head?

Well. Now she could add shuffling in the attic where there was none, imagining a vague shift of movement in the cellar, just because there were a few dark corners.

And the book—she honestly didn't remember leaving it on her desk.

Allison realized she had clenched both hands, had to force them to relax. Dammit. She had fought so hard to climb her way out of the nightmare that had consumed nearly two long years of her life.

She refused to go down that dark road again.

"Hey—you okay?"

Allison blinked. She hadn't noticed him walking over to her. "I was... just thinking."

In his eyes, she saw the questions, and then the flicker of the moment when he decided not to push.

He scribbled something down on his notepad. "It'll be a couple of weeks before I can get back to you with an estimate."

She responded with a slow nod. The things that had been happening—maybe she hadn't imagined them. That meant there was another possibility here. This house—her house—could be haunted.

Even with what she had read and studied on the paranormal, Allison wasn't sure whether she believed in ghosts. The doctors had assured her it was impossible to see or hear the dead.

That kind of thing just didn't happen.

She jolted when a loud *thump* came from the attic. Her gaze zipped up, then over to Paul.

He frowned. "Yeah. I heard it."

"Let me go up first."

"You won't get an argument out of me." Allison handed Paul the package of light bulbs she'd bought at the grocery store. She'd been right at his heels when he'd rushed out to his truck to grab a high-powered flashlight and the crowbar he called "an equalizer."

Now she was more than willing to let him climb up into that dark space without her.

The slow thud of his boots against the plywood floor above grew faint, then stopped.

"Paul?"

She gave it just two seconds. Heart tripping, Allison rushed up the steps, ignoring the creaks and sags beneath her feet. His hand shot out from the dark and took hold of hers, keeping her balance steady as she crossed into the shadows. "Sorry. Didn't mean to frighten you."

Relief flooded out of her in a huge sigh. "Okay. It's okay." In that instant, when she peered past the beam of his flashlight and through the dim circle of light cast by the single bulb overhead, Allison felt a draft of chill air.

It was gone before her body could react to the cold.

His hand, she realized, was still holding onto hers. "Did you find anything?"

"Yeah." He released his grip on her hand. "Nothing to be alarmed about, though."

Aiming his flashlight into a dark corner, Paul went over to where an old barstool had toppled onto its side and picked it up, set it out of the way. "Couple more stacked against the wall back here. This one must have shifted and fallen off."

Logical, she admitted. "I had some help settling in this past weekend. They had to move most of this old furniture around." What little she could see now in the faint light made the attic seem like the inside of a junk shop. "I guess organizing the space up here hasn't exactly been at the top of my list."

Paul gave her a quick smile. "Can't do it all in the first week." He swept the light over a clutter of furniture, some boxes. "Since we're up here, let's make sure there's nothing else stacked that's going to come crashing down."

"Good idea."

He stepped around her to where he'd propped the crowbar against the wall, and scooped the package of light bulbs off the floor. "Hang on a sec while I get some light in here."

Nodding, she moved back, and as the bulbs flicked on, a subtle glow began to chase away the shadows. A definite improvement. The downside, though, was that she could actually see the thick layers of dust that was making her nose itch.

"That should help." Paul switched off the flashlight and set it on the floor, along with the empty package.

"It's better," Allison agreed. "But..." She glanced around the wide, deep space, and, for no apparent reason, shivered. "The space still feels dark."

A frown moved across his face. "You're right." He glanced over at the west wall where someone—Mr. Treadwell, she assumed—had nailed slats across the only window in the room. "Any reason to keep those boards up?"

"Not really. The inspector told me the window was fine. I have no idea why it's covered."

"Much as I can remember"—Paul reached for the crowbar— "Bill's mom had it done. Think she was worried about us kids sneaking up here to play and taking a dive out the window."

Made sense. Still...

Allison cringed from the high-pitched scraping and creaky protest of wood. The kids were grown, had moved away from home long ago. Strange, the Treadwells hadn't bothered to let a little warmth from the sun into this musty attic.

Paul put more force into the job. As the boards began to peel back from the wall, daylight streamed through the window a section at a time, drawing her eye to the strong line of his jaw, the flex of muscle beneath denim. Allison blinked and shook her head, yanking her focus in another direction.

Her gaze skidded to a halt on the tiny object that glimmered on the floor.

She stooped down, got a tingle in her belly.

Well. Wasn't that something? It had been right here the entire time. Must have fallen out with the diary. Or when Steve had turned the chair on its side. It was just small, and the room had been dark.

They had missed it.

She plucked up the tiny, brass key and slipped it into her pants pocket, frowning when she noticed the water.

"Uh—Paul?" Allison dipped a finger into the puddle that was seeping into a gap between the floorboards. "Could you come over here for a second?"

He dropped the last piece of wood onto the pile he'd made, then crouched down beside her. In that instant, when he glanced down and then flicked his gaze up to hers, she caught the jolt in the middle of all that blue.

She hadn't imagined it.

Paul took her hand, pulled her to her feet. Then grabbed his flashlight, swung the beam in a slow arc over exposed rafters and plywood. "I don't see where the water's coming from." He aimed the light directly above them. "We've had a lot of rain lately. Could be a seam in your metal roof needs caulking."

Or the inspector had missed something, and the roof required major repairs.

"Caulking," Allison echoed. "Hope it's something that simple."

With a soft, grateful sigh, Allison leaned back in the wonderful old claw-foot tub. Every muscle in her body slowly went limp in the hot water. She gazed out the small window at the darkness dotted with pinpoints of twinkling starlight, listening to the stillness around her and hoping it would last.

The idea of having this vintage farmhouse all to herself seemed less attractive now than it had just a few days ago.

Allison lathered her washcloth with the herbal body wash she liked to use. She'd been tempted to ask Paul to stay for dinner, just a simple gesture to show that she appreciated his help. But she had shied away from it. She barely knew him. Then there was the niggling of raw lust she felt whenever he looked at her a certain way. That and his staying for a while longer would only have delayed the inevitable. The meal would end, and he would leave. She would be alone in this big old house.

Stop it.

Filling her lungs with a determined breath, she glanced around at the cozy space she had made her own—a hand-painted ceramic soap dish and towel rings, brushed with feathery strokes in warm autumn tones of gold and rust, the miniature Artisan pottery jars she'd placed along the windowsill.

This was her home, now. There would be no running back to Nashville. Although her dad expected her to do just that.

Damned if she'd prove him right.

She squeezed more of the creamy body wash onto the cloth, scrubbed the back and sides of her neck until the tension that had crept into those muscles began to ease. She was strong enough to work through whatever was going on here. And there *was* something going on with this house. Toni, and Lilly Jameson, the sweet, elderly woman who owned the craft shop, obviously thought so.

Haunted. Was it possible?

Allison brushed back a stray curl that had worked loose from her hair clips, ignoring the water that trickled down the side of her face. If Mae Davis had heard any rumors of things here going bump-in-the-night, she'd kept them to herself. Who could blame her?

Paul knew, or at least suspected something was off.

With a shiver, she realized her bathwater had turned cool. Allison pulled the plug and got out, then snatched a towel and patted her skin dry, chasing back the goose bumps. She slipped into her sleep-shirt and went through the nightly ritual of cleansing, moisturizing.

The eyes that looked back at her from the other side of the mirror were shadowed with fatigue.

It hadn't been that long ago when she'd stared at her reflection in another mirror and noticed the first faint signs of panic beneath the exhaustion. Terrified of what she had seen, or what she *thought* she had seen.

Her gaze slipped down to the tiny, brass key she'd set on the vanity. Tammy believed that finding the diary, after decades, had been some strange act of Providence.

Could it really be that simple?

Or that complicated, Allison mused.

She grabbed her comb, waged the usual battle with her tangle of curls. Her mind took a short skip back to the thump overhead in her studio, the frown that had etched its way into Paul's blue, blue eyes.

Yeah. He knew something.

Hadn't he mentioned that he'd grown up with Bill Treadwell? His gaze had drifted out the window in the kitchen when he'd admitted to spending a good amount of time in this house. She had sensed something brooding just below the surface of his quiet, solemn tone.

And he lived just next door. Her neighbor to the east, as it turned out.

A small detail Mae had neglected to mention.

Allison picked up the key, then switched off the light and padded into her bedroom. Leaving the bedside light on, she took the diary from the drawer on her nightstand and snuggled under the covers.

"Tell me what's going on," she murmured when the tiny key clicked in the lock. "Help me out, here."

CHAPTER 10

BIRTHDAY PARTIES, SUMMER VACATIONS—ALL THE normal stuff. The Treadwells seemed happy, Allison mused as she slowly sifted through pages that spanned several years. The only hint of trouble was Bobbie Jean's son, Bill, and his sidekick in crime, Paul. Those two had been quite a pair. One shenanigan after another.

She felt a smile tugging at the corners of her mouth, imagining the energy it must have taken to keep up with two rambunctious boys, and turned the page, found a blank sheet. Then another. Frowning, she thumbed forward, finally coming to an entry that took her well into the following year.

August 6, 1975—

I couldn't believe my eyes when I saw him getting out of the car. I don't think he noticed me staring, though. At least, I hope not.

What is he up to? Why come back after all this time?

Whatever the reason, it can't be anything good. The man has no soul. He is nothing but pure evil.

Evil. An icy shiver bolted through her, right down to the tips of her toes. Allison stared across her bedroom, into the shadowy corners, telling herself that what she had just read most likely had nothing to do with whatever was going on here, in this time.

The only way to know for sure was to keep reading.

Weary—and even more uneasy—she pulled her gaze back to the diary.

August 8th—

Two days now since I saw him getting out of that car. I keep waiting for the evil to come knocking on our door. It's like standing on the razor-thin edge of a bottomless, black pit, struggling to keep my balance.

I suppose I should count my blessings, but I know better. He's biding his time, waiting for the right moment.

Or has he already talked to Jay without my knowing it?

Maybe. Maybe.

I caught Jay watching me today while I was hanging out the laundry. He turned his head away.

This is tearing me apart. I wish to God that I could just drop this pretense. But our Bill, he's the innocent in all of this, still just a child. Only, not Jay's child.

My son can never know what a twisted, evil man he comes from. I will NOT let that happen.

God. Allison wasn't sure what she had expected to find, but this certainly wasn't it. She moved her focus off the looping, feminine script and looked around the room. Not just a bedroom, but a cozy, intimate space where Bobbie Jean and Jay Treadwell had made love, made children. Or… one child, she supposed.

For a moment, she felt like an intruder in her own home, and had to shake her head slightly to clear the awkward sensation.

Allison glanced down at the page again. Evil…

Why would Bobbie Jean ever let herself get involved with a man like that?

The guilt the poor woman must have carried all those years. And her husband—had he gone to his grave without ever learning the truth?

The son, Bill, did he know now?

Secrets could eat you up from the inside out, no matter what end of them you were on. Allison knew that firsthand.

She held back a sigh, refusing to stray down a road that would only depress her. One day, she'd figure out a way to convince her dad that she didn't want—didn't need—his protection. Only the truth.

The truth. Where her mother was concerned, that had always been something beyond Allison's reach.

Why?

As it had so many times over the years, that question burned in her head for a long while, until her eyes gradually began to close. She was barely aware of the diary slipping from her grasp.

Sometime in the middle of the night, she rolled over and switched the bedside light off.

The drizzle had started not long after Paul pulled himself out of bed this morning. And it was still coming down. A persistent light rain seeping through a gray fog.

With his back to the sunshine-yellow walls that on most days seemed cheery, he sipped coffee at the counter in his grandmother's kitchen and gazed out the window above the sink. The miserable weather mirrored his mood.

How many times had the dream jolted him awake last night? He'd lost count, but he couldn't seem to shake the image that was still rolling through his head like an abbreviated film clip: the little girl's face—pale, scratched—magnified by the telescope lens as she darted through the woods, green eyes wild with terror.

That was decades ago, and, as it had a habit of doing, life had gone on. The passage of time had managed to dull the worst of those memories. Until he met Allison Weathers.

He glanced over his shoulder when he heard the soft shuffle of his grandmother's footsteps, and felt his mouth curve. Up at seven, sharp, her habit ever since he could remember. She had even taken time to do that thing she always did with her snowy-white hair—gather it up into a soft, elegant puff. A "bouffant," he believed, is what she called it.

Annie Bradford might be a petite, small-boned woman with a nature like a warm, gentle breeze, but time—and the nasty summer cold she had caught—had hardly slowed her down at all. Paul thought she must be the most spry and beautiful eighty-something woman on the planet.

The glance she sent in his direction was both amused and curious. "My favorite grandson. Good morning."

"Morning, Gran." He walked over to the stove as she put the teakettle on, gave her a peck on the cheek. "And I'm your only grandson."

The glimmer in her blue eyes made him smile. "Hope you don't mind me letting myself in."

"Of course not." Her eyes narrowed, still sparked with amusement. "But you must have better things to do than to check up on an old lady. I'm fine," she added softly, with a dainty sniffle. "Just a pesky cold—the tail-end of one, at that."

Even with his dark mood, she had managed to tug another smile out of him. His gran had a way of doing that with most folks. Her upbeat way of looking at the world was highly contagious.

He went over to top off his coffee while she fixed the herbal tea she liked. The simple routine grounded him, reminded him that there had always been this—the everyday normalcy of life.

His foundation.

Settled at the antique table he'd refinished for her a while back, his grandmother sipped hot tea, gazing at him over the rim of her china cup. "What's on your mind, dear?"

"That obvious, huh?"

"I'm afraid so."

Paul heaved a sigh. He wasn't sure where to begin. Hell, he wasn't entirely sure, now, whether his mind had played some kind of nasty trick on him.

His grandmother's deep-blue eyes held a steady gaze. She would wait, he knew, for as long as it took him to get on with it.

And dammit, he should—get on with it. He had permits to pull, a slew of jobs to check on.

Paul took a long swallow of coffee, then went over and settled into the chair across from her. And told her about Allison Weathers.

"Well," she said after a while, "we were wondering who bought the house."

"Yeah. And I guess the resemblance could be just a fluke. They say everyone has a double somewhere."

Annie lowered her cup to the saucer. "But you don't believe that's the case here."

Paul thought about that for a minute. "If it was only a question of Allison's resemblance to the girl, I'd have to say it's just one of those things. But..."

He shook his head. "Hard to believe there's not a connection here."

The soft lines on his grandmother's forehead deepened as her focus shifted past him, the gentle curve of her mouth stretching to a grim line. Last summer, she had scoffed at him for converting the old barn on the north end of her property into cozy living quarters. *All this trouble just to keep an eye on an old woman,* she had told him.

Paul was glad now that he had ignored her and moved himself into "The Barn," as they had officially christened it. And not just because his grandmother was getting on in years. Her living alone next door to the Treadwell farmhouse had been a concern.

82

Strange things happened over there.

Annie gave another small sniffle as she rested her unwavering gaze on him. "I suppose it could all just be coincidence."

"Maybe," Paul admitted. "The house is old. Might be an issue with the wiring or the connection at the main breaker that caused her to lose power during the storm." He shrugged. "As for her having to cut the heat on—maybe she's cold natured. Could be her central air needs an overhaul."

And that, he told himself, was bullshit.

Allison had turned three shades of pale the second she'd noticed the book that had somehow found its way off the shelf and onto her desk. *A Study of the Paranormal.*

And damned if he could explain the water up in her attic. No sign of where it might have dripped down from the roof. He'd remembered, though—just a flash from the past that had hit him the minute he'd crouched down beside her to have a look—Bill's dad, a strong, towering man back then, standing in the kitchen with his wife, a mug of coffee in one big calloused hand while he scratched his head with the other. *Blasted water up in the attic. Darned if I can figure where it's coming from.*

Paul drummed his fingers on the table, shook his head again. "Look, Gran, we both know there's something going on with that house—still. I just need to know how—or if—Allison fits into it all."

"I understand. But in the meantime, don't you think you should at least warn her?"

Paul sipped his coffee without tasting it, and sighed. "Yeah. I do." He stared down into his cup, wondering how he could tell a woman he hardly knew that the house she had just bought was haunted. Then there was the one small detail he wouldn't be able to dodge. For decades now, he had thought that *she* was the reason for that haunting.

Even as he mentally went through the theory, none of it made one iota of sense. Allison Weathers was a living, breathing woman. A woman who had stirred much more than his memories.

It wasn't just a sexual thing, Paul thought. Although that was definitely there. But the minute he had looked past the guarded wariness in her green eyes, had caught the underlying sparkle there, like sunlight on emeralds, he had felt a stronger, deeper pull.

Shit. He had to step back from that. Things were already complicated enough.

Paul looked back over at his grandmother, who sipped the last of her tea with the patience of a saint. "She's going to think I'm crazy."

Smiling, Annie reached across the table and patted his hand. "I doubt it. In any case, you mentioned that Miss Weathers seemed tense. She may already suspect that something about the house isn't quite right.

"As for the other…" His grandmother lifted her shoulders in a faint shrug. "You should just come right out and ask her."

Paul felt the slightest of curls tugging at the corners of his mouth. And there was no humor behind it. "Guess I could."

But the little girl he had met just a few brief times all those years ago… Christ, he couldn't even remember her name. She was long gone. Deep down, he knew that. Or at least, he had known it.

Now, he wasn't so sure. He wasn't sure about any of it.

The weather had ruined any hope she'd had of going for a run this morning, so Allison took some time to answer a few e-mails and return a call from one of her friends in Nashville. She'd wanted desperately to blurt out everything that had happened since the move. But how could she have put it?

The book… I don't remember leaving it on my desk. And there was a noise in the attic. Shadows in the cellar are moving. I heard… a voice.

Babbling. Words strung together in rapid succession, spilling off the tongue of a woman on the verge of losing her sanity. She'd half convinced herself otherwise, that there was something odd going on here, but now, running through it all in her head, dammit, she just wasn't sure.

On a weary sigh, Allison managed to shove back the niggling doubt. She started up the stairs to her studio with her second cup of coffee, not ruling out a third. All those hours of reading last night had made her head groggy, her eyes sore.

About the only thing she'd come away with was the awkward feeling of having dug around in a dead woman's personal business.

She couldn't help but wonder, though, if Bill Treadwell's natural father was still alive.

Nothing you need to go poking your nose into.

She had enough issues of her own.

Movement flashed in the corner of her eye. She jumped. Hot coffee splashed over the rim of her cup, missed her hand by inches. Allison froze at the head of the stairs. A shadow, lightning quick, had just darted into her bedroom.

Run was the thought that raced through her head, but she couldn't get her feet to cooperate. Trapped inside her own body, panic swelled in her while her heart did a wild and crazy drum roll in her chest.

She tightened her grip on the cup, felt the realness of it, something tangible in her hand. Then concentrated on taking slow, deep breaths, until her erratic heartbeat began to settle.

Okay. Better now. Allison scanned the hall, the doorway, for more movement. What she did notice was the warm cast of light against the walls. Because of the dreary weather, she'd left the lights on in the foyer, and she wasn't entirely sure, now, that she hadn't just seen her own shadow crossing over the bedroom door as she moved up the stairs.

To prove the point, she waved a hand, relieved to see the vague silhouette of four fingers and a thumb shifting along the wall.

"Jesus," Allison muttered, and pulled out the napkin she had tucked in her pants pocket, dabbed up the spilled coffee. Didn't take much these days to have her jumping out of her skin.

It seemed silly now, but she detoured over to her bedroom, left her cup on the dresser while she checked the closet. Then took a quick look in the bathroom before tossing the wadded napkin into the small trashcan next to the vanity.

Alone. She was alone here.

Back in her bedroom, she reached for her cup, then stopped short. Frowning at the corner of dull-colored paper that peeked out from under the dresser, Allison bent down to snatch it up.

Her breath hitched. The old faded photograph in her hand...

She didn't remember taking it out of her jewelry box.

Think. Just... think for a minute.

Allison absently reached up with her free hand, brushed a finger over one of the small gold hoops that dangled from her ears. This morning she'd gone through the motions of getting dressed with her head in a haze. Still, if she had so much as glanced at this particular photo, she would remember.

Wouldn't she?

In the mirror above the dresser, her own pale, haunted face looked back at her through eyes clouded with doubt. Was she losing herself again? There had been no emotional trauma to fracture her mind. A catalyst, the doctors had told her. There was always a catalyst.

Paul. She wanted to believe he at least held some of the answers. Or maybe she had sensed something from him that just wasn't there.

Control, Allison reminded herself. Squaring her shoulders, she shot a defiant glare back at the mirror. She could either let the situation bury her, or take control. Because there were no options here, no second – or third chances to get it right.

She gazed down at the pretty, young woman in the photograph. Hair the coppery red of a new penny fell in soft curls just past her shoulders. Although time had yellowed the photo somewhat, the woman's smile brightened everything around her.

A mischievous smile, Allison thought as she reached for her cup, sipped. Even so, the woman in this photo had always seemed lonely. Lost, somehow.

Lost. Like Allison's *Dead Man.* The forlorn, half-human thing she had created from clay by reaching down into the darkest part of her.

Gazing into the depths of the green eyes staring up at her from the photograph, Allison shuddered.

Was that what you wanted, Mother? To be so… alone?

For just a second, she could have sworn she heard a faint whisper. Nothing discernable, more like a soft rush of air that had brushed past her ear.

She tilted her head, listening. Then jumped when thunder boomed, dumping a hard rain onto the metal roof.

Allison let loose with an oath and shoved the photograph into the pocket of her pants, grabbed her cup. A part of her wanted to ignore the deluge. Paul had promised to be here around six this evening to work on the attic stairs, and to take another look at the leaky roof.

By that time, she might have a small flood up in the attic.

She rushed down to the kitchen, grabbed a flashlight. Halfway up the rickety attic stairs, she stopped, stared at the closed door looming ahead of her. She didn't want to go in there alone.

That, she knew, was just the little-girl-fear-of-the-monster-in-the-closet talking. If something in this house wanted to harm her, it would have already done so.

Wouldn't it?

She switched the flashlight on and hurried up the rest of the way before her nerve faltered. Dust had her scrunching up her nose to ward off the itching tickle as she moved through the dim light cast by overhead bulbs. The ungodly hammering of rain against the metal roof was like the rapid beat of a drum in her ears. Hard and unrelenting.

Should be a cinch to spot a leak.

Allison stopped where she'd found the puddle of water, aimed her flashlight at the floorboards, and swung the beam up to the exposed rafters. Brows knitting, she ran the light over every square inch above her, then into the corners, along the entire attic floor.

Dry. Every board up here was bone dry.

Chewing at her bottom lip, she ventured over to the window, gazed out at the rain. From this height, she was several feet above the treetops, had a clear view of the window beneath the gable on the house next door.

The Atkins' home, she realized. With the right pair of binoculars, anyone could see straight into her attic from that window.

Before she could back away into the shadows, a muffled ringing drifted up through the open door. The phone in the kitchen.

Allison switched off the overhead lights and raced down the attic stairs, nearly losing her footing when they wobbled. She swore the next time she drove into town she'd remember to replace the cordless phone that had conked out on her.

Breath coming hard and fast, she dropped the flashlight onto the kitchen counter and snatched up the receiver. Through the faint crackle of static on the line, a television played low in the background.

"Hello?"

Click.

She pulled the receiver away from her ear, and frowned. A wrong number. Someone had just dialed a wrong number.

CHAPTER 11

"**S**HE'S HOME."

He nodded, smiling, then grunted from the strain on his biceps as he finished the last repetition of curls. At his age, keeping the muscles in shape was getting to be a real bitch. He blew out a short breath, dropped the weights onto the floor. "You know what to do."

Her bony old fingers strayed up to a loose button on her dress. "Are you sure—?"

"Dammit, woman!"

She jumped back, nearly toppled over the ottoman. He almost split his gut trying to keep from laughing, but caught himself, sucked it up and put on his pity-face, glanced around the shabby room. His gaze stopped to linger on the threadbare rug, then drifted over to the stained, lumpy cushions on the couch.

Sure enough, the old bag's eyes were tagging right along with his. Damn, he was good.

"You want to live like this for the rest of your life?"

She shook her head.

"Then get on with it."

He reached into his shirt pocket and pulled a cigarette from the pack, lit up, then exhaled a fine stream of smoke into the air, watching her bony backside as she shuffled out of the room. Glancing down at the cigarette balanced between his fingers, he saw the fresh blood that had covered his hand last night. Wet. Red. Sticky. A messy business.

He had run into a small, unexpected problem.

The rattle of dishes and pans shattered his thoughts. He scowled, eyes going to slits as his focus slid over to the open doorway that led to the kitchen.

Something would have to be done about her. Soon.

Because most of his recording sessions started in the afternoon and stretched out late into the night, Steve Kincaid normally didn't come into the studio until just before noon, usually around eleven. But he'd made it a point to be here early this morning to catch up on some paperwork.

He'd been at it for a while now, and he hadn't accomplished squat. The clutter on his desk seemed to be growing.

He sighed, raked a hand through his hair. A good administrative assistant would have this cleared up in no time. The problem there would be coming up with the money to pay one.

Not that he was short on cash, but he was still expanding, building the business. Most of what he had put aside he'd earmarked for equipment upgrades and purchases, advertising. And he was hoping to move Jeff Parker into full time, get him more involved on the mixing and production end of things.

Steve tapped his pencil on the desk. Just a cluster of small-business growing pains. He could do a lot worse.

A rap on the door distracted him from the pile of paperwork. Tammy breezed in, and his mind stalled. Long, dark hair pulled back with a silk scarf that left just a few uninhibited, wavy strands to frame her face. A hint of cleavage peeked past the v-cut of her rose-colored blouse.

His gaze skimmed over full lips painted a soft, sugary pink. Just how was he supposed to work with her standing there looking like his favorite candy?

He hadn't thought it possible, but she looked even sexier now than she had this morning when he'd reluctantly dragged himself from his bed and left her sleeping. If that wasn't enough to grab a man's attention, she was holding two large, steaming go-cups of cappuccino.

"Tell me that's White-chocolate Mocha you've got there."

"It is." She bent over, brushed his cheek with her lips.

Smiling, Steve took one of the cups. "Thanks. I thought you had to work today."

"I've got a little time before I have to be there." She settled into the corner chair, eyeing the disaster on his desk. "If you'd quit spending the big bucks on all that new equipment, you could afford to hire me. Then I could handle all the important things, like keeping that mess on your desk straight.

"And if you were a good boy"—Tammy shifted her gaze over to the cup he held—"I'd bring you cappuccino every morning."

"Every morning, huh? Before or after—?"

She cut him off by raising her own cup in a toast. "Drink up."

He did, and savored the warm, mocha flavor, looking forward to a major caffeine buzz. It would help him concentrate. Something he'd been having a hard time doing these last few days.

While she sipped, Tammy studied him over the rim of her cup. "I guess your sister is settled into her new house by now."

"She's getting there. I got an e-mail from her this morning." He held a hand up when her dark green eyes sparked. "And before you ask—no, she didn't mention the diary."

"Hmm. That doesn't necessarily mean she hasn't opened it." Tammy leaned forward, grinned. "I told her to call me when she did. I don't think she will, but I'm dying to find out what's in it."

Steve smiled. "I'm curious about that, too. But knowing Allison, she's probably still sitting on the thing, trying to make up her mind." He remembered scanning the few, short sentences she had shot off to him in her e-mail. She'd seemed... distracted. "I figure getting organized, plus having to turn out pieces for the Atlanta show, will keep her occupied for a while."

"It is a big house," Tammy agreed. "And I know the show's important to her."

Steve nodded. For Allison, just about everything was riding on that show. Her career, hell, her entire financial future.

Scary.

What on earth had she been thinking, moving out to the middle of nowhere? Away from her network of friends. Taking on the responsibility of an old house that size. The place was huge. And isolated. Hidden away in the middle of all that land like some outrageously spooky Victorian castle.

He stared across his office at nothing in particular, told himself the move was what Allison had wanted. It was a done deal.

Tammy gave him a soft smile. "You're still worried about her."

"Yeah." He had been from the moment they had driven off in his van and left her standing in the driveway looking after them. "I know Allison is a big girl. She's got to make her own decisions. The trouble with that is she's still fragile."

Although she'd never own up to it. Not in a million years.

For what was probably the umpteenth time, Steve wondered if his sister even realized just how much like their dad she really was. Stubborn. Had a head like a brick wall whenever she made up her mind about something.

Tammy crossed her legs, the sexy, gold ankle bracelet she wore catching a glint from the overhead lights. "I know you haven't told me everything. But is there anything I can do to help?"

Steve sighed, shook his head. "Not that I don't appreciate the offer. But there's really nothing I can do, until I talk to dad. He's still out of town on business."

"And your mother—she doesn't know anything?"

"If she does, she's not giving it up."

Frowning, Tammy leaned forward. "Do you really think your dad will? Give it up, that is."

"Probably not." Steve paused, weighing his words. "The only thing I know for sure is that the old man didn't convince Allison to start seeing all those doctors just because she was grieving over her husband."

"You think there was another reason."

"Damned right. And I think that whatever made her so fragile is still there—even if it's only in her head."

That was the root of it, wasn't it? The chord that kept the same old song playing.

How the hell could he help her if he didn't know the tune?

He took a deep breath to knock back the frustration, and shook his head again. "She's taking on too much, way too fast. I don't like that she's living in such an isolated area."

"I agree. But we both know why your sister chose that town."

Yeah. The conversation she'd overheard between their dad and his mother, just before their grandmother passed away.

Eyes narrowed, Tammy tapped a slender finger against her cup. Steve could see the reels in that pretty head of hers spinning. "The private investigator Allison hired—you told me he wasn't able to find any evidence that proved her mother had ever been anywhere near Dawson Mills." She glanced over at him. "Doesn't quite fit."

"Yeah. Well." Steve stared into his cup, brooding. "I think there's probably a lot we don't know about that."

"Like what?"

He smiled—zero humor there. "I'm not sure. But I intend to find out."

The rain had slowed. The steady patter against the arched window was like a soft underlying rhythm to the moody, acoustic melody that drifted from Allison's small stereo. She sat hunched over on the stool, working at a pace that matched the music. It felt good to have her hands in the moist clay, to narrow her focus down to a pinpoint as she molded the shape of a woman's body, massaged rough edges into soft curves.

She stopped for a moment to stretch her back, then glanced over at the sketch that had taken her the rest of the morning to complete. One slender arm hung limp at the woman's side, the other stretched upward, fingers groping.

Like the desperate, twisted branches on her oak tree.

Her gaze shifted up to the eyes. Wretched. Empty. Unlike the photo, they held no hint of humor, just the dull, blank stare of a desolate woman who had lost everything—her husband, her child, and, ultimately, herself.

"What happened, Mother?" Allison murmured, her voice cracking on that last word. "Where did you go?"

She felt her heart wrench, had to close her eyes, and gave it a moment to put the emotion aside. For now. Tomorrow, though, she would give Toni a call, set up that date for pie and coffee at Wilma's.

Then what?

Well, she would just have to persuade Toni to use her reporter's resources to help find Beverly Kincaid. Even if it meant casting suspicion on Allison's dad.

Allison reached for her water bottle, took a healthy swallow, then went back to work, carving angles and smoothing curves, getting the piece to that first point of life. When her hands began to feel the strain from those muscles working nonstop, she took a small break to flex her fingers, then leaned back, studied her progress.

Briefly, she wondered what her dad would think about the solemn, clay image. Then decided she honestly didn't care.

She picked up her sculpting tool, began defining melancholy eyes, then worked her way down to smooth out a slender nose, and carved out the grim slit of a mouth.

It took a while for the knocking downstairs to break through the zone where her creative mind had retreated.

"One second," Allison muttered as she ran the tool along the side of the neck, then across and down, rounding the shoulder.

Downstairs, some determined person with lousy timing kept banging on her front door.

"*All right.*" She put her sculpting tool down and wiped the clay from her hands, switched off the music. She wasn't wearing her watch, but knew that it was too early in the day for Paul. Even if he'd managed to catch a break in his busy afternoon, he wouldn't have just swung by without phoning first.

And beating down the damned door to get her to answer didn't quite seem his style.

Shrugging off her irritation, she draped a damp cloth over her work and hurried down to the foyer.

The woman had short-cropped, mousy-brown hair, peppered with gray. She was maybe five-two and painfully thin. A faded, shapeless housedress hung on her skeletal frame like an old sack.

If a good gust of wind were to come along, it might just carry the poor woman away.

Allison scanned the thin face: heavy lines accentuated by a thick layer of face powder that didn't quite hide the ugly, yellowing bruise on her left cheek. She tried not to stare at it.

"Hope I didn't catch you at a bad time." The woman sent her a brief smile, then held out the Tupperware container she had tucked under one arm. "Thought you might like some chocolate chip cookies."

"Thank you." Suddenly conscious of the dirty smock she wore, the clay caked under her fingernails, Allison took the container. "Please, come in out of the rain."

The woman nodded agreeably and stepped into the foyer, waited for Allison to shut the door. "I'm Ellie Atkins."

Atkins. Allison bristled.

"Me and my husband, Jared, live next door. Guess you could call me the welcoming committee." Ellie's smile didn't quite reach her dull brown eyes.

She's wondering if I know about that annoying little habit of hers—spying on her neighbors.

Old bat.

"Yes, well. I'm Allison Weathers." She paused, forced a smile. "Would you—like some tea or coffee?"

"No, no." Ellie waved a hand in an absent gesture. "Can't stay long. Just wanted to come by and say howdy, see if you might be interested in meeting some of the other ladies in town. That is"—she craned her neck to get a good look up at the second level—"if your husband doesn't mind. I'm assuming he's at work."

"I... live alone." Allison cringed inside when Ellie's eyes lit with curiosity.

"Well, then. There's no reason for you to stay cooped up in this big old house by yourself."

"Actually, I'm afraid you've caught me working."

"Nonsense. A girl's got to have a little social time. I'll just wait right here while you put those cookies away. Then we'll get going."

Get going. She wasn't going anywhere with this woman. Now, or ever.

"Our ladies club meets down at the Community Center in town every Thursday." Ellie eyed the streaks of dried clay on Allison's smock. "We've got a little time. You go on upstairs now, get into something a bit dressier."

Okay. The woman wasn't going to take no for an answer. It occurred to Allison that the formidable Jack Kincaid, staunch businessman, had absolutely nothing over this scrawny, aging busybody.

She got a nasty jolt of déjà vu; saw herself struggling to hold on to her ideals, God, her identity, against her father's iron will. She felt the first, small rush of panic. Then a jab of irritation.

It took a long, slow, steady breath before she could summon a measure of forced control. "I'm afraid I can't today. I have a contractor coming by later this afternoon."

Ellie's brows darted into a V. "You sure that's not something you can't put off?"

Allison nodded, managing a half smile. "But I appreciate the cookies. Let me just put them into something. I wouldn't want to keep your container."

Against her better judgment, she left Ellie Atkins alone and hurried to the kitchen, setting a speed record transferring cookies into a ceramic jar.

She rushed back to the foyer, relieved to see that the woman hadn't budged. "It was nice to meet you," Allison lied without a smidgen of guilt, and handed her the container. "But I won't hold you up. I know you don't want to be late for your meeting."

Frowning, Ellie nodded, then turned to leave. She paused, her thin fingers wandering up to a button on her dress. "Sure I can't talk you into coming with me? The ladies will be awfully disappointed."

Disappointed? "They were... expecting me?"

Discomfort—or maybe it was a good old-fashioned dose of embarrassment—flickered over Ellie's face. "Guess news travels fast in a small town."

Huh. Allison wasn't aware that she was "news." Then again, Mae had warned her.

Ellie opened her mouth to say something, but, apparently, decided not to push it. She gave Allison a vacant smile, then shuffled off to the ancient, rusted station wagon parked in the driveway.

It took forever for the old engine to sputter to life.

Allison sighed, shoulders slumping as she watched the old heap roll out of sight.

CHAPTER 12

A PROMISING RAY OF SUNLIGHT STREAMED through a part in the clouds. The rain, just a drizzle now, sparkled like diamond droplets against Allison's bedroom window. She slipped into silky, dark slacks and a sleeveless, cream-colored blouse, then checked under her fingernails to make sure she'd scrubbed away all the hardened clay. And thanked God for the wonderful invention of the shower. There was nothing quite like a good, pulsing spray of hot water to relax the muscles and rejuvenate the mind. Something she had been desperate for after having to deal with the likes of Ellie Atkins.

Welcoming committee. Right.

After she had shut the front door on the old busybody, she'd marched straight back to the kitchen and dumped the cookies into the trash. A juvenile thing to do, but it had made her feel better. Much better.

Allison took a quick look in the mirror above the dresser to check her makeup, then worked a comb through her hair; told herself all this attention to her appearance had nothing to do with Paul.

Yes, he was attractive. And she had to admit that whenever he fixed those intense blue eyes on her, she had trouble holding onto a single, coherent thought.

But her heart was still so full of Ken.

Not willing to stray down a road that would only draw the aching to the surface, she shifted focus, checked her watch. Paul wouldn't be here for another hour. There was no reason, really, to hold off until tomorrow to phone Toni.

She picked through her purse, found Toni's business card. Then, before heading downstairs, checked her hair one last time for any stray curls.

While she waited for the receptionist to put the call through, Allison eyed the hideous fluorescent fixture in her kitchen, imagining it gone.

Progress, she reminded herself, took time. And patience.

She moved over to the window above the sink, stretching the phone cord as far as it would go, and gazed out at the light rain. Despite the interruptions, she'd had a productive day's work. Late tomorrow evening, or first thing the next morning, she should have this latest sculpture ready for firing.

The plan had been to send the remaining sculptures to Atlanta in one shipment. This particular piece, though, wasn't something she wanted to keep around the house to dwell over.

"Hey, there. I was just thinking about you. Great minds, huh?"

Allison smiled. "I guess." She caught the muffled words in the background. "If this is a bad time, I can call back in the morning."

"No, we're good. I was just tying up some loose ends." Toni chuckled. "Call me crazy, but I thought I'd try to get home while daylight's still burning. Just for a change." She paused. "Speaking of home—you get settled in yet?"

"I'm just about there." Allison debated on how much, if anything, to say over the phone. She decided to keep it short. The convoluted subject of her mother was something that required a face-to-face. "I'm actually calling to collect on that pie and coffee."

"Yum. Apple pie. I've been looking forward to that. And there's something I wanted to talk to you about, but—could you hold for just a second?"

"Sure, go ahead." Allison heard a soft rustle as Toni's hand slid over the receiver, more muted words.

"Sorry about that. Listen, I'd just about kill to get to that pie

ASAP, but I'm working on something that, well, let's just say it's going to require all of my focus."

"Sounds intriguing," Allison said.

"Yeah. And that's not the half of it. So—how about next Wednesday? Around ten-thirty? That'll get us in before the early lunch rush."

Well, she had waited all these years. A few more days wouldn't make much difference. "That's fine. I'll see you then."

Allison hung up, then opened the freezer and rummaged, deciding on chicken breasts for dinner. Over pasta, she thought, with Portabella mushrooms and pearl onions, in a light cream sauce. Along with a good bottle of white wine.

Since Paul had committed his free evening to helping her with the roof and working on the attic stairs, the least she could do would be to feed him.

She set the meat out to thaw, and frowned. Toni hadn't followed through on whatever it was she had wanted to talk to Allison about.

Something else, she supposed, that would just have to wait a few days.

"I came up here earlier, when it was raining hard." Allison's gaze followed Paul as he moved up another rung on the ladder he had brought in. The beam from his flashlight swept along rafters that were still bone dry. "I didn't find any water."

Frowning, he switched off his flashlight, climbed down. "I still want to check the seams on the roof. The rain's stopped, but it's probably slick up there. We'll have to wait a day for the metal to dry."

Paul took her elbow, steered her toward the door. "I want you to wait until we get those stairs fixed before you come up here on your own again." He gave her one of those quick smiles that made her pulse skip. "And I'm going to get on that right now."

Tempted to prod him for whatever information he might have

about this house, she managed to hold back. Dinner first, a nice casual meal and a little wine. It would relax them both and give her time to think more about how to approach the subject.

Allison sucked in a sharp breath when the wobbly stair beneath her sagged and she pitched forward. She grabbed frantically at the air. Felt the solid strength of Paul's arms wrap around her. "You okay?"

Her head still reeling, she blew out a shaky breath. "I think so. Guess I just lost my balance for a second." She looked up into those blue eyes. His face was too close. *He* was too close.

She pulled back. "Better now. Thanks."

Paul gripped her hand, released it only when her feet made the transition to the sturdier hardwood floor.

Chivalry, Allison mused. Nice to know that it was still around.

"I'll just... leave you alone now, and let you get started on those stairs."

He nodded. "Shouldn't take me long, maybe a couple of hours."

Allison busied herself in the kitchen, tuning in to the vague creaking of the front door as it opened and closed when Paul went out to his truck to get whatever tools he needed. After a few minutes, she heard the front door open and shut again, followed by the rustle of activity as he hauled everything up the stairs.

Drizzling olive oil into her large skillet, she smiled. It'd be nice to have someone to share a meal with, some conversation. Lately, she had felt so alone here, in this big old house.

Well, not completely alone, she admitted, hoping Paul would shed some light on that. Because she refused to accept the alternative.

The blast of icy air came from behind her. Allison went rigid as the chill snaked up her spine. It was like being thrust into the middle of a dream, she thought with an odd detachment as she watched her own shaky hand lower the spoon she held, heard the hollow clink of metal against the saucer.

She forced herself to turn around.

Scarred, laminate counters, scratched cabinets, a chipped linoleum floor under the stark glare of fluorescent light. Her grandmother's Wedgwood salt – and pepper shakers and sugar bowl rested in the middle of the table.

Everything in its place. Normal.

"I know you're here," she half whispered in a tremble.

No shadows this time, no small, faint voice.

"Okay." She took a breath. Better now. Steady. "Either show yourself, or go away."

The room stared back at her in blank silence.

"Did you hear me? Just—go away!"

Allison whipped back around to the stove, her tension easing as the ice in the air faded. Maybe she couldn't control this, but, apparently, she could at least communicate with… whatever it was.

A sick churning started in her belly. She swallowed over the sour taste of fear. Hadn't she tried to convince herself of that in the past? When she had woken in the middle of the night and imagined her dead husband standing at the foot of her bed?

"I am *not* losing my mind," Allison muttered, and wished she could believe that.

Put it away. For now, just put it away.

She managed to do just that, and took her time with the preparations to get everything right, to give her mind time to settle. And to give Paul the time he needed to do his job. Once the chicken and sauce were on simmer, the asparagus and pasta nearly done, Allison went into the dining room to set the table.

From the hutch, she pulled out her grandmother's good china and silverware, the expensive linen napkins she had purchased several years back on a whim. And after a slight deliberation, the crystal wine glasses her dad had brought back from Germany.

She stepped back to survey, and frowned. Pretty. Almost elegant. It was too much. Too over-the-top for just a casual dinner.

"Wow." The word came out in a soft rush of air.

Allison whirled around. Paul had stuck his head in, had a brow cocked as he scanned the artistic placement of fine china, silver, and crystal. She felt her cheeks flush, hoped her face wasn't turning red. "I guess I went a bit overboard. It's been a while since I've had company over for dinner."

She made a move toward the table. "I'll just change this up. Or we can eat in the kitchen, if you like."

The quick humor in his blue eyes had her flustered. "No, no, don't change a thing. It's nice. I'll just put my tools away and get washed up."

Allison nodded. "Okay, then. I'll get the wine."

"This is delicious." Paul forked up the last bite of pasta and chicken, some asparagus tips, savored.

"I'm glad you like it." Smiling, Allison set her fork down and sampled more wine. She had to admit she'd outdone herself in the kitchen this evening. "There's more if you want seconds."

He shook his head. "I'd love it, but if I take another bite, I won't be able to move." Paul reached for his wine glass, sipped. "You look nice, by the way."

The flush returned to her cheeks. Allison told herself it was the wine. "Thank you. You wouldn't have thought so earlier. Working," she explained when he cocked a brow. "I always manage to get clay all over myself." Layers of it, she thought, picturing the hard, brown crust caked under her fingernails, the smudges on her hands, her face, and streaks over her arms.

Her smock had probably looked as though she'd been in a mud fight. Definitely not appropriate attire for the Ladies Club.

You go on upstairs now... get into something a bit dressier.

Allison frowned. How had Ellie Atkins known that the master bedroom was on the second floor?

An assumption, maybe. Or at one point over the years, the old busybody had wormed her way into the Treadwell's home.

"Something wrong?"

"No, I'm sorry. My mind wandered for a minute." She took a small breath, decided it was now or never. "Can I ask you something?"

"Sure."

"You spent a lot of time here, with Bill Treadwell, and you live next door. Have you..." Her nerve faltered as she heard her own voice trail off.

Blue eyes steady on hers, Paul lowered his glass to the table. "Have I—what?"

Guarded caution, Allison thought. And maybe it was just her imagination, but she could have sworn she'd sensed a spark of tension in the air.

She took a hefty swallow of wine for courage. "Have you ever noticed anything strange about this house?" There. She'd said it.

Eyes narrowed, he leaned back in the chair. A sigh, barely perceptible, escaped him. "Define 'strange.'"

Define. Oh, yeah. She could. In detail.

Allison rolled the wine around in her glass for a moment, then drank. Paul was rock-solid. Steady. The kind of man who would help because it was in his nature to do so. He'd proven that over the short time she had known him.

Did she really want to drag him into the middle of her own uncertain world?

It could lead to a string of complications.

But there was no backing off from this. She wanted—*needed*—answers. Either way.

"I don't think I'm alone here. I've... seen some things, heard noises I can't identify."

For the longest time, he sat with his head tilted to one side, gazing past her while his broad shoulders rose and fell with slow, deep breaths. Inside, Allison cringed. Was he trying to decide how much, if anything, to tell her? Or did he think that she was just a bored female with an overactive imagination and too much time on her hands?

"It's an old house," he finally offered. "There's a lot of history here, a lot of memories. I suppose it would be easy to get caught up in the feel of it all, wondering about the past, the people."

Allison knew denial when she heard it. She was intimately familiar with it. Hadn't she lived with it, slept with it, Christ, *battled it* for years?

To ease her dry throat, she took a drink of wine. Then another. "I admit that the long history here captures my imagination. It's one of the things that first drew me to the house." She paused, searching for the words. "And I realize that old houses tend to be drafty, noisy. Wood sometimes creaks. Plumbing pipes might rattle or groan." She held his gaze now, not shying away from those intense blue eyes that seemed to peer past the surface, into the deeper part of her. "But I think it's more than that."

Paul swore under his breath, nodded. Then picked up his glass and drained it. "You mind?" he asked, reaching for the wine bottle.

Allison gestured for him to go ahead. She watched him pour, sip. Could see his mind turning.

"A few months before Mr. Treadwell died, he told my grandmother this house was haunted. Said the ghost here kept waking him up in the middle of the night. I think that kind of thing had been happening for a while—years, maybe. It really had him spooked. Hell, it had us all spooked."

He paused to take another drink of wine, and Allison reached for her own glass again. Haunted. She didn't know whether to feel relieved about that or not. Didn't she recall reading something about unsettled spirits, stirring up their anger?

Yes. She wondered now if she had done that by opening Bobbie Jean's diary. "Can you tell me anything about this ghost?"

"Now that," Paul said, "is where things get tricky. Do you—or, I guess I should say, did you—by any chance have a sister?"

She didn't get where he was going with this, but shook her head. "No, no sister. Why do you ask?"

"No sister," he repeated, ignoring her question. "Prior to your trip here to look at the house, have you ever been to Dawson Mills?"

"Not that I recall." Allison tried to think. "I guess it's possible I may have travelled through town, but if that's the case, I was too young to remember. Again—why do you ask?"

For what seemed an eternity, he searched her face. "You remind me of a girl I met a long time ago. Here—in this house. She was just a child."

"Okay," Allison said slowly, still not sure where this was leading. Then it clicked for her.

Head spinning with possibilities, she had to take a second to absorb, to reason. *Had* she been here before? Had her mother brought her to this small town? If so, why?

She helped herself to a healthy swallow of wine. "You think I'm that girl."

He sighed. "At first, yeah, I did. But—it's impossible."

"Impossible. Why?"

"Because." Eyes shaded now the same cobalt of his denim shirt, Paul stared down into his glass. "She's dead."

CHAPTER 13

"Dead," Allison murmured. "Are you sure?"

"As much as I can be."

She just shook her head. "What does that mean?"

Paul got up from the table, paced. "It's complicated. I was just a kid at the time. I don't even remember the girl's name."

"But you remember her face?"

"Yeah, well." He went away for a minute. "That face—it's hard to forget."

The darkness that clouded his eyes sent a shiver through her. Allison pushed her chair back and went over to him. "Can you tell me what happened?"

Paul sighed. "I could, but it's jumbled." He tapped a finger to his head. "Up here. Bits and pieces. Like I said—it's been a long time."

He rested his hands on her shoulders. "I know the idea of having a spirit roaming around your house is unsettling. But I don't think she wants to hurt anyone. She just—"

"Wants us to know she's here." Allison stepped back from the hold he had on her, frowning. The book that had somehow made its way onto her desk had an entire chapter dedicated to the earthbound dead. Disembodied spirits trapped between a world of human existence and some other, unknown place.

She had read that chapter over and over again, searching for answers, but had found it just too incredible to believe. After a while, she stopped seeing Ken, or what, she supposed, had been a vague, translucent image of him.

A memory, she had thought at the time. Just a fading memory.

Chewing at her bottom lip, Allison glanced at Paul. He'd moved next to the window that overlooked the back lawn. From there, he could see clear to the edge of the woods. "This girl—do you suppose she's..." At a loss, Allison just shrugged. "How do I say this? Maybe she needs help getting to wherever it is that we're supposed to go when we die."

The look he gave her was one of mild surprise, followed by a slow shift to reflection as he came back over to her. "I think you're right. And I've got a couple of friends who may be able to help with this—identify her, at least. I'll get in touch with them; see if I can shake something loose."

"Okay." Allison drew the first steady breath she'd managed in quite a while.

"I'll swing by here tomorrow after work. Hopefully, I'll have more information by then. Meantime"—Paul gripped her shoulders with the gentle pressure of a man who meant business—"if you need anything—anything at all—call me. Even if it's the middle of the night."

He touched a finger to her lips when she started to protest. "I'll leave my cell phone on. You've got the number. *Call me.*" He gave her shoulders a soft squeeze. "Promise."

Because she desperately needed the support, Allison nodded. "I promise."

Paul switched the lights on in the spare room he used as an office, set aside the blueprints he had carried in from the truck. He put his coffee mug on the desk and settled into the chair, scrubbed a hand over his face. And wondered if he had done the right thing.

It had been hard to sit there with Allison, after sharing an excellent meal and a bottle of good wine, while he watched her grapple with the little he had told her. She had seemed so vulnerable. He'd wanted to fold his arms around her, protect her. But he had kept his distance.

He hadn't lied, not exactly. He had just decided to keep certain things to himself, at least until he could make some sense of it all.

Paul took a slow sip from his mug, tried to sort through the jumble in his head.

No sister… have you ever been to Dawson Mills?

Not that I recall.

"Not that you recall," he muttered and shoved the chair back, paced over to the window. A fat yellow moon had broken through what was left of the hazy cloud cover. His gaze drifted over the open ground, back to the edge of the woods. He had always thought the moonlight eerie, the way it cast an unearthly glow over the night and drew out the shadows.

After the police had gone, and things had more or less settled down, his parents had followed him up to his bedroom to tuck him in. Paul lost himself in the memory for a second. He'd waited for the door to shut, gave it a few minutes, then pushed the covers back, padded over to the window. The moon was out, full and round, spilling pale blue light over the ground, into the woods.

For most of the night he'd sat by that window, his face pressed to the glass, wondering. Waiting.

The girl, he remembered, couldn't have been more than seven or eight at the time. She'd be about Allison's age now.

Well, he was just guessing at the age—Allison's, anyway—but he imagined he was close.

Paul heaved a sigh, and went back to his desk, glancing over at the prints he had brought in. He'd promised the homeowner an estimate by tomorrow.

Just sitting here wasn't getting the work done.

He took a long swallow of coffee, hoping the caffeine would

kick in soon, then unrolled the prints, stared down at the blue lines and angles on the stark-white page. He'd seen it—the sheer terror in those wide, green eyes. No one could have convinced him otherwise. The girl had to have been frightened beyond any rational thought.

She'd been just a child at the time, but the trauma—dammit, it would have stuck with her.

Unless…

He drummed his fingers on the desk. *Blocked*, he realized, and swore. The brain had a way of shutting out the bad stuff.

What were the odds that some deep part of Allison's subconscious had steered her back to this town, to that house?

Possible, he thought. More than possible. Jay Treadwell had never described the ghost that had haunted him. Paul had just assumed it was the girl.

For a moment tonight, he'd wondered if the spirit roaming that old house could be Bill's mom, but the idea just didn't track. Whatever was going on there had started before the woman had died.

So where did that leave them?

"I need more information." He checked his watch. Too late to be calling anyone, but tomorrow was several hours away, yet. A lifetime.

He grabbed the phone and punched in Bill Treadwell's number, relieved when his old friend assured him that the late hour was no problem. "The kids are having a sleepover at the neighbors', so we had dinner out, took in a movie. Just walked in the door, actually." Bill paused. "What's up?"

Now that he had Bill on the line, Paul wasn't sure where to start. "Some… things have come up. I need your help sorting through them."

"I'll do what I can. What's going on?"

"You remember when we were kids; you got that telescope for your birthday."

Silence dropped like a rock.

"Listen, Bill, I hate to bring this up."

"Then don't."

It wasn't that simple. Ignoring the situation wouldn't make it go away. Not this time. "I really don't have a choice."

Bill huffed out a breath. "I don't—hang on." He said something to his wife that Paul didn't quite catch, then gave it a minute. "I don't know why you're stirring this up after so long a time. But let it go, man. Just let it go."

"I can't. You know what we saw."

"I know what you *thought* you saw. For all of maybe three seconds, we got a glimpse of a little girl running through the woods. The rest of it? Hell, I didn't see anything else. Neither did Cliff."

The quiet hum of the long distance connection slipped between them. Paul didn't bother to explain that their friend, Cliff Barlow, later admitted to seeing more than what he had let on. Chickenshit, Paul had thought at the time. But he supposed he couldn't blame Cliff. They had all been so young.

"And yeah," Bill admitted, "I think it's strange the girl just disappeared after that. But you remember what the sheriff told us."

Sure. The family had headed down to Texas. No one seemed to know exactly where. He hadn't bought it then, and he sure as hell wasn't buying it now, even if Allison Weathers did turn out to be that little girl.

Something about the whole story was still... off.

"I guess you don't remember," Paul said, hearing the edge in his own voice, "the torn piece of her blouse they found down by the creek."

"Snagged it on some brambles while she was playing," Bill countered. "That's what the sheriff figured, and I have to go with that. There was no blood, remember? No real sign of foul play.

"And before you get revved on that crazy ghost theory again, the answer is still no. We never experienced anything out of the ordinary at home—ever." Bill paused. "Toward the end, Dad took a lot of medication."

"I'm aware of that." This conversation, Paul decided, was going nowhere. "Look, I just need to know if you remember the girl's name."

"Sorry, pal. Can't help you with that."

Can't, or won't?

"What about your sister? They played together a few times. If I could get her number—"

"I'm afraid I can't do that. She's had a rough time of it, emotionally, since Dad died. Dredging all this up would just upset her." Bill sighed. "I'm sorry, but it's late. I really have to go. Take care."

"Yeah. You too."

Shit. That went well. Paul grabbed his mug, glowered into it when he tasted lukewarm coffee. What he needed right now was just to shut it all down. Go upstairs to the master loft and collapse into bed. Or maybe stretch out on the sofa here in his office.

First thing tomorrow, he'd hunt down Cliff Barlow. Not that he expected Cliff to remember the girl's name. He'd had less contact with her than any of them. But Cliff was a detective now for the Sheriff's Department. He would have access to all the old case files.

And would fight Paul all the way on this. A case closed for decades, the file probably stuffed into a box and shoved back into a musty corner. Considered better forgotten by some.

"Fuck that." Paul shoved his chair back. Whatever information was in that file warranted another look.

He damned well intended to make that happened.

The echo of an owl hooting somewhere deep in the woods made him shudder. It was a lonely, eerie sound, like something lost, he thought. And wasn't that strange? Because owls were creatures of the night. Predators. They never lost their way.

From behind the bushes, he shifted his position on the damp ground. His ass had gone numb from sitting for so long. He eyed the girl's house, quiet and still now. Under the moonlight, it seemed to jut out from the darkness. Reminded him of a Gothic castle in one of those old horror movies.

Bradford, he supposed, fancied himself as some kind of knight-in-shining-fucking-armor.

He rubbed the back of his neck where the ache had been crawling around for a while, felt the familiar stab of pain that signaled another one of his headaches. And swore.

Getting to the girl now would require a slight change in plans.

A breeze brushed past him, stirring the fine hairs on his arms. For a second, he wondered where it had come from, that breeze, but then lost the thought. His mind didn't always work right when the pain in his head got bad.

And this was shaping up to be one mother of a migraine.

He pressed his fingers to his temples, then blinked. *Where was I?*

It took a minute for the answer to pop through the blank spot in his head.

Oh. The girl. Eyes narrowed, his gaze shifted back to the house. First, he'd have to dispose of Bradford. Something he should have taken care of years ago.

CHAPTER 14

T o Toni, the office seemed too quiet, even for a Sunday. *Dead zone,* she thought, and made a face at the morbid reference as her fingers tapped away at the computer's keyboard. But, yeah. The *Times* just wasn't the same without that buzzing, weekday rhythm—phones ringing, the chatter of interns in their cubicles soliciting subscriptions.

Funny how she missed the noise.

She stopped typing and sipped the last of her coffee before it got cold. Just outside her door, the copier hummed as it snoozed. Toni reached inside her desk for the notes she'd jotted down during Friday's meeting with her dad. He'd kept his voice low, the door to his office closed and locked. Scanning the pages, she frowned. The words, sentences, half-formed thoughts she'd scribbled had one hell of a weight. She could literally feel it hanging over her.

"Not anything you didn't sign up for," she muttered. Sure, her dad had given her an out, had hoped she'd take it. Toni just wasn't the type to toss in the paddle mid-stream. Neither was he. And because he knew when his daughter had her mind set, he hadn't wasted any time in getting down to business.

If my suspicions pan out, digging up the dirt will put both our butts at serious risk, kiddo. Anything you write down or record, lock it up.

She'd already figured as much, but hearing him say it had some-how put the danger up front and personal, where it needed to be.

The small safe she had at the condo, in her closet, was no good. Not with her niece visiting for the summer.

Toni tapped a finger on her desk. She had to be careful there, didn't she? With Jenna. The girl's... talent, for lack of a better term, had developed at an alarming rate. Sans control.

Several times over the last couple of weeks, Jenna had unwittingly reached into Toni's head, plucked out a random thought.

Freaky.

"Okay, Harper." She blew out a breath. "Stash it."

She shoved the notepad back in the drawer, locked her desk. It took some time, but she managed to push any thoughts on commercial development and sketchy funding into their own compartment, for now.

After completing the last of the revisions on an article for tomorrow's deadline, she reviewed her work, then sent it off as an e-mail attachment to her dad. Leaning back in the chair, Toni massaged the knotted muscles in her neck while her gaze roamed her cramped office.

Dull, cream-colored walls displayed an assortment of old photographs. A visual black and white history of the *Times,* some of the pictures taken just after Toni's great-grandfather had purchased this building.

She took in the rest of it. The standard beige carpet one would find in most offices—clean, but worn. A small visitor's chair. Crammed into a corner, there was a two-drawer metal file cabinet with a slight dent in its side.

The strip of sunlight that shone through the skinny window lured her focus away from the four walls and took her mind off to some faraway beach. White sand, a cloudless blue sky. Minimum clothing and plenty of suntan oil. Endless margaritas.

"Toni?"

She shot around in the chair, hissed out a breath when she saw her dad's assistant standing in the doorway. "*Kara.*"

"Sorry. I didn't mean to startle you. I saw your car out front, thought I'd pop back here and say hi."

Toni waved it off. "Don't worry about it. I was just…"

"Daydreaming, I think is the word." Kara's caramel-brown eyes twinkled behind her bifocals. "Where were you?"

"The truth? On a remote beach, soaking up the sun. Sipping, I might add, on the first of many frozen margaritas." Toni tilted her head, smiled at the petite woman who stood in front of the desk. The conservative dress Kara wore in cornflower blue picked up the highlights of her soft, silver-gray hair. Small pearl studs on her ears gave the overall look a simple elegance.

And here she sat, offspring of the man who owned this paper, wearing the old T-shirt and faded jeans she had yanked on this morning, the ensemble topped off with a pair of scuffed sneakers—no socks. Jeez.

"So, what are you doing here? Don't you get enough of this place during the week?"

Kara chuckled. "That's a fact. But I was halfway home from church when I realized I'd left the recipe book I brought in a while back on my desk." She took a seat in the small chair across from Toni, set her purse down. "I knew I'd need it today. Guess my memory's not what it used to be."

"Cut it out," Toni said. "You run circles around the rest of us. I don't see how you keep up with it all." She shook her head. "You're amazing, and you know it."

Kara smiled, lines fanning at the corners of her eyes. "I do all right for an old lady. But—why are you here? Any work that needs doing on a Sunday is usually something you tackle from home."

Before Toni could respond, Kara frowned. "It's this business with your father."

Yep. Sharp as ever.

"Well, you can't say anything, and that's fine. I'll keep the questions to myself. But if there's something I can do to help, please let me know."

Help. Toni nodded. She could use some of that. "Actually, there is some research I need done. There's an old Victorian farmhouse outside of town on Dawson Creek Road. Belonged to the Treadwell family. Are you familiar with them?"

The map of fine lines on Kara's forehead deepened as her lips pursed. "Can't say as I know—or knew, I suppose—any of them personally. But a friend of mine lives out that way. She was best friends with the wife, Bobbie Jean."

Kara just shook her head. "A real shame, her dying so young."

"Yeah, it is. Must have been hard on the family. I heard it was a massive heart attack."

"That's right. My friend, Alma, helped Jay see to the kids after his wife passed. It took the poor man quite a while to get over the sudden loss." Kara sighed, a gentle rush of air. "I married my George when I was eighteen. We had three children, nearly fifty years together. Good years. I think, when he passed, a small part of me went with him. I miss him every day."

"I know. I know you do." The feisty little woman who ran the office and kept them all in line was gone. Replaced by someone Toni didn't recognize. She wanted the other woman back. A good, strong hug, she thought, would do it. But not before it made them both tear up.

"Well." Kara managed a smile. "Enough about me. I can tell you that Jay never remarried. I suppose Bobbie Jean was the only one for him."

"It happens," Toni admitted, shoving Ray out of her head when he popped into it. And damned if he didn't creep right back in. Thick, jet-black hair around a tanned, rugged face. Startling, blue-green eyes that made her heart pound with just a look. Dangerous eyes.

Kara—bless her—pulled Toni's focus back. "I heard a woman from Nashville recently bought the house."

Toni nodded. "Allison Weathers. I met her the other day. I liked her. Anyway, it's just curiosity at this point, but—Ray's men responded to a few calls out that way. Apparently, Jay Treadwell kept insisting the house was—"

"I know, I know. Ghosts, haunted." Kara shrugged. "I'm not sure I believe in that sort of thing. But when you've been around as long as I have, you learn to keep an open mind."

Brows knitting, she tilted her head. "What about your sources at the Sheriff's Department? Can't they give you any information?"

Toni scowled. "Can, but won't."

"I see." A sly smile played over Kara's lips. And yeah, the twinkle in her eyes was back. "I'll just have a talk with my friend. Then I guess we'll see what we see."

The sun warmed her bare shoulders as she jogged along the side of the road. With the humidity up from all the rain, Allison had opted to wear shorts and a sleeveless crop top. The woods, she knew, would be much cooler because of the dense tree cover. But the idea of venturing in there alone again made her uneasy.

She picked up the pace, rounded a long curve, heading down the last stretch of road that would lead her back to the house. Her nice, quiet, peaceful house. The last couple of days, she'd experienced a welcome lull in the unsettling activity there.

A disembodied spirit roaming her house. Jesus. How was that possible? Could all the doctors, with their years of medical training, be wrong?

Paul seemed to have accepted the idea. But now that she'd had some time to think it through, Allison just wasn't sure. Admitting there were such things as ghosts meant that she had squandered nearly two years. Hopeless, lost. Drifting through a dark void with her brain in a medicated fog, until what was left of her husband had faded away.

She swallowed over the burn in her throat, refusing to dwell on that now.

Still, on the off chance that she had stirred a dead woman's anger, Allison had left the diary in the drawer of her nightstand, untouched.

She zipped around a patch of loose gravel. The landscape changed when trees and underbrush gave way to an open field of tall grass. Allison angled her face to catch the light breeze that had come up. Ghost or not, whatever had been trying to communicate with her, and scaring the hell out of her in the process, had been quiet.

Since Paul had started coming over, she realized, and frowned.

Her lungs working to keep up now, Allison adjusted her pace to a moderate jog, then slowed to a walk, so she could think without the added effort of having to focus on her breathing. After Paul had left Thursday evening, she'd half expected whatever was there with her to finish the business it had started earlier in the kitchen. But there had been no icy chill. No shadows. No voice.

The house had seemed almost too quiet.

Allison watched a butterfly flutter past her and settle onto a fencepost. Maybe the calm would last. She wasn't betting on it, but, for now, would try to stay positive. She'd had two productive days without interruption, had managed to finish the sculpture she'd started, get it fired and crated, and labeled for shipment.

Evenings she'd spent with Paul. He'd found no leaks in the roof, so, still a puzzle. But just with him being there, the world had seemed right again. Sturdier. Normal.

Allison smiled at the memory as she walked under the warm sun. Other than mentioning that he was still waiting to hear back from a friend about the girl, they hadn't talked of ghosts or haunted houses. Instead, they'd chatted like old friends about work, the weather, and life in general while he helped hang the last of the paintings she'd left stacked in the foyer.

After, they had watched old movies on TV, eaten popcorn, and munched on the most delicious oatmeal-raisin cookies she had ever tasted—compliments of Paul's grandmother.

Allison slowed when the lovely, old two-story cedar farmhouse that belonged to Annie Bradford stretched into view. The gardens, a blooming riot of color, swept along the gentle curves of a postcard-picture lawn. She took a deep breath of fresh, country air, tilted her head up to the blue, blue sky. A hawk soared in swooping circles above the treetops before it zoomed off.

Life here had the potential to be better than good.

Hadn't she known that?

Yeah. She had just needed a reminder.

She wasn't sure where Paul fit into that life, not yet. But she enjoyed his company. For now, that was enough.

Her heart slammed into her throat when the animal darted out from the tall grass just inches in front of her and stopped. The little dog she'd seen in the woods—thick, black fur still matted and filthy—whimpered and wagged its tail.

"*Jesus.*" Allison put a hand to her chest. "You scared the life out of me!"

The dog cocked its small head and whimpered again.

An apology, in doggie language. It tugged at her heart. Allison studied the poor little thing. The dog still looked as though it hadn't eaten a good meal in weeks. "Have you been out in the woods all this time?"

Those soulful brown eyes looked up at her with such sadness… Boy, was she in trouble.

In a slow, smooth motion, Allison lowered herself to a half-sitting position, her weight balanced on the balls of her feet. "Would you like to come home with me?"

The dog wagged its tail.

"Guess that settles it." She reached for him, then paused. "You are a 'him,' aren't you? Because we don't need a bunch of puppies running around."

Allison glanced under the animal's sunken belly. Yes. A male. That made things easier for both of them. Either way, though, she wouldn't have left the poor thing here to starve.

The dog back-stepped, growling low in its throat when the dull roar of an engine slowed behind them. Allison glanced over her shoulder just as Paul's truck eased to the side of the road and rolled to a stop. She waved. "It's okay, boy. He's a friend. Now, let's get you"—she turned, reached, grabbed a handful of air, and muttered—"home."

Where did he go?

Paul walked up to her, helped her to her feet. "What are you doing?"

Allison just shook her head. "I was going to take that stray dog home, give him a good meal and a bath. Apparently, he had other ideas. What?" she asked when he frowned.

"I didn't see any dog."

She shrugged that off. "I think the poor thing's been lost for a while now. He's probably just wary of people in general."

"Could be. He's quick, I'll give him that."

He was. The little guy had pulled the same vanishing act on her out in the woods. She noticed now the shadow over Paul's eyes, the tight line of his jaw. "What's wrong?"

His gaze drifted past her. "Were you out for a run?"

"Was. I'm heading back to the house now. Tell me what's wrong." It took her a second, but when he sighed, she got it. "The girl. You heard back from your friend, is that it?"

Silence drifted in.

"Why don't you let me give you a ride home? We'll talk there."

They rode the short distance in silence, Paul with his jaw set, eyes straight ahead on the road. Allison gazed out the passenger window at rolling fields separated by patches of woods, the occasional farmhouse. Theories—none of them good—ran rampant through her head.

By the time they pulled up to the house, tension had knotted the muscles in her neck and shoulders. She rubbed the back of her neck, tilting her head to one side to stretch out the kinks.

"Headache?"

"Getting one." And the inside of her mouth had gone dry. Swallowing was like gulping stale air. "I should probably take some aspirin."

"Then let's get you inside." He hopped out, opened the passenger door for her. As he followed her back to the kitchen, the ache turned into a nagging pain that crept up the back of her skull and throbbed behind her eyes. Allison wondered if she looked as shaky as she felt.

"Mind if I grab a Coke?"

"Help yourself." She rummaged through a cabinet, found the bottle of aspirin.

"Water for you?"

"Please." She popped two pills into her mouth and took a long swallow from the bottle he handed her, the cold water like heaven on her parched throat. Allison leaned a hip against the counter, gave herself a second to steady. "Tell me what you found out."

Paul took a pull from his soda can, then paused. "This is going to take a while. Why don't you go ahead and have your shower first? Give those aspirin a chance to work."

What little patience she'd mustered during the ride home exploded from her in a fireball of irritation. "*I don't want a damned shower!*" She slammed the bottle down on the counter, sloshing water everywhere. "I—"

So much for keeping a calm head.

"I'm sorry."

"It's okay." He rested a hand on her shoulder. "Go on up, get under the hot water for a few minutes. You'll feel better."

Allison gazed into the shadows that lingered over his blue eyes. "Will I?"

He was right. A hot shower had done wonders. For the physical part of her, anyway. Mentally, Allison felt like a wreck in capris and a cotton blouse waiting to happen.

She opened the fridge, got drinks for both of them, then, with a deep breath to steady, went into the living room. Paul stood by the fireplace, gazing at the framed photograph of her and Ken that she had placed on the mantel. Under the subtle wash of sunlight shining through the leaded-glass windows, his honey-amber hair shimmered like soft gold. He'd turned back the cuffs of his white cotton shirt, exposing toned forearms bronzed by the sun.

For a moment, she couldn't seem to take her eyes off him.

Oh, Jesus. She had to put this attraction away. The timing was all wrong. To be honest, she wasn't sure whether it would ever be right.

Steering her mind back to where it should be, Allison set her glass of iced tea on the end table by the sofa, then handed Paul a fresh Coke.

"Thanks. I didn't notice this picture before. Your husband?"

"Yes." Puzzled, she studied him for a second. He'd told her about his ex-wife. Even though she had relocated to Washington, they remained friends, and still kept in touch. That alone spoke volumes about the man standing next to her. But Allison just hadn't been able to bring herself to tell him about Ken.

Mae, she realized. Mae must have told him.

"I'd been putting off going through a box of photographs. Last night, after you left, I finally got around to it."

She picked up the photo, gazed down at the warm hazel eyes, the boyish, crooked grin. "He was killed in an automobile accident.

It's been over two years, but..." Allison set the picture back on the mantel. A quiet sigh trembled out of her.

"It's hard losing someone you love." Paul put a hand to the small of her back and led her over to the sofa, sat next to her. "I lost my parents and younger sister when I was twelve."

"I'm so sorry." He'd mentioned that his grandparents had raised him, but hadn't expounded. She had wondered.

He nodded. "I was at summer camp when it happened. Drunk driver." His eyes went dark. "He was the only one who survived."

"That must have been rough."

"It was. My dad's parents were there for me—that helped. They put their house up for sale, moved into ours so I wouldn't have to deal with any more drastic changes.

"My grandfather's gone now. I'm grateful that Gran is still with me."

And still living next door, Allison mused, picturing the hanging swing on the wide front porch of Annie Bradford's farmhouse, the lazily paddling ceiling fans. Gardens graced with the same loving care that had nurtured Paul. She was curious about the barn he had remodeled—his home now.

He gave her a soft smile when she mentioned it. "Guess it's what you'd call modern-rustic. Hardwood floors, granite counter-tops in the kitchen and bathrooms. A huge deck off the back. I'll give you a tour sometime."

"I'd like that." And she appreciated that he had managed to put her at ease. But it was time to move on.

Allison sampled her iced tea. "So. About the girl. Talk to me."

Nodding, Paul scrubbed a hand over his face. "Looks like I may have run into a wall, trying to identify her." He sent her a sideways glance. "There are some things I didn't tell you before."

She frowned. "Like what?"

"First, I need you to understand something. There were too many questions I didn't have answers for, still are. I knew what I had to say would only confuse you more." Paul just shook his head. "I suppose I wanted to save you from that."

Trying to protect her. Why did that seemingly good intention always lead to lies or half-truths? Did he think she was fragile? Had he just assumed that her delicate mind couldn't work through a conflict?

Oh, she could tell him a thing or two about conflict.

To push down the irritation that had shot through her, she focused on keeping her breathing slow, steady. "Tell me all of it. Now."

"Yeah. Guess it's time I did just that." He took a quick sip of Coke, ran a hand across the back of his neck. "I was just a kid when it happened. Ten years old and thought I knew pretty much everything." His mouth curved—a faint smile that didn't quite reach his eyes. "Bill had just turned twelve. Anyway, school was out for the summer.

"I think..." Paul narrowed his eyes. "Yeah. It was a Sunday, late afternoon. We'd had a baseball game right after church, had just gotten back from the park. Bill's mom stayed home, wasn't feeling well. But she insisted on riding into town with his dad and sister for ice cream, said the change of scenery would do her good."

As anxious as she was for Paul to get to the heart of it, Allison let him take what she thought was the long way around. When she'd been lost in that dark place, reliving each small detail of the events that had put her there had helped her to crawl her way out.

It had been a slow and painful process.

"Bill talked his parents into letting him stay home. We wanted to check out the telescope he'd gotten for his birthday. Another friend who lived down the street at the time came over, helped us set up outside."

Looking past her, Paul frowned. "A thunderstorm came up out of nowhere. It was raining—hard. We had to move the telescope up

125

to his sister's room." He glanced back over at her. "That would be the room you're using for a studio now."

Allison nodded. "The arched window would have given you a broad view."

"It did. Back then, the underbrush was spotty in places. We could see fifteen, maybe twenty feet into the woods. There were three deer, a doe and two little ones. They were just standing there, grazing on some bushes. Made us all jump when the doe jerked her head up and they shot back into the woods.

"A few seconds later, we saw her. The girl," Paul said when he caught the question in Allison's eyes. "She bolted out from behind some trees, zigzagged around the brush. I swear she was moving like Satan himself was after her."

"What—?"

He held a hand up. "We zoomed in on her just for a second, but it was enough. She was terrified." He stopped, and when his eyes met hers, Allison shuddered.

"We swung the telescope over, tried to see what she was running from. Bear don't usually come this far down from the mountains, but occasionally one or two will wander this way."

Bear. Dear God. She had jogged right into the woods, oblivious, had never even considered the possibility of something like that. Allison put a hand to her throat. The image in her head made it difficult to swallow. "Was it? A bear?"

"That's what we thought at first, but no." Paul dropped his gaze. The shadows in his eyes were back. "We didn't see the guy's face, but judging by his height and speed..."

"A man," Allison murmured. "You saw a man chasing her."

"Yeah. We all stood there for a minute, couldn't move. Shock, I guess. Once we snapped out of it, I ran home, got my dad to call the police."

He sighed. "They found a torn piece of her blouse down by the creek."

"And the girl?"

"No, nothing."

Allison frowned. "So it's possible she could still be alive."

Paul reached over, gave her hand a squeeze. "I swear, when I first saw you, I couldn't believe it."

"Because I remind you of her." She paused, trying to work through it. "I understand why you wouldn't be able to forget that poor child's face. Even if she had lived, though... It's been decades. What makes you so sure she'd look anything like me now?"

"Believe me, I've asked myself that same question." Paul shook his head again. "I know it doesn't prove a thing, but you're a mirror image of the girl's mother."

Her heart tripped. She gripped his arm, squeezed. "Her mother. You met her mother?"

"Yeah. I—"

"Wait. Just wait." Allison bolted off the sofa, ignoring wobbly legs that threatened to give way under her. "I'll be right back."

She rushed upstairs, grabbed the faded photograph she had put back in her jewelry box. Her mind raced right along with her pulse. Hope, like a tiny flame, had kindled inside her. She knew better than to let the fire rise, was still reminding herself of that as she thrust the picture at him.

When the frown clouded his face, Allison knew she had her answer.

"That's her."

CHAPTER 15

"MY MOTHER." ALLISON SANK DOWN onto the sofa before her legs could buckle.

"Are you okay?"

"I'm—just give me a minute."

"Sure." Paul set the photograph of her mother on the low table in front of them and went over to one of the windows, gazed out.

The questions were like a barrage of explosions in her head. It was too much, just too much. Her mother, the girl no one seemed to be able to identify—it all made a horrible kind of sense. And no sense at all.

Shaking, Allison got to her feet. "I need some air. Mind if we take this out on the back porch?"

Watching her, Paul nodded, then followed her out. They sat in the wicker chairs, setting their drinks on the table between them. He took a slow scan of her face. "You don't remember being here before, but the connection to this—your mother—can't be a coincidence."

Allison gazed out across her back lawn, to where the domed tops of Black-eyed Susans swayed in the light breeze. The birds were singing, happy in their minute-to-minute world.

He reached over, brushed his hand along her arm. "Talk to me."

Talk. She could barely breathe. Allison rubbed her hands over her face and sighed. "There was an accident. I'm not sure how old

I was when it happened. Most of my memory around that time is muddled. But I was young."

"What *do* you remember?"

"Not much, to be honest. Definitely not the accident, or the few days leading up to it." Allison dredged up what little memory of that time she had. Her eyes had fluttered open to a blur of light and shadows. God, she'd been so scared. Then her vision began to focus. She'd found herself in a bed with metal bars on the sides, in a room with a white-tiled floor that smelled of antiseptic. Her head felt thick and groggy. It had taken a tremendous amount of effort just to move her small arms.

She reached for her iced tea and drank. It did nothing to calm her. What she needed was a shot of whiskey. "I was in a coma for nearly a week. When I woke up in the hospital, Mother was gone. Just"—her breath hitched—"gone."

Because she needed the silence, just for a moment, she let it settle between them. "Dad won't talk about it. All these years, the only thing I've been able to get out of him is that he blames my mother for what happened."

Allison glanced sideways at Paul. Her gaze followed his to the distant line of trees that marked the edge of the woods. How many times over the years had he looked out onto those same woods, past the vibrant colors of autumn, the dull winter browns, or the budding life of spring and summer, and wondered?

As many times, she imagined, as she had gazed down at the faded photograph of her mother, wanting—no, *needing*—answers.

"I told you that I moved here to get away from the city. That's true, but... there's more."

He pulled his focus away from the woods. "I'm listening."

She blew out a breath. "When Mother left, my dad hired a private investigator to find her. He traced her here, to Dawson Mills." Allison frowned. "A few months before I bought the house, I hired my own investigator."

"No luck?" Paul guessed.

"No, none."

Needing to move—to do something—she got up and went over to the porch rail, angled her face up to the warm afternoon sun. Her life was changing again. She could feel it. What little stable ground she'd found since coming here had begun shifting beneath her.

Careful what you wish for. How many times over the years had her dad tried drumming that into her head?

She hadn't wanted to listen. Still didn't.

"How did you meet my mother?"

"It was the same day we saw you—the girl—through Bill's telescope. Early that morning." He got up and stood next to her, scanning the woods. "I came over here to get my baseball bat. The game," he reminded her. "Your mother was just coming out the back door. She was in a hurry, barely noticed me."

With her mind spinning through the jumble of information, Allison had almost missed the significance of what he had just said. Then it clicked.

"My mother—what was she doing here?"

"I don't know. At the time, I didn't think to ask. I was... just a kid." Paul heaved a sigh. "I'll never forget her face, though. The look in her eyes. Like a cornered animal." He shook his head. "Something, or someone, had her running scared."

Running scared. She got a mental flash—hushed, angry voices behind her parents' closed bedroom door, her own small hand moving away from the doorknob as she turned to tiptoe back down the hall. Her belly jerked into a knot.

"Did you tell the police?"

"Yeah. But I'd walked up onto the back porch just as she was coming out the door. They figured I had probably startled her." He shook his head again. "I know there was more to it."

Allison gripped his arm when a sudden movement stirred the dense undergrowth at the western edge of her property.

"What is it?"

Frowning, she squinted. "It's gone now, but…" She pointed at a cluster of bushes. "I saw a flash of something dark."

"Stay here."

Before she could argue, he shot down the steps, dodged the picnic table, and bolted across the lawn. Heart hammering, she watched him disappear into the underbrush.

"Ouch."

"Sorry. I know it stings." Allison waited for Paul to lean back in the chair, and with a gentle touch, continued to dab the alcohol-soaked cotton ball over the red, puffy scratch on his arm while he winced. Then did the same to his scraped elbow. "All done."

"Thanks. Guess you didn't expect to have your kitchen turned into an emergency room, huh?"

Smiling, she set everything on the counter, tossed the used cotton balls into the trash. "I'd hardly call a few scratches and scrapes an 'emergency,' but no." She washed her hands at the kitchen sink, grabbed a paper towel to dry them. And was still smiling when she turned back around.

For a moment, while she'd cleaned the light streaks of blood from his arm, the tall, muscular, blue-eyed man with the killer smile had turned into a small boy. "I'm sorry you were hurt."

He waved it off. "Damned tree jumped right out in front of me."

"Of course it did." She didn't bother to remind him that it was impossible for a tree to jump out at anything, much less a dead and rotting one that had already fallen to the ground. "And I'm sorry you ruined your shirt."

Paul looked down at the smudges of dirt on white cotton, the tear in the sleeve, and shrugged. "It's just a shirt." He shook his head. "Dog had to be a magician in his last life."

"I suppose so." All this trouble because she hadn't realized the dark flash of movement in those bushes could be the stray dog that kept popping up. She had panicked. "How far did you follow him?"

"Not very. My up close and personal with the tree put a hitch to the chase." He shook his head again. "I don't think I'd've caught him anyway. Rascal's quick. I was lucky just to get a glimpse of him."

Allison nodded. The little stinker had an irritating tendency to vanish before you could blink. "Would you like another Coke, or some iced tea? If you're hungry, I could put a sandwich together."

"Just water for me, thanks."

She grabbed two bottles of water from the fridge, passing one to Paul as she took the chair next to him. She was calmer now. Collected. "We should finish our conversation."

"I agree." He took a long drink. "Like I said, I think there was more to your mother's reaction than her just being startled. Bill's mom came out on the porch about that time. She looked worried. She gave me my bat, told me to get on back to the house."

Paul frowned. "Whatever was going on, Bill's mom kept it to herself."

A secret that had followed her to the grave. Allison shuddered.

"The girl was here for only a few days, a week at best. Staying with someone in the area." Paul slanted a glance in her direction. "I don't know who. All the sheriff would tell us was that the father got a job somewhere in Texas. They packed up and headed that way."

"Father," Allison echoed. The knot in her belly was back, twisting a little tighter. But "staying with someone" was hardly her dad's style. Jack Kincaid was a man who required privacy, was accustomed to the comforts money could buy. As far as she knew, he'd never had to answer to anyone. The money—and there had always been plenty of it—had come from his own lucrative business investments.

Paul covered her hand with his. "You have any relatives down that way? In Texas?"

"Not that I know of. I don't remember my mother's parents,

though. We never had any contact with that side of the family after she left."

Allison moved her hand away from his. She felt herself drifting into some kind of weird, mental fog where nothing was real. Had her entire life been a series of smoke and mirrors?

Fighting the sigh that rode on a hot ball of anger, she took a drink from her water bottle.

Paul angled in the chair to face her. "I talked to Bill Treadwell. He couldn't remember the girl's name. I think she came over to play with his kid sister a couple of times."

"Were you able to get in touch with her—the sister?"

He shook his head. "Bill really didn't want me to go there. She's still having a hard time accepting their dad's death."

And Mae Davis, Allison knew, wouldn't give out that information without consent.

"I doubt his sister would remember much, if anything. She was so young." Paul sighed. "The friend who was with us when it happened is a detective now for the Sheriff's Department. You'd think he'd want answers. He hasn't put a lot of effort into hunting up the old case file."

"Don't talk about it, and it'll just go away," Allison murmured.

"Something like that."

Rage spiked in a hot rush to the top of her head. If the clouded look Paul gave her was any indication, Allison thought that her anger was probably radiating off her in waves.

She didn't care. When the words came out, her voice was quiet, calm. Chilling. "My father is a rich and powerful man. Determined. I think he would do just about anything to keep the truth from me."

Allison took a sharp breath to stop the shaking. "A nice, fat sum of money would probably ensure that the man I hired to look for Mother kept silent." A short laugh trembled out of her. "And, hell, why stop there? With his political connections, he could very well control the entire police force in this area."

Paul frowned. "I think... before we jump to any conclusions, we should consider the possibility that your father was just trying to protect you."

There was that damned word again.

Allison gazed through the large bay window. A squirrel scampered under the warm golden light slanting across her lawn. The sun had shifted well to the west. Soon the afternoon would be gone. "There was an argument—I think. My parents. I don't recall what was said, just the anger."

She paused, struggling to remember more, and getting nothing. "Mother may have left and taken me with her. I have no idea why she chose Dawson Mills, but... Once my dad located us he would have come for me."

Paul nodded. "And if you were traumatized by whatever happened in those woods, he would have wanted to spare you from remembering that. What?" he asked when she frowned.

"I went jogging the other day, into the woods. There was an area down by the creek..." She shook her head. "It seemed familiar. Nothing I could put my finger on, just a vague sense of something."

Allison let out the sigh she'd kept pent up. "I've got to know what happened in those woods."

"Yeah, same here." Paul shoved out of the chair, paced. "You mentioned your stepbrother helped you move in. Does he have any influence with your father?"

"I don't know. I doubt it. But until I have a better idea of what I'm dealing with, I don't want to drag Steve into this."

He stopped, gazing out the window above the sink. "You're probably right. I have to wonder, though, about your mother's connection to this town. Could be she stayed with relatives here. If that's the case, she might still be somewhere in the area. We need to try to locate her."

So she was back to where she'd started. Armed with more information, maybe, but still at square one. "Actually, I know someone who might be able to help with that. I met her the other day." She told him about Toni Harper.

He nodded. "I did some remodel work for her dad a while back. She's solid. You can trust her."

Deep down Allison had felt that, but it was good to hear. On her feet now, she laid a hand on his arm. "Thank you. For working through this with me."

He reached up, brushed a stray curl away from her face. "I wouldn't have it any other way. I'd like to be there when you talk to Toni, but—*Christ*." Paul raked a hand through his hair. "I forgot to tell you. I'll be out of town for a few days."

She couldn't explain the punch of panic she felt. Or the instant aloneness. She only hoped it didn't show.

"My grandmother's sister took a nasty fall. Doctors put her on bed rest for a week. She lives in Virginia. Gran refuses to fly, and there's no way I'm letting her take a bus up there."

"When are you leaving?"

"In the morning, early. I'll be gone just long enough to get her settled in." He rested his hands on her shoulders. "I hate like hell to leave you alone."

For a moment, this close to him, Allison had a hard time finding her voice. "I'll... be fine."

"If you're not"—he gave her shoulders a gentle squeeze—"call me on my cell. Even if you just need to talk."

"I will. And remember to keep those scratches clean."

Releasing his hold on her, he grinned. "Yes, ma'am."

Allison set their water bottles on the counter, and went with him into the foyer. Opening the door, she paused. "If I am that girl, and this house really is haunted..."

"Whose spirit is trapped here?" He frowned. "Good question."

Soft moonlight had slipped into her bedroom through a part in the curtains. Allison jerked at the bedcovers and rolled onto her side, a jumbled bundle of nerves that stared at the muted glow coming through the window. Her head was beginning to throb from all the questions that had been racing around up there for the last several hours.

And she'd let herself run out of chamomile tea, dammit. Something that rarely happened.

She made another effort to quiet her mind. And failed. Miserably.

She should call Steve. He'd be up, probably at the studio. Twice, before climbing into bed, she had picked up the phone, and had to remind herself that dragging her brother into this wasn't a good idea.

Still wasn't.

With Paul out of town, she was on her own. At least until she could talk to Toni.

Allison shoved the covers aside and went over to the window, peered out. The silvery light that washed over her back lawn flowed right up to the edge of the woods. A vast, softly glittering sea of absolute stillness.

It made her feel small and alone, all the silent, unmoving space.

What was she doing here, really?

She could believe fate had led her to this small town to find a rhythm. To settle. But stumbling onto this house in the process...

No, not a coincidence.

Shadows of tree leaves fluttered over the moonlit ground with the breeze that had come up. Those shadows, she thought, were a lot like memories. Dormant until something came along to stir them.

Her gaze drifted back to the darker mass of woods. Somewhere, buried deep in the back of her brain, were long forgotten fragments of her past. She wondered now if those hidden pieces of memories had brought her here, to this place.

It fit. God, it fit.

Allison glanced back at the vague silhouette of her nightstand, to the drawer there, where she'd tucked the diary away. Hadn't she read that the burden of unfinished business sometimes held a spirit to this world?

Yes. And Bobbie Jean had died so suddenly.

It wasn't just the fear of sparking a dead woman's anger that had kept Allison from reading further. After what Paul had told her, the idea of what she might find on those pages terrified her.

What did that say about her?

"Not much," she muttered, and closed the curtains.

Her dad had known all along that she'd bolt when the going got rocky.

Well, she wouldn't, not this time. Maybe she had faltered for a few hours tonight, but she refused to crawl inside herself and hide.

Armed with that, Allison climbed back under the covers and switched on the bedside light, reached into her nightstand drawer. She propped the plush, down pillows behind her, then opened the diary to the page she had bookmarked, and paused.

She hadn't mentioned the diary to Paul. She'd have to, though, wouldn't she?

There was no way around it.

She pulled her focus back down to the looping script. And froze when she heard muffled voices downstairs.

CHAPTER 16

ER HAND DARTED OVER TO the bedside light and switched it off, throwing the room back into a muted glow of moonlight. Trembling, Allison strained her ears to catch any minute sound.

Nothing. Nothing but the ragged murmur of her own unsteady breathing.

She hadn't imagined those voices. She'd left her bedroom door open, just a crack, enough for the sound to reach her. Not the same distant, airy plea she'd heard in her studio, but hushed—solid.

Heart hammering, she groped for her cell phone and flipped it open. Jolted when the display didn't blink on.

Damn. Damn, damn. She'd forgotten to plug in the charger.

What now?

Sitting helpless in the dark just wasn't an option. It unnerved her even more than the idea of confronting whoever was downstairs.

Allison pushed the covers aside, crept out of bed, and fumbled around for her purse, found her pepper spray. She tiptoed over to the door, easing it open just wide enough for her to slip through. Then stopped.

There. Again. It sounded like...

Children.

Impossible.

Gripping the rail, she rushed downstairs through the pale wash of light that shone through the overhead windows in the foyer. One bare foot touched down onto the hardwood floor, and the cold slammed into her, a chilling wall of ice. The bitter freeze went straight through to her bones, filled her lungs. Racked with shivers under her lightweight sleep-shirt, Allison wondered why her breath didn't frost in front of her.

Ears perked, she took a cautious step forward and bit back an oath when a floorboard creaked. Her head jerked around at the earnest mutters that shot out from the kitchen.

Young voices.

Jesus. How did they get in?

As she hurried toward the kitchen, a niggling in the back of her brain told her the drop in temperature might have something—*everything*—to do with that. But when her hand darted around the corner and groped for the light switch, the cold was gone.

In less than a finger snap, she realized, but didn't have time to question.

Squinting under the harsh, fluorescent light, Allison glanced around. Nothing was out of place. And the deadbolt on the back door—still thrown.

Her gaze zipped over to the door that led to the utility room—open a few inches.

Hadn't she closed that door?

She took a breath to steady. "Hello?"

The absolute silence that followed was deafening.

"I know you're in there. Come on out."

Allison gave it a minute, then, with a finger poised on her pepper spray, started for the utility room. She glanced over at the phone on the wall. Maybe she should call the police.

No. No, they were just kids.

Little thieves, she thought, and narrowed her eyes.

Or just bored, snuck out of the house. Giving the new lady in the neighborhood a good scare.

Well. A phone call to the parents would straighten this out. If not, she wouldn't hesitate to bring the law into it.

Nudging the door to the utility room open with her foot, she flicked on the light, and found the cellar door swung back all the way on its hinges. Allison swore. She didn't want to go down there. She really didn't. She'd seen enough late-night horror movies to know it wasn't a good idea.

And she wished now that she'd taken just a second back there in the kitchen to phone Paul.

No. She shook her head. He was leaving in the morning. Early. She wouldn't drag him out of bed.

She could do this.

Moving past the clutter of cleaning supplies, she reached around into the dark opening, flipped the light switch. And stood there staring into the pitch-black.

Great.

She stuck her head in, shuddered from the damp, chilly air that came off the concrete below. "Come out of there—*now!*"

There was a rustle of movement, the shuffle of small footsteps. Followed by a long stretch of silence.

Okay.

Scowling, Allison stomped back into the kitchen, then grabbed her flashlight from under the counter. She had half a mind to phone the police after all, teach the little brats a lesson.

She shoved the impulse aside and went down to the cellar, shivering from the chill that darted up her spine as the beam cut through the darkness. God, it was cold down here.

With the rough concrete scraping against the bottom of her bare feet, Allison clutched her pepper spray in one hand while she gripped the flashlight with the other, and inched forward. Dust motes floated along the narrow beam of light, cobwebs shimmered. The old boiler in the corner next to the air-handling unit popped out in stark, metal relief.

She swung the beam up to the horizontal windows that lined the top of the west wall, scanned the locks. Satisfied, she blew out a short breath. "Okay. Game's over. I'll give you just two seconds to come out."

A mocking silence answered.

Either she'd delivered the ultimatum with zero authority, or the little sneaks were getting a kick out of watching her work at this.

Probably both.

Allison spun around on her heel, wincing when the concrete dug in, then aimed the beam under the staircase. And went rigid. An industrious spider, busy spinning a web in the corner, had gone still as stone when the light hit it. She hated the way spiders seemed to have a sixth sense, as if they knew you were thinking about swatting them with the first thing you could grab.

Of course, they knew. And this one was staring right back at her. She could feel it.

Cringing, Allison lowered the light and backed away. She eased into the corner where the old boiler stood, skimmed the light along the area behind it. A frown moved over her face. More cobwebs, layers of dust. That was it.

There wasn't enough space between the air-handling unit and the wall for even the smallest person to squeeze into.

"Where did you go?" In the stillness, her half-whisper sounded hollow. And when had the temperature changed? The air down here still felt damp, clammy, but the cold was gone.

I need to get out of here.

She turned, and when the beam angled across the dirty concrete floor, something glimmered there under the light. Allison set her pepper spray aside, crouched down. Then dipped her fingertips into the small puddle.

Water.

Where—?

Her head jerked around at the sudden sound of scratching. Pulse tripping, she yanked herself up, backed out of the corner, and ran the beam in a fast, wild arc over the room.

Thumping now. Against glass.

She swung the light up to the windows.

There... Over there. A dark, wet snout pressed against the other side of the glass, the small, familiar face covered in a tangle of matted, black fur. Soulful brown eyes transformed by the light into two unearthly glowing orbs.

The dog thumped its paw against the glass again.

"*You!*" Allison darted up the stairs, losing her grip on the flashlight, ignoring it as it bumped and rolled down to the concrete. She flipped the deadbolt on the back door, flew out onto the porch. Then skidded to a halt.

A gauzy line of clouds had drifted across the moon, leaving only patches of wan light over the ground. In the distance, beneath a trace of that moonlight, about halfway between the middle of her lawn and the edge of the woods, stood a small boy.

She felt the familiar pull of his gaze, and recognized the bright gold hair—the boy she'd seen while jogging, the kid Steve had caught messing around in her back yard.

Allison hurried down the steps, conscious of the dewy grass beneath her bare feet, the cool, damp breeze shifting her hair around.

He would bolt before she could get to him. She just knew it.

Oddly enough, he didn't. The boy stood there, wide eyes fixed on her, waiting.

Chilled from the cold that had crept into the air, she stopped just a few feet in front of him, took a deep breath to steady her thudding heart. The tattered overalls and old, holey T-shirt he wore looked thin as rice paper.

She glanced down at his bare feet: filthy.

Keeping a wary eye on her, he tilted his head. The poor child had the shaggiest hair she had ever seen. And under the soft moonlight, what had seemed like shadows across his pale face just moments ago were now heavy smudges of dirt.

Her heart melted. "Hi. I'm Allison. What's your name?"

The boy just stood there, eyes the midnight blue of sapphire watching her.

Okay. She'd try another tack.

"Where's your little friend?"

She waited through the silence while the damp grass chilled her feet right up to the ankles. The air was like ice now on her skin. Allison was tempted to grab the kid and shake him.

Finally, he lifted his small shoulders. "She's scared."

"Scared. Of me?"

He shook his head, and the wind stirred in a frigid gust that made her shudder. The moisture in the air was thick now. She could smell the rain. Allison glanced up at the clouds when thunder rumbled, jolting when the small black dog bounded out from behind a tree.

"*You again.*"

The dog half wagged its tail, but eyed her with caution, whimpering when the air crackled behind another roll of thunder.

"It's okay, Scooter." The boy crouched down, rubbed a hand along the animal's matted fur. He glanced back over his shoulder, then up at Allison. "They're watching you."

Every inch of her skin prickled. "Who's watching me?"

His small, pale face solemn, the boy pulled himself back up. Allison was suddenly conscious of the chill wind stirring again, the subtle whisper of tree leaves. An unsettling reminder of just how vulnerable she was out here in the dark.

"*Who?*" she demanded. "Who's watching me?"

"The bad man... and—" The boy cocked his head. "I have to go now." He turned back toward the woods, the dog at his heels.

"Wait!"

For one brief moment, she had the horrible feeling he would just ignore her and keep going, that she wouldn't be able to stop him. Whatever information he had, he'd take with him into those woods.

A small sigh of relief escaped her when he stopped and turned back around, but before she could utter a word, the shaggy, blond hair, the somber, dirt-smudged face, the tattered T-shirt and worn overalls—all of it—gradually began to fade. Until...

Dear God. She could see right through him.

"Find us." The dim echo of a whisper. "*Please.*"

Allison felt her mouth move, but no words came out as she stared into the empty space where the boy and his dog had been just seconds before. Her mind ordered her to go back inside—now, but her brain couldn't seem to get the signal to her feet.

Then, as if someone had flicked a switch, darkness swallowed up everything around her as the clouds rushed in, erasing the last of the moonlight. An angry wind shoved her hair back and whipped her sleep-shirt around her legs. She shuddered under the force of it as the first cold, heavy drops of rain splattered her arms and face.

CHAPTER 17

H E PARKED THE CAR ON the side lot of the convenience store just outside of town. Then sat there for a minute or two, staring at the gray-painted block wall through bleary eyes. He'd never been one to race old Mother Nature into the day. Waste of energy. Besides, he figured there were already enough bright-eyed go-getters in the world, too obsessed with earning a dollar to know better.

Well, he'd beaten them all to it this morning, hadn't he?

A funny thing, necessity. It made a man go against his grain.

Yawning, he struggled with the stubborn door until it finally swung open. He hated this car, piece of shit. But he supposed it ran a little better than his truck.

Still, it was a damned shame he'd had to sacrifice the truck. A man belonged behind the wheel of something that could at least haul a substantial load of supplies, or… other things.

He more or less sleepwalked into the store for a cup of black coffee and a pack of smokes to jump-start his system. He hadn't intended to be up late last night, had just wanted to check on the girl, see what she was up to.

But the moon had been out, for a while anyway, and she'd given him quite a show.

He shook his head as he poured coffee into a large paper cup, deciding he wanted a pack of those powdered-sugar donuts. She was a strange one. Standing out there in the middle of her yard, wearing that little pink nightie. Carrying on a conversation with thin air.

The girl had a screw loose. Maybe two.

He picked through packages of donuts, found one that felt fresh, and was just about to head to the front of the store when the bell over the door chimed. The chubby, clear-eyed girl behind the counter—one of those irritating go-getters—said in a cheery voice, "Morning, Paul. You're out and about awful early, even for you."

"Hey there, Cathy. Yeah, I am."

He froze right where he stood, turned his back to the counter and pretended to browse the aisle. His gaze slid up to the round security mirror in one corner of the ceiling. Bradford went over to the cooler, grabbed a small container of orange juice. Then headed for the coffee, poured a cup, snatched a few napkins, and took it all up to the counter.

The clerk, being the chatty sort, asked where he was off to this early in the day.

Driving his grandmother up to Virginia, to visit her sister.

Well now. Wasn't that interesting?

Smiling, he edged a little closer to the front of the store, stood behind the rack of chips.

"That's sweet of you, looking after your grandmother like that." The clerk gave Bradford a bright smile. "Will you be gone long?"

He shook his head. "Gran'll be there for a couple of weeks. But I can't spare more than a few days off from work—got a lot going on."

A few days. His own smile broadened. More than enough time to finish up and then do what needed to be done.

By the time Bradford made it back to town, it'd be too late. Much too late.

Sunlight beamed through the small window in her bathroom.

Allison squinted at her reflection in the mirror. Haunted eyes with faint, gray crescents beneath them gazed back at her from a chalk-white face.

She looked horrible. And felt even worse. Her stomach had tied itself into one big knot.

Someone was watching her. *A bad man.* That's what the little... *Go on, say it... dead boy* had told her.

Not the kind of information she could take to the local county Sheriff's Department.

Allison blew out a shaky breath and bent over the sink to splash cold water on her face. All those agonizing hours she'd spent under the care of well-meaning doctors, drugged just about into oblivion, convinced that she had lost her mind...

She had been wrong. They had all been wrong.

Ken, or his spirit, she supposed, hadn't meant to frighten her. He had only wanted her to know that he was all right, that he loved her. She knew that now.

What she had seen last night was no hallucination. God, she had even *talked to the boy.*

With an effort to stop her hand from trembling, she reached for a towel, blotted her face dry. *Find us.*

They had led her down to her own cellar.

The idea of what had probably happened to those kids made her sick inside.

Shoving the disturbing image out of her head, Allison went back to her bedroom, then slipped into a pair of capris, a sleeveless blouse, and some comfortable flats. A trace of cold still lingered in her bones. She hadn't been able to shake it, wouldn't, she realized now, until she found the little dead boy and his friend.

Jesus. Do you know how crazy that sounds?

Yeah. She did. But she couldn't just close her eyes and pretend none of it had happened, wish it all away.

Allison plucked the comb off the dresser to tackle her curls.

Looking into the mirror, her gaze settled on the small drawer in the nightstand. How many hours had she whittled away last night? Cowering under the covers, staring at her locked bedroom door, with the lights blaring, while the rain pounded the roof. Reading more of a dead woman's diary had been the last thing on her mind. All she'd wanted, really, was just to hear Paul's voice.

He was probably miles away by now, could only worry. She refused to put him through that.

But she was out of her realm here.

Allison stopped fiddling with her hair. Steve had always done his best to help her. She couldn't be certain, though, that he wouldn't take whatever she told him straight to their dad. With good intentions, sure, but—no. No, she couldn't drag him into this.

Since the list of available help was short, that left Toni Harper. And Wednesday, Allison thought, frowning, just wasn't soon enough. Although with what she'd sensed from the woman, Toni might be willing to juggle her schedule.

She's solid. You can trust her.

Yes, she had believed Paul, and she would trust *him* with her life. Until just this second, Allison hadn't known that.

She gave her haggard reflection one last glance, deciding this was as good as it would get today, then snatched up her purse and found Toni's business card.

Halfway out her bedroom door, Allison stopped, swung back around. Then reached into her jewelry box and grabbed the faded photograph of her mother.

Toni took a swallow of coffee, eyeing Allison over the rim of her cup. "Sure you don't want to do this at my office? We'd have more privacy."

Allison glanced around the café. The morning rush at Wilma's appeared to be over, so it was fairly quiet. The booths next to them were empty. Even though she knew it was just a desperate illusion, being out among people made her feel, well, normal. And safe. Hadn't she always heard that there was safety in numbers?

"I think we're okay here."

"Your call." Toni paused for a second, still watching her with sharp, curious eyes. "So, tell me what's going on."

Nodding, Allison took a sip of coffee, then sat back while the waitress came up to serve their apple pie.

"You ladies need anything else?"

"We're fine for now," Toni said. "Thanks, Jolene." She watched the efficient waitress hurry over to take an order from a customer sitting at the counter, then turned her alert, brown eyes back to Allison, and waited.

Allison picked up her fork, speared off a chunk of pie, toying with it. The scents of brewed coffee and food cooking had done nothing to whet her appetite. "I really don't know where to start."

"The beginning usually works for me."

The beginning. Allison sighed. "You've got to promise me that you'll keep what I tell you to yourself."

"Now you've really got me curious. But yeah, whatever you say stays between the two of us." Toni took a bite of pie, gestured with her fork. "So—give, already."

Taking herself back, Allison went through her family history, relaying what little information she'd gotten from the private investigator she'd hired. "I was going to ask you to use your resources to help locate my mother, but..." She shook her head. "It's more than that now."

She blurted out the details of what Paul had told her, what they had worked through together.

Toni took a slow sip of coffee, then set her cup down, tapped a finger on the table. "I have to go with Paul on this. Your mother, the girl, your accident—it all strings together. Can't be just a coincidence."

She leaned back, eyes narrowed. "You both believe the house is haunted."

Don't you? Allison wanted to ask. She helped herself to more coffee, willing the caffeine to do its magic, and glanced around. Not a soul within earshot. Still, she kept her voice low. "I talked to one of them last night."

Toni's brows shot up. "A ghost?"

Allison nodded. "It started the day I moved in. Hearing things, seeing shadows. And the house would get cold for no reason."

It took her a while to get through what had happened last night, because even now,—especially now—sitting here in the light of day, it all seemed like some bizarre nightmare.

Toni just shook her head. "Wow. A ghost. I'd heard rumors, but—to be honest, I'd planned to do some research there, then talk to you about it."

"So, you do believe me."

"Yeah. And I'm wondering what's up with the water you found in the attic, the cellar." Frowning, Toni stared down into her cup for a second. "This guy who's supposed to be watching you—did the dead kid give you a name, a description?"

"No, nothing." Allison felt her heart skip. Hadn't she thought, just the other day, that someone was following her? "Actually, something odd did happen..." She told Toni about the old truck with the dark, tinted windows. "He didn't follow me home. I thought I'd just imagined it."

"Maybe. But there's usually a reason why we notice things. I figure something—other than an old heap with tinted windows—made you uneasy."

"Instinct," Allison murmured.

"Yeah. We all have it. Trouble is we don't always listen to what it's saying."

She knew that, didn't she? Allison had ignored her intuition before, had suffered the consequences. She shook her head. "I don't get the connection, though, between the boy and this man who's supposed to be watching me."

The answer to that jolted through her just as she'd finished putting the thought into words, and it shook her to the core.

Toni caught the look on Allison's face and nodded. "The boy, and the other kid—the girl; this guy may have killed one or both of them. Or at the very least been involved somehow." She absently tapped a finger on the table again. "The kid said, 'they.'"

"Yes, and whoever 'they' are—"

"They're worried," Toni finished. "Think about it. Those kids led you to the attic and down to the cellar for a reason."

Allison dipped her head. She'd done more than just think about it. She'd obsessed over it half the night. Wondered why the boy hadn't simply told her what he needed her to know.

The spirits never gave up all the answers. She had read that. Something about keeping the natural order of things in balance.

The diary, she knew now, was part of that balance.

"The day I moved in, we... found something up in the attic." Allison went through what she had read. "I don't usually snoop around in other people's business, but I was hoping to find some answers." She lifted her shoulders. "Or at least a clue."

"I get that. Really." Toni frowned again. "I'm wondering what had Bobbie Jean so terrified of her son's biological father. You didn't by any chance bring the diary with you?"

Allison bit back an oath. "I can't believe I didn't think of it."

"Don't be so hard on yourself. Considering what you've been through, you're doing fine." Toni gave her a wry smile, and forked up another chunk of pie, waiting as an elderly couple walked past their booth. "I'd like to go back to your place, have a good look at the diary. But I've got to follow up on something that, well, just can't wait.

"So, let's do this: read through the rest of it as soon as you get home. Then I want you to hide it."

It took her just a second. Allison shuddered from a chill that had nothing to do with the temperature. "You think whoever's watching me might be looking for the diary."

"It's possible. Got to admit, though, the logic doesn't follow. Why didn't he search the house when it was vacant? It was on the market for—how long?"

"Six months." Allison sipped her coffee. "I've driven into town on errands a few times. I would have noticed if someone had been in the house while I was gone."

"My thoughts." Toni paused. "Another thing—we're probably stretching on the time frame. We know Bobbie Jean died years—decades—back."

"And at this point," Allison said, "we have no idea when those poor kids died."

"Right. But what we do know is this: it's likely they're both listed in a database as missing." Toni blew out a long breath. "That really sucks for the parents, the relatives."

Yes, it did. Going through the days, living life, because that's what time forced you to do. And somewhere in the middle of it all, hanging onto a thin fragment of hope.

"Find us," Allison murmured, and, with her heart sinking, looked back over at Toni. "The cellar?"

They both nearly jumped out of their skin when someone nearby cleared her throat. Allison's gaze zipped up. Her shoulders slumped when she saw their waitress—what was her name? *Jolene*—hovering.

"Uh—you ladies want a refill on the coffee?"

Toni made a show of peering into her cup. "I'm good."

"Me, too." Allison dredged up a smile.

"Right. Well." Jolene set their check on the table. "I'll just leave this. No rush—really." She hurried off, glancing, twice, over her shoulder.

Toni scowled. "Probably not much chance of that one keeping her mouth shut. But don't worry. I think I can fend off the worst of the gossip." She swallowed the last of her coffee. "Meantime, we need to identify the kid you talked to, find out who he is—*was.*"

Allison slid her plate aside. What little appetite she had

started with, she'd just lost. "What kind of monster would murder innocent children?"

Toni sighed. "Unfortunately, there are some sick, evil bastards in this world." Her eyes went to slits. "You own a gun?"

Allison shook her head.

"Got a dog, any kind of security system?"

Chewing at her bottom lip, Allison shook her head again, slowly. Steve had suggested an alarm system—in jest. Why hadn't she taken the idea seriously? Living miles from town, with acres between neighbors, she was pathetically vulnerable.

"You should at least consider taking a trip to the local animal shelter. It's about five miles past the north end of town. Get a dog—a big one. And if it were me, I'd be on the phone to an alarm company by the end of the day."

"I'll do that," Allison murmured, more to herself than to Toni.

A hum of activity slipped through the silence that fell between them. Some of the tables and booths toward the back were occupied now. Early lunch crowd, Allison supposed. She glanced over at the counter, caught their waitress yanking her gaze away.

Great. Just great.

"Another thing"—Toni reached for the check—"goes without saying, our otherworldly source won't garner much attention from the Sheriff's Department. Not of the serious kind, anyway. But just as soon as we figure out a way to get around that part of it, we'll have to talk to the police."

"About what?" The deep male voice jolted them. The man had come up like a wolf stalking its prey. Silent, slinky, unnoticed.

He looked down at Toni with eyes that were a piercing swirl of blue and green. Eyes that reminded Allison of an ocean somewhere off a tropical beach.

A stormy ocean.

Toni scowled up at him. "*Ray.*"

CHAPTER 18

A SMILE CREPT OVER HIS TANNED, rugged face. Allison knew it was rude to stare, but couldn't seem to pull her gaze off the angry, jagged scar that started below his left ear and ran half the length of his jaw.

"I repeat, what do you need to talk to the police about?"

Toni slanted him a look. "When did you start listening to conversations that are none of your business?"

Those stormy eyes sparked, but the smile held. He just stood there—all six-foot and some-odd inches of him, if Allison was any judge—looking down at Toni. Allison shifted her attention to the badge pinned to his denim shirt, then to the holstered gun he wore on a thick leather belt.

Toni sighed. "An article, Ray. We were discussing an article I'm considering for the paper. Operations of our local police force, keeping the small-town peace."

The woman was quick. Allison had to give her that.

Toni's gaze flicked over to her. "I'm sorry. This is our sheriff, Ray McAllister." She glanced back up. "Allison Weathers. She's new in town."

His focus swung over to Allison. "That right?"

She nodded, wondering if she looked as awkward as she felt. He was far from the typical small-town sheriff. Broad in the chest and muscular under the denim he wore instead of the standard uniform. His hair, the true, pure black of midnight, fell just past the collar of his shirt.

And, God, that radiating gaze of his made her want to crawl off into the nearest corner.

Allison blinked, found her voice. "I… just bought an old Victorian farmhouse out on Dawson Creek Road."

She saw it—a flicker of something in his eyes. Then it was gone. "That would be the old Treadwell place."

"Right. And it's a great house." Toni flashed a broad smile. "Now, I'm sure you want to grab a table before the lunch rush hits."

One corner of his mouth stretched up in a slow curl. He nodded. "You ladies have a good day. Miss Weathers, hope you like our town."

"I'm… sure I will."

For a moment, Allison thought he would slip into the booth behind theirs, but he walked away, took a seat at the counter. She blew out a small breath. "Wow."

"Yeah. He is a bit intense, isn't he?"

"*A bit?*"

"Okay. Understatement." Toni pulled a couple of dollars from her wallet, dropped them onto the table. "We got yanked off topic there for a while, but I wanted to tell you that I'll poke around, see if I can find some information on any missing kids in the area. We know the boy had a dog. That might help." She shook her head. "Sure wish you'd been able to get a picture of the kid, though."

A photograph. Of a spirit? Allison wondered whether her digital camera would have picked up the boy's image, or captured only the vague, shadowy outline of trees under the pale moonlight.

"I could sketch him."

"A sketch. That's good. It'll give me something to work with." Toni pursed her lips, tilted her head. "I'm just going to throw this out there. You remember the other day—in the craft store—I mentioned that my niece, Jenna, is different from most kids her age."

155

So much had happened since then. Allison had to take a mental step back and think. "Yes. I do remember you saying that."

"Well, what I didn't tell you is that Jenna sometimes... knows things." Toni paused, frowning. "How can I put it?

"Guess you could say she gets a sense of events, thoughts, whatever. Either as they occur, or afterward."

Just a short week ago, Allison might have laughed at that, brushed it off. She wasn't laughing now. And she had read about this.

"You mean she's psychic."

Toni nodded. "Jenna has what she calls 'flashes of insight.' Other times, she gets images, like a two or three-second film clip running through her head."

"That must be unnerving."

"I'm sure it can be, at times." Toni's smile was rueful. "The kid's stepfather thinks she's just plain weird. Spending the summers with me gives her a chance to get out from under the microscope."

Poor thing. Allison could definitely sympathize with the girl. "Your niece's—what do I call it? Ability? Is that something she inherited?"

"It is. From my grandmother on my mother's side." Toni shrugged. "My sister, Kate—Jenna's mom—doesn't have a psychic bone in her body. Ditto for me. Go figure." Her brown eyes deepened to the shade of strong coffee as her focus drifted over to the sheriff. She scowled. "Sorry. Ray has a habit of distracting me. It's irritating."

"I can imagine." Allison had noticed the heat sparking between the two of them the second they had locked eyes. It wasn't a sexual heat.

"So here's where I was headed on the thing with Jenna—I think she might be able to help us. It's up to you."

Allison took a moment to consider. What did she have to lose? Nothing. Absolutely nothing.

"I think I'd like that."

"Good." Toni gave her a resigned smile when two women settled into the booth behind them. "Guess that's our cue. I'm working late tonight, so I'll run this by Jenna first thing in the morning and give you a call."

Nodding, Allison started to get up, then stopped, reached into her purse. She had almost forgotten about the photograph. "I scanned the original on my computer this morning and printed a copy. My mother." She passed the picture to Toni.

"Beverly Kincaid," Toni said, reading what Allison had jotted down on the back. "Maiden name, Sorenson."

"That's as much as I can give you." Allison just lifted her shoulders. "It's all I know."

"Well, it's a start." Toni tucked the photo into her purse, and they headed for the register. She held a hand up when Allison reached for her wallet. "Uh-uh. I owe you, remember?"

Allison smiled. "I think it's probably the other way around now. And I want to thank you for… everything. I don't know what I would've done without your help."

"It's okay." A waitress hurried over to ring up their ticket, then handed Toni her change. "Depending on how things shake out, I'll try to check in with you later this afternoon. If not, we'll talk tomorrow morning for sure."

At the door, Toni stopped, turned. "Allison? *Be careful.*"

"I will."

Instinct—that same, intuitive sense they had discussed earlier—had Allison glancing back at the counter.

Ray McAllister was watching her.

Toni pulled her Mustang out of the Town Hall's parking lot and headed left on Jefferson Avenue. Off and on for the past couple of hours, while she'd sat in on a meeting of the Zoning Commission, she'd been trying to place the man sitting well to the back of the room. He wasn't a local. But there was something about those almond-shaped bourbon colored eyes, his long, narrow face...

She'd seen him before.

But where?

Tapping a finger on the steering wheel, she glanced into the rearview mirror at the midday traffic that rolled along. It'd come to her. Eventually. Meantime, she had other issues competing for a front slot in her head.

Ray topped the list.

She'd tossed around the idea of calling him just as soon as she got back to the office, taking her chances and laying it all out. They could be dealing with a killer here. A killer who had his eye on Allison.

But... A ghost. Straight from the mule's mouth, Ray didn't believe in the "psychic bullshit," or anything to do with the paranormal, for that matter. It would require some creative brainwork on her part to come up with a credible story. One that he could fit comfortably into the nice, tidy black-and-white world in which he existed.

Lips pressed into a tight line, Toni just shook her head. Damn Ray McAllister. He could be so close-minded. "Pigheaded," she muttered. It was going to cost him one day.

If she could just get him to take off the blinders for half a second...

Right. And tomorrow, come sunup, Old Man Casey's pigs would take a flying leap over Dawson Creek.

Toni pulled the car into her parking spot in front of *The Times,* noticed her dad's space was still empty. She'd hoped he'd be back by now. They had mapped out the plan for tonight, but she wanted to go over it again. Make sure it was solid.

There would be no margin for errors.

She swung the door open, walked over to her mail slot, and sifted through the few pieces there. Kara looked up from her computer over the rims of her bifocals. "You're back."

"Finally. Anything going on?"

"Well, the sheriff called. He wanted you to phone him when you got in."

Toni would just bet he did. She had another vision of those pigs flying over the creek but kept it to herself. "Okay. Thanks." She paused when she caught the frown flitting over Kara's face. "Something wrong?"

"I'm not really sure." Kara glanced back in the direction of the cubicles where the summer interns were working, and kept her voice low. "That little matter you asked me to look into yesterday? I had lunch with my friend earlier. We need to talk."

It was immediate, that tiny zap to the system. Like a split-second electrical jolt to the nerves. Toni called it her own internal alarm system.

It had just chimed loud and clear.

She nodded. "Have someone cover the phones. I'll be in my office."

She detoured into the small break room, grabbed a cup of coffee, and continued down the narrow hall, trying to keep her mind tethered. But the possibilities, theories, had already begun to spin through her head. She had to give Kara credit—the woman hadn't wasted any time.

Toni set her cup on the desk and stashed her purse, checked her voicemail. Two messages from Ray. One hang-up—probably him again.

She could just imagine the daggers shooting from those blue-green eyes when he'd reached her recorded greeting a third time. And she'd switched her cell off during the meeting. So he tried the main number, spoke to Kara.

The man had no patience.

Shaking her head, she sighed, then leaned back in the chair, spotted her dad's assistant coming down the hall.

"I'm just going to close this." Kara pulled the door shut behind

159

her and took a seat in the small visitor's chair. Concern shadowed her softly lined face.

Lips pursed, she folded her hands in her lap. "My friend—Alma—swore to me that none of the Treadwells ever mentioned a thing about ghosts or the house being haunted. But there was *something* going on there."

Kara paused, absently brushing a hand over the slim-line, navy skirt she wore. "A few weeks before Bobbie Jean died, she was upset. She wouldn't say what was bothering her, but whatever it was had her frightened."

Frightened. Paul had said the same about Allison's mother, Toni remembered. And Bill's mom—she'd looked worried when she'd come out to the porch to give Paul his baseball bat.

"Alma believes the stress was too much for Bobbie Jean's heart." Kara frowned. "Do you know about the young girl who went missing back then?"

Toni nodded. "I've heard the story."

"Then you know the family supposedly moved to Texas."

Leaning forward, Toni folded her arms on the desk. "You're going to tell me that's not the case."

The pause in the air carried a tangible weight. Toni took a swallow of coffee, ordered herself to keep patient while Kara shifted in the chair.

"According to Alma, Bobbie Jean let it slip that she saw the girl a few days after the family was supposed to have left town."

Toni sat up straight now. "Did she say where?"

"Unfortunately, no. No details. But something else struck me as odd. Alma went over to the Treadwell's for coffee shortly after that. Jay had run into town for something, and the kids were outside playing, so it was just the two women. They were at the kitchen table. Bobbie Jean seemed distracted. Anxious. She kept looking back at the door to the laundry room."

When Toni arched a brow, Kara nodded. "In that house, the access door to the cellar is off the laundry room."

The cellar. Well, well. Toni took another swallow from her cup, wishing she'd been able to get her hands on that diary.

Gazing past her, Kara pursed her lips again. "About a week later, Jay had a crew down there. They put up brick walls, poured a concrete floor. Strange, don't you think?"

"Yeah. I do." Toni sat back, studied the petite woman. Sharp mind, good instincts coupled with a healthy dose of curiosity. Great qualities. But in this instance those particular assets spelled trouble, with a capital T. "I appreciate your help on this, but I need you to step away from it now."

She saw it coming—the protest at the edge of Kara's lips—and shook her head. "I wouldn't have put you on the trail had I known before, but—there may be other things, people, involved here. It could be dangerous."

Toni studied the feisty, diminutive woman across from her. "Have you spoken to anyone other than your friend about this?"

"No, no one."

"Good. You'll want to get in touch with her ASAP, tell her to keep what the two of you discussed to herself."

Eyes narrowed, Kara nodded, and got up to leave. She stopped at the door and turned, pointing a finger at Toni. "Seems to me you've been treading into some awfully deep waters lately. Watch your step, young lady."

Toni tilted her head in a slow acknowledgement, gaze following the tiny woman as she walked away. Kara had the determination of a bulldog whenever she scented a subject worth pursuing. She also knew when it was wise just to back off.

Small wonder that Toni's dad would beg or bribe to keep his assistant happy with her job.

She went over and shut the door. Back at her desk, she pulled the photo of Allison's mother from her purse. Marveled at the genetic stamp. If not for the age difference, the two women could have been twins. So, yeah. She got why seeing Allison for the first time had seriously scrambled Paul's head.

Toni glanced at the back of the photo, then turned to her computer, opened the Internet browser. Probably wouldn't find much on Beverly Sorenson/Kincaid. The father would be a different matter, though. Wealthy, prominent businessman. Political connections.

High profile all the way. And with the right search criteria, she just might be able to track through the history, pick up some information on the first wife.

Her direct line rang a couple of keystrokes into the search. Toni glanced over at the display on her phone and swore.

Ray.

Timing, she noted, was everything. As usual, his sucked.

She tuned out the ringing, finished running the search. And grinned.

"Jackpot."

CHAPTER 19

THE DOG SAT UP IN the front passenger seat of Allison's Explorer, his large head half hanging out the window she'd lowered for him. Ears flapping back in the breeze, his pink tongue lolled out. She could swear he was grinning.

Happy to be out of doggie jail, she supposed. Who could blame him?

As she drove, she reached over to make sure the seat belt wasn't too tight around him, then stroked his soft fur. He was a Saint Bernard mix, white with chocolate-brown markings, a bit of gold and tan here and there. A pretty animal with an even temper.

He looked like a Ben, Allison thought, glancing over at him. Or maybe a Henry. But changing his name would only confuse the poor thing. He'd been through enough.

Although the irony of the dog sharing a name with Allison's dad hadn't escaped her.

"Well, Jack. Just one more stop, then we can go home."

Home. The word seemed hollow now. She'd rather be headed anywhere than back to that huge, old house.

For the last few hours, though, Allison had been preparing to do just that. A mile or two before the animal shelter, she'd spotted a strip mall, had gone in to buy a cordless phone. Then, because she'd left her pepper spray and flashlight in the cellar, had no intention of going back down there on her own, she'd had to replace them.

She'd picked up a cache of batteries while she was at it.

After, with Jack in tow, she'd stopped in at the pet store she'd noticed. And spent a small fortune. A collar and leash, two large bags of kibble. Rawhide bones and other assorted goodies, along with a king-sized doggie bed.

They were set now, except for the fixative spray she'd forgotten to buy last week for her charcoal sketches.

Allison pulled up to the front of Lilly Jameson's craft shop, eased the window up a bit on Jack's side. "I'll just be a minute."

He gave a low, throaty chuff, and then another one of his happy-dog grins that nudged a smile out of her.

A trace of that smile lingered as she swung the door open and stepped into the cool, central air. Lilly looked up from behind the counter and beamed. "Well! You're back!"

Nodding, Allison managed another faint smile. "I need some spray sealant. For charcoal sketches?"

"You'll find that on the second aisle to your left. Just holler if you need help."

"Thank you." Allison skirted around a few customers who were browsing the display of picture frames, and grabbed a can of the brand she usually bought, then paused, took another off the shelf before heading up to the register.

"Find what you needed?"

"Yes, ma'am."

"Good. I do try to keep a variety of stock." Lilly rang up the purchase, handed Allison the bag and her change. "We missed you at our Ladies Club meeting last Thursday."

The Ladies Club. It seemed a lifetime had passed since Allison had opened her front door to the scrawny, irritating woman with mousy-brown hair. She'd almost managed to forget about Ellie Atkins. Almost.

"Not just us old biddies, you know," Lilly said. "Several of our members are young ladies about your age."

"It wasn't that. I just—" Allison glanced back at the door,

hoping Jack hadn't slobbered all over the front seat by now. "Mrs. Atkins caught me in the middle of something. To be honest, I didn't know about the meeting beforehand."

Lilly chuckled. "That sounds like our Ellie. And if you haven't figured it out already, the woman tends to root around in other people's business. But she's harmless, really." Her soft blue eyes darkened. "That husband of hers is another matter. Jared. Have you met him?"

Allison shook her head, trying to think past the jab of panic.

"Well, take my advice and stay away from him." Lilly glanced over at the women who were still picking through the picture frames, and lowered her voice. "Jared tends to tip the bottle with a heavy hand. He's a mean drunk."

There it was again—that nasty jab of panic. Allison felt a tremble as the image popped into her head: the ugly, yellowing bruise Ellie Atkins had tried to cover with a thick layer of face powder.

Beneath the fear, though, there was outrage, even a pang of sympathy for the woman. "I... appreciate the warning. I'll certainly keep my distance."

Lilly nodded. "I think that's best."

When she pulled around the last curve in her driveway, Allison's stomach balled up into a knot. The house loomed ahead like something out of a bad dream. Or a horror movie. A silent, mammoth structure left shadowed by pockets of deep shade when the late-afternoon sun had slipped off to the west.

The house was too still. Too quiet. The windows were like dark, malevolent eyes watching her.

She cut the engine. She didn't want to go in there. Hell, she didn't even want to get out of the car.

Jack gave a soft whine, the tip of his huge tail thumping against the seat.

"Okay, boy." Allison reached over, released his seat belt. Then hurried around the front of the car and opened the passenger door, jumping back when the dog shot out of the seat. She was left standing there, holding the leash, while the newest member of her family headed for a nearby tree to hike his leg.

She felt small, and exposed, waiting in the big open space, with the breeze tugging at her hair, birds chirping softly from somewhere above her.

That under-the-skin prickly feeling, like raw nerves sparking, began creeping over her.

Allison cast a wary glance over her shoulder at the dense cluster of pines and undergrowth that separated her land from the Atkins' property. An abusive drunk. She wondered if he drove an old red truck with tinted windows.

After she'd left the craft shop, she'd been tempted to head straight to the Sheriff's Department, but how could she have put it? That a little dead boy said there was a bad man watching her?

The image of Ray McAllister eyeing her in stony silence, the scar on his face made even more visible by a smirk, had kept her driving right past the town limits.

She turned her gaze back to the dog, realized that she was clutching the leash hard enough to have her nails digging crescents into her palm. The sheriff had to know about Jared Atkins. This town was just too small to keep something like that a secret. Murder, though, was a different matter.

There was no way she would walk right into that huge, silent house, arms full of boxes and bags, without first taking the dog in to have a look around.

Allison drew a breath that shuddered out in a sigh. She had managed to wander straight back into the life she'd left behind, hadn't she? Looking over her shoulder, around corners. Jumping at the smallest movement or sound.

And this time around, she could forget about jogging to help settle her mind—couldn't risk it.

Like living in a prison, she thought. A haunted prison.

When he finished his business, Jack surprised her by padding right back over to her. Allison reached down and stroked his massive head. "I guess we can do without this, for now." She dropped the leash back into one of the bags, grabbed her purse and keys. Then, keeping an eye on her surroundings, headed up to the front porch, the dog at her side.

In the foyer, she shut the door behind them, turned the deadbolt, and took a moment to glance around, to listen.

The house felt... empty.

She couldn't be sure, though.

"Come on, boy." Allison led the dog around the main level, working toward the kitchen. Heart thumping, she paused at the cellar door, muttering an oath as she yanked it open.

Jack poked his snout into the dark, cavernous opening. He took one disinterested sniff of the damp air that wafted up, then turned his big brown eyes up to her and wagged his tail.

Good enough. Her entire body slumped with relief, then jolted when the phone rang. "Jumpy," she muttered, glancing down at the dog.

She rushed over to the wall phone, felt the calm flow through her when she heard Paul's voice.

"I would have called sooner, but the signal on my cell was in and out. The mountains." A hush settled over the connection. "Are you okay?"

She wanted to tell him everything, just blurt it all out. The worry would keep him tossing and turning half the night. She couldn't do that to him. Not now, not over the phone.

"Hey. Tell me everything's okay."

"Sorry. I—"

A sudden, heavy-handed knock on the front door sent Jack in

a spin and made her jump. Allison could barely hear herself think over the barking as the dog zipped past her. She had no idea an animal that large could move so fast.

"That's definitely not the stray mutt I chased off yesterday," Paul managed over the din.

"No." But she didn't have time to explain. "I need to get the door. Can I call you right back?"

"Go ahead. I'll hold."

Grabbing the new pepper spray from her purse, Allison hurried toward the barking. At the door, she called out to whoever was on the other side to wait just a second, and took hold of Jack's collar.

His barking diminished to low, throaty growls.

"Let's just see who it is before we open the door." She steered the dog around to one of the windows, breathing a small sigh when she saw the large brown truck in her driveway. The courier. Of course. She had scheduled a pick up for today, to ship the sculpture she'd finished to Maison's Gallery in Atlanta. She had forgotten all about it.

Allison got Jack settled down, then took care of the shipment, and went back to the phone.

"Sorry for the interruption. And the noise." She paused. "I know you're wondering about the dog."

"The thought did cross my mind."

She decided to keep it simple, told him with everything that had happened she needed the company. Allison described the dog, painting what she thought was an accurate mental picture, right down to the colorful markings. "He's a rescue—from the animal shelter. His name is Jack."

"Jack. Well, I'm glad you're not alone."

"Me, too." She glanced over to where the big dog had sprawled out on the floor next to the table. Yes, she had company now. And no one would be able to get within ten feet of her, not without her knowing about it.

That didn't necessarily mean the house was secure.

It took her only a second to decide whether to ask for Paul's input. "I want to get a security system installed. Could you recommend someone?"

Twisting the phone cord around her finger, she waited through the stretch of silence. She'd just given it all away, hadn't she? With one simple question.

Maybe a part of her had wanted to do just that. Even though the tiny voice of reason inside her head had insisted that she hold off, at least until she could talk to Paul without a phone line and miles between them.

His deep sigh was like a weight against her ear, and on her conscience. "What are you not telling me?"

While Jack sprawled on the floor, working a rawhide bone, Allison sat back on the sofa, her feet tucked up under her. And tried to focus. With what little broken sleep she'd managed to get last night, the long day, the stress, her brain was beginning to feel numb.

Still, she had forced herself to climb the stairs to her studio, had finished the sketch for Toni. It was a good rendering, Allison admitted. She had captured the dead boy's image right down to his tattered clothes and filthy, bare feet. Getting the likeness of his little dog, Scooter, onto paper had given her some trouble, though. When it came to the poor thing's sunken belly, her hand hadn't been able to get past her heart.

After a while, she'd managed to put those emotions aside. One look at her drawing and anyone who knew those two would recognize them in a heartbeat.

Yawning, she took the diary off the end table, brushed a finger over the embossed, gold script on the cover, and frowned. The nightmare she'd lived through these past twenty-four hours—she hadn't been able to keep that from Paul. But the diary...

Once she started down that road, Allison would have to tell him about Bill. How could she not?

A shock like that, about his lifelong, childhood friend, wasn't something she could just blurt out over the phone.

She had given him enough to worry over.

Her gaze drifted up, scanning the silent space that she had filled, with Steve's and the others' help, with her own furniture, knickknacks. She had looked forward to making this huge old house a home, had welcomed the solitude.

Now she wanted anything but.

Not that she and Jack would be alone for much longer.

Allison wasn't quite sure how she felt about letting a man she had never met spend the night in her guestroom. But it was either that, or Paul would be driving back to town tonight. She didn't want him risking the long drive over those winding, mountain roads in the dark.

Glancing at her watch, she blew out a small breath. Stan Michaels—the man who had run one of Paul's construction crews for about six years now—would be knocking on her door, an overnight bag in hand, within an hour.

An hour. She opened the diary. That didn't give her much time.

August 13, 1975—

It stormed last night, so heavy that I thought the sky had opened up to let loose the end of days. Jay wasn't home. He'd gone into town on an errand and gotten stuck there with the bad weather. And the kids were asleep.

I thought I heard someone knocking on the back door, and wondered who on earth would be crazy enough to come out on a night like this.

Deep down, I knew.

Evil in the guise of a man. I suppose he'd been waiting for just the right time to catch me alone. He was never one to get in a hurry, for anything.

I didn't want to answer the door, but what choice did I have?

So I went into the kitchen, shaking inside. When I opened the door, there was nothing but an empty back porch and rain pouring down from the pitch-black sky in torrents. And the wind... Lord, I'll never forget the way it howled and moaned. The loneliness of it sent a shudder right through me.

Then I saw her. At the edge of the woods, running. Just a flash of her when the lightning lit up the ground.

The girl.

My heart nearly stopped.

For a moment, while I strained to see past sheets of rain sliced by the violent wind, I half expected the girl's mother to come scrambling out of those dark woods, frantic.

There was no one.

The police told us they had moved on to somewhere in Texas. That was three days ago.

I knew better. So, I think, did Paul.

Dear God. Allison had to take a minute to get her shaking under control. She rubbed her hands over her face, blinked. Her first night alone in this house... the storm had knocked out the power. The lightning had given her just a glimpse of the thing running at the edge of the woods.

A stray dog, she'd assumed.

A dead dog, Allison had come to realize.

Now she suspected that what she had seen bolting through all that rain was neither.

She glanced back down at the looping, feminine script. A girl. One who had left town three days before. Or maybe not.

A spirit, then?

Not if that girl was Allison.

She closed her eyes for a second, tried to think. Was it possible that she had seen herself? Some sort of weird, mental flashback?

A vision?

The psychic arena was Toni's realm. Although, Allison remembered reading that an emotional or physical trauma could awaken latent abilities. She hadn't realized it then, but shortly after she had lost Ken, she'd been able to see and talk to the dead.

She wondered now about the other child—the girl who had been with the dead boy. *Scared,* he'd said. She hadn't shown herself to Steve, either.

Why?

Questions racing through her head, Allison got up and paced over to a window, turning when she heard rawhide thump against the hardwood floor. Jack whimpered, his big brown eyes on her, watching her every move. He'd done the same the entire time she'd unpacked the boxes and bags she'd brought in from the car.

Even from the utility room, with his head lowered over his bowl of kibble, he'd kept an eye on her while she sat at the kitchen table with her own supper. Worried, she supposed. Probably because his former owners had abandoned him.

That was sad, but his home was with her now. And just having him here made her feel not quite so alone, more secure. Hopefully, she would do the same for him.

"It's okay, boy. I'm okay."

The dog cocked his large head, studied her for a while longer. Then wagged his tail and went back to his rawhide.

Allison ran a finger along the leaded glass as she peered out at the twilight shadows. Psychic. It was such a foreign concept to her. Aside from her—what was it called?—mediumistic ability, could she possibly have some sort of extrasensory perception?

It would explain a lot.

Where had this... talent come from? Would it help her work through the nightmare her life had become in the last week? Or only confuse her more.

Her gaze shifted to the deeper mass of shadows at the western edge of her lawn. A few hundred yards beyond the thicket of pines and underbrush stood a sad-looking, two-story farmhouse in desperate need of a good coat of paint.

A subtle hint, she thought, of the abuse that went on behind those walls.

Allison squinted from a quick, bright flash. She swung her gaze in that direction just as the headlights rounded the last corner of her driveway.

CHAPTER 20

WITH JACK'S BARKING THROTTLED BACK to low growls, Allison kept her grip on his collar as she inched the front door open. The man who stood beneath the amber glow of her porch light ran a hand through his short-cropped, chestnut hair, and gave her a cautious smile. His eyes were like Tiger's Eye marbles—deep chocolate brown flecked with gold.

She nudged the door open a little farther. "Stan?"

"Yes, ma'am." He pulled his wallet from the back pocket of his jeans to show her his driver's license.

Satisfied, Allison stepped aside to let him in, tightening her grip on the dog's collar when he gave another warning growl. "I'd better introduce the two of you." She softened her voice. "Jack, this is Stan. Say hello."

"Hey, buddy." In a slow move, Stan reached out to let Jack get a good sniff of his hand, then scratched the dog behind his ear when he wagged his tail.

Well. That was easy enough. Allison glanced at the overnight bag Stan had set beside him on the floor. "Would you like to take your bag up to the guestroom?"

He scanned the second level. "Actually, if it's okay with you, I'd like to bunk on the sofa. Not that I don't appreciate a comfortable bed." Those tiger-eyes lit up with a quick, affable smile. "But I'll be able to keep a better ear to things from the first floor."

Of course. She hadn't considered that. "Whatever you think is best."

With Jack padding behind them, she led Stan to the living room. He set his overnight bag on one of the chairs and looked around. Age wise, he had a few years on Paul, she thought. But he was fit, had the rock-solid build that came from doing good, honest manual labor.

She imagined he could take care of himself in just about any situation.

"I really appreciate you coming here on such short notice."

"Not a problem. Paul would do the same for me."

Yeah, she was sure of that. She wondered now if Stan had gotten the chance to eat something before driving out. "If you're hungry, I make a fair sandwich. Or I can order pizza. And there's soda, a pitcher of tea in the fridge, whatever you'd like."

"I've already eaten, thanks." He gave her another quick smile. "Glass of iced tea would be great, though. Just let me check the windows and doors first, make sure everything's locked up."

She had already been through that routine—twice. But it wouldn't hurt to have another set of eyes look things over. "I took Jack on a tour of the house when we got home. We... didn't go into the cellar." Allison paused, wondering how much Paul had told him. "For whatever reason, the light down there stopped working. I just replaced the bulb a few days ago."

He frowned. "I'll take a look at it. Why don't you point me in that direction?" Stan reached into his overnight bag, pulled out the kind of heavy-duty flashlight Allison assumed he'd use on the job. Then, after a brief pause, he took out a small zippered case, opened it.

The compact steel cylinder and barrel, the sleek, black handle caught her off guard.

"A gun."

"Just a precaution." He dropped the case back into his bag, and tucked the gun into the waistband of his jeans. "I have a permit."

Then he knew how to handle the weapon, had been instructed in the safety and legal issues. The man had come prepared. Allison had to give him that. She nodded. "The cellar's off the utility room."

When they walked into the kitchen, her eyes vaguely registered the brief shock of harsh fluorescent light. She half expected the temperature to plunge, to catch the flit of a shadow. But everything seemed normal.

Or was that just another desperate illusion? Had the fear rooted itself so deep inside her that it had dulled her senses?

Maybe. And that in itself was another kind of fear, wasn't it? She would be... psychically blind to whatever chose to come at her.

Not all spirits were benevolent.

The dog followed them as far as the table, then plopped down next to it and sprawled out, nudging a smile from her. She supposed he'd found his spot in this room.

"Through there?" Stan gestured toward the door she had left open so Jack could get to his bowls, and Allison nodded. She went with him into the utility room, stepping aside while he opened the narrow door that led down to the damp, chilly darkness. She reached for the package of light bulbs on one of the shelves, stopped short when he flipped the switch and light below popped on.

The look he shot her was half frown, half speculation. "Could be a loose wire. I'll check it out in the morning."

The morning. Yes. Somehow, things always seemed safer in the broad light of day. Allison waited at the threshold while he descended the stairs. The dank air drifting up clung to her skin. She shivered. Not from the cool dampness, but from the idea of what might lie beneath all that concrete.

There was something horribly wrong about walking over two— maybe three, with the dog—small bodies.

A muted curse floated up when the light below flicked off. "Got to be a short in the wiring," Stan called up to her.

Or not, Allison thought, and shivered again.

She watched the beam of his flashlight float around in the dark until it finally began rising in her direction.

"All clear. Found this on the floor." Stan handed her the flashlight she had dropped... was it just last night? Her perception of time was beginning to unravel.

"Thank you."

"Sure." He pulled the cellar door shut. "I promised Paul I'd phone. First, though, I want to look at the rest of the house. Then if it's okay with you, think I'll take the dog for a walk, check the outside perimeter."

On a pause, Allison glanced at the gun tucked in his waistband. "I'm sure you know what you're doing with that, but please be careful around Jack."

"Of course."

Searching those friendly tiger-eyes, the quick smile, she had to remind herself that Paul trusted the man. That should be good enough for her.

Jack would need to go out before bed, anyway.

"I'll get his leash." The words had barely left her when she had to hold back a yawn. Her eyelids suddenly felt heavy. She set the flashlight on the utility shelf, then remembered the pepper spray she'd left down there. And decided it wasn't important.

Half past nine on a Monday night and the streets in this suburban Nashville neighborhood were already rolled up tight. The quiet was a nice change, Steve thought as he turned the van onto his driveway. One of the reasons he'd chosen to live outside the metro area. Sure, he loved every second he spent around people and music, noise in general, but there were times when a man needed to get away from all that, wind down.

Tonight, though, the slower pace hadn't been able to work its magic on him. There was too much clutter in his head.

He let loose a sigh that had been building for some time now, cut the headlights and engine. Then just sat there for a minute. It had been eating at him non-stop—the history he'd finally been able to drag out of his dad about Allison and her mother.

None of it was good.

He understood why Allison had kept certain details about her mental illness from him. Who wouldn't? But what he just couldn't get his head around was why the old man had—

Dammit, you're not going there again. Not tonight.

Nothing he could do about any of it until morning.

Gaze trailing the moths that fluttered around the glow from the porch light, he took a breath to center, then climbed out of the van. The warm air felt good on his skin. Zero humidity tonight. That was a plus.

He glanced up, scanned the dark vastness dotted with white glimmers softened by moonlight, caught the mellow-sweet scent that drifted over from the flowerbeds next door. Somewhere in the distance, a dog barked—nothing annoying, just the canine version of happy-to-be-alive.

Summer. You had to appreciate it.

Steve unlocked the door, trying not to wake Tammy by rattling the keys. He managed to get one booted foot inside before he felt the punch of arctic air.

Man. He shivered, surprised that his breath wasn't puffing out ice crystals. Sometimes he thought Tammy was part Eskimo. Kept her apartment like the inside of a freezer, didn't she? Twenty-four/seven.

That was why he usually insisted they spend the night at his place. For all the good it did.

Must be love.

Aware of the lopsided grin pasting itself to his face, he locked up, left his keys on the small table by the door. The grin still with him, Steve went over to adjust the thermostat, then turned off the lamp she'd left burning for him and headed to the bedroom.

A narrow strip of moonlight fell across the carpeted floor, slanting up at an angle onto the bed. He stood there for a second, watching the covers rise and fall with her steady breathing. The soft light picked up just a hint of her gorgeous, olive skin and shimmered over all that dark hair.

She was something. Beautiful, he supposed. And sexy as hell, even when she was fast asleep.

You've got it bad, Kincaid.

That, he told himself, was a dangerous road to travel down at this particular stage of his life. He wanted to build the business, concentrate on getting himself squared away financially. They could take their time. Get to know each other better.

Then, down the line... who knew?

Right now, he needed to focus on getting this thing with Allison out into the open and resolved.

Steve closed the narrow gap in the curtains, then slipped out of his clothes, slid into bed. Onto cold sheets. He snuggled up for body heat, and Tammy stirred beside him.

"You're home early," she murmured, her voice soft from sleep. Her hand reached through the dark to brush his cheek. "Is something wrong?"

"Long day, that's all. Decided to cut out and leave it with Jeff." He took her hand, pressed his lips to it. "Sorry I woke you. Try to go back to sleep."

Staring up into the blackness, he listened for the soft, rhythmic breathing that would tell him she had drifted back off. It didn't happen. He could feel those dark green eyes homing in on him.

"You"—Tammy reached over, switched on the lamp—"are such a liar."

She had him.

"Yeah. I am."

She pulled herself up, propped the pillows behind her, and leaned back while Steve did the same. Letting the silence sink in, Tammy slanted him a look. "You going to tell me what's wrong, or do I have to torture you?"

His gaze skimmed her soft mouth, drifted down to full breasts beneath a pale blue, baby-doll top that was whisper-thin. He grinned. "Torture, huh?"

She rolled her eyes. "Is that all you ever think about?"

His amusement fading, Steve shook his head. "No. It isn't." He looked over at her, realized that he needed her input, that… release, he supposed. "I managed to corner Dad this afternoon, had a talk with him."

"About your sister."

"Yeah."

She waited through the stretch of quiet, giving him the space and time he needed. Steve wondered if she even knew how much he appreciated that about her.

"Dad can be stubborn as hell. It was like yanking teeth, trying to get anything out of him. But he finally gave in." His gaze drifted across the room. "I almost wish he hadn't."

"Is it that bad?"

He shrugged. "Depends on what you believe, I guess. I told you Allison's husband was killed in a car accident. Dad says shortly after that, she started… seeing him."

"You mean his ghost."

"That's what they call it. So, yeah." Steve raked a hand through his hair, blew out a breath. "All this time—the doctors, therapy, medications—I thought it was just to help get her through the grief. Hell, if I'd have known, I would never have yanked her chain about the old man who died in that house coming back from the dead."

Tammy reached over to brush the hair from his forehead. "But you didn't know."

True. Still, he had planted that small, ugly seed in Allison's head, made her wonder, worry.

Damned if he could do anything about it now.

"Allison was about a breath away from losing her mind. Dad thinks she's still too fragile to be on her own."

"And what do you think?"

Steve just shook his head. "I think she's been through a lot. And, yes, her mental state is still probably a bit shaky."

Lips pursed, Tammy ran a slender finger along the quilt. "Some people believe we go on after death—that our spiritual selves continue to exist." She looked over at him. "I'm one of them."

"And I get that. I do. But to actually *see* a ghost." He shook his head again. "It gets worse. Turns out, Allison was having regular conversations with her dead husband."

A frown shifted over Tammy's face. "I'm not saying this is the case with your sister, but I've heard there are people who can communicate with the dead. They're called 'mediums.'" She gave Steve a knuckle-punch in the arm when he slanted a look at her. "I'm serious. They're sensitive to spirits."

Her frown deepened. "It's probably nothing, but last weekend, when we helped your sister move in—it was just after they delivered the pizza—we walked into the kitchen, and I swear she nearly jumped out of her skin. Allison said the room was freezing. She had goose bumps all over her arms. I didn't feel it, but Jeff noticed a slight change in the temperature when he came in from the back porch."

She glanced sideways at Steve. "Supposedly, if a spirit's nearby, the temperature will drop. You don't think—?"

He sighed. "What I *think* is that her AC probably needs to be checked."

Biting her bottom lip, Tammy nodded. "That's what I told her."

Steve let the silence hang for a minute. He wanted all of this to go away. It wasn't that he didn't love Allison. Hadn't he always run interference for her with their dad? And for over two years now, he'd constantly worried about her.

Shallow, maybe, but he wanted his damned life back.

Tammy rubbed a hand over his arm. "Are you okay?"

"Yeah. I'm just concerned about her." And the ghost thing wasn't the half of it. He reached for Tammy's hand, linked his fingers with hers. "There's more, but it's complicated."

She waited, watching him. Steve scrubbed a hand over his face. "I'm having a hard time, myself, absorbing what Dad told me." He forced a smile. "Before I lay it on anyone else—"

"You need to talk to your sister. I understand."

Nodding, he gave Tammy's hand a gentle squeeze. "Figured I'd call her first thing in the morning, tell her I'm coming up for a visit."

"Will you be leaving tomorrow?"

"I need to. Jeff's already said that he'd handle things at the studio."

Tammy gave him a light kiss. "You know I'll come along for moral support."

She would—just like that. And it wasn't that he didn't appreciate the offer. Steve put an arm around her shoulder, drew her in. "Thanks, but this is something I need to do myself."

After she had turned off the lamp, he lay there, eyes wide open, listening to her soft snores and staring a hole through the darkness. Trying to tamp down the anger that had started to boil inside him. He hated this feeling, the under-the-skin seething that made him want to punch something. If Allison did somehow manage to find her mother after all these years, the situation could turn deadly. His sister might be in serious danger.

Just because their dad hadn't thought she was strong enough to handle the truth.

A truck in the driveway. Not Bradford's truck—he was out of town.

Whose, then?

He swore, moved farther back into the dark cover of under-brush. He'd had no choice but to push his schedule up. The old woman had started to go weak-kneed on him. Another day and she'd have seriously screwed up his plans.

He'd been forced to rush things, do what needed to be done. Now this.

Mouth turning down in a scowl, he looked back over at the truck. Damned if he didn't have another fly in the syrup.

Well. He would just have to wing it.

He slipped a hand into one of the side pockets of his pants, grinned when he felt the extra syringe snuggled there, right next to the other. Being prepared was his specialty.

Now if the moon would just stay behind the clouds.

Anticipation kicking his heart rate up, he moved deeper into the brush several yards, then started his approach toward the rear of the girl's property. To keep from getting off track, he used the glow of the back-porch light she'd left on as a guide.

Closer. He had to get a little closer.

He crept forward, stopping to wait a bit whenever a pine cone or twig crunched beneath his boot. Then crouched down behind the last layer of brush that would keep him well hidden.

So many windows, he thought, scanning. Several on the first level. Soft light shone out onto the night through some of them. Others, the dark ones, were more inviting.

The breeze that had come up stirred the trees above him, made the shadows move across the yard in the wash of light coming from the porch. He watched those shadows, kept his eyes on what was moving out in that yard. And he hated to admit it, but the damned place was starting to give him the willies.

He got just two steps away from open ground, then stopped cold. Eyes narrowed, he studied the darker, solid mass moving just beyond the edge of the light. There was an ache now at the back of his neck. He put his hand there, rubbed; tried to keep the pain from crawling up to his head.

Then the voice floated over to him, on the wind, it seemed.

For a second, he thought he'd imagined the voice. But then the edge of the light caught the man pacing a small area of ground, a cell phone to his ear.

Well now. He reached into his pocket, drew out one of the syringes, his mouth curving.

It seemed that his luck had just turned.

CHAPTER 21

Toni settled in behind her desk, took a greedy swallow of coffee. Her third cup. It had taken two just to get her moving this morning and on the road.

Her head was still in a haze.

Sooner or later, the caffeine had to kick in.

Barely registering the hum of activity outside her office door, her gaze moved over to one of the old black-and-white photographs on the wall, where two grinning, gangly boys stood in front of the ancient, brick building that housed the *Dawson Times*. Their bicycle baskets were loaded down with folded newspapers.

Her dad and Jim Stevens. Long before Jim ever thought about running for political office, Toni mused and took another swallow of coffee. Before he'd started swindling the local hardworking farmers out of their land. Land that had been in their families for generations.

And didn't that just suck?

Mayor Stevens. He'd walked into the basement of the old church last night with the other men, and she'd nearly dropped her recorder. But she'd kept it together, stayed crouched in the narrow, cramped pantry.

Frowning, Toni tapped a finger on her desk. She'd spent half the night in that damp, musty basement, listening. Waiting. They'd debated over commercial development, costs. But not one of them had uttered a single incriminating word.

She'd wondered if someone had spotted her getting out of her dad's car and him driving off. A stretch, but maybe.

Well. At least she knew now who the players were. That was a darned good start.

Toni glanced over at the time display on her phone, considered giving Allison another call, but then decided to hold off. It was just a few minutes past nine, and she'd already left a voicemail, figured Allison was still sleeping. Yesterday the woman looked as though she could use a twelve-hour shot of some serious snooze time.

"Couldn't we all," she muttered, and logged on to the network. Since she'd met her deadlines for this week's edition, Toni went back to her research on Jack Kincaid. She'd already scanned through several press releases—business ventures, social events. Nothing on the first wife. Yet.

But something else had grabbed her attention.

She pulled up the article she'd accessed yesterday just before leaving the office and, eyes narrowed, studied the picture.

Couple of decades back, a charity event. The stern-looking man, probably in his late thirties, was Jack Kincaid. He wore a sleek, tailored suit that, even at the time, probably set him back more than what Toni brought home in a month.

Must have been born smug, she thought. But Kincaid's arrogance wasn't what had caught her eye.

She zeroed in on the man standing behind Allison's father. Much younger than Kincaid by a good ten years. There was nothing in the article to identify him, but...

Toni flipped through her mental files, grabbed the image of the man she'd noticed during the meeting yesterday at the Town Hall. Took another long look at the face in the photograph.

Yeah. The eyes gave him away. Those almond-shaped eyes.

She sent a copy to the printer, stashed that in her purse. It was a long shot, but Allison just might recognize the guy.

Revved now, Toni downed the last of her coffee, accessed the paper's database. There'd been no local kids reported missing since she had worked here, going on ten years now. Unless she counted the time when the Tyler boy climbed into the hayloft of his parents' barn and fell asleep.

Still, key in the right search criteria and she might pick up a link to one of the surrounding counties.

How far back should she go?

Toni huffed out a jittery breath, thinking she should have stopped halfway through that last cup of coffee. Then plucked a year out of the air.

This was going to be like frog gigging in the dark without a spotlight.

After an eternity of peeling away at the layers of old news, she finally got a hit in a local paper two counties over. Toni scrolled through the story, found the pertinent information. And sighed.

Kid was too old. Sixteen. And he'd been located. Hoofing it down the highway, with his thumb out. Headed to Florida.

Her vision began to blur from staring at the monitor non-stop. She blinked, pinched the bridge of her nose.

"You don't answer your phone, do you?"

Toni jumped, jerked her head around. Ray's hulking form filled the open doorway. On an oath, she grabbed the phone. "Who let you back here?"

He held a hand up. "Before you go jumping down Kara's throat, I threatened to arrest her if she warned you I was coming back."

Toni snorted. "I'd like to see you try." Eyeing him, she cradled the receiver. "What do you want?"

He walked up to her desk, folded his arms over a chest that— well. Impossible to ignore the rock-hard muscles under the denim, she thought, irritated that her mind had taken the small detour.

"You don't pay much attention to your messages, either. I left three."

Toni shrugged. "I've been busy."

One side of his mouth curved, then the other. She'd never been able to decipher that look. The last time they'd butted heads, she'd pretty much decided it was a smirk.

Ray pulled up the visitor's chair and had a seat. He leaned forward, leveled his eyes on hers. Beneath the startling blue-green, she saw the storm brewing and checked the urge to squirm.

"You want to tell me what's up with the new girl?"

She played dumb. "New girl..."

This time he did smirk—no mistaking the smug look.

"What's all the talk about dead kids?"

Shit. The waitress over at Wilma's—Jolene—hadn't wasted any time.

Maybe she should just lay it all out, here and now. Cards on the table. Toni searched his face. He wouldn't believe a word of what Allison had told her, not without physical evidence.

"I don't know what you're talking about."

Ray just shook his head. "A person moves to town, starts talking about dead kids, people get nervous."

"People." Toni tapped a finger on her desk. "You mean Jolene. Since when do you listen to gossip?"

Fire flashed in his eyes. The scar on his jaw stood out like a jagged bolt of white-hot lightning. "Don't screw with me."

Her gaze locked onto his. A standoff. Wasn't the first, probably wouldn't be the last, but it was pointless.

So end it. Now.

"People with big ears sometimes tune in on the wrong part of a conversation. Things get taken out of context." Toni reached into her mental file box, grabbed a fragment of what she'd learned about Allison's past. "Her family—Allison's—suffered a tragedy. It was a long time ago."

Ambiguous, she admitted, but not a total lie. "And it's none of your business. Now. If you don't mind—" She checked her watch, physically jolted when she saw the time.

Almost noon. Allison hadn't returned her call.

Toni snatched up the phone just as her direct line rang. It was her niece, Jenna. No hello, how are you, or what's up, just: "It's your friend, the one you told me about this morning—Allison."

Panic came hard and fast. "What about her?" Ignoring Ray's heavy stare, Toni gave the pause that followed just two seconds. "Jenna?"

"I'm here. I… think something's happened."

Jenna. He should have known. If there were anything at all out of the norm stirring, Ray would bet his badge Toni's niece was involved.

"Psychic, my ass," he muttered. Something about that girl just wasn't right. And it had nothing to do with the so-called paranormal garbage.

Scowling, he steered the Jeep through the downpour that had come up from nowhere while the wipers made a futile attempt to swipe back the rain bulleting the windshield. He'd sat there, across from Toni, watching the color slowly leave her face after she'd picked up the phone. Then—and it had been like a switch flicking off—she was herself again. Slid her hand over the mouthpiece, informed him that the call was personal, and he should get back to doing whatever it was he typically did this time of day.

She'd topped off the suggestion with a quick, sharp smile that had stopped just short of those sexy, doe-brown eyes.

The woman was infuriating, just plain stubborn.

Ray whipped into his allotted spot in the parking lot behind the courthouse, made a dash through the rain and up the stairs to the second floor. He stopped at the front desk to check in. Then headed toward his office.

As was the case most days about this time, there was minimal activity in the bullpen. He had just two deputies in—one on the phone, the other sifting through a file cabinet. Ray nodded at them.

As jobs went, his wasn't half bad. For the most part Dawson Mills was a quiet, peaceful town.

So why did he have the nagging feeling that was about to change?

Frowning, he detoured over to the small alcove where they kept the coffee machine, poured himself a cup—a lousy substitute for a late lunch—then settled into his office. He took the first swallow of caffeine and leaned back in the chair, watched the rain hammer against the narrow window. He'd heard that a single woman had bought the old monstrosity of a house outside of town. And just the other day, a couple of his deputies had mentioned that Toni had made a few subtle inquiries about the place.

He picked up a pencil, tapped it on the notepad in front of him. Then let it drop.

Allison Weathers. Young. Attractive. And skittish as a newborn colt.

What was she hiding?

"Sheriff? Got a second?"

Ray glanced over at the open doorway. Tanya Lewis, the newest deputy on his team, had poked her head in. He motioned for her to grab a chair. "What's up?"

"I just got off the phone with Joe Dean. The owner of that sports bar outside of town?" She pulled one of the chairs over to the front of his desk, had a seat. And when she fixed her big blue eyes on him, his concentration took a small dive. She had the kind of soft, full mouth that could really tempt a man. Then there was all that smooth, creamy white skin. Hair the color of spun gold.

She filled out the uniform in all the right places, too. Big bonus there.

Back in his Academy days, they sure hadn't made them like Tanya Lewis.

And he was straying too damned far down the path. Ray yanked his mind back to business. "There a problem at the bar?"

Tanya looked down at the notepad she'd brought in. "One of

his waitresses hasn't shown up for work in a couple of days. They've been calling her cell and home phone, but no answer. No one seems to know where she is."

He sat up a little straighter. "Has anyone been out to her house?"

"Yes, sir. One of the other waitresses stopped by there—twice." Tanya checked her notes again. "Woman in question is Jessie Conner. Fiftyish. No living relatives, according to Mr. Dean. She left the bar early last Tuesday evening, just before eleven. Wednesday is her usual day off, and she'd put in for a couple of vacation days. They expected her back at work Saturday."

He took a minute to roll it around. He knew Joe Dean. A rough, crude man, thick in the middle, and in the head. And he knew the bar. The place was a dump. Catered to the local drunks, along with a few of the town's businessmen who preferred dingy atmosphere and cheap whiskey.

A person gets a little time away from that, it'd be damned hard to come back.

"Could be that she just decided to take a few extra days."

Tanya nodded. "That's what I'm thinking."

Ray took a swallow from his cup, studied his newest deputy—strictly from a professional angle now. She was sharp. Capable of a lot more than running just a routine patrol. "I'm going to let you handle this one." He caught the spark in her eyes. "Grab some backup and take a ride out to the bar. You know the drill. Talk to everyone there. Check out Conner's residence."

"I'll get right on it." Tanya pulled the chair back over to the corner, paused on her way out. "Sheriff?"

He cocked a brow. "Yeah?"

"Thanks."

Tough, but he managed to keep his mouth from twitching. "Don't thank me, Deputy. Just do your job."

He watched her walk away, her back and shoulders ruler-straight with purpose, then huffed out a short sigh.

Dead kids. A missing waitress.

The nagging feeling was back. The one that told him his nice, quiet town probably wouldn't stay that way for much longer.

At least with the thing on Jessie Conner, they had some cooperation. He doubted he'd get that lucky where Allison Weathers was concerned.

Swearing, Ray grabbed the phone, buzzed the front desk. "Bring me whatever files we've got on Jay Treadwell."

He downed the rest of his coffee and shoved out of the chair, paced over to the window. Honest to God, he hadn't known whether to grab Toni and try to shake some sense into her, or kiss that stubborn streak right out of her. Of course, the last time he'd tried kissing her into submission it had backfired. She had walked out on him.

Bad move on his part.

He stared out at the dreary rain. Secrets. He hated the blasted things. And lies—he hated those even worse.

Toni was up to her pretty, little neck in both.

An overturned farm truck and pigs on the loose. Only in Dawson Mills. Toni slapped a palm against the steering wheel and hissed out a breath. Too bad her psychic niece hadn't foreseen this mess.

It doesn't work that way.

"Yeah, yeah," she muttered, then grabbed her cell phone, scowled at the rain that ricocheted off the cars lined bumper-to-bumper in front of her as she tried to get a signal. She'd have better luck reaching Allison with a couple of tin cans and some string.

She stared down at her hands gripping the wheel, ordered herself to get the adrenaline under control. Jenna had gotten only a brief flash. Vague. Whatever that strange place-out-of-time had wanted Toni's niece to see had been lost in a psychic fog. They were working strictly off a sense of something here.

Could be nothing. This psychic business was open to interpretation. Experience had taught her that.

And with the storm, maybe the power was out, the phones down. Still, she'd feel a hell of a lot better if Ray were here.

Out of frustration more than hunger, Toni shoved a hand into her purse and yanked out the package of peanut butter crackers that had been there for who knew how long, and washed a couple down with the lukewarm remains of the soda she'd grabbed on her way out of the office.

Up ahead, taillights blinked—a blur of red through the rain— and traffic started a slow roll forward.

About damned time.

When she reached the top of a hill, she noticed the lights were out at the small market on the right and felt herself relax a little. The drive down Dawson Creek Road was even more promising. Hard to tell during the day, but it appeared that none of the houses in the area had power.

There was a good chance the phones were down.

Toni turned onto Allison's driveway, keeping a light foot on the gas as she followed the winding concrete. Rain pounded the windshield faster than what the wipers could push it back. Out on the lush, rolling lawn, tall trees swayed from heavy gusts of wind, their twisted branches whipping back and forth.

Crazy, maybe, but the trees seemed angry.

She shook off the creepy thought and rounded a wide curve, passing a mammoth oak. Toni had to do a double-take when the house stretched into view. She'd heard the place was huge, but... overwhelming was more like it. Intimidating.

The cramped space of her two-bedroom condo suddenly seemed cozy, inviting.

Her gaze zipped over to the white truck parked behind the Ford Explorer she'd noticed Allison getting into when they were leaving Wilma's. Work truck, she thought. Toolbox on the back. Toni took

193

a quick inventory of her mental files, grabbed the image of a dark blue truck, Paul's company logo on the doors. And he was out of town for—what? A few days, Allison had told her.

Frowning, she pulled to a stop, then switched off the headlights, squinting past the blur of wipers and rain. Not the single flicker of a candle behind one of those dark windows. No sign of movement.

She glanced down at the display on her cell phone and swore. Still no service. And no pepper spray, she remembered. She'd left it in her bedroom on the dresser.

Lot of good it did her there.

She wished now that she had slapped those metaphorical cards down on the table, told Ray about Allison. Sure, mention the dead kid and anything else she had to say would fly straight past his ears, but he wouldn't have let Toni come out here alone.

Hindsight. It wasn't worth much.

She switched off the wipers and engine, slipped the keys into the front pocket of her slacks, and grabbed her cell phone—just in case. Her mind, two steps ahead of her, already had her sprinting toward the back of the house as she stashed her purse under the front seat and popped the trunk.

Toni sucked in a breath, dashed out into the downpour. Swiping soggy strands of hair away from her face, she leaned into the trunk, the rain pounding her backside, and grabbed a flashlight, the tire iron.

Another oath rushed past her lips when she punched the flashlight on and nothing happened. Toni tossed the useless thing back into the trunk. Gripping the tire iron, she scanned the rows of dark windows, blinking back the hard rain, then dashed across the yard. And jolted when thunder boomed behind her.

Ironic, how a simple offer for pie and coffee had led to this.

Jenna would call it fate.

Toni thought it was just plain bad luck.

CHAPTER 22

CURSING THE RAIN AND TRAFFIC that had held him up, Paul whipped his truck around the winding curves in Allison's driveway, felt the wheels sliding on slick concrete. The minute he'd cleared the mountains and gotten a signal on his cell, he'd called Stan. Voicemail. The same with Allison.

Neither of them had returned his call.

"Damned storm." He eased off the gas as the truck rolled through several inches of standing water. Once the heavy clouds had moved in and the rain had started, he'd lost service on his cell. Could be the phones had gone out on this end as well. Maybe the knot that had been twisting in his gut for the last hour was just a reaction to all the worry that had piled up in his head.

He took the last curve faster than what he should have and felt the bed of his truck start to slide. Paul fought the wheel, managed to get control before the truck could fishtail. Through the wind-blown rain, he glimpsed a woman darting around the corner of the house, a tire iron in her hand.

He glanced over at Stan's truck, his gaze shifting to the silver Mustang, the vanity plate. Toni Harper.

Scanning the house, he swore. The place was too still.

The knot in his gut twisted tighter.

Paul killed the engine and headlights. He shoved out of the truck, zipped across the yard. Large drops of rain exploded against his skin, his hair, and seeped into his T-shirt and jeans. He was drenched by the time he reached the back porch.

In a blur, Toni let go of the screen-door handle and whirled around, tire iron poised to strike. Her dark brown eyes flashed, then dulled, narrowed. "Bradford. You scared the hell out of me."

Before he could open his mouth, she shook her head. "Never mind. I don't know what you're doing here, but I'm glad you are. Here," she clarified, then swiped back the wet hair from her face. "I couldn't reach Allison, got worried. That truck in the driveway—"

"Stan. He works for me. I sent him over here after I talked to Allison yesterday."

Nodding, Toni let out a small breath as he made a move for the door. "Wait. Take this." She handed him the tire iron.

Thunder rumbled behind them just as a heavy gust of wind dumped a spray of rain onto the porch. Paul eased the screen door open, shared a glance with Toni, then reached for the doorknob.

The shock was a punch that knocked the wind from him. Fear gnawed at him with vicious teeth as he took in the chaos. Drawers pulled out, cabinets flung open. Silverware and dishes, pots and pans—the rest of it—strewn over the counter and floor.

"Shit," Toni muttered.

Allison. Goddammit. With Toni at his heels, Paul rushed across the room, dodging the mess. A *thump* in the utility room stopped him in his tracks.

Toni bumped into him. "Sorry—sorry." She frowned at the deep rumble of barking that had started upstairs. "A dog—locked in one of the rooms, by the sound of it."

"Yeah." His gaze shot toward the foyer, then back to where the thump had come from. Paul eyed the closed door, tightened his grip on the tire iron. "Stay here."

"No way."

He heaved a sigh. "Fine. Just—keep back." The barking revved up to frantic howls, grating on nerves that were already raw. Paul yanked open the door to the utility room. And swore. He shoved the tire iron into Toni's hand, then knelt down, scanned the tightly wrapped layers of Duck tape that bound Stan's wrists and ankles. A wide strip of the same gray tape covered his mouth.

Stan grunted. Relief and frustration flashed in his eyes. The angry, purple bruise on his left cheek had Paul muttering another oath.

"We need to get the police out here." Toni pulled a cell phone from the pocket of her slacks and flipped it open, scowled. "Where's the phone?"

"Kitchen. On the wall, next to the fridge."

She grabbed a flashlight off one of the shelves. "I'll check the rest of the rooms downstairs while I'm at it."

Paul nodded. "Be careful." He reached for the strip of tape that covered Stan's mouth, met the man's eyes; got the go-ahead. Then began peeling it back.

Eyes watering, Stan hissed out a breath past raw lips. "*Fuck.* Son of a bitch came up behind me, shot me up with something. Knocked me out."

"Allison?" Paul pulled the Swiss Army knife from his pocket, went to work sawing through the tape.

Stan shook his head. "I—give me a second. Dizzy." He took a couple of breaths. "I was outside—the back, just got off the phone with you. Last thing I remember is my knees buckling." He glanced down at the pieces of tape, flexing numb fingers. Then pressed a hand to his swollen cheek, winced. "Think I hit the porch steps."

Sighing, Stan closed his eyes for a minute. "Bastard took my gun."

The panic spiked another notch as Paul tried to shove it back. He ordered himself to keep his head. Otherwise, he was useless here.

He helped Stan to his feet, raked a hand through his wet hair. *Christ, Allison...*

He could see her now, close to him, the fear shadowing her green eyes the instant he'd told her that he was leaving town.

No. No, not fear. More like a quiet hysteria.

And he had walked away, left her alone in this house.

Paul made a move toward the door just as Toni stepped in. "We're on our own—phones are down. And the power's still out." She shifted her focus. "Stan, right? I'm Toni. You okay?"

"I'll make it. Thanks."

Nodding, she propped the tire iron against the doorjamb. Paul searched her face, aware that he could no longer hear the dog's howling over the sound of the wind and rain beating against the house. "What did you find?"

"Nothing we didn't expect—rooms downstairs are trashed." Her dark brown eyes went to slits. "I'm betting he took her. Allison's smart. She wouldn't have told him where to find it."

His chest tightened. "Find *what?* What are you talking about?"

From somewhere in all the blackness, a dull scraping noise reached her ears. A pathetic whimper escaped her lips. She struggled to open her eyes, but couldn't.

They were like lead weights.

What's wrong with me?

Fighting through the heavy haze that had settled over her brain, she was dimly aware of her rigid muscles, of the damp, chill air around her.

And the spongy surface beneath her felt gritty, lumpy.

Where am I?

Still unable to open her eyes, Allison willed her arms and legs to move. Wasted effort. All she could do was lay there, listening.

A man's voice. Distant. Rough.

More scraping noises.

Then... another voice. Softer, hushed, but with an anxious edge to it. Vaguely familiar.

Snatches of blurred conversation.

Not enough... energy... to listen.

With a small sigh, Allison let herself sink back into the haze. She felt the sluggish thumping of her heart straining to keep the life pumped into her as the fuzzy image of a big dog with a happy grin swirled through her brain.

Jack.

A single tear slid down her cheek. Muddled thoughts and voices faded. Then her mind drifted back into darkness.

"She was going to hide this." Toni pulled the diary from the drawer on Allison's nightstand, then looked back over at Paul. "Apparently, she never got the chance."

"Apparently."

If Toni had noticed his clipped response, she didn't show it. Using the small towel she'd grabbed off the kitchen floor to grasp the handle, she shut the drawer, then switched off the lamp that had flicked on a few minutes before when the power had finally blipped back on.

He didn't have to ask why she hadn't taken the same precautions before she'd laid her hands on the damned journal.

Paul moved over to the window, glancing out at the dreary sky that had temporarily stopped dumping water. He watched Stan lead the dog around on the leash, and had to ask himself—again—why Allison hadn't told him about the diary.

That bothered him more than he cared to admit.

He turned, leveled his eyes on Toni. "Tell me again why we shouldn't hand that journal over to the police."

She glanced down at her watch, huffed out a breath. "I can't get into the details with you now. We've got maybe twenty minutes before Ray—the sheriff—gets here. But, like I said before, there's a good chance that whoever took Allison"—she held up the diary—"was looking for this."

"Yeah. I got that." He'd waded through the destructive chaos in the other rooms on this level and in the attic.

Paul glanced around. Covers pulled up neat on the bed. No drawers yanked open. Nothing in here seemed out of place. Just luck, really, that there had been a big dog on the other side of this door. If not, the bastard would have easily found what he was looking for.

He wouldn't have had a reason to keep Allison alive.

If she played it right, she could buy some time. He hoped Allison realized that. Christ, she *had* to know it.

"We go through the journal, we at least get a clue as to who this guy is—best shot." Toni shook her head. "I really don't want to take the chance that the damned thing might end up sitting on a shelf in the evidence room. Do you?"

It took him maybe half a second. "No."

"Good, good." She started for the door, then paused. "I don't know whether she had time, but Allison was going to sketch the dead kid, something we could use to help identify him."

Paul frowned. He hadn't noticed a sketchpad in the middle bedroom, but they hadn't really looked. At the time, they'd been just rushing through the rooms to make sure Allison wasn't lying on the floor somewhere, hurt—or worse. "Let's go back into her studio, see what we can find."

They stepped around boxes of charcoal sticks and colored pencils, tubes of oil paint, brushes and other artists' tools that littered the floor. Toni glanced down at the pile of rubble in the corner, next to the empty shelves: pieces of broken sculptures. "A damned shame." She pursed her lips. "Makes me wonder, though. If he was searching for the diary, why waste time busting up sculptures?"

"Temper." And Paul hoped to God that Allison hadn't been on the receiving end of it, that, like Stan, she'd been out cold, oblivious. Because the bastard had sure torn through the house in a rage.

But—he had missed this. Paul reached for the drawer in the side of Allison's worktable, and stopped. "Toss me the towel, will you?"

Toni pitched the towel in an overhand arc. He caught it, opened the drawer. "Got something here."

She was next to him before he could look back up. Taking the sketchpad from him, Toni flipped the cover back and frowned.

The breath caught in his throat. He hadn't felt this from Allison—the deep, all-consuming darkness that must have been pent up inside her to draw something like this. Writhing, contorted limbs in a frantic grab for the sky. "Scariest damned tree I ever saw."

"Yeah. Right out of a nightmare." With a visible shudder, Toni flipped the page back. Then nodded. "This is him—the dead kid."

The solemn face framed with shaggy hair had a smudge—dirt, he imagined—across one cheek. Blank eyes, with an odd, flat shine to them, stared back at Paul. A chill snaked through him.

"This is his dog." Toni tapped a finger on the image of the small scruffy animal near the boy's bare feet. "Scooter."

His heart tripped as he slowly repeated the name. Allison had told him about the dog. Dead. Ghost-dog. For just a second, his throat had locked up. He'd caught only a glimpse of the animal, but the dog had seemed... solid. Alive.

Welcome to my world. Her reply had been a soft apology.

"That's the dog I chased." He told her about the movement in the underbrush when they'd been standing on Allison's back porch. How he'd run through the woods after the animal, until a fallen tree had stopped him. "Thought the dog was having some sport. He kept looking back at me."

"Leading you," Toni murmured. "What direction?"

"Toward the property next door. The Atkins' place."

"Atkins... I've heard the name." Eyes narrowed, she cocked her head. "Jared Atkins?"

"Yeah." Paul frowned. "Yeah."

A torturous few seconds of silence slid by while she studied the sketch. "We need to go back down to the cellar. How long will it take you to get that light switch working?"

"Less than a minute or two, if it's just a loose wire behind the plate."

She gave him a sharp nod and closed the cover on the sketchpad, tucked it under her arm. "I'll stash this in my car with the diary."

"The tire iron," Paul reminded her.

"Right. Left that in her bedroom." Toni checked her watch. "We'd better hurry. Ray catches us inside, he'll hang us both."

Jared Atkins. It had taken every ounce of restraint Paul could muster to keep from making tracks in that direction. But he had to play this smart. He'd wait for nightfall—it would come early, because of the weather. Then—

"Hey." Toni snapped her fingers in front of his face. "Are we going down, or do you want to just keep standing here?"

"Yeah."

She arched a brow. "To what?"

Paul scowled. He flipped the light switch to test it, frowning down at the dim glow that popped out from the gloom. "Huh. It's working now."

"I see that." Holding the flashlight Paul had given her for backup, Toni followed him down the stairs. "Stan's putting the dog in your truck, since you've got a bench seat. He'll probably stay out there for a while himself. Fresh air's helping to clear his head." She paused. "I'm thinking, under the circumstances, he was damned lucky."

"I agree." Paul took the flashlight from her, aimed the beam into the dark corners. "But only because whoever took Allison had to search the house, get her out of here, take her... somewhere."

Toni nodded. "And Stan never saw the guy's face, so he can't identify him. Easier and quicker just to tie him up, leave him."

She glanced up at the stingy amount of gray light that came through the overhead windows, and shifted her gaze to the single lighted bulb. "It's gloomy as hell down here."

"Yeah, it is." Paul shook off the musty dampness, then ran the beam along the brick walls and shadowed edges of the floor. "No patch work that I can see. If someone was buried down here"—he stopped, willed himself not to picture what might be directly under their feet—"they poured concrete after the fact."

"I thought that might be the case, but we had to check." Toni frowned. "I think we both know Atkins' history—he's a drunk with a temper, takes all that pent-up anger out on his wife. In my opinion that says 'coward' with a capital C."

She shook her head. "The dead kid told Allison 'they' were watching her. And I'm just not getting that Atkins could have pulled this off without help."

"You're probably right," Paul admitted, then had to backtrack. "But I'm wondering—why take the risk now, with someone living here? After Jay Treadwell died, this house stood vacant for months."

"We wondered the same—Allison and I. Maybe he did, though. Search the place, I mean, and didn't find anything. If what we suspect about Allison's past is true, if she's been here before, doesn't remember..." Toni shrugged. "Murky, but there's got to be a connection here."

"Good point." Paul moved over to the old boiler in the corner, with Toni following. She stood on the tips of her toes, trying to see, while he maneuvered his way around the tight clearance between the wall and the boiler.

He aimed the light onto the brick, traced over the cobwebs that clung to the wall. Then shifted the beam down.

"Pepper spray," Toni said when the light bounced off the small canister on the floor. "Allison's."

Paul reached for it. Then froze. He angled his head to get a better look. A section of the brick wall behind the air-handling unit hadn't been mortared.

"Take this." He shoved the pepper spray into her hand, motioned for her to move back, and began working his way out of the tight corner. In the breath of space, where the air-handler butted up to one side of the boiler, the beam of his flashlight picked up more of the same—loose brick, stacked.

Toni's gaze trailed his. "What is it?"

"I'm not sure." They stepped around to the side of the air-handler, found a small square of bricks that Paul managed to pry from the wall with just a few scrapes to his knuckles. He slanted the light into the opening, frowned when the beam traveled without bouncing off earth or rock.

Toni's eyes narrowed. "You know anything about the tunnels that are supposed to be in some of the cellars in these old houses?"

"Tunnels... Civil War era, right?"

She nodded. "During that time, some of the more prominent landowners put their remaining slaves to work digging underground tunnels that would lead up into the old abandoned mine shafts."

"Yeah, I remember hearing the stories. Escape routes." Paul switched off his flashlight and stepped back, still frowning. "This house was built in the early nineteen hundreds. But that was after—"

"A fire destroyed the first. Exactly. I did some research. The original structure was built in the eighteen fifties."

Yeah. Yeah, he remembered now. And he couldn't believe it had never dawned on him that the Treadwell's house might be sitting on one of those tunnels. It might explain a few things.

He blew out a breath. "We need to slide this unit out from the wall. I'll run outside, see if Stan's up for lending some muscle."

"That won't be necessary."

"*Dammit.*" Toni whipped around. "Ray."

CHAPTER 23

"**A**RE YOU OUT OF YOUR *mind?*" Ray jerked his focus off Toni just long enough to glance back at the monstrosity of a house. It would take his CSI team at least another couple of hours to finish combing through the place. "What the hell did you think you were doing in there?"

Leaning against her car, arms folded over her chest, Toni huffed out a breath. Her gaze shot over to where Bradford was giving his statement to the deputy, then back to Ray. "We were just—"

"*What?* Contaminating a crime scene?"

Dark brown eyes smoldered as her face went to stone. A look he knew all too well. As far as she was concerned, this conversation was a done deal.

Red lights flashed against a drab sky as the ambulance pulled down the driveway with Stan Michaels in tow to the ER. Ray looked over at the van parked on the grass. At least Kincaid had stayed put. The guy hadn't been happy about it, but he had done what Ray had asked.

He shook his head. "Dammit, Toni. We don't have time for games."

She sighed, nodded. "You're right. I'm sorry."

The small smile she gave him made his heart kick. It irked him to no end that she could still spike his blood pressure with just a look. "I want you to get into your car, wait until I'm finished here.

Then we'll take a trip downtown. You're going to tell me what you know about Allison Weathers—the truth this time."

"The truth." Toni swung the driver's side door open. "All right. But you're not going to like it."

He didn't care much for the ominous sound of that.

Ray headed for the van, glancing up at the overcast sky when thunder rumbled. More rain on the way. If he was a superstitious man—which he wasn't—he might wonder if all these storms that had cropped up lately were some kind of omen.

That particular brand of nonsense was Toni's department.

He moved in a wide arc past Bradford's truck to keep from stirring up the big dog that had finally settled down. The young man behind the wheel of the van fixed a pair of wide eyes on him that were just this side of frantic.

"Mr. Kincaid."

"Steve. And—I need to know what's happened to my sister. Is she—?"

"All I can tell you at this time is that the house has been vandalized. Your sister appears to be missing."

"*Christ.*" Kincaid ran a shaky hand through hair that was already disheveled. "I'm too late."

Frowning, Ray lowered the volume on the radio clipped to his belt, muting the static. "What do you know about this?"

Kincaid just shook his head. "I'm not sure. It's... complicated."

Complicated. There was a lot of that going around.

Squinting against the mist that had started, Ray looked over at his deputy and Bradford moving up to the porch for cover. "I'm going to ask you to wait here for a while longer. Then I'll need you to follow me downtown, so we can get your statement."

"Sure, sure." Kincaid glanced past him. "The man standing on the porch—you said he's a local contractor?"

"That's correct. Told us he's bidding some renovation work for your sister."

The sigh was long, the nod slight. "Guess that tracks. Allison was planning to fix up the place, build a studio out here. She's an artist."

Maybe, Ray thought. But the connection between Allison Weathers and Bradford—whatever it was—went much deeper than casual business.

Kincaid pulled his focus back to Ray, and for a moment, it seemed that his eyes didn't quite know where to settle. It was the scar on Ray's jaw. It made most people uncomfortable initially. Some never quite got used to it. Ray sometimes found it hard not to do a double-take himself whenever he looked into a mirror or passed a storefront window that caught his reflection just right.

His radio buzzed. "You there, Sheriff?"

Sam Harris. One of the deputies Ray had sent around to question the neighbors.

"Hang on, Sam." He held up a finger to Kincaid then stepped away from the van, kept the volume low. "Go ahead."

"We've got plenty of curiosity from folks in the area, but no answers. No one saw a thing." Sam paused at the burst of static. "We didn't find anyone home at the Atkins place. I figure Old Jared's probably up to his usual, holed up in a bar somewhere."

He waited through another pop of static. "One of the neighbors said the missus works nights at the hospital—part of the cleaning crew. You want us to take a ride out that way?"

Ray considered. If anyone around here had noticed something unusual in the last few days, it'd be Ellie Atkins. When it came to other people's business, the woman had a long nose.

"Go ahead and take a ride out there, talk to her. Let me know what you find."

"Will do, Sheriff."

A drop of rain splattered against his arm. Then another. Ray went over to the Jeep, grabbed his slicker and tugged it on. His deputy on-scene slid the clipboard that held Bradford's statement onto the dash of his cruiser, donned his own slicker, then came over. "Sheriff."

Ray nodded. "Carl. Learn anything from Bradford that he didn't tell us initially?"

"Some. But I'm not sure how much it's worth. He kept insisting we look at Jared Atkins for what happened here."

Ray cocked a brow. "Why is that?"

"Well, the old man's a violent drunk, beats his wife. And he lives right next door. I assured Bradford that we're aware of the history there, but I just don't see Atkins having the energy or the ambition for something like this."

No, he wouldn't. Ray figured that aside from taking the occasional swing at his wife whenever the mood struck, Atkins was doing good just to haul his carcass out of the chair and stumble down to the bar.

"You get a number where we can reach Bradford's grandmother to verify he was out of town?"

"Yes, sir."

"Okay." Ray swiped the rain back from his face. "I've got two people scheduled for interview. I want you to head back to the office, give me a hand with that."

Carl tapped a finger to his forehead in a salute, then slid into his cruiser and pulled away. With the rain coming down like fury now, Ray dashed up to the house to check with CSI. He brushed the water from his slicker, and watched as Bradford shoved one of the large bags of dog food they'd found in the utility room into the cab of his truck.

Ray's temper sparked again. Sending an employee into a potential situation with a damned gun. And now said gun was in the hands of one pissed off individual.

Playing amateur detective. Or hero.

Trouble. The man was going to be nothing but trouble.

Bradford climbed into his truck, and the engine roared to life. Ray grabbed his radio, tagged his deputy.

"Go ahead, Sheriff."

"Change of plans, Carl. I want you on surveillance tonight."

With the rain bulleting down, Ray was doing good just to see a few feet in front of his Jeep. It made the ride back to town a slow go. He used the time to run through the scene in his head again. The dog had kept her bedroom upstairs off-limits. Nothing in there—purse, expensive jewelry in the ornate box on the dresser, or the rest of it—had been disturbed.

But the big-screen television setup with Bose surround sound had to be worth a few thousand. And there were plenty of other accessible toys. State of the art stereo, DVD player. Laptop and printer sitting on her desk in the library. Digital camera on a nearby shelf.

The only thing that appeared to be missing was Allison Weathers.

Whoever had torn through the house hadn't found what he was looking for. Kincaid knew what that was. If Toni and Bradford didn't, they at least had a damned good idea.

A hot rush of anger spiked through him. Secrets and lies. Ray swore.

With the wipers on full, knocking back the rain, he followed the last stretch of 285 onto Main. Ray pulled into the front lot at the courthouse. He waited for Toni and Kincaid to park, then caught up with them.

They rode the elevator up to the second floor in silence, Kincaid raking a hand through his wet hair. Ray brushed the water from his slicker. Behind him, Toni shifted. Tension radiated off her like a heat wave.

She didn't want to be here.

Tough.

The elevator bumped to a stop, and the doors slid open to a hum of activity—phones ringing, muted conversations.

Busy night. The storm, probably.

Ray glanced across the bullpen when the door to the back stairway shoved open and Deputy Lewis came in, stopping just long enough to leave her wet slicker on a peg by the door. She walked over, gave Steve and Toni a cursory nod, then brushed the rain from her face. "You got a second, Sheriff?"

He nodded. "Go on back to my office. I'll be there in a minute."

Ray steered Toni over to a metal chair in the waiting area, then flagged one of his deputies. "Make sure she stays put—and no phone calls." Ignoring the daggers shooting from her dark brown eyes, he took Kincaid across the hall into the conference room. "I'm going to have you wait here. I won't be long. Meantime, can we get you something to drink?"

Kincaid sank into one of the chairs at the long table, scrubbing a hand over his haggard face. "A Coke would be great. Thanks."

On his way to Vending, Ray shrugged out of his slicker and draped it on a peg. He got the soda, took it in to Kincaid, and managed to get maybe two steps past Toni when she hissed out his name. He turned, heaved a sigh. "What is it?"

She glanced at the deputy assigned to watch her, then yanked her gaze back to Ray, eyes narrowed to sharp slits. "No phone calls? You're treating me like a common criminal."

Not quite. He could have charged her with obstruction, tossed her obstinate butt behind bars.

Ignoring the curious looks from his people, Ray kept his tone even. "You've got just one choice: cooperate. Or I'm going to show you how we *do* treat criminals around here."

"I'm allowed to make a phone call."

He nodded. "Yes, you are. But not until I say so."

Ray turned to his deputy. "Keep an eye on her."

Still feeling the heat from Toni's anger—and his own—he

stopped to grab some coffee and headed to his office. Tanya stood up from the visitor's chair she'd moved in front of his desk. Ray waved her back down, then shut the door, settled into his chair.

"Sorry to interrupt, Sheriff, but I think Jessie Conner may have gotten herself into some trouble."

Joe Dean's missing waitress. He leaned forward. "What have you got?"

"One of the other waitresses—Irene Stevenson—told us that Miss Conner had taken her car in for repairs. The garage on Main Street. She was supposed to pick it up sometime Wednesday. It's still there. Mechanic said she never called in."

Tanya flipped through her notes. "Seems Jessie Conner is dating a married man. Miss Stevenson was the only one who knew anything about the relationship."

Or the only one willing to talk, he thought. "The Stevenson woman, was she able to ID the boyfriend?"

Tanya shook her head. "Unfortunately, she never saw them together, never got his name. But—" She paused, blue eyes homing in on him. "Miss Conner did let it slip that he'd be coming into a pile of money. Soon."

Ray cocked a brow. "She happen to say where the money was coming from?"

"Guess that would have made things too easy. But, no. Just that they planned on leaving town together as soon as he got his hands on it."

She glanced over at the storm still raging outside when thunder rattled the window. "We drove out to Miss Conner's residence, found the landlady letting herself in."

"Behind on the rent?" Ray guessed, and she nodded.

"Irene Stevenson is the only reference listed on the rental app. And the landlady isn't aware of any relatives, or even that Miss Conner is in a relationship."

Frowning, Tanya drummed her fingers on his desk. "Here's the thing—we checked inside, the place is rented furnished. Landlady verified nothing was missing. And no sign of a struggle. The closet and dresser drawers were cleaned out, toiletries gone. But some of the other personal items were left behind. Nothing we could get any information from, like an address book or any documents, just a few dishes, a small stereo and some CDs, things of that nature."

Ray took a swallow of coffee and glanced over at the time readout on his phone, briefly wondering how much trouble Toni was giving his deputy. "If Conner expected to come into money, she might have figured on replacing everything once they got to wherever they were headed."

"Maybe. But I don't think that's the case."

He eyed her for a second, could almost see the wheels in her head turning. "What makes you say that?"

"Well, her cat was still there. Poor thing was starving."

She shook her head when he frowned. "I know what you're thinking, but the landlady told us Jessie's had the cat for years. Rescued it from the animal shelter when it was barely five weeks old."

Tanya leveled her gaze on him. "She wouldn't have left that cat behind."

Dimly aware of the snatches of conversation around her, the occasional phone ringing, Toni ignored the deputy intent on watching her. She looked up at the large round clock on the wall. Light from the overhead fluorescents created a glare, in spots, on the glass that covered the stark-white face. The red second hand ticked in a slow, jerky motion past the black markings.

She shifted in the hard chair, blew out a breath. Every tick of the hand on that clock closed the window of time they had to find Allison just a little more. And all Toni could do was sit here.

But if she had read Paul right, he wouldn't be able to step back and let the police handle this. He'd want answers. Tonight.

Hearing Ray's voice behind her, she turned and saw him heading back toward the bullpen with the new female deputy. Toni had gotten just a glimpse of the woman earlier, but she was sure getting an eyeful now. Golden blonde hair cut short in a no-fuss style. Dark blue eyes—clear, alert. A tight body with hourglass curves. And the woman wouldn't have to stand on the tips of her toes to look Ray straight in the eye.

She wasn't sure how she felt about that.

Her gaze made a quick jump down to the woman's left hand. No ring.

Miss Perfect gave Ray a smile before veering off to her desk. Toni scowled, reminding herself to focus on what was important here—Allison.

At this point, the quickest way to her just might be through Jenna.

She tapped a finger against her thigh as Ray tucked the notepad he held under one arm and refilled his coffee cup. When he started for the conference room, Toni jumped up from the chair. The deputy assigned to watch her moved around his desk and had his hand on her shoulder before she could take a step. "Sorry, ma'am. You're going to have to sit back down."

"I just need a minute with the Sheriff."

Frowning, Ray made a sharp detour. "Is there a problem?"

"No, no problem." Toni slanted the deputy a look, shrugged her shoulder from his grip. "I need to call Jenna. She'll be worried."

Ray took a slow swallow from his cup. "Thought maybe you'd already done that."

"I did—from the landline, just after I phoned you. That was several hours ago." Toni shook her head. "I tried checking back with her before we left Allison's, and on the way in. Couldn't get a signal on my cell. The weather."

Ray eyed her for a second, then nodded to his deputy. "One call—that's it." He looked back at Toni. "Keep it short."

Lowering herself into the rigid chair that was beginning to

feel like a block of concrete beneath her butt, she grabbed her cell phone from her purse. The signal was there, but weak. Toni ignored the calculating stare on her, and punched the speed dial for her home number.

Because words had an annoying habit of travelling through the air to perked ears, she gave Jenna just the basics. "I don't know how much longer I'll be here. Have you been able to pick up anything else on Allison?"

Silence. Then her niece's short, faint sigh. "I tried but… all I get is blackness. It's like a wall that makes my mind feel trapped and… heavy, I guess. Then the darkness shifts, lightens to gray, and goes to black again."

"I'm not sure what it means."

Toni wasn't either, but she had a hunch. If she was right, they still had time.

Jenna sighed again. "This is never easy, you know?"

"I know, sweetie" Like working a puzzle, she supposed. With one eye closed and a hand tied behind your back. She glanced over at the door to the conference room. The stepbrother,—Steve— maybe he could provide some insight.

For a second, she wished she'd been able to morph into a fly, follow Ray into that interview.

The deputy tapped his watch, and Toni raised a finger. "I have to go. Just try to relax. That usually helps, right?"

"Sometimes." Jenna paused. "Did you get the diary?"

"Yeah. I'll be there with it as soon as I can." Toni disconnected. The minion assigned to watch her had his back to her now, digging through a file cabinet. She grabbed Paul's business card from her wallet, was just about to key the number in when a hand swooped down and snatched the phone from her.

Ray's deputy flashed a broad smile. "I'll just hold on to this until you're ready to leave."

CHAPTER 24

WHILE RAY WENT THROUGH THE motions of getting comfortable at his desk, Toni pulled up one of the visitor's chairs and sat. The cheese crackers she'd gotten from Vending earlier weighed on her stomach like gravel under a sea of Pepsi.

Ugh.

She glanced out at the darkness beyond the window, making a small wager with herself on how much longer he would hold her up. The good news was the rain had finally slacked up enough so that it wasn't pounding against the glass.

About damned time.

Ray pulled a fresh notepad and handheld recorder from one of the drawers, the movement just enough to draw her focus. Toni glanced at the empty spot on the corner of his desk where he'd kept a framed photo of the two of them. The absence of it put a small ache in her throat.

She told herself to get over it. Life was a lot smoother without all the emotional upheaval.

His eyes steady on her, Ray tapped the eraser end of his pencil on the desk. "I'm going to say this just once, so listen up. If I think for one minute that you're withholding information, I'll toss your butt behind bars. And you will *stay there.* Got it?"

So much for sentiment.

Could be a fine line, Toni thought, switching mental gears, but she didn't consider the diary and Allison's sketchpad "information." Not in the literal, technical sense.

The hitch there would be if Allison's brother happened to mention finding the diary to Ray.

She blew out a breath. She'd just have to deal with the fallout, if and when. "Yeah. I got it."

With a sharp nod, he switched on the recorder, then recited the interview– and case introductions. "How well do you know Paul Bradford?"

Toni lifted a brow. Of all the questions he might have led with, she hadn't expected that one. "Well enough to trust him, if that's what you're getting at."

She ignored the flash in his eyes. "I met Paul last summer. He built the library addition on my dad's house. In fact, Mayor Stevens—" She glanced at the area map pinned to the wall, and scanned the large block marked for commercial development along the northern section of 285.

Backdoor dealings. The term her dad had coined for the questionable business transactions. She wondered if they had lured Paul in as an investor. They might have sweetened the deal by giving him the contract on the construction.

There was always a fall guy. Always.

"Tape's still running," Ray said, his gaze boring into her.

"Yeah—sorry." Toni shifted in the chair. "The mayor recommended Paul's work. My parents were out of town during most of the construction, so I was the go-to. Paul was easy to work with, and he did a great job for a reasonable rate. Dad was more than pleased."

She shrugged. "He has a stellar reputation. What more can I tell you?"

The hush that dropped had her fighting the urge to squirm.

"Whoever tore through that house was looking for something. You got any idea what that is?"

"I don't have a clue," Toni lied, bracing for the fallout that, apparently, was going to hit much sooner than she'd anticipated.

When it didn't, she breathed a small inward sigh.

Ray took a long swallow from his cup. "Tell me what you know about Allison Weathers."

Time to fess up. Toni looked down at the recorder. The tunnel... had to be a link there, why the dead kid had led Allison down to the cellar. But unless Ray could ditch the blinders he wore like a bad habit long enough to see the pattern, the truth would do more harm than good.

"Before I get into specifics... The open area behind the air-handler in Allison's cellar... You *are* going to have your men check it out."

His eyes flashed fire. "You need to let me worry about handling this investigation."

"Fine." Toni sucked in a quick breath, then got on with it. She gave Ray a physical description of the boy, leaving out the small detail that the kid was no longer breathing. She was still working her way up to that.

"The boy admitted having a friend with him—a girl, who had run back into the woods. Scared, is what he told Allison."

"So, you're saying—what?—a couple of kids broke into her house?"

"Not exactly."

His broad shoulders rose and fell in a long, smooth motion. She had maybe a second or two at best before he exploded.

"Thing is—cryptic as it sounds—we're fairly certain the kids led Allison down to the cellar for a reason. The tunnel," she added when he cocked a brow.

She paused to backtrack, told him about the old red truck that had spooked Allison. "Kid warned her that a man was watching her. At one point, he said, 'they.'"

Ray heaved a sigh. "And it never occurred to either of you

to report any of this to the police." Before she could open her mouth, he grabbed the pencil, scribbled a note. "I don't suppose the boy happened to mention any names, or how he knew she was being watched."

Not exactly, Toni reflected, but the kid's dog had sure tried pointing them in a certain direction.

She bit down on the words just as Jared Atkins' name was about to roll off her tongue. Paul had already mentioned Atkins to Ray's deputy. And after mulling over the theory, she'd found a huge hole there. She'd heard enough from Lilly Jameson and some others around town to know that Atkins was dimwitted, temperamental, and just plain mean. If he hadn't found what he was looking for, he'd have most likely beaten Allison senseless. He wouldn't have had the patience to drag things out.

It just didn't fit.

Toni shook her head. "Specifics would've been nice, but no."

"Okay." He scribbled another note. "Kids probably live somewhere in the neighborhood."

"I doubt it."

His gaze shot back over to her. "You seem fairly certain of that."

"Yeah, well." Toni glanced at the tiny glowing, green light on the recorder and wished he would shut the darned thing off. "We're... not sure about the girl—Allison never got a look at her—but the boy..."

There was no way to soften the blow.

"He's dead."

"Dead." The scar on his jaw bulged. "You want to tell me just how and when that happened?"

If only. Toni lifted her shoulders. "See, that's just it—we don't know. We think he's probably been that way for a while now."

The shutters in his eyes slid down, his personal defense mechanism. A handy little invisible stone wall that kept anything remotely connected to the paranormal from sneaking past his thick skull. Toni sighed. "A ghost, Ray. Allison talked to a ghost."

He made a rough sound, then shut the recorder off, fixing a hard stare on her. "A ghost. And you believed her."

"Yes, dammit. Why is that so difficult for you to accept?"

"Because it's bullshit. There's no such thing as a ghost."

She nodded. "Yeah, well. I guess Jay Treadwell was imagining things, too. He thought the house was haunted."

Toni ignored the glare he shot in her direction. "You might want to reconsider how you look at the world. Because right now, that 'ghost' may be the only connection we have to finding Allison. And from what I've been able to put together, I'm almost positive whoever was watching her murdered that poor kid—probably the girl too."

Her eyes went to slits. "Now the creep has Allison."

Silence dragged, his gaze glued to hers, until he finally scrubbed a hand over his face. "Off the record—are you aware that Allison Weathers spent nearly two years in a psychiatric hospital?"

She had to grapple for words. "No... I... didn't know that."

The deep, black void around her began to lift, slowly becoming a blend of shadows. Allison had a dim awareness of the faint scent that lingered around her. Old, stale earth.

And her skin, she noticed with an odd sort of detachment, felt clammy.

For a moment, she had the peculiar sensation of drifting, then felt the muscles in her arms and legs twitch, and her eyes fluttered open.

Darkness—everywhere. She couldn't see a thing. Panic fisted in her chest, pounded there.

Where am I?

Trying to focus through the haze in her head, she groped to pull herself up, and realized that she was lying on a bare, lumpy mattress covered with a layer of grit. She was still dressed but... her feet were chilled, the tips of her toes like ice.

Her shoes. Where were her shoes?

Allison struggled to a sitting position. Her head took a spin, and she rode it out, gripping the edge of the filthy mattress with a shaky hand, taking slow, shallow breaths.

She remembered now. Stan—coming back in with the dog. Then he'd stepped outside again to phone Paul. And... What?

Allison rubbed a hand over eyes that felt puffy and sore. There was a dull ache in her head, but it was nothing compared to the queasy churning in her stomach. It took a mountain of effort to get past the nausea, to reach through the fog in her brain, but she remembered taking Jack upstairs to get him settled. Then shutting her bedroom door, so he wouldn't pad after her.

Jack. Her breath hitched. She had left him alone.

And Stan... What had happened to him?

The rest of it flashed through her head. Back downstairs to make up the sofa. Then—into the kitchen.

Dark. She called out to Stan, reached for the light switch.

The shuffle of footsteps behind her. Trying to scream as the rough, calloused hand clamped over her mouth.

And the struggle. She had felt a slight prick in her arm and then a burning sting. Seconds later, her mind shut down, and she sank into absolute blackness.

Dear God. How long had she been unconscious?

I... have to get out of here.

Allison swallowed over the horrible dryness in her throat. She eased her legs around. Small, jagged rocks poked at her bare feet as they touched down onto hard-packed earth.

Damp earth. The air was thick with a cool, musty smell she could almost taste.

The realization of what that meant slammed through her. She was deep under the ground, a cavern of some kind.

No one would ever find her. No one.

She choked back the urge to scream. Think. She needed to think.

No time. From the other end of what seemed to be a long corridor, a small round light flicked on. Heart thundering, her gaze darted around the pitch-black then back to the spot of light floating toward her.

Do something.

What?

Run.

To where?

Anywhere.

The light flicked off, followed by the echo of a muffled curse.

Now. She scrambled off the mattress, fighting another wave of dizziness, and pitched forward, arms flailing through the black, empty space. Allison cried out as she went down, wrenching her ankle. Muttering an oath, she bit back the pain, tried to get to her feet but couldn't.

The light flicked on again. Closer now and still moving toward her. In the dim glow cast by the broadening beam, she caught shadowy glimpses of rock and tree roots, compacted earth, and sobbed.

She was going to die, right here. Alone. Deep under the ground.

They would never find her body.

Allison shivered from a draft that came up from nowhere. For one horrifying moment, she envisioned her soul trapped between this world and the next, wandering for an eternity through a pitch-black grave.

Lost.

"*No,*" she murmured. There had to be another opening down here somewhere. A way out.

Bracing against her throbbing ankle, she scooted on her bottom. Sharp rocks waged a stinging assault on her palms and bare skin

221

below the hem of her capris as she dragged herself toward the faint flow of air she'd felt.

Her heart kicked when the walls of earth around her popped out from the blackness. She jerked her head around. And froze.

The light was on her now. Harsh, blaring in her eyes, blinding her. Allison squinted up at the black silhouette behind the light. A monster. Masquerading as a man. She could barely make out the vague shape of him—tall, broad through the chest. But she could feel his eyes on her.

Eyes that knew her. She sensed that as well.

He reached down, grabbed her arm, and jerked her to her feet. Allison screamed when pain shot through her ankle.

"Shut up."

Whimpering, she choked back the sobs, then cried out again from the fierce pressure of his fingers digging into her arm as he yanked her over to the mattress.

"I said shut up!" He shoved her down.

Unable to stop shaking, Allison clamped her bottom lip between her teeth. She was afraid to look at him, yet, powerless to take her eyes off him.

He pulled a small foldout chair from the darkness and, with single-minded determination, dragged it in front of her, then lowered himself onto it. The flashlight clanked against rock when it met the ground with a hard plunk, the beam pointing up. Allison shifted her gaze to his face where shadows blended with the light. Time had etched a map of deep lines across his forehead and beneath his eyes. Heavy grooves bracketed a harsh mouth.

He might have been handsome once, just a trace of that was still visible. But the years, along with his cruel nature, had stamped a bitter hardness into his features.

"You don't remember me. I'm disappointed."

The words were like a slap. Allison searched his eyes—two pools of black ice. She didn't know this man, this… monster.

"I don't understand any of this."

He shook his head. "You're lying."

"No—I—"

His arm lashed out, the back of his hand striking her face with brutal force. Allison screamed as her head jerked back. He grabbed her chin, yanked. Behind the amusement that flickered in his eyes, she saw a shadow of something much darker. "Where is it?"

It. The diary.

Had he not searched her house?

This close to him, with his hand on her, she couldn't think straight.

Trembling, Allison pulled away from his grasp and put a hand up to her stinging face. Glared at the bastard. "I don't know what you're talking about."

"Now, see. You're lying again. And that's going to piss me off—again." A thin slice-of-a-smile crept over his face. Her pulse skipped. She knew that arrogant look. The man wearing it had been behind the wheel of a battered truck with tinted windows.

"You got a knack for playing games, girlie. Just like your mother."

Mother. Allison swallowed, hard, as he reached into his shirt pocket and pulled out a photograph. She watched him rip the faded photo she'd left on her desk in the library after scanning it. Pieces of her mother's image fluttered to the ground like feathers carried on a breeze.

Questions twisting around speculation raced through her head. She shoved it all back. Focus. She had to focus on staying alive. Giving the monster the information he wanted sure as hell wouldn't accomplish that.

He would kill her in a heartbeat.

And he'd know if she were lying again. She'd have to use the truth, just not the whole of it, to steer him away. Hopefully create enough doubt so that she remained an asset.

"I... think it's somewhere in the house."

He grinned, eyes bright. "I knew it. The room upstairs." A scowl wiped the grin away. "Couldn't get in there. Damned dog nearly took my head off. I'd've shot the sonofabitch, but anybody within a mile of the place would've heard the gun go off."

Jack. A sigh shuddered out of her. Her dog was all right. For now.

She looked back into those cold, empty eyes. Stan... Was he still alive?

The monster cocked his head. "Let's back up a minute here. You said, 'somewhere in the house.'"

"Yes. Buried, I think. In the cellar." As soon as the words were out, she realized her mistake. Afraid to breathe, Allison scanned his face—a blank page. She grasped at the only straw she'd been able to gather—a pitiful arsenal—and hoped to God she had guessed right. "I was so young. I... need time. To remember."

Those two chilling pools of black fixed on her, unblinking, for the longest time. Finally, he nodded. "You've got twenty-four hours."

A day. Time enough to find a way out of here.

Relief flooded through her like a balm.

A mental institution. Typical of Ray to drop a nasty shocker like that into her lap and then hold back the details. Toni steered the car north, down Main. Wilma's Café rolled by—shut down for the night, just the one, outside light burning. "Dammit, Allison. You should have told me."

Turning into the narrow strip of parking lot that spanned the Creekside Inn, she spotted the Ford van with Davidson County tags parked in front of a room where dim light leaked through a part in the curtains. It hadn't been difficult to find Kincaid. Dawson Mills wasn't exactly a hot travel destination, just a one-night stopover or drive-through for tourists on their way to the Smoky Mountains. There were only two motels in the area. The other was about five miles north of town, a sad, sagging structure with chipped and peeling paint that rented rooms by the hour.

Toni pulled beside the van, grabbed her cell phone to make sure the ringer was on. And jumped when it rang in her hand. She flipped it open, recognizing the number from Paul's business card she'd punched in a short while ago, when she'd left a voicemail.

"Good timing. I was just about to—" Music struck up in the background, followed by the clinking of glass and muffled laughter. She frowned. "Where are you?"

"Hold on a sec."

The noise on the other end fluctuated. Then hinges groaned as a heavy door swung open, and the music stopped.

"I'm tracking what might be a lead."

"A lead. That's good." Toni paused. She figured Paul could take care of himself, but odds were better than even that they were dealing with a killer. "Is Stan with you?"

"He made a good argument for coming along, but no, he's still pretty shaky. I took him to my place. He's staying there tonight."

Her gaze moved across the parking lot where shadows crept along the edge of the light. "Goes without saying, but watch your back."

"Always."

"Okay." She switched gears. "Now—about that lead. Share."

Paul blew out a breath. "We're going to have to put that on hold. I need to get moving, just wanted to return your call. It might be late, but I'll get back to you, let you know what I come up with."

And that, she thought, would just have to do for now. As for Allison's stint in the psych ward, Toni kept the question to herself. Kincaid would probably be a better source there anyway. "All right. But before you go—I had to tell Ray about the dead kid, couldn't get around it."

"And?"

The sigh vibrated past her lips, a small explosion. "He more or less stalled on me." Ray was a good cop, though, and this was his town—peaceful, for the most part. He wouldn't tolerate having that balance upset. "It won't keep him from doing the job."

"Let's hope." A heartbeat of silence skipped in. "You plan on looking at the diary tonight?"

"Absolutely. But first, I've got another line to tug—Allison's brother."

"That might not be a good idea. She wanted to keep him out of this."

Protect him. Toni glanced over at the door to Kincaid's room. "I think that's reason enough to find out what he knows."

"Yeah. Yeah, maybe you're right."

"Okay. We'll both do what we do. Call me, and—be careful." She disconnected and shoved out of the car, breathing in the clean, crisp scent the rain had left behind. Toni rapped on the door, waited. Rapped again.

The door inched open. Dark brown eyes peered out at her from a weary face shadowed with a day's growth of facial hair. He wore the same jeans and T-shirt she'd seen him in earlier, somewhat wrinkled now. Socks but no shoes.

One brow rising, he raked a hand through sandy colored hair that was already tousled. Toni mustered up an apologetic smile. "I realize it's late, but I was hoping we could talk." She paused. "You do remember me?"

He nodded. "Toni Harper. You're a reporter for the local paper. Sheriff said you might try to look me up."

Of course he did. She had to shove back the jab of annoyance. "This is not about me digging for a story, I swear. And I know you've had a long day, you're stressed. But we really need to talk."

Toni met his silence with a shake of her head. "Look, Allison called me, asking for my help with... something." She glanced around. "I'd feel a lot more comfortable talking about this inside."

Suspicion waged a small war behind his dark eyes as he scanned her face. She ran a quick tally on her odds of coming out at the winning end. Not good. He surprised her by stepping aside, gesturing toward the table and two chairs in the corner. "Have a seat."

"Thanks."

The room was larger than what she might have imagined, and it lacked the usual hotel-room staleness that tended to linger beneath the scent of air-freshener. Toni took a quick scan. Microwave, mini-fridge, the standard coffeemaker and supplies. There was even a pamphlet on the table with instructions on connecting to the wireless network.

Steve pulled a can of Coke from the small fridge. "Want one?"

"Please." She shook her head when he held up a glass. "Can's fine."

He handed Toni her soda, took the chair across from her. The small, overhead light magnified smudges of fatigue under his eyes. "The name's Steve Kincaid. But I'm guessing you already know that."

"Yeah." She popped the pull-tab on the can and drank, letting the caffeine fizz its way through her system.

Steve took a swallow from his own can. "How do you know Allison?"

As was her habit, Toni started to jump right into it, but told herself to slow down, gain his trust. So, keeping the dead kid out of it for now, she gave him just the basics, up to the point where she had agreed to meet Allison at the café in town.

"Your sister thought someone was watching her."

The frown moved in, creasing his forehead. And when his gaze drifted past her, Toni had to wonder—again—just what he was doing here. "Allison didn't mention you were driving in."

"I tried calling her this morning to let her know, left a voicemail. Got worried when I didn't hear back from her." He huffed out a breath. "The trip was last minute. Some... things came up."

Things. She tapped a finger on the table. "Can you share?"

He studied her, weighing her. "Not really, no."

Mind clicking on how she could get to this from another angle, Toni nodded. "Guess I'll have to respect that. But since we're all working toward the same goal here, can you tell me if Allison has any enemies, maybe someone from her past? Or someone who might have followed her here?"

There—a spark in those deep-brown eyes. Then it was gone. "Not that I'm aware of." Steve sighed, shook his head. "I've already been over this with the sheriff."

"I get that. But it's possible something might have slipped by you. Repeating the details could jog your memory."

Mouth firm, he fixed a bland stare on her. She gave it just two seconds before switching the bait on her line. "I know about her stay in the psychiatric hospital." Toni remembered now that Allison had started talking to the dead shortly after her husband's accident. Guessing, she added, "No one believed her—about the ghost."

She saw the truth of it on his face, and couldn't even begin to imagine what the poor woman had suffered. Convinced that her mind was slipping away, grappling for any tenuous thread of reality.

Had they medicated her?

Probably.

The struggle back would have been a long, dark, solitary road. In Hell, you were on your own.

"Allison asked me to help figure out who was watching her."

On a sigh, Steve ran a finger along the rim of his Coke can. "No police. But she trusted you." His focus shot back to her. "Someone she's known for all of—what?—a few days?"

"The circumstances are complicated."

"Complicated." A slow smile curved his lips. "Believe me, after what I've learned over the last couple of days, I know all about 'complicated.'"

He did. She could see the stress of it in his eyes. Feeling her way, she took a small leap. "My niece is waiting up for me. I had arranged for Allison to talk to her tonight." Toni paused, hoping he would be open-minded about some things. "I thought that Jenna—my niece—might be able to help us. She's what you might call 'intuitive.'"

"You mean psychic," Steve guessed, surprising her for the second time tonight. "My girlfriend's into that sort of thing."

"And you?"

He shrugged. "Honestly? At this point, I'm open to just about anything. And I'm guessing you want me to talk to your niece."

"It might help."

Another frown moved across his face as he leaned back in the chair. "Assuming your niece is wired differently from most of us... I don't much care for the idea of someone poking around in my head."

"Who would? I can assure you it doesn't work that way with Jenna. She won't invade your privacy." Toni helped herself to another quick sip of the cold caffeine. "The short of it? Based on whatever you tell her, Jenna should be able to pick up emotions and certain images that belong only to Allison. It just might give us the edge we need to find her."

He took what felt like an eternity to mull it over. "Guess it's worth a try."

"So, you'll come with me tonight, talk to my niece?"

Steve nodded—no hesitation now. "Yeah. Yeah, I will."

CHAPTER 25

S HE'D TRADED WORK CLOTHES FOR loose pants and a comfy, cotton shirt, had ditched the headache that had blindsided her on the way home by wolfing down a sandwich. Toni felt almost human again.

Now—if they could just get on with it.

Watching Steve and Jenna sitting across from her at her small dining table, heads bent in murmured conversation, Toni tapped a finger against the side of her cup, and breathed in the heady aroma of coffee before taking a deep swallow. Seconds slid into costly minutes. Necessary, though, to give Steve whatever time he needed to feel comfortable with this, with Jenna.

It was beginning to work. She could see the gradual transformation—discomfort, doubt, morphing into something more like curiosity as he leaned back in the chair and tilted his head, sipping from his soda can.

Toni had to hand it to her niece. The girl had a way of putting people at ease.

Steve took a chocolate chip cookie from the plate Jenna had put between them on the table. "I guess dealing with the psychic thing can get freaky at times."

Jenna just smiled, the warmth of it drifting up to soft, silver-gray eyes that reminded Toni of a calm winter sky. She brushed a delicate hand over raven hair cut in a pageboy style, glossy against her porcelain complexion. "Sometimes. But… the ability… has always been a huge part of my life." Her slender shoulders moved in a shrug. "I'm still learning."

"And you're doing just fine." Toni plucked a napkin from the holder on the table, helped herself to a cookie.

"If I am," Jenna noted, "it's because of you and Mom, the support there."

Toni gave her niece a faint smile. Had to be rough, wandering between the here and now and wherever the visions took her. It'd be a constant struggle just to keep a mental balance.

"No one believed Allison." Steve sighed. "But you already know that."

"Yeah." Taking another swallow of coffee, Toni shifted her gaze to the darkness beyond the window that overlooked her compact patio during the day, wondering what Paul had managed to turn up, if anything. And Allison, assuming the creep had drugged her, had to be conscious by now.

Trapped. Scared. Hurt, maybe.

"Do you think she's still alive?"

Sharing a glance with her niece, Toni nodded. "We do." For a moment, she was tempted to grab the diary, plop down on the padded, leather sofa in her living room, and dig through whatever information Bobbie Jean had left behind. But—that was a cart, horse thing. There had been a man—the "father"—who had supposedly found work in Texas. Not Jack Kincaid. Someone had brought Allison and her mother to Dawson Mills. Who? And why?

That was the key.

Steve had the information. Or at least a part of it.

Time, she thought, to get things rolling. "We found this in Allison's cellar." Toni pulled the pepper spray from her pants pocket, set it on the table.

Steve frowned. "I'm guessing the sheriff doesn't know you have that."

"No. But I doubt he would have gotten much from it." She

231

gestured toward her niece. Jenna held the pepper spray, eyes closed, slim, delicate fingers probing the canister.

Within just a few seconds, Toni caught the familiar flicker of her niece's eyelids.

"There's… something." Jenna took a small breath. "It's vague. A feeling. Uneasiness, I think. And… water." She opened her eyes, brows lifting.

Toni nodded. She hadn't mentioned the water to her niece, so—yeah, they were moving in the right direction. "Allison found a puddle of water in the attic. It'd been raining hard. She figured maybe a leak in the roof."

"But she found more water down in the cellar." Jenna lowered her gaze to the small canister in her hand. "A leak. No. No, that's not right."

Steve had kept silent, munching on the cookie, taking a few hits of soda while his focus darted back and forth between Toni and her niece. He just shook his head now. "I'm trying my best to keep an open mind here, but I really don't see how this is getting us any closer to helping Allison."

Under different circumstances, Toni would have to agree. But in Jenna's world, pieces of the puzzle always had those undefined edges, murky shapes that never quite fit together at first glance. If Steve was going to be of any use to them, they'd have to keep him calm, centered. "I know it seems like we're dragging, but the psychic… process, for lack of a better word, is tricky. Everything—sounds, images, whatever—is open to interpretation."

His gaze drifted past her. "My girlfriend once said something like that."

"Okay. Let's just give it a few minutes."

She looked back at her niece. "The water—can you tell us what it means, where it came from?"

"I can try." Jenna closed her eyes and began turning the canister in her hands. Toni had to shake off the chill when her niece's thin, pale face went as still as death, as though everything inside her had just shut down. She'd seen it before, Jenna going deep, probing. It never failed to spook her.

Then—the frown, flitting in and out. Another flicker of the eyelids.

Shoulders slumping, Jenna sighed and opened her eyes. "I'm sorry, I'm just not sure." She set the pepper spray back on the table. "But I think it's important."

"Important—how?" Toni asked.

"The water has… something to do with Allison, with her past." Jenna shifted her soft gray eyes onto Steve, searching.

"I have no idea. I—hold on." His fingers drummed a light rhythm on the side of his soda can. "There was an accident, she was just a kid."

Toni nodded. "Allison told me about it. Sketchy on the details, though."

"Coma," Steve said half under his breath. "Messed up her head. She doesn't remember much." He scowled. "Dad does, but he's not giving up any details."

Bitter, Toni remembered Allison telling her that, blamed the mother for whatever had happened. Or was it something more?

Shifting in the chair, Jenna gazed back down at the pepper spray. A shadow swept across her pale face. "The connection there, with the house, the cellar… It may not be what we're thinking."

Toni nearly dropped the cup she had raised halfway to her mouth. She juggled it back down to the table before hot coffee could slosh over the rim, her mind scrambling through her theory, ticking off the details. Kara's research on the house. The dead kid. The forgotten piece of Allison's past. Convoluted at first glance, but it had all seemed to line up. *Seemed* being the operative.

What were they missing?

She shook her head. "You're telling me those two kids aren't down there?"

"Wait a minute." Steve jerked a hand up. "Wait just a damned minute. What the hell are you talking about?"

She told him, straight out. Then watched the color drain from his face.

"You're saying the kids I saw in Allison's back yard are... *dead? Ghosts?*"

"I know it's a lot to take in, but, yeah. We thought they were buried in the cellar." Toni glanced over at her niece. "I'm not really sure of that now."

He blinked, just once. Panic rolled across his face in waves. "You think whoever took Allison murdered those kids." Steve raked a shaky hand through his hair. "Jesus Christ." He pushed to his feet, paced over to the window, stared out at the wall of darkness. "Sheriff asked me if I noticed anything unusual the weekend we helped her move in. I couldn't think. Just couldn't get my thoughts together at the time, you know?"

"I understand, believe me. And just so we're all in the same loop here, I told the sheriff about the kids. But he'll have to look at physical evidence, hard facts."

Toni gave it a moment while Steve kept his eyes fixed to the darkness outside, letting what she had just told him slowly sink in. He was a million miles away. "If there's anything at all you're holding back on this end, now's the time."

He dropped his gaze down to the potted ivy on the plant stand next to him, studied the heart-shaped leaves, as if, by some miracle, he'd find answers there. "Yeah. Yeah, I guess it is."

The headlights on the cruiser that had been trailing him for a while were gone. Nothing back there now but a dark and desolate, rain-slicked highway.

Steering his truck past the Hilltop Market, Paul shifted his gaze from the rearview mirror to the road in front of him. Hadn't surprised him much that the sheriff had put a tail on him, but it had pissed him off. A waste of valuable resources.

Time wasn't something they had a lot of.

He blew out an explosive breath. Every lead he had followed to Jared Atkins tonight had been like slamming straight into a brick wall. After he'd gotten Stan and Allison's big dog settled in, Paul had cut through the woods on foot to the back of the old man's property, and found the place deserted. Then he had hit the bars, talking to customers and waitresses, the bartenders, local musicians. Hell, he had even barged in on a couple of backroom poker games.

No one had seen the old buzzard in several days. It made him wonder what Atkins had been up to.

The curves in the road began snaking tighter around the hills. Paul switched on the high beams, dropped his speed. There was nothing left to do now but head back to where he'd started, keep an eye out for Atkins.

By the time he made the turn onto Dawson Creek Road, the dark highway had started to hypnotize him. He blinked and shook his head, stifled a yawn. His mind felt thick, fuzzy from too little sleep and trying to make sense out of the jumble of disjointed information. It wasn't much of a stretch for him to imagine what the sheriff's men might find buried in Allison's cellar. Just the thought of it sat like lead in his gut. But her connection to the dead boy...

Could be just the house. Or maybe the poor kid had been waiting for someone who could communicate with him.

Because he didn't want to look too closely at that right now, Paul shook off the thought. On the other side of his window, farmhouses rolled by, dark silhouettes against an even darker background, separated by pastureland and woods. About the only things stirring out here were the moths that fluttered around the soft, amber glow coming off the few streetlights that dotted this long stretch of country road.

He switched to low beams, glanced down at the time readout

on the radio. Almost midnight. Toni should have gone through the diary by now.

Paul grabbed his cell phone, swore when he dropped it and the damned thing slid under the seat. He kept one hand on the wheel, leaned sideways, groped. Then jerked his attention back to the road as it curved and a dim outline of the Atkins' home stretched into view. Not a single light burning. No vehicles in the driveway, at least not that he could see from here.

Where are you, old man?

At the far end of the field, a strip of light spilled across the ground when the barn door swung open. Paul doused the head-lights and eased the truck onto the shoulder, cut the engine.

The light inside the barn flicked off.

He kept his eyes on the old man's vague shape swaying through the darkness up to the house, waited for Atkins to make it onto the back porch. Then gave it another minute before grabbing his Mag-Lite.

Paul slipped out of the truck, a damp breeze brushing across his skin, and paused. One wrong move on his part, and he'd most likely find himself staring into the barrel of a loaded hunting rifle. At the other end of that gun would be a nasty-tempered drunk with his finger on the trigger.

His gaze moved past the barn, to the dark mass of woods. In his mind, he could see the small girl, terrified, her mouth opening in a scream no one had heard. Paul took in a shuddered breath, and the image shifted. Haunted green eyes looked out at him from Allison's pale, pale face.

"Shit." He darted across the road and moved in a wide arc over the front yard, keeping his distance from the house. Rushing through the field, Paul dodged the old man's tractor, then sprinted up to the barn. The hinges creaked when he eased the door open. He glanced back at the house. Still no lights burning. Atkins must have staggered off to bed.

Paul slipped inside and inched the door shut. Breathing in the musty smells of neglect, he stuck close to the wall and began feeling his way through the pitch-black, boots scraping over the rough wood-plank floor.

Chilly in here, he realized. Too damned cold for this time of year.

He stopped, tried to get a sense of his surroundings. To his left the darkness shifted as a blur of shadow shot across the black space in front of him. Small, indistinct, just a shade lighter than all the darkness around him.

Movement without sound.

It took a second—shock, he supposed—for his brain to process what had just happened. Paul shook off the bitter cold and tuned his ears to the stillness. He kept his voice to a whisper. "You here, Scooter?"

Something rustled.

He grabbed the Mag-Lite from his shirt pocket and punched it on. A tiny field mouse jumped from behind a discarded paper cup, then scurried across loose boards that were scattered over the floor. Frowning, Paul swung the light up. The compact beam arced across a gaping hole in the floor of the loft, where some of the joists had collapsed. Recently, he thought. Atkins hadn't gotten the chance to clear the mess.

The heaviness that had been sitting in his gut for most of the night started to churn.

Sidestepping fallen boards, he hurried over to the narrow wooden stairs, tested them to make sure they would hold his weight. Then climbed high enough to scan the area with his light.

Cobwebs, layers of dust. A couple of storage boxes stacked on what was left of the floor. And there was something...

He angled the light onto a sagging section of floor a few feet in front of him. What had soaked into the wood was vague, had just a hint of reddish-brown left to it. Diluted. Scrubbed down, he thought, and brushed a finger over the stain.

Dry. It had been here for a while.

The breath he hadn't realized he'd been holding rushed out. Not Allison's blood. Whose, then?

The boy's?

Aw, Christ.

Paul rushed back down the stairs, the beam from his Mag-Lite bouncing over a clutter of ancient tools and equipment that probably hadn't seen the light of day in decades. He couldn't remember when Atkins had added a floor to this old barn—too many years back to count. And he wasn't sure whether it was important.

What mattered, right at the moment, was what the old buzzard had been doing out here this time of night. That, and there was a damned good chance they'd been wrong about the human remains encased behind the loose brick in Allison's cellar.

Pulse racing, he set the Mag-Lite down, began shoving fallen boards to the side. Then pressed the flat of his hands along the floor, feeling for loose planks.

The draft snuck up on him. Paul groped for the light, pointed the beam where he thought the breeze had come from. He had just enough time to register that the window at the rear of the building was open before something struck the back of his head with the force of a sledgehammer.

Blinding light exploded in front of his eyes. Then everything went black.

Unbelievable.

Eyes gritty with fatigue, Toni stared down at the legal pad on the table in front of her, scanned the notes she'd scribbled. She didn't doubt for a minute that Bobbie Jean was somehow linked to this. But there was a chance—a strong one—that whoever took

Allison wasn't looking for the diary at all, probably wasn't even aware that it existed.

Could this get any more complicated?

She slanted a look at her niece, caught the slight shrug. "We're missing something. Two men—shot and killed, no witnesses. Your dad had a good idea who the murderer might be. What did he know that the police didn't?"

Steve pulled his gaze off the darkness beyond the window that overlooked Toni's patio, then settled back down at the table. He blew out a breath. "It's muddy. When Beverly—Allison's mom—took off, Dad called a friend of hers, thinking he'd find her there. Turns out the woman had left town the same day with a man she'd been dating. It was right after the story on the murders hit the news.

"According to Dad, the woman's mother thought there was something off about the guy. I got the feeling she was afraid of him."

A slew of theories scrambled through Toni's head. "Did your father say something specific to give you that impression?"

One side of his mouth curved. "It was more what he didn't say."

Nodding, she tapped a finger on the table. Still, it was a mile's worth of supposition. "You said the two men who were killed happened to be diamond brokers."

"Yeah. From New York, on a layover in Nashville. Couple of days before, they'd made a substantial buy from a mine in South America. Police found the paperwork for the purchase on them."

"But no stones," Toni said, catching the flit of a frown on her niece's face. Steve had told them that his dad was sure the diamonds had never been sold, were still somewhere in the area. How would Jack Kincaid possibly know that?

She put the question to Steve.

Darkness, like a thundercloud blown in by a swift wind, rushed across his face, settled into his eyes. The muscles in his jaw tightened.

"He knows. Believe me. I have no idea how, but he knows."

Steve shoved a hand through his hair. "The guy had been in

Nashville for maybe a month, wouldn't say what had brought him there or where he'd come from." He paused. "But it's a sure bet he ended up here. The private investigator Dad hired trailed the woman to this area. She used her credit card to pay for their gas."

"So he was able to locate Allison and her mom from there." Toni frowned. "This woman—did you get her name?"

Steve shook his head. "Dad wouldn't say. About all he'd tell me was that he drove straight here, took Allison back to Nashville." He nodded when Jenna lifted a brow. "I know. It doesn't play right. They never caught the guy. He could have still been in Dawson Mills at the time. I don't get why Allison's mom would stay here, hell, why Dad would let her."

Beverly Kincaid couldn't have known, Toni thought. As for her husband, well. She shared a glance with her niece. "It's possible your father didn't connect the murders until after he'd taken Allison home. You mentioned earlier that he and Allison's mother argued the night before she left. About what?"

"I have no idea." Steve stared down at the empty soda can on the table in front of him. "Dad refuses to talk about it."

"Is he aware of what happened here?"

"Not yet, as far as I know. Sheriff asked me not to contact anyone, said he'd take care of it."

"Okay." Toni took a minute to run through it all in her head. Behind them, the compressor on the fridge in her tiny kitchen clicked to life with a low hum. She listened to the indistinct buzzing of it, brushing a finger along the side of her cup, trying to corral the information from all the different sources and force it into a halfway cohesive theory.

Jenna's slender shoulders rose and fell with slow, steady breaths, her soft gray eyes locked onto Steve. "Why would they come to Dawson Mills?"

He shrugged.

"The guy had to be from here," Toni said, "or knew someone in the area. If he's back, looking for the diamonds—"

"They could be buried in Allison's cellar," Jenna said. "The tunnel."

Steve cocked a brow. "What tunnel?"

"Actually, it just might be a small section of earth that someone shoveled out." Toni tried to call up a mental picture of the space they'd found down there. She'd gotten only a glimpse. "I'm not sure how far back it goes, but the sheriff's men are supposed to be taking a closer look."

Frowning, Steve shook his head. "I was down there a couple of times, didn't notice anything like that."

"You wouldn't have. It's behind the air-handling unit." What, Toni wondered, did the dead kid—the boy—have to do with any of this? And his little friend, the girl... How did she fit into it all? *Did she?*

Toni downed what was left of her second cup of coffee. "Jenna, I need you to take a look at something." She pushed up from the chair. The shadows under her niece's eyes stopped her short. "Are you up for it?"

"I'm a little tired, but I'll do whatever I can to help."

"Good girl. I'll be right back." Toni headed down the hall to her bedroom and grabbed the sketchpad she'd managed to smuggle in past Steve. Poor guy, he'd been like a walking zombie coming up to her front door.

Frazzled nerves could do that to a person.

It all came down to roadblocks, she thought. Jack Kincaid had put up just enough to keep them guessing.

She detoured over to the nightstand where she'd left her purse, took out the picture she'd printed off the Internet—Jack Kincaid, and a younger version of the man she'd noticed sitting at the back of the room while the Zoning Commission debated over commercial development.

Coincidence?

Hardly.

She tucked the picture under her arm with Allison's sketchpad, frowning when the hour changed on her digital clock. When had she last spoken to Paul?

Toni pulled her cell phone from her pants pocket and checked the recent calls. Hours ago.

The frown etched deeper across her face, but she shoved the speculation back before it could take up residence in her head. When time mattered, progress tended to move about as fast as a snail.

She flicked the light off and hurried back to the dining room, smiling when she saw the fresh cup of coffee waiting on the table. Toni sat, blew at the steam, sipped. "Thanks for this."

"Sure." Jenna took the sketchpad from her.

"Allison's?" Steve guessed.

Toni nodded, then, to keep things simple, lied. "She gave it to me at the café."

She slid the printout across the table, over to Steve. "The man standing just behind your father—do you recognize him?"

"I'm not sure." His eyes narrowed. "This was taken a long time ago, but... yeah, he works for Dad." Steve looked back up at her. "What's he got to do with this?"

"That's what I'm trying to figure out." Toni told him what she knew, which wasn't much. "Can you give me a name? Tell me what he does for your dad?"

"No, to both. But you can bet your ass—" Steve glanced at Jenna. "Sorry." He turned back to Toni. "I'll get some answers, count on it."

Toni set the printout aside as Jenna lifted the cover of Allison's sketchpad. The girl's face clouded the minute her gaze locked onto the first drawing. "A tree," she murmured, and ran a finger along the blank oval shape Allison had left in the trunk.

Not the drawing she had wanted her niece to focus on, but the girl's psychic antenna had homed right in on the dark, squirming tangle of branches. Medusa-like demon-arms snatching invisible prey from the sky.

It happened in a blink—Jenna's already-pale complexion blanched to chalk-white. Her slender body went rigid. Those gray eyes, wide open, stared straight ahead into nothing.

Steve's gaze shot over to Toni. "What—?"

"Wait. Just wait."

Seconds crawled into minutes. She wanted to reach out, put a hand on Jenna's arm and break the connection that was keeping her niece in an eerie limbo. But she held back.

Jenna's small frame suddenly jerked as a clear stream of fluid gushed from her mouth, spilling down the front of her pale yellow blouse. Toni jumped up, grabbed her niece by the shoulders, and shook her. "Jenna!"

Steve was half out of his chair, but froze when Jenna began clawing blindly at the air, strained gurgling coming from deep inside her throat. "She's choking!"

Shit. Oh, shit. Toni shook her niece harder. *"Dammit, Jenna!"*

With a shuddered gasp, Jenna slumped back in the chair.

Eternity was a concept that had always seemed unfathomable. A measure of time without measure. How could anyone really grasp the meaning of it? Toni believed she had come as close to comprehension as she'd ever get within just the last ten minutes, while she'd watched, helpless, as Jenna struggled to fight her way back from whatever hell the vision had thrown her into.

She dimmed the overhead light in her living room, then sat on the sofa next to her niece, and handed her a glass of juice. The girl was still deathly pale. "Are you sure you're all right?"

"I... think so." The glass shook in Jenna's hand when she raised it to her lips. She swallowed, winced.

Toni glanced over at Steve sitting in the chair across from them. He hadn't uttered a word for several minutes, was still wild-eyed. She pulled her focus back to her niece. "This physical interaction—has it ever happened before?"

"Never." Jenna brought a hand to her mouth, coughed.

"What happened?" Steve leveled his eyes on her. "What did you see?"

"A girl. A small girl, with red hair, I think." Jenna drew a slow, rasping breath. "There was water. Deep water. I was—" She shook her head. "The girl, the girl was drowning. I felt it, but... I saw it happen, too. It was almost as if I were standing off to the side, watching myself drown."

An icy chill made tracks up Toni's spine. "The girl, you mean. You were watching the girl."

"Yes. But it felt more like..." Jenna lifted her shoulders. "A memory. I think I experienced someone else's memory."

"Christ," Steve murmured. "I don't pretend to understand any of this, but is it possible that you tapped into Allison's head?"

Biting her bottom lip, Jenna searched his face. "No. No, I don't think so." She glanced around the room. "The sketchpad... I need to see the other drawing."

"Maybe we should hold up on that."

"I'm all right." Jenna met Toni's silence with a calm, steady gaze. "I want to do this."

Steve lifted a brow, and, against her better judgment, Toni nodded. He grabbed Allison's sketchpad off the table, passed it to Jenna, then settled back into his chair. When the somber, dirty little face stared up at them from the page, his shoulders slumped. "That's the kid I caught messing around in Allison's back yard." He looked up at Toni. "But you already know that."

Head bowed, Jenna brushed a finger over the dark smudge that marred the boy's cheek. "Poor thing."

The quiet sadness in those two simple words ripped through Toni.

"He tried to help the girl, but... There was a man. He broke the boy's arm, then..." Jenna sighed, a soft release, just a whisper. "He killed him. And the dog, he killed the boy's dog."

Toni rested a hand on her niece's arm, gave it a gentle squeeze. "Can you describe the man?"

"No, all I got was... the knowledge."

Steve frowned. "How is that possible?"

A trace of a smile crossed Jenna's lips. "I wish I knew."

Drained past the point of exhaustion, Toni reached for the cup she'd set on the end table and took a deep swallow of coffee, hoping the caffeine would kick-start her adrenaline. "Were you able to get a sense of where the boy was when... he died?"

"Not really. It was the same when I saw the girl—I was caught up in the emotions and physical sensations. The surroundings were just a haze." Jenna breathed another small sigh. "I'm sorry."

"You did your best." Steve's voice was weary, his eyes even more so.

Gulping down coffee, Toni tried to think, frowning when a thought finally popped through the fog in her sleep-deprived brain. "We assumed the girl was dead. But, I'm a bit confused." She held a hand up when Steve opened his mouth. "Go with me on this for a minute."

She turned to Jenna. "In your vision, you saw a girl with red hair, drowning—Allison, we believe. That would explain the accident, the coma." Toni rubbed at her bleary eyes. She backtracked, laying out the thoughts spinning through her head. "Steve got a glimpse of the girl, but only in the shadows. The morning she went jogging, Allison caught just a flash of the same girl, or thought she did. All she really saw was the red hair. In both instances, the girl was with the dead kid—the boy."

Nodding, Steve stared back down at the drawing. "And you

said the kids were together the night the boy warned Allison that someone was watching her."

"Yeah. She heard the girl, but never saw her." Toni shifted to face her niece. "Any thoughts?"

Lips pursed, Jenna gazed at her hands folded in her lap. "I wonder... Maybe the girl is, I don't know, an echo. Of the past. A memory."

"A memory," Toni repeated.

"Yes." Jenna looked over at Steve. "The sense of drowning I felt when I saw your sister struggling under water—I believe that came from Allison. But the actual memory..."

"Belonged to the boy." Toni had to smile.

"That's right. It's possible he's holding on to the memory of her, somehow projecting that. So we can..." Jenna shook her head. "Make the connection, I guess."

She offered Steve a sympathetic smile when he made a rough sound. "There's something else. The water Allison found in her attic and in the cellar has to be another connection. I think the boy was trying to help your sister remember."

It tracked, Toni admitted, and had to marvel at the world she lived in, where following a lead from the dead actually made sense. She raised her cup to her lips, scowled when she swallowed the dregs, and set it down. Numb with exhaustion, she ran a hand over her face. "As much as I want to, I don't think we're going to find Allison tonight. We've put together some solid information, but before we talk to the sheriff, I need a little time to sort through it all."

"Yeah, my head's spinning." Steve huffed out a breath. "It's just so damned frustrating, though."

"I know." Still, Toni needed some down time, a couple hours—max—of sleep. Then she'd be able to sift through the diary with a halfway clear mind.

"So, Steve, can I give you a call first thing in the morning?"

"Sure." He pulled his wallet from his hip pocket, handed her a business card. "My cell number's on there. Or you can phone the hotel. Either way."

When he moved to get up from the chair, Jenna gripped his arm. "Be careful—*please*."

CHAPTER 26

THE SUN WOULDN'T BE UP for another hour yet, maybe longer. He'd felt rain coming in the damp air when he'd walked out of his hotel room. Steve gave the wheel a sharp jerk and swore when a strong gust of wind sent the van skating across the center lane. He hated driving on these dark and winding mountain roads. Navigating them during the day with a clear head was one thing, but he was running on just a couple hours of sleep.

His brain felt like a worn, flaking piece of recording tape that had passed between the rollers on one of those old reel-to-reel machines one too many times.

Still, he was doing something. Lying in his bed at the hotel, staring a hole through the ceiling, just hadn't been an option.

At least he'd had the choice. That was more than he could say for Allison.

He felt the anger chipping away at him again and wanted to punch something. All these years, their dad, in his infinite wisdom, had kept the truth from his daughter. The ugly past he'd hidden from Allison was coming back to haunt her now.

Secrets had a way of doing that—hurting the innocent. And if that wasn't bad enough, he'd sent one of his men here.

Why?

"Dammit, Dad," Steve muttered beneath the whir of the transmission as the van climbed a steep curve. Was he doing the right thing here? Rambling down a desolate highway through Nowheres-ville in the frigging predawn hours.

He hadn't been able to get that damned tunnel off his mind. Another thing—blame it on stress—he'd forgotten all about the diary they'd found stashed up in Allison's attic, until the image of it had slammed him right out of a fitful sleep.

More secrets. Had to be something there.

Chances were the journal had already found its way to the Sheriff's Department, which, Steve admitted, was where he should be headed. What he'd learned about Allison last night was vital. But how could he put it? That he'd gotten it all from a psychic?

Right. With his own eyes, he had witnessed Toni's niece doing... whatever it was that she had done, and he still found it hard to believe.

Then there was the ghost thing.

And the girl—nothing but a memory. A dead boy's memory. Of Allison.

It was just too weird. Hell of a long way from physical evidence or hard facts.

When he reached the crest of the hill, the small market that made the awesome pizza popped into view. Steve huffed out a short sigh of relief. Even though all the lights inside were off and the parking lot was deserted, after driving through miles of darkness, the glowing sign was like a huge Welcome mat.

Bleary-eyed, he blinked to keep focused and steered against the wind, headlights glaring out onto the long stretch of highway. If Allison was still alive—and he had to believe that—maybe, just maybe they could get to her before the bastard who took her—

He shoved the thought from his head, just couldn't go there. Ever.

The turnoff for Dawson Creek Road came up fast, a small, obscure street sign set back several feet off the highway. Steve hit the brakes, cut the wheel hard to make the turn.

Christ. How did anyone manage to find his way around out here?

Landmarks, Steve-O. You're in the country now. It's all about landmarks.

Tammy had told him that when he'd shot past the turnoff the first time out here. Remembering it now nudged a smile out of him. He took a trip back for a second, and saw himself sitting in his van, in Allison's driveway, gazing numbly at the nightmare of flashing red lights. He'd had an actual physical ache for Tammy that had nothing to do with sex. He had needed her there with him as much as he'd needed the breath in his lungs.

That had both surprised and shaken him.

Hours later, when he'd finally made it back to the hotel, he'd just had to phone her. A smile crept over him again. Her voice had been like mellow music to his raw nerves.

Steve slowed his speed to keep from zipping past Allison's property, and rolled along through the pitch-black. He had to ask himself again what had possessed her to settle in this particular area. Moving to Dawson Mills, well, he got that. The thing with her mother. But why not buy a place closer to town? There was nothing out here but sky and woods, and these damned roads that went on forever. Even the streetlights were few and far between.

None of that, he reminded himself on a sigh, mattered now.

He spotted her mailbox on the left, made the turn into the driveway, and followed the winding stretch of concrete, headlights flashing over trees bending in the wind.

To the west, lightning pulsed and lit up the sky.

Steve pulled to a stop, cut the engine and headlights. He scanned the vague, shadowy line of crime-scene tape that was whipping in the wind. The place felt... empty. Cold. Like a mausoleum.

Be careful...

"Yeah." The word brushed past his lips in a whisper as he shuddered. He hadn't forgotten Jenna's warning. How could he? It had shocked him right down to his bones. And he'd seen enough from her to know that he needed to take it seriously.

Dammit, Sis. Why couldn't you have just stayed in Nashville?

Steve scrubbed a hand over his face and summoned what little energy he had, then grabbed his flashlight. The sheriff had told him that his people weren't finished going through things here, they'd be back tomorrow. Meaning today.

He had maybe a couple of hours at best.

He slipped out of the van and ducked under the line of crime tape, found the front door padlocked, couldn't get in through any of the windows. With the strong wind shoving at him, Steve headed around to the back porch. His eyes had adjusted to the dark just enough to make out the vague shapes of furniture there: couple of chairs, a small—

Fuck! He hissed out a breath against the stinging bite in his shin where he'd bumped into the sharp edge of a wrought-iron plant stand. Then froze.

Something had moved out in the yard.

His thumb jerked instinctively toward the button on his flashlight, but stopped. *Not a good idea, Kincaid.*

He gave it a minute, stood rigid, ears perked.

Nothing but the rustle of tree leaves.

Okay. Had to be a rabbit, or some other small animal.

Still spooked, he turned his back to the unsettling sounds of things he couldn't see stirring in the wind and groped his way along the porch. Steve inched the screen door open, holding his breath when it creaked. His hand brushed up against a padlock fastened to the door—no big surprise there—and none of the windows would budge.

Locked tight.

The cellar windows, then. He'd have to crawl under the porch to get to them.

Shoving the wind-tossed hair from his eyes, Steve felt his way down the steps. He managed to shimmy on his belly about halfway under the porch before he heard the footsteps behind him.

"Get up." A deep, male voice—gruff. "Don't turn around. And don't make any quick moves. Keep your hands where I can see them."

Not a cop, Steve realized. Would have identified himself.

Heart kicking into double-time, he backed out from under the porch, got slowly to his feet.

"Drop the flashlight." The voice was right behind him now, a few feet, maybe.

Close enough. Steve took his one chance and whirled around, swung the flashlight in an arc, aiming for the head. In a flash, the sharp, steel blade slipped into him with frightening ease. He grunted from the rush of burning pain in his gut and the dull pressure as the blade was jerked back, felt the warm, sticky wetness pumping out of him.

He doubled over, crumpled to the ground. *This... isn't happening.*

Dimly aware of the man standing over him, the rain that had started to mist his face, Steve fought to get his breath, fought to hang on. But he was going numb all over. And he was cold. So cold.

In one long moment of deafening silence, he felt himself slipping away, and let go of a weak, jerky sigh.

Allison... He couldn't help her now.

And Tammy. *Oh, God... Tammy.*

They hadn't had enough time together. It wasn't fair.

In Ray's book, there was no such thing as coincidence. Events were like lines that connected the dots, eventually closing the pattern. For Allison Weathers, Dawson Mills hadn't been just a spot on the map chosen by the random stick of a pushpin. The same went for the scum who had most likely trailed her back here.

He took a deep swallow of coffee and gazed out the window in his office, mentally connecting those dots that Steve Kincaid had brought to the table. Below, the traffic light at the corner of Main and Jefferson swung in the wind as a few early-morning commuters drove by, headlights slicing through the rain.

The pattern wasn't coming together. Some of those lines just weren't tracking right. Missing dots, he thought, scowling, then gulped down more coffee.

Ray heaved a sigh, went back to his desk. He rubbed a hand across weary eyes and took another look at the fax that had come through just a while ago.

Harold Rush. Age fifty-one. Hard-faced with a square jaw. Thin lips. Small, dark eyes.

Rush had stalked, raped, and killed two women in Nashville. And according to what Ray was reading, the man liked to play with knives, had a nasty habit of leaving his victims disfigured to the point where visual identification was next to impossible.

The guy was a real piece of work.

He glanced up at the rap on his door. Detective Cliff Barlow stuck his head in. "Got a minute, Sheriff?"

Ray waved him in.

"I just finished going through the Weathers case file." Cliff pulled up a visitor's chair, then opened the folder he'd brought in. "The kid who supposedly warned her—there's got to be someone in the area who knows him."

Unless the boy had never been there to begin with. But they couldn't ignore the lead. "Follow up with that. Keep me informed."

Nodding, Cliff shoved a hand through the thick, coarse hair he wore a bit longer than regulation. "Figures, I take a few vacation days and the stuff hits the fan."

That might not be the half of it. In any case, Ray had to agree. Until now, there'd been very little in this town to keep a detective busy. The truth was Cliff usually spent the majority of his on-duty time patrolling. "You get a chance to review the Conner file?"

"The missing waitress. Yeah. It's possible she took off with her boyfriend, but…" Cliff shrugged. "Around here, two women go missing in the same week, there's got to be a connection."

Ray slid the fax across his desk. "Take a look at this."

Cliff scanned the page, dark brows knitting. "Rush escaped a couple of weeks ago." He glanced up at Ray. "You're thinking he followed Weathers here. If that's true, we've got a bigger problem on our hands than what we realized."

"Agreed." And Toni had worked herself right into the middle of it. She had no idea what she was dealing with. Ray looked over at the time on his phone as thunder rumbled outside. He'd left her a voicemail this morning, hadn't heard back from her.

He'd give it a bit longer.

"The photograph of Weathers found at the scene—" Cliff thumbed through the pages in the file. "They didn't get a clear set of prints off it."

Ray scowled. "No, dammit." And they hadn't been able to pull a match yet through the database from any of the prints found on-scene. At this point, looking at Rush for this was like tracking a line to a dot that may or may not be there.

The Nashville Police had found photographs of Rush's victims in his apartment, and he'd been carrying a picture of Allison Weathers the night he'd assaulted her. The one piece of evidence Ray's CSI team had managed to find so far was a photo taken of her while she was jogging into the woods. It had fallen between the porch steps around back. Dropped during the struggle with Stan Michaels, he thought.

"Weathers never got a look at Rush. He came up behind her, slipped a pillowcase over her head."

"I read that in your notes. Off-duty officer happened to be in the area, saw what was going down." Cliff paused. "All things considered, I'd say the lady got lucky."

Sexual assault, a knife held to her throat. Ray had to go with "ditto" on the luck. Allison Weathers had no doubt suffered emotional scars, but she had come away from the attack with her life.

"At the time, there was an ongoing investigation related to a similar case. They kept Rush's face out of the media."

"So Weathers wouldn't recognize the guy if she passed him on the street."

Ray smiled—no humor there. "Probably not."

"Well, hell. Assuming we're on track here, someone in this town must have seen the sonofabitch at one point."

"You'd think."

"And there's nothing on the vehicle?" Cliff flipped back another page in the file. "The old truck, tinted windows."

"Just what's in the report." One of Ray's men had passed the truck heading out of town a few days back, hadn't thought much about it. Old vehicles in this area were common enough, driven mostly by the local farmers or their kids. "Anyone running patrol today will be checking with the convenience stores, the café. Maybe we'll get lucky there." Ray finished off the last of his coffee, the bitter dregs going sour on the way down. He hadn't bothered to eat this morning, had lost count of how much caffeine he'd consumed.

Enough so that his stomach was telling him to slow down.

"A bulletin went out to the state police. They figured Rush would head for Mexico. He's got family in one of the Texas border towns."

"Texas," Cliff repeated, frowning.

Ray cocked a brow. "Ring a bell with you?" Those dark, coffee-colored eyes that met his sparked. There was a pause—just a beat.

"Maybe." Cliff drummed his fingers on the edge of Ray's desk. "The photograph of Allison Weathers... it wasn't in the file. I'm assuming you still have it."

Nodding, Ray pulled the clear evidence bag that held the photo from his desk drawer, passed it to his detective.

Cliff took one look at the picture, and his face seemed to fold. "Aw, shit."

He had drugged her again. A smaller dose. Her head wasn't as groggy as it had been after the first time he'd jabbed the needle into her arm and she'd come to in this godforsaken place.

Allison swallowed past the sour taste in her mouth, the trickle of saliva a tease of moisture in her parched throat. There was a gnawing pain in her stomach from being empty too long. Her joints and muscles ached. The damp cold had settled deep into her bones. Her insides shivered with every breath.

She pressed her fingertips lightly to the swollen side of her face that still ached from the force of his hand, and winced.

Focus. She had to focus on the positive—she was alive.

For how long?

Allison stared into the silent blackness, felt the oppressive weight of it. No one had come for her. No one would.

A day. He had given her twenty-four hours. How much of that time had she been unconscious?

She shifted, cringing from the pain that shot through her swollen ankle when it brushed against an odd lump beneath the mattress. Frowning, she worked a hand under the gritty material, groped. And grabbed what felt like a square container, then two small plastic bottles, a narrow cylinder cold from the ground. Metal, she thought, pulling everything from under the mattress, and frowned again.

Who had left these things?

She grasped the cylinder, whimpered when her thumb found a button and punched it, flooding the darkness with a bright, compact beam of light.

On the ground in front of her were two bottles of water and a plastic, covered container. She snatched up one of the bottles and twisted the cap off, gulped so fast, she nearly choked. Then yanked the cover off the container, tossed it away, and with another small whimper, fell on the sandwich inside, tearing off chunks with her teeth, not bothering to chew before she swallowed.

A tear slid down her cheek as she crammed the last bite into her mouth, the bulk of bread and meat hitting the pit of her stomach like a ball of lead. The monster had reduced her to something wild and ravenous. An animal.

Allison choked back a sob. The heavy lumps of undigested food lurched in her stomach. She struggled to keep it down, and gave a violent shake of her head, trying to dislodge the image there. Black eyes... a thin-lipped smile.

You got a knack for playing games, girlie. Just like your mother.

She didn't know what he'd meant by that, wasn't sure she wanted to know. But this was no game.

With a trembling hand, Allison reached for the second bottle of water, took small sips, then grabbed the flashlight, scanned the walls of rock and earth. Her odds of surviving this were next to none, she knew that. But, dammit, she had to try.

The same branch of this cavern that had brought her here would lead her out.

A string of muffled curses shot out from the dark. Allison switched the flashlight off, felt around for the water bottles, and shoved everything under the mattress. In the distance, a pinpoint of light flicked on.

She froze. The light expanded, growing brighter as it moved toward her through the darkness in a swift, deliberate, bobbing rhythm.

Evil snaking a trail to her.

Fear clawed through her, nipped at her. Shuddered out of her. She told herself that she could do this. She could face the monster again.

He brushed past her, swinging the flashlight, and grabbed the foldout chair, slumped into it, mouth turned down in a scowl. The windbreaker he wore was wet, slick with what she assumed was rainwater.

He shoved the hood back. His gaze dropped to the ground beside her, eyes going to slits. Allison's heart jumped.

The container... Oh, no.

The words stammered past her lips. "Th-thank you... for the sandwich."

Dark, hard eyes shot back to her. "What else did I bring you?" His voice was quiet thunder.

She looked away. "Nothing."

"Lying bitch!" Before she could move, his hand was around her throat, squeezing the life from her. Gasping, Allison clawed, dug her nails into his wrist.

He didn't let go, but loosened his grip.

"All right," she choked out, and managed to stretch her arm far enough to fumble under the mattress for the water bottles. "Just this." She sucked in a wheezing breath. "Just the water."

His gaze slid down to the bottles, lingered for a moment. He shoved her back, his dark laugh trailing the ragged whine that escaped her.

The fragile Allison—the woman who'd been helpless to stop the world from crashing down when she'd lost her husband—begged her to put an end to this, just give him the information he wanted. Maybe he'd let her go.

But the woman who looked at that same world now with a clearer focus wondered if she could move quick enough to grab his flashlight and beat the bastard unconscious with it.

A warning jab of pain shot through her swollen ankle. Allison sucked in a breath, felt the burning reminder of the hand that had banded around her throat, and gave up the fantasy. She pulled herself back up, met his hard, brutal stare.

There was something wrong with him. With his eyes. They

couldn't seem to focus on any one object for long. He raised a hand, massaged his temple. "We've got too damned many people sticking their noses in our business here." The hand working his temple lowered, clenched into a fist. "Bradford won't be coming for you."

Allison jolted. "Paul? What have you done to him?"

He slanted a look past her, into the darkness. The chill that crept through her was like icy fingers around her heart, squeezing.

Paul. She had dragged him into this nightmare. He hadn't been able to get out. Her breath hitched. This *was* a game. The monster was toying with her.

Soon he'd be bored.

She scanned his face—sharp angles and harsh planes, half shadowed where the glow from the flashlight didn't quite reach. Her best chance of survival was to become a proactive player. In the end, if she lost, it would at least be on her own terms.

"You were right, before. I lied."

His focus zipped back to her.

"What you're looking for, I… know where it is." On a prayer, she drew herself up, met his cold gaze. "If you want it, you're going to take me out of here—*now.*"

That thin, arrogant smile spread in a slow, smooth motion as he slid a hand under his windbreaker. In a flash of movement light glinted on razor-sharp steel. Terror slammed into her, oozed out through the pores of her skin in tiny beads of sweat. Had fate, in a matter of months, led her right back to what she thought she had escaped?

Was this how the circle would close, after all? Was she destined to die at the end of a blade?

Allison said another silent prayer and forced her eyes away from the knife. "Go ahead. Kill me. But you'll never find what you're looking for. You need me."

His eyes sparked, dulled. Then he swore, gave a tight nod. "Tonight, then." The look he shot her had Allison pressing her lips together before the protest could escape. She'd pushed the bluff about as far as it would go.

He tucked the knife away, and she slumped with relief. "Try anything—screw with me—you'll end up just like your friend."

Paul. Oh, God.

Or Stan. Or... *Please, not Toni.*

She fixed her gaze on his, searching those two bottomless black pools. "Who are you talking about?"

"Now, that's a good question." He reached into the pocket of his windbreaker and pulled out a wallet, flipped it open, held it under the flashlight. "Kincaid. Steve Kincaid."

No. No, this... monster was lying. Steve was in Nashville. With Tammy and Jeff. Working in his studio.

He tossed the wallet onto the mattress. Allison snatched it up. In the shadowed light, Steve's face grinned at her from the tiny picture on his driver's license.

Everything inside her stopped and then broke loose all at once. A desolate moan whimpered out of her, a sound less than human, triggering a flood of tears that blinded her. The scream shot like lightning through her mind and exploded from her throat, *"You bastard!"*

Within the last ten minutes, the wind had turned fierce, slamming the rain against his office window at an angry slant. If it kept up, there'd be a rash of fender-benders. Or worse, Ray thought, remembering the semi that had lost traction last night on the slick road.

He pulled his mind back to the business at hand, then, leaning back in the chair, skimmed over his notes, ran through a quick, mental recap of what Cliff had just told him. A young girl—no one had seemed to know who she was, or where she had come from. Then the incident in the woods, and she was gone. Just like that. Supposedly left town with her parents, headed for somewhere in Texas.

To Ray's way of thinking, the outcome of that decades-old investigation had turned out to be just a bit too convenient.

He studied his detective. "You and Bradford both believe that girl is Allison Weathers."

Cliff stared back down at the photograph. "It's got to be her."

Yeah, given what he'd learned from Steve Kincaid, Ray had to agree. The pattern was starting to come together. He didn't like what he was seeing. "Why didn't you mention this sooner?"

Cliff sighed. "Bradford wanted me to hunt up the old case file, look into the girl's identity. That was right before I left town. He wouldn't say why he'd suddenly decided he needed the information.

"To be honest, I figured he'd just gotten a bug in his cap, the way some people do when they get to thinking too hard. Stirring up old ghosts."

Ghosts. Ray flinched at the term. Then felt the heat rush through him. "Bradford never said a word about this when we questioned him. You got any idea why?"

"I don't have a clue." Cliff paused. "The report stated that he seemed to think Jared Atkins was involved."

And they'd had no luck tracking down the old man or his wife. Ray frowned. "Probably nothing to it, but no one was home at the Atkins' place. Supervisor at the hospital where the missus works told us she'd put in for vacation time. She has relatives in Memphis, might have headed that way."

"I read that in the report. I'll check in to it." Cliff grabbed the small pad and pencil from his shirt pocket, jotted down the note. "If I remember right, one of the men on Dad's bowling team was a deputy at the time. I'll get in touch with him. Maybe he can tell us something."

He glanced back up at Ray. "The diamonds—you see a connection there with Rush?"

"Given the time frame, he's about the right age, so we can't rule it out. And according to his son's statement, Jack Kincaid's adamant about the stones being somewhere in this area." Ray took a mental jog back. An image of Toni popped into his head, sharp, sexy, doe-brown eyes narrowed on him. *The open area... in Allison's cellar. You* are *going to have your men check it out.*

Yeah, dammit. What they had found was a cavern that stretched along maybe twenty feet before ending abruptly. A cave-in. The earth down there was packed solid, hadn't been disturbed for who knew how many decades.

If the diamonds were buried somewhere beneath all that rubble, they weren't going anywhere.

Ray had men keeping an eye on the place. A screw-up in this morning's shift change had left the house unguarded for maybe an hour, but CSI had gone out to run a second sweep. If the scene had been compromised, he'd have heard by now.

He reached for his coffee mug, scowled when he remembered it was empty, and set it aside. "I want to look in to Kincaid Senior's background before we contact him, see if anything stirs."

Cliff nodded. "Got to be cautious there. The man has connections in high places."

"Then we do the research prior to questioning anyone. It's all we can do." Maybe they'd be able to pull a connection to the first wife. Assuming she was still alive.

Ray leveled his focus on Cliff. "We've got to play this by the book. I don't want any slipups here. And I sure as hell don't want to give this bastard a chance to get away.

"Have someone out front make copies of Rush's picture. I want it distributed to everyone in this department—today. And I want to have a look at the old case file. Any record going back that far should be stored in the basement. Get whatever help you need to find it."

"Right." Cliff grabbed the fax. He eyed the evidence bag that held the photograph of Allison Weathers, and scooped it up. "Think I'll take a copy of this over to the drug store. They've got one of those machines now that develops the film on-site. Might pick up a lead there."

Ray nodded. "Maybe."

Just as the door shut behind his detective, the interoffice line buzzed. He grabbed the receiver.

"I got Deputy Lewis on the line, sir. She says it's urgent."

"Put her through." Ray straightened in the chair. "What's up, Tanya?"

"Sheriff, I think we may have found Jessie Conner."

CHAPTER 27

THE GRIEF TORE AT HER heart, shredding her soul until she was numb. Through a stream of tears, Allison watched the blur of light bobbing at the end of the long tunnel. She pressed the back of her hand to her split, swollen lip and cringed when the pain ripped through her jaw where the blow from his flashlight had sent her head reeling back.

He'd wanted to kill her. In a heartbeat, she'd seen her own death play out in those cold, dark eyes.

A breath shuddered out of her as she swiped at the tears. She had managed to drag everyone she'd come in contact with into her own private hell. Now Steve was gone. She wasn't sure about Toni, but knew that Paul and Stan were hurt. Or worse. The big happy dog she had rescued from the animal shelter—*rescued? God*—had been in danger from the moment he'd hopped into her car.

Allison swiped back more tears. She had to survive, if for no other reason than to see that the bastard answered for what he had done.

Focus, she ordered herself. The only thing she needed to focus on was getting out of here—now.

After the light disappeared, she waited another minute or two, then grabbed the flashlight from under the mattress and punched it on. Pulling herself up, she tested her injured ankle. Sore, and still swollen, but it would hold. It had to.

At a hobble, she started down the tunnel, bare feet stinging from the bite of jagged rocks. The door stopped her in her tracks. Planks of wood framed by pressure-treated posts spiked into the earth.

"No," her voice trembled out in a whisper, then louder on the heel of a quaking breath, *"No."* Allison dropped the flashlight, putting every ounce of strength she could muster into digging her fingers in around the edge of the door. She pried, pulled, then pushed.

It didn't budge.

A whimper escaped her, building to a moan as she pounded a fist against the rough wood. Helpless to stop the tears, she slid, like something boneless, down to the cold, hard ground.

Other than what Allison had told her, Toni hadn't been able to glean much from the diary. A major cause for concern, that. But she had read slowly, had only advanced maybe a third of the way through.

So there was hope, yet.

Slowing for a curve in the highway, she switched the wipers on full as the rain hammered harder against the windshield. She glanced over at her niece in the passenger seat, a pretty, young girl in a pink T-shirt and jeans. Jenna should be spending the summer with friends, going to parties, sharing juicy gossip over the latest hunk on the high-school football team. Or not, Toni thought. Solitude was more her thing.

Either way, the girl at least deserved a shot at normalcy. Hadn't been much of that going around lately.

To make matters worse, one of their links to Allison—Paul—had gone looking for answers and hadn't come back. Toni was afraid that Steve might have done the same.

They rode the next few miles down 285 in silence, listening to the rain beat against the car while the wipers made a lame attempt to swipe it back. Once they reached Annie Bradford's house and Jenna was able to place her hands on Paul's truck, or his cell phone, she might be able to tap into his head.

Getting a connection to Steve was going to be a bit tricky. The business card he'd passed to Toni hadn't turned out to be much of a conduit.

She looked over at her niece again. Jenna stared out the side window, gray eyes solemn. Neither of them wanted to say what they were both thinking. "Steve... Can you... sense him at all?"

Jenna dropped her gaze. "No." Her lips trembled. "I shouldn't have mentioned the tunnel in Allison's cellar. He went there—we both know he did."

Maybe, Toni admitted, sighing. Probably.

"Whatever has or hasn't happened, it's not your fault. So don't think for one minute that—"

Jenna shook her head. "I'm *supposed* to be psychic." Her breath hitched. "And the best I could do was—*what? Tell him to be careful?*"

Be careful. Hadn't Toni said the same to Paul?

Yeah. Look what had happened there. At one point last night, between the time they had last spoken and the predawn hours, he had vanished.

Toni kept her eyes on the rain-slicked road in front of her. What could she say to lift the weight from her niece's young shoulders? She could fall back on the old litany—no psychic was ever a hundred percent accurate. Those were just words strung together, hollow in the wake of any one of a number of possible, gloomy realities.

The truth was that Toni, not Jenna, had pulled Steve deeper into the situation.

The second she opened her mouth to remind her niece of that, her cell phone rang. Toni glanced down at the caller ID. Ray. They'd been playing phone tag for a while this morning.

"I'd better take this."

With a jerky nod, Jenna swiped the wetness from her eyes that threatened to spill over into tears, and turned back to the window.

Toni flipped her phone open, punched the speaker on. "I can't talk long. I'm driving."

"Then just listen. We may have identified the man responsible for Allison Weathers' disappearance. He raped and killed two women in Nashville." Ray paused. "Dammit, Toni, you need to step away from this."

A suspect. But... sexual assaults?

She arched a brow at her niece, who was frowning. Biting her bottom lip, Jenna shook her head slightly, shrugged.

He could be moving in the wrong direction, Toni thought. She had to tell him what they had worked through last night. The down side of that was one mention of her psychic niece and he would drop the shutters, slam up the stone wall he hid behind.

They needed a face-to-face.

She glanced down at the phone when static crackled out of the speaker. "You still there?"

"Yeah. I talked to Stan Michaels this morning, and Bradford's grandmother. She found Bradford's truck in her driveway."

Toni knew that. Wasn't about to admit it, though. Paul's grandmother had called her just after they'd talked to Ray. She'd heard shaking, and tears, in the poor woman's voice. Hours before she had boarded the first flight home, Annie Bradford had felt that something had gone horribly wrong.

"You got any idea what Bradford was up to last night?"

Nothing concrete. It irritated her now that she hadn't pushed a little harder when she'd had the chance. Toni told Ray what little she knew, that Paul wasn't specific about the lead he was tracking.

"Michaels said pretty much the same." He sighed. "Where are you?"

"Driving." She glanced over at Jenna. Soft gray eyes, clouded with worry, gazed out at the rain. "I was with Allison's brother for a while last night."

A muttered curse floated out of the tiny speaker.

"I'm afraid I let it slip about the tunnel in her cellar." She shook her head when Jenna shot her a look. "Steve didn't answer the phone in his room this morning, or his cell. He wasn't at the hotel when I stopped by. According to the clerk there, he hasn't checked out."

"Goddammit, Toni."

Jenna flinched. Toni blew out a short breath. "There's something else." She told Ray about the man she'd noticed during the zoning meeting. "He seemed familiar. I couldn't place him, but Steve recognized him from an old picture I printed off the Net." She paused. "He works for Allison's dad."

Silence hovered like a weight ready to drop.

"You didn't get a name?"

"Steve couldn't remember. He was going to look into it, but…" She let it go at that.

Ray's voice came at her in a quiet fury. "Where are you?"

"I told you—driving."

"Where?"

"Working, Ray. I'm working."

"Fine. Just so you know—my men are at Weathers' house now. You get anywhere near the place, you'll be spending some serious time in a jail cell."

He disconnected.

"Well. He's pissed." Toni slowed the car to steer over a section of highway where water had pooled, and felt her niece's eyes on her. "What?"

"I was the one who told Steve about the tunnel."

"Yes, you were. I wanted to keep things simple, and I can handle Ray. You have enough to deal with."

Jenna inhaled, let it out, her breath barely a murmur under the noise of the rain. "It's all so complicated, isn't it?"

"Yeah, sweetie. It is."

Complicated wasn't the half of it. Things had spiraled out of control. First Allison, then Paul. Now Steve.

Toni pulled her eyes off the road long enough to look over at her niece. If Paul was hurt—or worse—and Jenna physically experienced whatever he had suffered…

"I have to do this. You know that."

Anger sparked Ray's blood as he stood in the pouring rain with the wind whipping against his slicker, just a few yards away from the lake where they had found Jessie Conner's body floating face down. On the far side of the lake, Tanya Lewis and the other deputies battled the weather, trying to get a fix on a vehicle that may have rolled into the water.

Murder. It was always ugly. And always personal.

Ray figured that working as a waitress in Joe Dean's dump-of-a-bar for next to nothing, and hustling tips, Conner might not have been doing much with her life. But, dammit, she was a human being.

She had deserved better.

He swore, swiped the rain from his face, and headed over to where the M.E., Matt Johnson, was working on Conner under a tarp they had strung up. Cliff had no idea how right he'd been about the stuff hitting the fan. CSI had just found a trace of blood the rain hadn't washed away near Allison Weathers' back porch. Blood that hadn't been there yesterday.

Now both Bradford and Kincaid were missing.

And Toni… Christ, the woman just wasn't going to back off from this.

Ray swore again. How had he let the situation get this far out of his control?

He yanked his focus back and ducked under the tarp, making a conscious effort to breathe through his mouth when the stench hit him. Doc Johnson was bent over the body, face grim as he worked under the bright, battery-powered lights.

"Matt." Ray glanced down at the bloated body, had to steel himself. He hadn't known Jessie Conner, but he had a good idea that she wouldn't have wanted anyone to see her like this. His gaze tracked over to the left side of the skull that had caved from a heavy blow. Blank eyes, embedded in wax-like, distended flesh, stared out at him, almost accusing, from beneath a glazed-over, milky film, the left pupil blown.

Doc Johnson shifted solemn, pale-blue eyes onto Ray, the lines on his face, his graying hair, more prominent under the harsh light. "That suspect you mentioned earlier—no sign of any knife wounds on the body."

Ray nodded, still conscious of the putrid odor that didn't seem to faze the doc. "You got any idea on time of death?"

"Hard to say until we get her on the table, but I'd estimate five, maybe six days." Matt covered the body, then stood up, stretched his neck. "You said a high school student found her?"

"That's right. He was out here fishing with a buddy a couple of days ago and lost his wallet, came back to look for it."

"In this weather?"

Ray shrugged. "Kids. I figure it worked in our favor, though, him driving out."

"I suppose it did. Guess the boy was pretty shook up."

"Yeah." Ray remembered the kid's face, pasty white, how every inch of his lanky frame had trembled. "His parents had to drive out and pick up his car, take him home."

Sighing, the doc reached over and shut the lights off. "And here I thought I was going to retire in a nice, peaceful town where murder's just something you read about in a mystery novel."

He fixed a hard gaze on Ray. "You need to catch this bastard."

"Believe me—I intend to do just that."

"I know, I know."

A gust of wind sprayed rain under the tarp. Matt shifted a quick step over to dodge the brunt of it. He looked back down at the motionless form, signaled to one of his men. "I've done all I can here. We'll go ahead and bag her." He glanced at the activity across the lake. "Think I'll stick for a while longer, though, just in case our Miss Conner had company."

Ray moved away to let the doc finish his job, and spotted Cliff's cruiser rolling down the gravel road. Cliff got out of the car, yanking the hood of his slicker up. He huffed out a breath, glancing over to where Ray's people were working. "Got here as quick as I could."

Nodding, Ray motioned toward his Jeep. "Let's get out of the rain for a minute."

They climbed in, and, dripping water, shoved the hoods of their slickers back. Ray briefed his detective of the status on-scene. "Lewis and her partner were on their way to check Conner's residence again. They spotted the kid's car—abandoned—from up on the road, drove down to take a look."

Cliff raked a hand through damp hair. "If we're right about Rush, I don't see the connection here—not his MO."

"No, it's definitely not his style. And I want to focus on finding Conner's boyfriend." Ray paused, homing in on another line. "This murder could have been something Rush hadn't planned on."

"A situation that caught him off guard," Cliff noted. "Forced him to improvise. Conner may have walked in on something, seen or heard something she shouldn't have."

That, Ray thought, could lead them right back to Allison Weathers. "You have any luck with the photograph?"

Cliff shook his head. "No one at the drugstore remembered seeing it. The clerk who usually develops the film was out on a doctor's appointment. I left a copy with the manager." He pulled his cell phone from his shirt pocket, checked the signal. "Should hear back from her sometime this afternoon."

And they were still looking for the old case file.

"It might take a while," Cliff said. "Filing system back then wasn't the best."

There was that, and Ray remembered most of those old records had gotten shuffled around when they'd built the new courthouse and moved everything over. They might spend weeks digging around down there, come up with nothing but dust and paper cuts.

The good news was that Cliff had managed to track down his dad's bowling partner.

"Joe Saunders. I think we may have hit on something there. He didn't work the case, but he remembered the deputy who did saying that Atkins knew more than what he was letting on."

Atkins. Ray frowned. "Did Saunders happen to recall the deputy's name?"

"Yeah, but the guy's retired somewhere up north. We'll have to track him down." Cliff paused. "It was just the one deputy and the sheriff working the scene. Sheriff passed away a few years back. I was about to hunt up Bradford when you called."

Ray stared past the sheets of rain sliding down his windshield. A little late now, but if he had bothered to push Bradford at all about Jared Atkins, he might have gotten some of the answers they needed.

He had screwed up.

He brought Cliff up to speed on Bradford and Kincaid, told him about the blood CSI had found. "No sign of Kincaid's van."

"Shit," was all Cliff could manage.

"I had Carl trail Bradford until around three this morning. He had to pull off—that overturned semi near the Old Mill bypass."

Cliff heaved a sigh. "I heard the driver didn't make it."

"No, he didn't." Ray wondered how many others in his once peaceful town they'd be adding to the body count before the week was out. "Carl drove past Bradford's after he'd finished up, spotted his truck in the driveway. The lights in the house were off. He figured Bradford had called it a night."

For a moment, Cliff sat back with his arms folded, dark eyes narrowed. "Truck in the driveway, no sign of foul play."

"Yeah. And Bradford hit the bars last night. My guess is he was looking for Atkins."

Cliff shot Ray a sideways glance. "Maybe he found him."

Or the other way around, Ray thought, not sure where Rush fit into the picture. He checked his cell phone, swore when he noticed the red light that indicated he had lost service. They were down to just radio communications now. "I've got a man keeping an eye on Atkins' place. If anything stirs, we'll know it."

He grabbed the door handle. "Let's see if they've made any progress out here."

They darted back into the rain, and the radio clipped to Ray's belt squelched. "Go ahead, Tanya."

"Sheriff, we got it—the vehicle. It's coming up now."

"We're on our way."

They'd made it halfway past the north point of the lake when a battered red truck with tinted windows began rising out of the water from the end of a tow chain. Ray shared a quick, sharp look with Cliff as they picked up the pace.

Deputy Lewis hurried in their direction, caught up to them about ten yards from where they were towing the vehicle out of the water. She swiped the rain from her face, aimed grim, blue eyes on Ray. "We got another body."

Ray swore, motioned for her to keep moving. "Any luck on the ID?"

"Yes, sir. One of the deputies was able to identify. It's Jared Atkins."

Settled in a comfortable chair, next to her niece and across the table from Mrs. Bradford, Toni glanced around the quaint, country kitchen—walls the warm yellow of the summer sun, windows bordered by delicate, lace curtains embroidered with tiny daffodils. The room suited Paul's grandmother, a slender, petite woman, no more than five feet in height, her stylish bouffant of pure white hair soft as a cloud against the pale sky blue of her dress.

Toni drank from the tall glass of iced tea in front of her. The rain had finally stopped, but outside, thunder rolled as if all hell was about to bust loose. She looked over at Jenna, hoped the looming storm wasn't a sign for what might be coming next.

Annie Bradford's hand trembled as she raised the china cup to her lips and sipped hot tea. Her eyes, like her grandson's, were an intense, brilliant blue, which, Toni guessed, would normally spark with energy. Today they were racked with worry.

"Paul phoned me yesterday, to let me know what had happened to that poor girl. He didn't want me to hear it from the police." On a sigh, she lowered her cup back to the saucer. "I don't like planes, but I couldn't stay away. I... didn't tell him I was coming home. I knew he'd try to talk me out of it."

"We'll do our best to help, Mrs. Bradford," Jenna offered.

Paul's grandmother gazed into Jenna's soft gray eyes, searching. "I'm sure you will, dear. Your aunt mentioned that you have... a special talent."

"Yes, ma'am. Sometimes—not always—I'm able to see things that have happened, things I normally wouldn't know about because... well, because I wasn't there."

No mention of the premonitions, Toni thought, or the spooky mind-reading thing Jenna had been tapping into lately. Her niece had kept it simple. Smart girl.

Annie took another sip from her cup. "You have an unusual gift. I can't say I understand it, but I do believe there are things beyond our realm of knowledge. Some of them," she added softly, "just aren't meant to be explained."

The back door opened on a short rap, and Stan Michaels came in with Allison's big dog. The bruise on the man's face looked worse than it had yesterday, but Toni imagined that was the least of his worries right about now.

Eyes bright and tongue lolling, Allison's dog cocked his huge head at Jenna, then padded over to her, wagging his tail. "Jack likes you," Stan noted.

"I like him, too." She stroked the dog's large head, grinned. "Jack. What a name for a big pooch like you."

"Deputy outside is about done with Paul's truck," Stan said to Mrs. Bradford, and about the time she nodded, Toni's purse rang, or rather, her cell phone did.

She twisted around, to where she'd draped her leather Hobo bag over the chair. The purse was too big, really, something she'd bought on a whim and seldom used, but today she'd needed the cavernous compartment inside.

She reached in, past Bobbie Jean's diary, and fished out her phone.

Ray again.

"I need to take this. I'll just be a minute." She scooted her chair back, went into the living room. "Yeah, Ray."

"What the hell are you doing there?"

Irritation spiked. She'd recognized the deputy outside when they'd pulled up. Apparently, he had done the same with her. Hadn't taken him long to get on the phone to his boss.

She took a deep breath to quell the anger. "I don't recall you mentioning anything about staying away from Paul's grandmother."

He swore. "Is your niece with you?"

"What—your man didn't tell you?"

"Dammit, Toni, just answer the question."

"All right. Yes, I brought Jenna with me."

Ray swore again. "I want both of you to stay put. I mean it— stay inside. I'm headed that way."

"What's going on?"

"Not now, babe. Not now."

The protest was rolling off her tongue just as he disconnected. She frowned, flipped her phone shut. She didn't like the shaking she had heard in his voice. He had sounded... vulnerable.

A word she would never use to describe Ray.

Still frowning, Toni went back to the kitchen. Stan was over by the window next to the door, peering through a part in the curtains. She moved beside him, sidestepping the big dog sprawled on the floor.

Her frown deepened. Ray's deputy stood on the covered porch, just outside the door, on full alert. Toni kept her voice low. "Sticking close, isn't he?"

Stan nodded.

"You didn't see or hear anything last night?"

"Not a thing. If anyone had come near Paul's place, or made the slightest sound, Jack would've gone ballistic."

Toni glanced over at Stan's truck parked at this end of the narrow, gravel lane. Her gaze followed the lane through the long stretch of rain-soaked land that led to the cozy barn with the covered front porch, lingered briefly on the redwood furniture, the barrel planters filled with blooming color. Behind the barn, the property went on for what looked like another few acres before butting up to a line of thick woods.

"This guy—whoever he is—might be closer than what we realized."

"Yeah. I thought the same. Annie tells me your niece might be able to get a handle on Paul."

"She's going to try." Feeling Jenna's focus on her, Toni gestured to Stan. Nodding, he moved away from the window, and took a seat next to Paul's grandmother while Toni settled back into her chair. She slipped her phone into her purse. "The sheriff called to let us know he's on his way."

All the color leached from Annie's face. She gripped Stan's arm. "Is it my grandson?"

How could Toni answer that when she had no idea herself?

It started with a slight quiver of the mouth, then the soft lines on Annie's face deepened as tears sprung into her blue eyes.

Shit. No. No, don't cry.

Stan put an arm around Mrs. Bradford's shoulder, and cocked a brow at Toni. All she could do was shake her head. "I wish I could tell you more. The sheriff asked us to stay inside. He'll be here soon. That's as much as I know."

She sighed. "I'm sorry."

Jenna managed a small smile. "Mrs. Bradford, do you still have Paul's cell phone?"

"Why, yes." Her hand shaking, Paul's grandmother reached into the pocket of her dress for the phone, her gaze aimed at Toni. "You were the last one my grandson spoke to before he disappeared. I know this because your number was the most recent on his call list. I believe that he trusts you." She paused after those final few words had trembled out. "I did as you asked, I didn't mention finding Paul's phone to the sheriff. I pray we did the right thing."

Toni dipped her head in a slow nod. If this worked the way it should, the phone would hold something akin to an energy signature. It might be her niece's only connection to Paul.

Jenna took the phone from Mrs. Bradford, then closed her eyes and began brushing delicate fingers over the small display, the keypad.

Holding her breath, Toni caught the subtle flicker beneath Jenna's eyelids.

A shadow moved over her niece's face. "There's a man, not Paul. It's dark. He's walking away from…" She opened her eyes, stared down at the phone in her hand. "A building. Or maybe a house. I couldn't see it clearly."

Toni urged her to try again.

Jenna drew a small breath, focused, and closed her eyes. Then cried out when her head jerked forward.

"What the hell?" Stan made a move toward her just as the big dog sprung up from the floor and whined. He whipped around, grabbed Jack's collar. "Easy, buddy."

Shaking, Paul's grandmother was out of her chair. "Is she all right?"

Already at her niece's side, Toni scanned Jenna's face—chalk-white. "I don't know."

On a moan, Jenna raised a trembling hand to the back of her head and winced. Toni focused on the girl's winter-gray eyes, saw shock there, and pain. "Tell me you're okay."

With a shudder, Jenna nodded. "I'm all right." She lifted her hand to her temple, pressed. Blinked. "It's Paul, he's... hurt."

Stan swore. Annie clamped a hand to her mouth on a muffled sob, and collapsed back into her chair.

Eyes blurred with pain, Jenna inhaled. "He's hurt, Mrs. Bradford. But... he's alive."

CHAPTER 28

OUTSIDE THE OLD HUNTING CABIN, thunder rolled and rumbled like something possessed. Jeans and shirt clinging to his skin from the heavy humidity, Paul gritted his teeth against the pain that hammered through his head, and shifted his weight on the plank floor, trying to position his body at a better angle against the cast-iron stove at his back. The rope that bound his wrists to one of the legs on the stove had cut into his skin, but he'd been working it for a while now, was beginning to feel the pinprick tingling of circulation returning to his hands.

He focused past his blurred vision, kept sawing the rope against the rough edge of the iron. The old drunk had really waylaid him. But he was still breathing.

Why? Why had Atkins left him alive?

What do you want from me, old man?

A bargaining chip, maybe. If Atkins had been watching Allison, he had seen Paul's truck in her driveway more than once, might have assumed there was a relationship in the making.

Not too far off the mark, at least from Paul's end.

To be honest, though, he wasn't sure how much of what he felt for Allison stretched back to a memory that was decades old, to the small, defenseless girl he hadn't been able to help.

The girl who just might be the woman who had come back to this town, to that house.

Paul glanced over at the only window in the room when thunder rolled again and the dull, gray light inside went a little darker. It would take the better part of an hour to make the trek out of here, back through the woods. But he knew the route well. He knew this cabin. As boys, he and Bill Treadwell had stumbled onto it while exploring the foothills.

The cabin was remote, hidden from view by thick undergrowth and a wall of trees. There was no way Jared Atkins could have lugged the weight of an unconscious man this far over the rough terrain. Not without help.

Atkins would have wanted to keep Allison close, though. Accessible.

But where, dammit? *Where?*

He shifted to ease the tension in his shoulders, and put more effort into working his hands free. Then froze.

The open space behind the air-handler in her cellar... If it led to a tunnel, that same tunnel would most likely run beneath Atkins' property.

"Under the barn," Paul murmured, then swore.

He blinked back the sweat trickling down from his forehead, and with a grunt, put all his strength into jerking his wrists apart, finally felt the rope give way.

Hold on, Allison. Just hold on.

Dark eyes narrowed, Cliff shifted in the passenger seat as the Jeep took the curves along the old two-lane county road. "I just can't see Ellie Atkins being involved with this."

"I'm having a hard time with that myself."

Ray had someone back at the department contacting the bus station and airlines, checking with Mrs. Atkins' relatives in Memphis to verify whether she had headed that way. The state police had a description of her, along with the pertinent information on the old station wagon she drove. Those lines, he thought, would most likely lead to nowhere. His gut was telling him that the woman had never left her house.

Several yards ahead, fog rolled across the road. He eased up on the gas, steered through it. They'd been hitting patches of this stuff off and on since the rain had stopped, which made traveling down the winding and narrow potholed road a slower go than usual. But coming in from the east had been their only option. It would keep anyone holed up at Atkins' place from spotting the department issued Jeep.

Meantime the clock was ticking. "Let's hope the trail you mentioned is clear."

"Depends on if the deer still travel that way. I haven't been on it since I was a kid." Cliff pushed a hand through his hair, glancing at Ray. "Worst case scenario? Maybe thirty minutes."

Nodding, Ray gave it more gas when they broke through the fog onto one of the few sections of road that didn't wind like a maze. The trail that started at the back of Bradford's land, maybe thirty yards into the woods, should take them straight up to the back edge of Atkins' property. To save time, he'd considered going in from Weathers' land, but had nixed the idea. They needed to keep the show of activity there to a minimum.

Gazing out the windshield, Cliff just shook his head. "The two of them together—Atkins and Conner—it should have clicked for me right out of the gate."

"Same here," Ray admitted. Dingy atmosphere, cheap whiskey, Joe Dean's was the kind of bar where a man could find a dark corner and drink himself into a blur. Right up Atkins' alley. He could see how Old Jared might have hooked up with one of the waitresses.

At one point, someone must have noticed Atkins chatting Conner up.

"What I don't get is what the hell she saw in him."

"Money." Cliff shot Ray a grim smile. "The diamonds."

"Yeah, there is that. And if we're right about Rush, he's been waiting a long time to get his hands on those stones. I don't imagine he'd be willing to share."

"No, I don't suppose he would."

When Ray pulled to a stop behind Toni's Mustang, his gaze slid up to the two-story cedar house. A ruby-throated hummingbird hovered over eye-popping colors that sprung from the flowerbeds. Wouldn't be hard for a man to get lulled into thinking that the days in this quiet, sleepy little town rolled along without too many bumps or scrapes.

A façade. It had sure as hell fooled him.

He scrubbed a hand over his face, pulled himself back to where he needed to be, and mentally ran through the setup again. Before he'd left Lewis and her partner to finish up at the lake, he'd had to shift his limited resources around. Of the two men posted to keep watch on Weathers' place, one—Riley—remained there, waiting for the order to move in on Atkins' property. The other officer was here, and would stay put. For now.

His CSI team, still working Weathers' house, was on alert.

Ray scanned the perimeter of Bradford's land, eyes darting up at the sound of thunder that rumbled down from the mountains. "Let's do this."

Allison turned her face into the filthy mattress as another round of tears flooded out of her. The cut on her swollen lip throbbed. Her jaw ached where she knew a bruise had bloomed. And the darkness around her seemed lighter somehow. Her entire body, she realized, felt... light.

Her breath shuddered out in shaky spurts as she felt the surrender sneaking up on her, the calm acceptance that she would die here taking over her mind, drifting through her like a quiet plague.

Still, the tears came. Angry tears.

"Don't cry, Allison. Please."

She jerked her head up at the sound of the soft, sad voice, and choked back a sob. She hadn't felt him coming up on her, not even a breath of chilling draft. Allison brushed back her tears, squinting against the abrupt light.

He stood just inches away, his small frame illuminated by an odd glow, shaggy blond hair and sober face like a beacon against the darkness. He wore the same paper-thin overalls and ragged T-shirt. His feet were still bare, and dirty. But there was no sign of his scruffy little dog.

"Go away," she half whispered to the dead boy, her own rasping voice unfamiliar to her. "Please, just… go away. I can't help you."

The boy sighed. "We're sorry about your friend."

"Brother," Allison gritted out, and her breath caught on another sob. "He was my brother." She looked down at her hands, visible under the peculiar glow coming off the boy. The pink stains from where she had grasped Steve's wallet were still there, on her palms, her fingertips. Dry now.

What was he doing here? Why had he left Nashville?

The boy held out his small hand for her. "You need to come with me."

"With you." The words came out on a broken sigh. If only it were that simple, just getting up and walking out. The monster who had imprisoned her in this cold, dark tomb had made sure there was no escape.

Had he done the same to Steve? Drugged him, trapped him, and then…

The thought she didn't want to finish trailed off as her gaze shifted up the boy's arm to where it bent at an impossible angle. Why hadn't she noticed that before?

"You're arm…"

"It looks funny, I know. But it doesn't hurt, not anymore."

Allison searched his face, skimming over the smudge of dirt there before settling on the serene eyes watching her, eyes that were different from when she'd first seen him standing on her back lawn under the moonlight. Blue, as before, but mixed now with a strange shimmering shade she couldn't even begin to describe, the colors pooling into a preternatural iridescence. She had the unsettling feeling that if she peered into them long enough, she would see her own reflection.

"Who are you?"

With Cliff beside him, Ray took the steps up to Annie Bradford's back porch, the humidity clinging to him like a second skin. He glanced at the darkening sky as Cliff scanned the distant edge of the woods, then gave his deputy on watch a sharp nod. "Everything quiet?"

"Yes, sir. I just checked in with Riley. He has a clear view of Atkins' property from the attic window next door. So far, nothing over there's moved."

"Okay." Ray brought him up to speed on the situation. "Keep your eyes open. No one in this house takes a step outside—for any reason." He jerked his head around at the sound of tapping. Toni's face was inches from the window. She crooked a finger at him. He stifled a sigh. "I'll be back in a minute," he told Cliff.

But no, it wouldn't be quite that quick, Ray realized as he stepped inside a kitchen dominated by three females, Bradford's employee—Stan Michaels—and Weathers' big dog.

Sprawled on the floor, the dog lifted its head and growled. "Easy boy," Michaels tossed over his shoulder. Toni's niece glanced up from whatever she was reading—a journal, by the looks of it—and pinned pale gray, somber eyes on Ray.

He held her gaze with his for a moment. The girl had always made him uncomfortable. Now, looking into that stark, direct stare, he got the sudden crazy idea that she could pluck every thought from his head.

"Sheriff, my grandson... We believe he's still alive."

Ray didn't have to ask who had put the cautious hope into Annie Bradford's head. He shot Toni a hard look. "We'll do everything we can to find him, Mrs. Bradford."

Toni moved next to him, kept her voice low. "We need to talk—it'll just take a second."

He jerked his head in a nod, then followed her into the hallway, sparing a glance at the collection of family photos displayed on the walls. "Make it fast."

He watched her eyes narrow—not in anger, her mind was clicking, condensing information.

She blew out a quick breath. "I hate to add fuel to a growing fire, and it might be nothing, but Lilly Jameson gave Paul's grandmother a ride home from the airport early this morning. With everything going on, Mrs. Bradford just remembered a little while ago that Lilly said she'd phone after she opened the shop, to see if there was any news on Paul."

Ray sighed. "She never called."

"No, she didn't. I spoke to the lady who works part time at the craft shop. When Mrs. Jameson didn't show up this morning, she got worried, tried calling her at home."

Toni shook her head when he lifted a brow. "No luck."

Ray swore. He grabbed his cell phone from the clip on his belt, checked to see if the service was back up, and contacted Dispatch, gave the order for the one patrolman he had free to swing by Lilly Jameson's residence. At the gentle touch of Toni's hand on his arm, he paused.

"Paul's been injured, but he *is* alive." She pulled her hand away when he cocked a brow again, and in less than a finger snap, reverted to the cool, distant woman who, nearly a year back, had crawled into his lover's skin. "We're not sure about Allison's brother."

Here we go. The psychic bullshit again.

Too much weirdness tied to this case. And damned if he

couldn't help but take a mental step through the clutter. There was Jay Treadwell, a delusional, dying old man, lonely, who'd resorted to conjuring up ghosts in his head for company. Then Allison Weathers had bought the place, picking up right where Treadwell had left off—seeing dead kids.

This from a woman who had been locked away—and rightly so—for claiming to have regular visits from her deceased husband.

Add to it the crumpled sketch they'd found in the trashcan in Weathers' workroom of *something* that appeared to be female, and the pictures she'd e-mailed to the art gallery in Atlanta... *Christ.* Grotesque images with eyes wide open in terror, or with an eerie emptiness. He couldn't figure which. Looking at the damned things had been like getting an up-close-and-personal glimpse into Hell.

The open book Weathers had left on her desk—*A Study of the Paranormal*—had sealed the idea for him that the woman was still seriously disturbed.

Ray just shook his head. "Listen—"

"No—*you* need to listen." Toni matched his glare with one of her own. "Mrs. Treadwell left a diary up in the attic. Allison found it."

He got a mental flash of Toni's niece looking up from the journal she'd been reading, and swore.

"She—Mrs. Treadwell—hid something for Allison's mother."

Ray had to ask. "And that would be?"

"A small ceramic replica of the Statue of Liberty."

"The diamonds."

"Yeah. We think Ms. Liberty's buried in Allison's cellar."

Ray swore again. "Behind the air-handling unit." He took her by the shoulders, squeezed. "I need to go."

"One more thing. The suspect you mentioned? Unless his name is Neil Brady—"

"The barn."

They both whirled around. Toni's niece was moving toward

them. Ray had to check the instinct to step back when she shifted a vacant gaze onto him. Those cool, gray eyes were like... two windows, he decided, with nothing on the other side.

"I... think Allison is under the barn."

Toni rushed over to the girl. "What barn, Jenna? Is she—?"

Jenna shook her head. "No. No, it's nothing like that. She's alive. But... the little girl, I may have been wrong about her."

Ray was a breath away from asking, "What little girl?" when Jenna frowned, her focus drifting past him, scanning some distant horizon only she could see. Her voice came at him in a whisper. "The Atkins' barn... I think there's some kind of tunnel under it."

Toni shot Ray a look. Oblivious, Jenna kept her blank stare fixed on some imaginary point. "Paul knows about the barn. He's headed that way now, through the woods."

She blinked, pulled her gaze back to Ray. "You'd better hurry, Sheriff."

Alone. Again.

Allison shifted her position on the gritty mattress, knowing it was useless but still trying to find a spot where the dampness hadn't seeped through from the cold ground. She clutched the flashlight, tempted to switch it on, if only for a brief moment, just to get a glimpse of something other than absolute blackness.

The small voice of reason in the back of her head told her to hold off, conserve the batteries. So she gave in to the darkness, let it continue to envelop her, *smother* her.

On a shaky breath, she cringed when the split in her lip peeled apart where the blood had dried. Allison dabbed at it with her fingertip and felt the sticky wetness there. She had shoved back the helpless acceptance of defeat, refused to break down again. Instead, she wanted to pound something, yell until her throat burned from it, until the echo of her own voice bouncing off the earth and rock deafened her.

One simple question—who are you?—and the boy had vanished before she could blink.

Why?

There was no sense of time down here, but every second alone in the darkness, with the musty dampness leeching into her lungs, felt like an eternity.

Having the dead for company, Allison decided, was better than being stuck in this godforsaken place with nothing but her own thoughts to haunt her.

"Joshua."

She started at the voice behind her and jerked her head around. Before her brain could register the boy's image, he was in front of her, the glow that radiated from his small body pushing back the gloom.

Allison squinted, adjusting to the light. There was still no sign of his dog. "Where did you go?"

When those odd iridescent eyes shifted to look over his shoulder, she got the sudden horrible idea that he would vanish again. "Please, don't—"

"Joshua Bauer. They called me Josh."

A name, at last. That still didn't tell Allison what he was doing here. What was his connection to her? Was there a connection?

She had so many questions for the boy.

"How did you die, Josh? The man who's keeping me here—did he kill you? Who is he?"

A frown shadowed his face. "I'll tell you everything, I promise. But we need to go now."

Go. To where, she wondered as the grief swept over her again. She blinked the tears back, and glanced at the long scratches on the side of her hand put there by pounding a fist against rough wood. Allison sighed. "Josh, I'm not like you. I just can't... sift through doors."

"I know that. But there's another tunnel." He glanced behind him. "Back there."

Hope surged through her and had her heart doing leaps. She strained to see. "Is it the way out of here?"

"It was, a long time ago."

He was leading her around in circles. Giving her vague answers that sent one question chasing after another. Allison struggled to focus on the miniscule place inside her where the calm centered, the small reserve of peace she had stored after finally crawling out of the nightmare that, for the longest time, had held her sanity hostage. That reserve had been her personal crutch. It had begun slipping away the day she had moved to this town, into that house. She hadn't been able to find it in a while. She couldn't find it now.

She met his steady gaze. It was like a beam on her. "What's in the tunnel, Josh?"

His eyes sparked—a pinpoint flash in the center of those two iridescent pools. "I almost forgot. You'll need the wire cutters."

She frowned. "You didn't answer my question. And—wire cutters? What are you talking about?"

He pointed at the mattress. "Under there. We don't have much time." The quick look he sent in the direction of the door was enough to put any questions she had on hold. Allison shoved her hand under the mattress, groped until she found what she was looking for. A simple tool, with long, pointed metal ends. Like pliers with a sharp edge. With the right angle and enough force, the tool could do some serious damage. Too bad she hadn't been able to get her hands on it earlier.

She had it now, though, didn't she?

Slipping the wire cutters into the pocket of her capris, she grabbed the flashlight and got to her feet. Darkness swirled with the light coming off the boy as her head swam, and she swayed.

"Here, let me help you." His small hand gripped hers. She jolted at the touch—solid, warm. Human.

289

How could that be?

Allison wasn't sure whether she wanted the answer.

For now, it was enough that he was here.

She took a breath to steady, then, keeping the flashlight off, let the boy lead her. The glow surrounding him cut a path through the darkness as she followed along with a slight limp, wincing whenever sharp rocks dug into her bare feet.

Her heart sank when she saw the crude but effective handiwork blocking her entrance to the tunnel. Here, instead of joining wood to pressure-treated posts, he had stapled barbed wire.

The bastard had caged her in. Like an animal.

A filthy, battered and bruised, ravenous animal that had grappled in the dark for an empty plastic container, and then licked it clean of crumbs. An animal that, halfway through its slow, defeated trudge back to its damp and gritty nest, had dropped its pants and left behind the strong stench of urine.

He had reduced her to that.

A hot rush of anger bolted through her, and Allison swore. Ignoring Josh's curious stare, she set the flashlight aside and grabbed the wire cutters from her pocket. Then went to work.

Arms and hands aching with fatigue, she continued to snip, pull, yank, ignoring the scratches and minor cuts she couldn't avoid, until the last of the wire fell away.

Allison swiped the sweat from her eyes and picked up the flashlight, then followed Josh through a cramped area where the tunnel made a tight curve, descending deeper under the ground at a gradual slope. The pungent smell of old, stale earth, more prominent down here, left a dank taste in her mouth. She had to work at swallowing past it. And it was a real effort now to keep her eyes fixed straight ahead. The narrow walls of rock and earth seemed to be closing in on her.

She shivered from the heavy dampness. "How much farther, Josh?"

"We're almost there."

Close—too close—behind them, something began scratching at the ground. "What is that?" Allison whispered, inching closer to the boy.

Josh kept moving, but glanced over his shoulder, his mouth curving. "It's probably just a mouse."

She tightened her grip on the flashlight, trying not to imagine a rodent scurrying across her bare feet as the tunnel steered them in a long arc to the left. When the walls widened, a draft, fresh and clean, brushed her skin.

Air. Her pulse raced. There had to be an opening down here. All she had to do was find it.

Working her way around Josh, Allison picked up her pace. She stopped short when an eerie soft, bluish glow suddenly filled the area up ahead. She could see the end of the tunnel now, where it fed into another cavern.

"Josh, what—?" She turned, found nothing but empty blackness behind her. On a long breath, Allison moved to face whatever was waiting for her. Her heart kicked when a small girl walked—or was it, *floated?*—out from the center of that odd blue light.

The girl took a few tentative steps forward, a timid smile on her freckled face. "Hello, Allison."

CHAPTER 29

S HE COULDN'T GET HER VOICE. It was stuck somewhere at the back of her throat. Allison just stared at the girl who appeared to be a bit younger than Josh. Something small and frightened hid behind the wide, green eyes that looked back at her.

Her gaze skimmed over the curly, coppery red hair that was tangled and streaked with mud, lingered for a moment on the generous splash of freckles across the petite nose. It was like looking into a mirror, seeing an untamed version of herself as a child.

She glanced at the raw scratches that marred the girl's forehead and one cheek, swallowed hard when her focus dropped to the criss-cross of deep cuts on the small spindly legs beneath faded red shorts. When she noticed the jagged tear in the girl's blouse, where a piece of fabric was missing, she felt a long, slow sinking in the pit of her stomach.

Paul's little ghost. Dear God.

Allison struggled to find her voice. "Do I know you?"

The girl glanced past her. Allison turned, and there was Josh, the glow around him faint against the darkness, but pulsing, growing brighter. His scruffy little dog—Scooter—stood beside him, wagging its tail.

Josh gave the girl a nod.

"My name is… Katie." The depth of sadness in those green eyes tore at Allison. "I'm your sister."

Because sound carried out here, both Ray and Cliff had muted their radios and set their cell phones to vibrate. They took just a second now to recheck their communications equipment, then made the trek past Bradford's renovated barn, along the section of land that was several acres wide, left in its natural state—thick with old trees and heavy undergrowth.

Ray brought Cliff up to speed with what he'd learned from Toni and her niece. He didn't bother to gloss over the psychic angle, just laid it out straight, what he'd witnessed, heard.

And felt like a damned gullible fool while he was doing it.

Cliff just shrugged as he matched Ray's pace. "Well, for Bradford's sake, I hope she's right. As for the rest—we've got to at least check it out."

Nodding, Ray batted at a mosquito that buzzed around his ear. The bombshell Toni had dropped just before the urgency in Jenna's voice had sent him scrambling out the door was still eating at him. There was a chance—a strong one—they'd been way off the mark looking at Harold Rush for this. "What about Neil Brady? That name ring any bells for you?"

"Not really. But if your ex is right about the guy—" Cliff broke off, frowning up at the hazy sky when the air vibrated with thunder, and his cell phone buzzed. He pulled it from his belt clip, glanced down at the display. "Drugstore."

Ray nodded the go-ahead.

"Detective Barlow." Cliff frowned. "I see. He's sure?" He slanted Ray a look. "All right. We'll send someone over tomorrow to take his statement. Thank you, ma'am."

Dark eyes narrowed, Cliff flipped his phone shut. "That was the manager at the drugstore. The clerk who develops the film remembered the picture of Allison Weathers, he thought she was attractive."

Ray cocked a brow. "And?"

"The woman who picked up the pictures paid cash, then took off—didn't even wait for a receipt. It hit him as strange, her running in and out like that. She usually talks a blue streak."

"Ellie Atkins." Ray heaved a sigh.

"Yeah."

Sister.

Allison had rolled that over and over in her mind as she'd just stood there, mouth gaping and legs threatening to buckle, staring at the girl. Barely aware of the dog sniffing at the flashlight that had fallen from her hand and clattered to the hard ground, she shook her head. "I can't—it's not—I don't—" Brows on the rise, she looked over at Josh. He sat on the ground, his back to the opening of the tunnel that stretched like a wide, dark yawn. The dog abandoned the flashlight and crawled into his lap. With a trace of a sad smile aimed at Allison, Josh stroked the animal's matted fur.

At a loss, she turned back to Katie. The odd blue light had dimmed. The girl wasn't quite transparent, but Allison could see now the vague shapes of rock and earth behind her.

Even though her mind kept insisting it wasn't possible, she couldn't ignore the mirror image of her much younger self. Genetics never lied.

"Why don't I remember you?"

Katie poked the toe of her sneaker at a pebble. "Grandma told me that Mama was still in school when I came along." She looked up, her frail shoulders lifting in a shrug. "It was before she met your daddy."

"Grandma," Allison echoed. "Mother's—?"

"No." Katie shook her head. "My daddy's mama, Grandma Callahan. She took care of me. Then she went to Heaven and..." The small voice broke off. "Daddy didn't want me."

Deserted by both parents, Allison couldn't imagine it. Unwanted, shipped off to the nearest relative. "Oh, honey, I'm so sorry." Without stopping to wonder whether her arms would slide right through the girl, she made a move to embrace the sister she had never known.

Katie took a step back. "When I first saw you down by the creek, under the big tree where we"—she glanced at Josh—"where we died..."

Seized by an icy chill, the rest of the words drifted past Allison as her mind tumbled back. The Giant Oak down by the creek, the rush of frigid air. The bushes stirring and—she shifted her eyes over to the dog. "I have to sit down."

Head in a spin, she lowered herself onto the ground next to Josh, waited for the dizziness to pass. The dog fixed hopeful brown eyes on her and wagged its tail. Allison half consciously reached over to stroke the animal's head, not surprised to feel the tangle of dirty fur beneath her trembling hand.

Nothing, ever again, would surprise her.

"Mama came for me, and the plane took us to your house." Katie poked at the ground with her sneaker again. "Your daddy was angry at Mama because... she never told him about me."

"They argued," Allison murmured as the memory began to surface. Her small hand on the doorknob, ear pressed to her parents' closed bedroom door. Before, talking through it with Paul, she had gotten just a mental flash of hushed, angry voices. Now she remembered the explosion of infuriated shouting, followed by the crash of glass shattering against the dresser mirror. Or was it the wall?

The silence in the air was like a weight on her chest. Allison had to force the breath in and out of her lungs. She fixed her gaze on her sister. *Her sister.*

"Katie, how did you die? Our mother—is she..."

"It was my fault." The words were a hollow echo as wide, sad eyes looked back at Allison. "He killed Mama, and it was all my fault."

Trying to breathe around the thick humidity was like taking water into his lungs. Paul swiped at the sweat that had pooled into his eyes and kept battling his way through the underbrush. The trek was a slow go. He was still dizzy, disoriented. Weak. His damned legs kept trying to fold under him.

He froze at the nearby sound of rustling, and faded back into the cover of dense brush. Then he saw the man—no one he recognized. Tall. Thick, black hair streaked with gray, heavy lines gouged into a hard face. Cold, dark eyes. The guy had a gun tucked into the waistband of his jeans, and with each stride, a long, ivory-handled knife nestled in a leather sheath bumped against his hip.

Headed straight for the cabin.

Paul took a quick survey of his surroundings. He needed an equalizer—a good-sized rock, or maybe a small, fallen tree branch. He'd at least have a chance of taking the guy out. Or not, he realized as the trees and greenery around him started to blur and tilt. He sucked in a breath, gave his head a shake.

Don't screw this up. Just... get to Allison.

Willing his head to clear, Paul kept his eyes on the back of the dark shirt moving away from him, until he could no longer make it out. He inched forward in a half-crouch, trying not to stir the brush, and shifted direction to veer west.

Coming in from this side was a crapshoot. It'd keep the guy from running up on him, but it would also steer him well past the direct route to Atkins' property, eating up more time.

He'd just have to move faster.

He picked up the pace, shoving damp hair back from his forehead, and zigzagged around trees, wrestled his way through the undergrowth, the heat and humidity stealing what little strength he had left.

When the woods opened to a clearing near the creek, Paul stopped for a second to catch his breath. He scanned the area, trying to decide at what point to cut back to the east, and spotted tire tracks. Deep, wide tread running a line through the rain-soaked mud that spilled off the shallow end of the creek. An ATV. It would explain how Atkins and his partner had managed to haul an unconscious man this far into the woods, over the rugged terrain. They'd come up to the backside of the cabin where the growth didn't run as thick, had lugged Paul maybe thirty yards at best.

And if he remembered right...

His gaze followed the tire tracks, to where they dipped down into the shallow end of the water and came back up on the other side. Yeah. An old logging road. It would lead him where he needed to go, maybe shave off some time.

Boots bogging down in the mud, Paul slid to the edge of the creek and splashed through to the opposite bank. Then hit the old loggers' road at a rapid gait.

He heard the frenzied buzzing of flies before he saw them. Caught the stench before he glimpsed the vehicle abandoned among the trees.

Aw... Christ.

Heart pounding, Paul eased up to the van, forced himself to open the door.

Blood. Everywhere. Lifeless eyes stared up at him.

He jerked back, put a fist to his mouth. And gagged.

CHAPTER 30

H ER MOTHER. DEAD. SHE'D KNOWN all along that it was possible, hadn't she? But as the torn pieces of photograph had fluttered to the ground, some small part of Allison had felt it.

Did you ever wonder about me?

No chance of asking that now.

There'd be no excuses, no explanations. No apologies.

A sigh trembled out of her, but even with the loss like a gnawing ache in her chest, the tears wouldn't come. Just a face in a photograph, Allison thought with another sigh, she hardly remembered the woman. Still, there was a hollow place inside her now.

Josh touched her shoulder, and she jumped. He'd been gone just seconds before. Vanished again. Why did he keep doing that—sifting in and out? Coming and going like a restless wind.

She shifted on the hard ground as he lowered himself next to her, felt the dog's cold, wet nose nudge her hand, and thought, *How odd.*

Ghosts that were... corporeal.

They were here for a reason. Unfinished business. It was what kept a spirit earthbound.

Why, then, had her mother moved on, leaving things unresolved?

Allison's gaze wandered over to the faint blue light, to the frail little girl who sat on the ground across from them, spindly legs tucked under her. She closed her eyes for a moment as the words, clipped, and bitter, came back to her: *I was trying to protect you.*

Protect me. From what, Dad? My sister? My own mother? The truth?

On a slow breath, Allison opened her eyes. What *was* the truth? She had only a glimpse of it. "How did it happen, Katie? How did Mother die?"

There was a moment—just a heartbeat as Katie glanced into the blackness behind her—when Allison caught the distant, plopping echo of what sounded like water dripping onto rock. She focused to see if she could tell what direction it had come from.

There was nothing now but stillness.

"After she argued with your daddy, Mama told me we were going away for a while. We came here, to this town, with her friend, Helen, and a man." A frown darkened Katie's face. "We didn't like that man. He was mean."

She paused, green eyes fixed in a solemn gaze on Allison. "Do you remember?"

"No. No, I—why would I?"

Beside her, Josh stirred. The dog lifted its head from his lap and whimpered. Picking at the tear in her blouse, Katie stared down at the deep cuts on her legs, and an image began forming in Allison's head—dark eyes sliding up to a rearview mirror, narrowing onto the woman and two small girls in the backseat.

Her heart fluttered in her throat. She knew those eyes, the same cold, bottomless black pools she had gazed into moments before learning that Steve...

"It was him. The man who's keeping me here." Allison looked at Katie for confirmation and got a nod. She suddenly realized that her mother had never left her behind. Confusion swept through her, trailed by anger at her dad, who, for a lifetime, had kept the truth secreted away from her.

The truth. Did she really want to hear it?

Allison pulled herself up and began to pace, ignoring the dull jabs of protest in her swollen ankle. She stopped, turned. "Tell me everything. I have to know."

Katie glanced toward the tunnel. The dog cocked its head, tail swishing against the ground. Josh had disappeared again. "We stayed at another man's house with Mama's friend, Helen, and the bad man." *Bad man.* The chill that shuddered through Allison nipped at her bones. "Mama... didn't want your daddy to find us."

No hotels then, or any form of transportation that could be traced. Had their mother been that terrified of Allison's dad? Or had her leaving been just a willful act of spite?

Either way, Beverly Kincaid had packed up her two small daughters and hopped into a car with a monster behind the wheel.

She'd been upset, Allison told herself, distracted. She hadn't noticed the evil lurking in those dark eyes, couldn't have known.

"Mama told us not to wander out of the yard but..." Katie shrugged. "I was bored. I... snuck into the woods, and followed the creek. There was a big house." She smiled now. "The girl who lived there let me play with her dolls.

"I went back the next day. Mama still didn't know, so I thought I'd go one more time. That's when—"

"I followed you," Allison remembered as she got a flash of tall trees with sun-dappled leaves, the bank of forest floor sloping down to a lazy flow of water that moved in a slow spiral over rocks.

Then the scene was playing out in her head, blurred around the edges, but there. Peeking through the bushes... The big house with the pretty, covered porch.

The Treadwell's house.

My house.

Her pulse kicked with the connection. And there was a little girl, she remembered now. On the swing, her long, blonde ponytail flying behind her as her legs swung forward, pushing her higher into the air.

Two boys tossing a baseball. Paul and Bill Treadwell, she thought, and shivered.

"Mama came after us." Katie worried with the tear in her blouse again. "She was really mad."

Yes. Allison could almost feel the fingers gripping her elbow, marching her back through the woods. The voice—a woman's—scolding. Then Allison's foot slid out from under her, and she went tumbling, tumbling, rocks and branches poking her, scraping her skin. A sharp pain in her shoulder. Then her head slammed against something hard and...

She raised a hand to the base of her skull, brushed her fingers over the long, narrow scar there.

Katie sighed. "You wouldn't wake up."

Humidity rolled through the woods like fog—heavy and steamy. Shirt sticking to his skin, Ray kept up the brisk pace behind Cliff and brushed the sweat back from his eyes. Then stopped dead in his tracks.

"Hold up a minute."

Cliff turned, slanted a look around. "What is it?"

"Thought I saw something." Ray zeroed his focus in on the thick patch of brambles beneath the grove of oaks to their right. "Over there."

Cliff's hand went to his gun as he scanned the underbrush. "I don't see anything."

Neither did Ray. Now. But off and on, just after they'd started down this trail, he'd gotten the kind of crawling-under-the-skin sensation that told him someone had their eyes on him.

He let loose with a silent oath at Toni and her niece, at himself. All the crazy talk about ghosts had him seeing things where there was nothing to see. "Probably just a deer. Let's keep moving."

They trudged through the brush—thicker along the trail than what they'd hoped for—dodging thorny bushes while the mosquitoes dove like mad bombers for Ray's skin.

Bastards were having a picnic.

He swatted one off his arm, checked his watch. "How much longer, you figure?"

Slapping one of the little bloodsuckers off his neck, Cliff glanced over his shoulder. "Fifteen, maybe twenty minutes."

That long. "Let's try for ten."

"You got it." Cliff huffed out a breath to put more effort into his stride, and when they picked up the pace, Ray could have sworn that he heard Jenna's voice in his head telling him to hurry.

Paul had been right, about some things anyway.

To take the weight off her ankle, Allison leaned against the wall of hard-packed earth and shifted as the exposed rock dug into her shoulder. With a tiny gust of a sigh, the dog sprawled onto the ground and looked up at her.

"Poor little guy," she whispered, and wondered if the animal was even aware that it had died.

Death, she had realized, wasn't the end-all. Far from it.

Allison brought a hand to her mouth and coughed. The ragged rattle that came from deep in her lungs where the damp chill had settled left a small fire in her chest. On a wheezing breath, she gazed into the blackness beyond the soft blue light that pulsed in a slow, rhythmic beat around her sister. Then considered, again, what Katie had told her.

Jack Kincaid wasn't the kind of man to backtrack. "Forgive and forget" was nothing but a tired, old cliché. Knowing that, Allison understood now the years of bitterness, could see why he'd held his wife responsible for the accident that had put their daughter into a coma.

Had it been sheer carelessness on her mother's part, or just bad choices?

Maybe some of both. Allison's dad would have seen it that way.

So he'd moved her to a hospital in Nashville where she'd eventually come to with her memory scrambled.

What she just couldn't wrap her brain around was why her mother had stayed behind.

"Your daddy was upset. Mama didn't want to go back to Nashville with him. She said we'd take a plane back to your house."

Startled, Allison searched those wide, green eyes. Either she had worn the question all over her face, or Katie had just read her mind.

Brows furrowed, Katie went over and scooped up the dog, cuddled the poor little thing. "It was getting late, and it was storming. Mama's friend, Helen, promised to take us to the airport."

But Helen had driven into the next town for something, Katie told Allison, and with the storm getting worse, didn't want to risk the dark and winding roads through the mountains.

There was another car, but it was old, not dependable.

They were stuck, Allison thought. There wouldn't have been a taxi service back then. That luxury had only recently come to Dawson Mills.

"Helen was supposed to be back the next morning. That's what they told us."

Allison slanted a sharp look at her sister. "They. Who are 'they'?"

Katie put the dog down when it squirmed in her arms, and the animal took off like a shot, into the blackness. "The bad man and..." She frowned again. "The man we were staying with. He was mean, too. That night, after Mama had gone to bed, I went downstairs to get a drink of water. I heard them talking in the kitchen."

Them. Allison wanted specifics—names—but there was something in the way her sister's gaze kept sweeping over the darkness behind her that told her just to wait, listen. So she kept quiet.

What had fed the evil for decades suddenly began to make a sad, sick kind of sense.

Diamonds, loose stones worth a fortune. Tucked away in plain sight, into one of those small unassuming statues of Liberty purchased by tourists.

The bastard who had drugged her and then penned her, like an animal, in this godforsaken place, who had murdered her brother, had killed two men in Nashville for those shiny stones.

A sigh shuddered out of her. She didn't need to hear the rest of it to piece together what had happened.

"I woke Mama up, told her what I'd heard. The next morning, when they were still sleeping, we found the statue in the attic."

A shadow moved across that young face. They couldn't get to the car keys without waking them up, and the phones were down because of the storm.

Trapped, scared. Desperate.

"Mama took the statue. The rain had stopped, and we went next door, to Mr. Treadwell's house."

Next door. Allison's pulse spiked. "Katie, who were you staying with?"

Brooding eyes looked up at her. "Jared Atkins."

Atkins. The name was like poison.

"Everyone had gone to church, except Mrs. Treadwell. She was… sick, I guess. She didn't have a car, and their phone wasn't working because of all the rain. Most of the other neighbors were at church. Mama was afraid to stay away much longer. She didn't want them to wake up and find us gone."

The awful sinking sensation that began in Allison's chest trickled down to her stomach and churned there. Her mother had assumed the diamonds, kept hidden, would guarantee their safety. It was a risk that had turned deadly.

She drew a quiet breath, felt the slow burn rise from her lungs again. "Mother gave the statue to Mrs. Treadwell."

Tears shimmered in Katie's eyes as her small head dipped in a nod. "Mama told me to stay with Mrs. Treadwell, but I was scared."

Knowing what came next, because, at that age, she probably

would have done the same, Allison made a conscious effort to soften her voice. "You snuck out of the house, followed her."

"I—I was hiding in the bushes, and I saw him—Jared Atkins." Katie brushed back a tear. "He killed Mama. In the woods, down by the creek."

Rage shot through Allison like liquid fire. She shoved away from the rough rock, fists clenched at her sides.

"I... couldn't scream." Another tear slid down Katie's cheek. "I couldn't move."

Paralyzed. Shock, and fear, could clamp down with a death grip, numbing the senses, the brain. Nothing left but the jerky thud of a heartbeat in your ears.

Allison shifted her gaze along the sad, scratched face. Such a brave little thing.

"The other man—the bad man who brought us here—came out of the woods, then. Yelling. Jared picked up a big rock and hit him"—Katie raised her hand to the side of her head—"here. I thought he killed him, too, but...

"I stayed in the woods, behind the bushes, for a long time, until the rain started again. Jared came back." Katie's image went translucent as it rippled in a shudder. "Mama screamed at me. In my head. She told me to run."

God. Oh God.

"He came after me." Katie's breath hitched on a sob. "He pushed my head under water. I couldn't breathe." Her gaze flicked over to the dim light that had popped on behind Allison. Josh and his dog were back. "Then you and Scooter were there. I'm sorry, Josh."

His smile was slow, solemn. "It wasn't your fault. We wanted to help you."

With a short bark, the dog pawed at one of the legs of Josh's worn overalls. "You're right, Scooter. I think it's time now."

Allison frowned. "Time—for what?"

He waited for Katie's nod. "We need to show you something."

CHAPTER 31

H E REACHED THE EDGE OF the woods and stopped, took a minute to get his wind and swiped the sweat off his face. The pain in his head was like pitchforks, stabbing fast and furious.

There'd been no warning this time, no crawling ache at the back of his skull. Just a blinding bolt of agony right to the head.

No damned wonder he couldn't think straight.

Hand moving to the gun in his waistband, he peered through a gap in the trees, and swore. What was he doing out here?

His gaze slid over the open field, lingered on the outbuildings before shifting to the barn.

Oh. Yeah. The girl. He had to get to the girl.

If Bradford hadn't beat him to it.

He swatted at the mosquito buzzing around his face and scowled. He had screwed up there, thinking Bradford might be useful to him.

Should have known better.

A rustling in the brush had him whipping his head around just as a rabbit darted past him. He sucked in a sharp breath when the vicious stab to his temple made the world tilt. With or without the girl, getting his hands on what belonged to him would require some maneuvering now. The place next door was still crawling with cops.

Another quick scan and he made a dash for the back of the barn. He yanked the small window open, cursing when he lost his balance going through and landed on his ass.

He pulled himself up, still swearing. He should be on a beach somewhere in Mexico with his toes buried in white sand, looking out at miles of blue water while he knocked back a cold one. Living fat off the good life. But the stupid fuck-up had lost his temper, murdered the girl and her mother before—

Wait a minute. That wasn't right.

Eyeing the fallen boards still scattered over the floor, he grinned. The girl was down in the hole, right where he'd left her.

He sidestepped the clutter, then dropped to his knees, started shoving the boards back. Sneaky piece of shit had lied about the girl.

The mother was a different matter.

On a grunt, he flung the last board to the side and started down the makeshift ladder. With his own eyes, he'd seen the life thrust out of the woman, had heard her neck snap like a twig.

It had pissed him off. Then.

Swallowed by the darkness, the dog was somewhere up ahead. An occasional bark—Scooter's way, Allison supposed, of telling them to speed things up—echoed back to them as she followed Josh and Katie through the narrow tunnel. She had to strain to see. The glow coming off the two small souls in front of her was just a stingy flicker now.

Allison gripped the flashlight tighter and shivered as they crossed through another icy pocket of bone-chilling dampness. They hadn't told her what they were taking her to see, hadn't needed to. She knew what was waiting for them.

She was in no hurry to get there.

Moments later a sound reached her ears—the faint, slow plop of water onto rock. Just ahead, dull, gray light winked, drawing her eye upward to the narrow opening where a sliver of—*yes!*—cloudy day broke through.

"Here," Josh said. The word seemed to float through the air, almost extinguished before it reached her.

Allison pulled her focus over to him, then to Katie, and on a hard swallow, looked down to where the dog sat shaking and whimpering. Next to the bones.

Hollow eye sockets stared up at her. She jerked her gaze away, but the images stayed with her, the same way bright spots tended to float and linger in the vision after staring into the sun. A trio of skulls, one adult, two children, teeth bared in a macabre grin.

Josh rested his hand on her arm, the touch weightless, like a feather. Allison took a quick, bracing breath, forced herself to look down again. Nausea rolled deep in her belly. The skeleton of a small canine and the pile of human bones... God. Their bodies had been tossed, one on top of the other, like useless waste in a landfill.

Even under the waning light, it wasn't hard to miss the marks on those bones, where small sharp teeth had gnawed.

She had to turn away. "I—I can't."

"Allison." Josh reached for her hand to pull her back. This time she felt only a vague, chilly draft brush over her skin. "You have to tell them where to find us."

"Tell *who,* Josh?" Allison choked back a sob as she spun around to face him. Her gaze flicked up to the strip of dull light that had managed to eke through the only hole left to the outside world when the tunnel had collapsed.

It would have been a way out. Once.

"I'm going to die down here."

"No." He shook his head, the shaggy ends of his hair lifting as though stirred by a breeze. "The sheriff—he's coming for you."

Her heart skipped, and then the reason for Josh's sporadic disappearances dawned on her.

Confused, Allison frowned. She'd spoken to Ray McAllister just once, in the café with Toni. The sheriff didn't seem the type to believe his eyes when it came to anything otherworldly.

Toni, though, would keep her mind and senses open.

Had Josh somehow managed to communicate with her?

Allison told herself it didn't really matter how the sheriff had come by his information. The point was that someone who could help her out of this nightmare knew where to find her.

Katie never had that chance.

She looked over at the forlorn little girl with the scratched face, legs marred with cuts. Her sister. The poor child had been lost for so long. And Josh...

Allison glanced down at the bones, sighed. Decades, they had waited decades for someone to find them.

As if it had read her thoughts, the dog whimpered, a lonely whine to remind her that he had stayed behind as well. She managed a faint smile. "Yes, you're a good boy."

They deserved resolution. Peace. Allison hoped she would at least be able to give them that. She desperately wanted to believe that her mother had managed to find the same, although she couldn't imagine how.

"Mother's death wasn't your fault," Allison said softly to her sister. "She couldn't have known what would happen, but she chose to come here. Just as she chose to take the statue and hide it away."

Katie stared down at the ground as she poked it with the toe of her sneaker.

"We don't always make the right decisions. Sometimes..." Allison's breath hitched. The grief was fresh again. Raw. A quick, burning stab to the heart as the bitter memory came into sharp focus. Icy roads, jammed interstates. She had begged Ken not to go into the office. He'd cupped her chin in his hand and kissed her, told her he'd be back before she knew it. "Sometimes... it's hard to know what to do."

She brushed back the tears blurring her vision. "You see that now, don't you?"

The smile was slow, but by the time Katie looked up, it had

reached her eyes. She nodded, and Josh took her hand. The dim glow that surrounded their two small souls faded to just a bare whisper of light.

"We've been here a long time." Josh smiled when Scooter padded over to him. "I think we're ready to go now."

Go. Allison had barely begun to know her sister. "Wait—I—"

"Don't let him find you here"—Katie nodded toward the bones—"with us."

Him. The monster. Allison wanted to look the stone-hearted killer in the eye, wanted him to know that she *knew*—everything.

"Who is he, Katie? Do you remember his name?"

For one sparse second, the light around them flashed brighter. In that instant, Allison saw the struggle cross her sister's face. Then the release.

"Neil," Katie whispered, her green eyes glancing past Allison. "He's coming."

Their images flickered, like a bulb just before burning out, and they were gone.

CHAPTER 32

Pulse pounding, Allison scurried down the narrow tunnel as the beam from her flashlight cut a jerky path through the maze of angles and curves. She bit back the pain spiking through her swollen ankle, and bolted through the opening where she had snipped the barbed wire. Josh had told her the sheriff was coming. She prayed—had to believe—that he would get to her before—

The blow came from nowhere, striking the side of her face. She cried out as her head jerked back. The flashlight flew from her grip, spinning light over shadows and rock in a dizzying strobe.

A hand grabbed a fistful of her hair, yanked with such force she thought her neck would shatter. Then the light popped on, a bright, ugly circle of it blaring in her eyes.

"*Bitch.*" He spat the word, lowered the flashlight just enough for her to get a good look at the face of the monster that intended to kill her. Allison pressed her hand to her throbbing jaw and glared back at him, memorizing the cold, cruel curve of his mouth, the dark, soulless eyes. If she ever got the chance to have a future, she would remember what evil looked like. And she would recognize it.

But if she were going to die, right here and now, damned if she'd give him the satisfaction of seeing fear in her eyes.

On a hard swallow to squelch the whimper that clawed up her throat, she forced her gaze to hold steady on his. "Hello, Neil."

The thin slice-of-a-smile he wore turned sly. "You remembered." He released his grip on her, and glanced over to where her flashlight had landed as she rubbed the back of her neck. His gaze zipped to the stretch of darkness behind the wire that had failed to cage her in.

He scowled. "Hand over the cutters."

Any hope she'd had of jabbing the pointed tips into the first vulnerable spot of flesh she could reach plummeted. With an inward sigh, Allison shoved her hand into the pocket of her capris and yanked out the wire cutters.

He snatched the tool from her, flung it to the ground. "What were you doing down there?"

She glanced at the gun tucked in his waistband, wobbled when she saw the sheathed knife that rested against his hip, and gave him a stingy portion of the truth. "Looking for a way out."

Before her mind could register that he had moved, he grabbed her arm. She jerked free, positioning her body to draw his eye away from the direction he had come, and in an effort to distract him, blurted out the first thing that popped into her head. "What happened to Helen?"

In the glow of his flashlight, darkness snaked across his face. He raised his free hand to his temple, massaged. Those brutal eyes went glassy. "Man traveling with a couple of women, two kids—family man. No flags there." His focus whipped back to her. "More trouble than it was worth."

He hadn't answered her question, but had at least confirmed her suspicions. All of them—Katie, Allison herself, their mother, probably Helen as well—had been nothing more than convenient camouflage. Once he had managed to trade the diamonds for cash, their lives wouldn't have been worth much.

Her accident had been a blessing in disguise. It had saved her life.

Hoping to buy enough time for the sheriff, Allison just listened as he stared past her, lost in the memory.

For a share of what the diamonds would bring, Jared had kept his mouth shut and given Neil a place to hole up. It was perfect. An isolated area away from nosy onlookers with big ears and prying eyes.

Then it all went to hell.

"You and that stupid sister of yours had to go traipsing into the woods." Under his breath, he muttered something unintelligible about the accident.

"All the damned attention." His eyes went to slits. "Your daddy was headed here even before your mama picked up the phone."

Yes, her dad would have started after them as soon as the private investigator he'd hired had tracked them to this area. If only he'd been able to locate them sooner. A day, just one short day might have made the difference.

A sigh shuddered out from the depths of her soul. So much death. Her mother, a half-sister she had never known. Josh and his little dog, Scooter. And Steve. God... Steve.

For what? A handful of shiny stones.

Then there was Helen, along with the men he had murdered to get to those diamonds. Allison had never known them, but that didn't make their lives any less important.

She knew there was a strong chance that Paul and Stan were on the long list of victims but just couldn't accept the reality of it.

"Your mama took advantage of all the confusion, got greedy. Helped herself to what didn't belong to her."

Greedy. No, that wasn't right. But Allison supposed the whys of it really didn't matter.

"Jared—stupid son of a bitch—killed her. She was no good to us dead." He brought a hand to his temple again, frowned. "He damned near put an end to me, busting me upside the head with that rock. When I came to, you—and your mama's body—were gone. Jared swore you were dead."

His dark gaze shot back to her. "How'd you get out of those woods? Who helped you?"

313

It took a second to click for her, but when it did, things began to make a bit more sense.

He thinks I'm Katie.

Her mind raced but just couldn't manufacture on the spot a convincing lie. All she could do was try steering his focus in another direction, and hope like hell it worked. "You must have been concerned about my sister, wondered how much she knew, what she would say once she came out of the coma."

The shift was subtle, but there. In his eyes. Allison breathed an inward sigh of relief. He grinned, a wicked flash of teeth. "Situation took care of itself, didn't it? Girl died before she made it back to Nashville."

Of course. True to his word, Allison's dad had tried to protect her. She imagined he'd made a sizable donation to the hospital here, to ensure the right information about his daughter found its way to curious ears.

He must have known about the murders in Nashville, the diamonds. Had he contacted the police?

What had possessed him to leave his wife and Katie behind?

While she puzzled through it, Neil studied her with cold calculation. "We figured the statue was buried somewhere near the spot where your idiot sister had her little accident. Never found it. Few days back, when I watched you run into the woods—" He scowled. "Damned thing was right next door the entire time, right under my nose."

So she hadn't imagined the prickling unease she'd felt as she'd jogged into the woods.

Instinct. We all have it.

The same perception was telling her now that he wouldn't kill her just yet. He still needed her. Allison wondered if the same held true for Jared Atkins. Probably not.

She took a breath to steady, kept her voice even. "I know where the statue is. You want it. I want information."

The sly smile was back. "I'm listening."

"The man you killed—Steve Kincaid—what did you do with his body?" Allison fisted her hands to control the sudden burst of shaking inside. "And—Paul Bradford, and the man who was with me the night you took me. Are they still alive?"

Those black eyes sparked. In a heartbeat, she was staring into the barrel of his gun.

"Chit-chat's over."

The barn door inched open. Atkins' partner stuck his head out. Paul ducked back into the woods and swore.

Allison.

He'd blown it, had made it probably a few hundred yards after cutting back to the east when his damned knees had buckled. His brain had just shut down. He'd come to, face in the dirt. The first thought that had slammed through him was that he'd never, *never* get to her in time.

His hands balled into fists as the bastard half dragged Allison from the barn, the barrel of a gun pressed to her head. She was limping, badly. The bruises on her jaw and cheek were an angry purple. Her bottom lip, swollen to twice its normal size, had a thin, crusted gash at one corner.

But it was her eyes—blind with fear—that grabbed his heart and shoved it into his throat.

The sickening image of what he'd found back near the old logging road flashed through his head.

Her brother.

Paul felt the muscles in his chest convulse. He couldn't let her end up like that.

Gaze skimming the field, he calculated the open distance between the nearest outbuilding and the edge of the trees. Considered the unknown factor—Atkins.

Where are you, old man?

Movement flashed in the corner of his eye—one of the sheriff's men, just at the back of the house. He followed the deputy's line of sight, homed in on Ray McAllister and Cliff easing around the side of the barn, their guns drawn. They were maybe ten yards from the tree line.

Close enough. Paul glanced back at Atkins' partner, then risked a slight move. Cliff picked up on it and slanted his boss a look, gave a short jerk of his head in Paul's direction.

McAllister froze, scanned the woods. The steely gaze that latched onto Paul warned him to stay put.

In that split second as Paul nodded, Allison stiffened, then, before realizing her mistake, turned her head back toward the barn just a fraction of an inch.

Atkins' partner whirled around, spinning her with him. "I wouldn't come any closer."

The sheriff and Cliff both stopped in their tracks. At the corner of the house, McAllister's deputy froze. Every muscle in Paul's body locked up.

"No one here has to get hurt," McAllister said. "Drop the gun. Let the girl go."

A bark of a laugh echoed back to Paul through the humid air. The hair on the back of his neck bristled. He'd heard that laugh before—the clipped snarl of a rabid dog—but couldn't place it.

Atkins' partner smirked. "I got a better idea. Both of you— back off." He pressed the gun barrel harder against Allison's head, ignoring her muted cry. And grinned. "Be one hell of a mess."

Her hand, riddled with scratches, began inching toward the sheathed knife. Paul felt his heart stop.

Fuck.

He bolted from the woods. McAllister yelled, *"Goddammit, Bradford—no!"*

Allison swiveled toward Paul and jerked free. Atkins' partner rolled to the ground; pulled the trigger. Rage roared from Paul, drowning in the deafening boom as Allison choked out a gurgled scream. Scarlet bloomed on her blouse. She crumpled. Then it was all a blur of movement—the gun swung away from her, aimed at Paul. McAllister and Cliff, the deputy, rushed forward. More shots fired.

The force of the bullet wheeled Paul around. A fire blazed in his chest, his mind went numb.

Then—nothing.

CHAPTER 33

S HE'D BEEN LUCKY. THAT'S WHAT the doctors had told her. The
bullet had gone through without doing any major damage.

Her bruises were almost gone, and the gash on her lip had
healed, but the wound would leave a scar. A reminder.

Good. She didn't want the memory to fade. Ever.

Allison leaned against the rail on her back porch, a slight breeze
lifting the ends of her hair. She watched a hawk floating in lazy
circles above the treetops. For a moment, she imagined herself soar-
ing over those trees, into the blue, blue sky, the wind against her
face as she rose higher, until everything below was just a blur of
color and texture.

An escape, she mused. Something that hadn't worked before,
and wouldn't now.

Still, she'd considered going back to Nashville. But there was
nothing for her within that grid of city lights, the flurry of activity.
Not anymore.

A corner of her mouth lifted when a squirrel scampered down
from a tree and darted across the lawn. Long before she'd remembered the connection, she had felt it, hadn't she? This town, the
house, her past—it all formed a small intricate circle.

A circle she had to step away from now. At least as far as this
house was concerned.

Behind her, the bustling sound of movers and packers wafted
out through the open kitchen door. It hadn't taken Mae Davis long

to find a buyer for the house. One of the subcontractors who would be working on the new development project north of town was relocating his family here. They had two small children and one on the way.

Soon the huge, vacant space would hum with laughter and energy. It was exactly what this house needed.

A cleansing, she supposed.

The screen door behind her creaked. She turned, and winced from the jarring pain in her side. Another reminder. She would be sore for quite some time.

Paul walked up to her, blue eyes locked onto hers. Careful to keep his right arm immobile in the sling, he lifted his free hand, brushed a stray curl away from her face. "Are you all right?"

Allison nodded. "Just sore. You?"

"I'll mend."

She could see that happening already. There was bulk beneath his denim shirt—the bandages, swelling—but a dose of healthy color had finally begun to replace the deathly pallor left by the loss of blood and the surgery on his shoulder.

He had risked his life to get her away from that monster.

"Paul, I—"

"Shhh." He lowered his forehead to hers, closed his eyes for a moment. Then his mouth was on hers, warm and gentle.

With an inward sigh, Allison let herself sink into the kiss. It was what she needed. *He* was what she needed.

There was no ugly twinge of betrayal, she realized as the rightness of it settled through her. Ken had loved her. He would want her to be happy.

His lips still like a warm, soft comfort against hers, Paul murmured, "I thought I'd lost you." He kissed her again, deeper.

He reluctantly eased back when the screen door gave another creak. Toni stuck her head out and grinned. "Guess my timing could have been better but—" Arms loaded with bags and juggling go-cups, she maneuvered out onto the porch. "I brought food."

She set everything on the table angled between two wicker chairs and motioned for Allison to sit. "You left this morning without having breakfast. Figured you could use something to eat."

"Thanks." Allison lowered herself into a chair one cautious inch at a time, trying not to make any sudden moves that would send another shock of pain through her side. She *was* hungry, she realized, and chose a club sandwich from one of the bags. Biting in, Allison thanked the fates—again—for putting Toni in her path. After leaving the hospital, she had taken Toni up on her offer to stay at the condo. Two women and a teenage girl were a bit of a strain on the compact space, but the close company had been a balm to her soul.

Last week Toni had put the condo on the market. Now, the three of them were moving into the pretty, four-bedroom house in town that her dad had inherited from his mother. The couple who had leased the house had relocated to Maryland just a few weeks back.

Timing, or fate, Allison wondered, picturing the spacious workshop in the back that Paul's crew would transform into a studio for her sculpting.

In little more than a week, Jenna would be going back home, getting ready to start school. That would leave just the two women, and Allison's big happy dog.

Toni took a chair, then plucked a burger and fries from the other bag, gestured to Paul. "You want?"

"Maybe later. You two go ahead." He settled onto the steps, looked out to the edge of the woods.

Handing Allison one of the go-cups and a straw, Toni sipped from her own cup. "Before I forget, Stan says hi. He told me to tell you not to worry about Jack. They're at the house now, with Jenna. Waiting on the movers." She glanced at her watch. "And since we managed to cram everything I own into one truck, they shouldn't have to wait long."

Allison nodded. She didn't know what she would have done without Stan. He'd stepped up, taken charge of her big dog, told her that Jack was welcome to stay with him for as long as she needed.

Sipping iced tea through the straw, her gaze wandered out to where the sun shone bright on a patch of Black-eyed Susans. The truth was she wouldn't have made it through this without any of them. Like links in a chain, she thought. Together they'd been strong enough to pull her out of the nightmare.

She hadn't been able to talk much about what had happened. She'd needed time to heal, physically. Then she'd had to take a long, slow look inside herself, sort through it all.

Afterward, she'd simply needed time *not* to think.

For the last couple of days, though, in her dreams, she'd found herself trapped under the ground in a frantic race down one tunnel and then the next, desperately trying to claw her way through earth and rock and rubble.

The one faint sliver of dull light was always beyond her reach.

With a shudder, she set her sandwich aside. Without Jenna's help, the sheriff would never have known where to look for her. That, Allison thought, along with Josh doing what he could to keep the sheriff focused on the path. Ray McAllister had admitted having the odd sensation of someone—or something—traveling alongside them through the brush. Always just out of eyesight.

A ghost guide. Although he'd never believe it.

Something that had been nagging at her for a while now chose this exact moment to jump from the shadowy corner of her mind, forcing her to examine it. Allison glanced over at Toni. "I understand why Bobbie Jean kept silent after Mother and Katie disappeared, but…"

She let it trail off there. A phone call, her dad had told her. The catalyst that had spawned decades of silence. It had started with the small piece of paper her mother had shoved into Mrs. Treadwell's hand, along with the statue.

Jack Kincaid's private number.

If anything happens, tell him… I'm sorry.

Allison's dad hadn't made the connection to the robbery and murders in Nashville until he'd spoken to Bobbie Jean. By then it had been too late for Katie and her mother. To keep his daughter safe, Jack Kincaid had launched his own investigation. Money and political connections had gone a long way. But not far enough.

In his heart, Allison's dad had known his wife and her small daughter were gone. Still, he'd kept up the search, hoping.

After a while, he'd moved on with his life.

What more could I have done? He had stared past Allison, eyes clouded with sorrow and regret, into a distant memory.

So the statue had remained hidden, tucked away in a narrow, rocky passage that wound beneath the earth.

Jack Kincaid had let the matter rest.

Bobbie Jean had never told a soul.

Allison sighed. "After a while, though, I would think that she would have gone to the police."

Toni shot them a quick look before dropping the equivalent of a bomb. "Your mother wasn't the only one who was afraid of Brady. He assaulted Bobbie Jean—sexually—shortly before she was married."

Allison took a second to absorb that. Revulsion churned in her belly. "Neil Brady… Bill Treadwell's biological father."

"I know it sucks," Toni admitted, "but, yeah."

Paul muttered, "Damn."

"Bobbie Jean was ashamed, scared to death, given the sort of man Brady was," Toni said.

Was. Past tense. Gleeful fury soared through Allison without shame as the scene flashed through her head—the cold, cruel face and black, empty eyes, the shudder of his last breath after the bullet struck.

God's own justice.

"I'm not sure whether the husband—Jay—ever figured it out," Toni added, "but I'd be willing to bet that Bill doesn't have a clue."

"He doesn't," Paul said quickly. "He would have told me."

Toni tipped her head in a slow acknowledgement. "Probably. And if it hadn't been for the diary, that particular secret would've stayed buried." She paused. "Can't say as I know what good will come of it from Bill's end."

Paul frowned. "At this point, I don't see any reason why he has to find out."

"My thoughts," Toni agreed. "We take the positive from it and go on."

Yes, the secrets Bobbie Jean had poured onto those pages had been a roadmap, Allison knew now. One that was meant for her.

She pulled herself up from the chair, walked over to the railing, and looked out onto the vast slope of land, to the shadowed woods beyond. "Without the diary, I don't know whether Jenna would have been able to..."

Find me...

Sadness stoked the small ache in her heart. It had been her sister's voice she'd heard that bright, sunny day, when she'd sat on the window seat in her studio. Just as she'd stopped sketching the jagged lines of the old oak tree, to brush a finger over the odd blank spot she'd left in the center of the trunk.

Paul got up and came over to her, covered Allison's hand with his, a gentle touch where the scratches from her assault on the barbed wire were still tender.

"It was a stroke of luck," Toni said as she rose to join them, "that your brother and his friend found the diary."

"No... Not luck." Raw emotion tumbled through Allison as

Paul eased his arm around her shoulders, drew her in. She leaned into the comfort of his strength.

Lowering her eyes, Toni inhaled, long, and slow. "I don't think I'll ever get past feeling responsible for what happened to Steve."

"Don't—" Allison began but couldn't finish. Her dad had looked down on his son lying cold and motionless on a steel table. A son who had held a world of promise, who had gone for his dream at full throttle, and damn the consequences. Music. Steve had always loved his music.

Her dad had cried when he'd told her.

They buried Steve in the family cemetery, next to their dad's parents. Just a body, Allison kept telling herself. A shell. She knew that, but it didn't make the loss any easier to bear.

She brushed back the tears blurring her vision. One of the men Paul had commandeered from his construction crew stuck his head out the door. "We're ready when you are."

Paul nodded. He drew Allison closer, gave her a gentle squeeze. "Let's get out of here."

CHAPTER 34

IT WAS AN ODD SORT of déjà vu, unpacking her personal things, putting clothes away in the closet and dresser drawers. Different, though, Allison thought as she finished with the small suitcase and set it aside. Tammy wasn't here, brushing her hand over the dark green marble that framed the fireplace. There was no fireplace. And Steve wouldn't be opening the door any second now to poke his head in and tell them to come up to the attic.

Think we found something.

The aching sadness was a weight on her chest that threatened to smother her.

Allison opened the window to let in some fresh air. Laughter, and the enthusiastic bark of her big happy dog, echoed in the still afternoon. Toni's niece tossed a tennis ball, laughed again as Jack scrambled across the lawn after it.

Life's subtle affirmation, she supposed, that it just kept moving on.

"Hey."

Allison whipped around and winced from the prick of pain in her side.

"Sorry—sorry. Didn't mean to startle you." Toni stepped up to her. "You okay?"

"I'm fine. Just a twinge."

"Had a few of those myself the last couple of days." Toni huffed out a breath. "It's nice having the bedrooms on the second floor, but I've been up and down the stairs so many times, I think my legs are starting to rebel."

She offered Allison the bottle of cold water she'd brought up. "Thought maybe you could use this."

"Thanks." Allison twisted the cap off and drank, aware of sharp, brown eyes homing in on her.

"You look a little pale. Why don't you take a break?"

Allison glanced over at the comfy chair one of Paul's men had placed in the corner for her. She was tempted to sink down into it, just for a while. But unpacking her personal items had somehow managed to whittle away the better part of two days.

More work than what she'd bargained for.

She wanted this last part of the move over and done.

"I'm fine. Really," she insisted when Toni arched a brow. "How are they coming with the rest of the furniture?"

"Well, since you obviously have a stubborn streak—which I can relate to, believe me—I'll answer that. It's done. Paul's still downstairs, but Stan and the rest of the crew just left. And I have to say it—my leather sofa looks great in the fourth bedroom."

Allison nodded. It had been a trick figuring out how to arrange two households worth of furniture into one. They'd finally opted to use the large bedroom as a combination office/study.

"I need to tell you…" Toni moved closer to the window, looked down at her niece and Jack. "I just spoke to Kara."

Her dad's assistant, the woman who'd been helping Toni try to locate Josh's parents. Allison drew a small breath. "And?"

"Took some doing, but we found the mother. His father passed away several years back. She remarried, so—different last name."

An article in the archives, Toni told her, had eventually led them to Josh's mom. "A group of kids, along with some of their parents, went camping during the summer—county just north of here. One of the boys—Josh—ran off after his dog and—"

"Got lost in the woods," Allison murmured. A soft explosion of air rushed past her lips. "Have you told the sheriff?"

"Yeah. I talked to him before I came up." More laughter drifted in through the open window. Toni paused, letting it fade. "I know this… situation isn't exactly what you'd planned."

"No, it isn't," Allison admitted. Plans could change in a heartbeat, though, couldn't they? The wind shifts and the clouds rush in. The air sparks and hums, and before you can even think about running, you're standing in the middle of a storm.

Her gaze roamed the cozy bedroom—hardwood floors in decent shape, a fresh coat of paint on the walls. In a few days, Paul's crew would begin transforming the musty, unused space in the workshop out back into a light-filled studio where she could sculpt, create.

"It isn't," she repeated quietly, "but I think it's what I need."

"Okay." Toni gave her an easy grin. "I'll remember that when it's your turn to weed the flowerbed out front, or—"

"Rake the leaves," Allison finished with a wan smile, looking out the window at the large oak tree that shaded the back lawn.

"Yeah. Definitely that. I don't do rakes—as a rule." Toni sobered. "Ray was just heading out the door when I spoke to him. He'll be here any minute now." Her focus latched onto Allison and lingered there. "If you're not ready to talk to him, we can wait."

Allison shook her head. "I can't avoid him forever." She had to listen to whatever the sheriff had worked through, had to sort it out in her own mind. And then put it all behind her.

Squaring her shoulders, she shut the window, then glanced toward the workshop at the edge of the property. And froze.

"Tell me again what you think you saw." The sheriff's gaze locked onto Allison like a beam as he settled into the chair across from her.

She shifted on the sofa, stroking Jack's large head when he nudged her hand with his nose and whined. Beside her, Paul stirred, and gave her arm a gentle squeeze just as Toni stopped pacing. Jenna leaned back in the overstuffed chair, pale gray eyes focused on Allison.

Allison sighed. "Sheriff, I—"

He held a hand up. "It's Ray."

She nodded. "Ray. I didn't imagine it."

"I wasn't saying you did. But the door to the workshop was padlocked, the windows locked. Nothing inside but a few shelves, some paint cans."

When he slanted Toni a look, she scowled. "Before you ask—again—the answer is still no. No one else has a key to the padlock. It's new—I just bought it the other day, to keep the building locked at night once they start construction." She shoved her hand into the front pocket of her jeans and plopped down on the loveseat. "At the risk of being repetitive, I'll mention—*again*—that Allison has the duplicate key."

Ray gave her a withering stare before turning back to Allison. "If I had to guess, I'd say you just happened to turn at the right time, caught the sunlight reflecting off a window."

Yes. A wink of light. Sunlight bouncing off the glass. The quick surprise of it had just startled her.

And that, Allison told herself, was just plain crap. The light on the other side of the window had winked in and out, but for a few seconds, it had floated.

How long had it taken her to accept the idea that the psychological shock of Ken's death had awakened a latent ability in her?

Over two long years.

She could see and talk to the dead. Not always, just, apparently, when she was needed. Or—when it was what *she* needed, Allison realized. When Ken had first appeared to her, she'd been out of her mind with grief, her own soul draining away, one tear, one sob, at a time.

It still terrified her, the thought of moving into that realm of shadows, but she couldn't run from it, not anymore.

There were times, though—and this was one of them—when she should probably keep what she had seen to herself.

"I think you're right. I'm sorry."

No one but Allison and Jenna seemed to notice the flicker in Toni's eyes. Paul covered Allison's hand with his. "After what you've been through, you're entitled to be edgy."

"That's a fact." Ray paused, keeping his gaze trained on Allison. "I spoke to your father today about the man he sent here to keep an eye on you."

"For all the good that did," Paul said flatly.

Allison shared a glance with him—a wordless agreement—as the last vestige of stubborn anger rippled through her. Her dad had admitted to placing a man here in Dawson Mills weeks before she had moved into the house. The only thing that had kept her fury from exploding was the stitches in her side.

Then the sheriff had told her about Harold Rush.

Her mind whisked her back to Nashville. She stepped out of Alain's Gallery, huddled in her wool coat against the icy December chill as she hurried across the dimly lighted parking lot. Then the dark cloth snapped over her head. A sharp, steel tip at her throat, filthy hands groping her.

With an inward shudder, Allison shook off the memory. Rush was back in custody. Thank God.

Her dad hadn't been aware that Rush had escaped. Still, she understood why he'd felt the need to protect her, but it damned well didn't mean she had to like the idea of being watched.

"Trevor Wilcox. He's been with Dad's company for years."

Ray nodded. "At the moment, no one seems to know where he is."

Allison frowned. "I thought he went back to Nashville."

"Maybe not," Toni said, and got a sharp look from Ray. "You remember I told you a while back I was working on something that required most of my focus. There's a chance Wilcox might be involved."

Allison didn't like where this was headed. "Involved—with what? How?"

"*'How'* is the question. As for the 'what,' well—" Toni glanced at Ray. "I'm afraid that's something I'll have to keep to myself."

Silence dropped like a lead weight. Paul sighed. "Tell me this, Allison's connection to Wilcox—any chance it could put her in danger?"

"I doubt it."

"But you're not sure." The quiet tone held just enough of an edge to spark a steely warning from Ray.

"Back off, Bradford."

Allison put her hand on Paul's arm when he stiffened, and shook her head. Now wasn't the time.

"We don't want to speculate at this point." Ray frowned at the long look Jenna sent his way. "I just wanted you to be aware of the situation. If you should see him—"

"I'll call you," Allison promised. "Immediately."

For the last twenty minutes or so, everything around Allison had seemed to stand still while her mind was held hostage in a dazed grip. She forced herself to focus as Ray finished telling them about Jared Atkins and the woman, Jessie Conner.

Murdered.

She'd known that much. But before now, the sheriff hadn't given her the details.

The monster who had called himself Neil Brady had ended their lives in the same barn where he had caged Allison deep under the ground. Probably while she was sleeping in her own bed.

Allison took a long drink of the iced tea Jenna had brought in after getting the dog settled upstairs. Shifting closer to Paul on the sofa, she caught the glances passing between everyone. "You knew. All of you."

"Not at first," Paul said. "I assumed the man I saw coming out of the barn was Atkins. But—" He gripped her hand. "There's only one thing that matters now. The blood I found in the loft wasn't yours."

That, Allison realized, was the simple truth of it.

Ray leaned forward in the chair. "I never would have believed Ellie Atkins had a hand in this, but the drug used on you and Stan Michaels came from the hospital where she works. Supervisor there verified the inventory in the supply cabinet was off." He shook his head. "She must have regretted getting involved with Brady. We believe she was headed to relatives in Memphis before he stopped her."

Regret, maybe. The softer, anxious voice that had floated toward Allison in the tunnel, when her mind had first begun struggling through the drug-induced haze, had held just a hint of remorse. A stab of conscience that had forced Ellie Atkins to risk leaving the meager bit of food, along with the water and flashlight, the wire cutters, under the filthy mattress.

Sunlight drifted through the window that faced west, bathing the hardwood floor in a golden hue. She recalled the stick-thin, mousy woman standing on her doorstep, frail, skeletal fingers trembling as they wandered up to a button on her worn and faded dress. The ugly, yellowing bruise her makeup couldn't quite mask.

Had Ellie Atkins ever had the chance to do anything *but* get involved?

"Do you think she knows about her husband?"

Ray frowned. "I doubt it. She's still in a coma."

Trapped in a dark void, with her mind screaming to get out. No one would hear. Allison shuddered. The sheriff had told them earlier that, on impulse, Lilly Jameson had stopped in to check on Mrs. Atkins after dropping Paul's grandmother at home. Ms.

Jameson had suffered a hard beating, had lost consciousness, but she had eventually come to.

Lucky. If you could call it that.

"If Lilly hadn't walked in on Brady when she did," Toni noted, "Ellie Atkins wouldn't have survived."

Allison took a slow sip from her glass. "I wonder why either of them did. Survive, I mean."

"He... panicked." Jenna fixed her pale gray eyes onto Ray.

He held her gaze for a long moment. "That would be my guess. We found them in one of the outbuildings on Atkins' property, bound and gagged." Ray glanced at Paul. "Next to the four-wheeler and trailer we figured Brady used to haul you through the woods."

Paul reached around to the back of his head where Brady had waylaid him. "He dealt with the women, then headed straight for the cabin." He flashed a bitter smile. "Son of a bitch would have killed me if he'd made it there a couple minutes earlier."

Everything inside her went rigid. Allison tried to shove back the horrible image of Paul's body slumped onto a dirty floor, blank eyes staring up.

"But he didn't," Paul told her softly. "He didn't get to me."

Ray nodded. "You beat him at his own game. And for what it's worth, according to Ms. Jameson, Ellie Atkins met Jared sometime in the early eighties."

"So she wasn't aware of what happened with Mother and Katie."

"That's right. At the root of it, she was in a bad situation with Atkins, needed money. My guess is Brady offered her a way out."

"The diamonds," Toni said. "Now that you've found them— what next?"

"Legally they belong to the men who were killed. I imagine they'll go to the next of kin." Ray shifted his focus back to Allison. "We had to shovel through twelve feet of cave-in. At least Brady had the good sense to put the stones in a pouch. Statue was shattered."

Shattered. The same went for the lives that had crossed paths with those damned stones.

Allison got a mental flash of her sister trembling and crouched behind the bushes as Jared—wild-eyed, probably drunk—murdered their mother. Neil erupting in a rage. A large rough hand darting down, grabbing the rock. Slamming that rock against Neil's head.

Had their mother drawn her last breath by then? Or had the final, dying part of her held some small measure of awareness?

She took a slow, ragged breath. "Neil was unconscious when Katie and Josh were killed. He really didn't know the bodies were down there with me."

"Maybe," Ray conceded. "Brady thought Atkins had lied about killing your sister. One good reason in that twisted mind of his to get rid of the old man. That and we believe Atkins and his girlfriend intended to get their hands on the diamonds."

Toni frowned. "I don't get how Atkins thought he'd have a snowball's chance of finding the stones after all these years. I mean, he couldn't have believed that Allison was Katie."

Ray hunched his shoulders. "You got me there."

"Enough booze in him," Paul muttered, "Atkins would go for just about anything."

The look Ray gave him said, *There is that.*

Toni's mouth curved. "Other than the diamonds, what was Brady's connection to Atkins?"

"Cousins." The stunned silence had Ray dipping his head in a nod. "Brady was a drifter, went back and forth between areas of Tennessee and North Carolina, Virginia. Few weeks ago, he got into a bar fight in North Carolina, nearly killed a man. He stole a truck, switched the plates, and landed here."

"Seclusion," Toni said. "And an area he was familiar with. Given their history, I don't imagine Atkins would have turned Brady out."

"No. But that connection stretches back long before the incident at the creek. At one point, they worked together on a construction site—the old Savings and Loan outside of town." Ray glanced over as Paul swore.

"I remember now. Dad gave them a job—cleanup crew. Mom picked me up from school. We stopped by the site, caught Brady and Atkins stealing tools out of one of the gang boxes. That was a couple of years before—"

He didn't have to say it. Before Allison's mother made the ill-fated choice of packing her two young daughters off and climbing into the car with a monster.

To give her husband time to cool down.

That was the irony, wasn't it? Allison's dad had been shocked about Katie, but had accepted the child. What he hadn't been able to get past was his wife's insistence on defending the girl's father.

A violent argument sparked by senseless, petty jealousy.

Although she didn't doubt for a second that sheer pride and stubbornness on her mother's part had escalated an already tense situation.

"Sheriff—Ray, were you able to locate Katie's father?"

"Not yet. We know he was living in New York at the time his mother passed. That's about as close as we've come."

A lot of people to wade through, Allison thought. A lot of years between then and now. Her dad had promised he would see to it that Katie and her mother would rest beside one another in the family cemetery. She wasn't sure whether Katie's father would care. He had never wanted her. But the man had a right to know.

"I'm still puzzled about something." Ray paused. "You were able to identify the remains in the cavern before our forensics team could even think about getting in there."

Toni rolled her eyes. The sheriff either didn't notice, or chose just to let it go. "Our M.E., Doc Johnson, confirmed that one of the minor victim's arms had been broken but was never set. How could you have known about that?"

Allison managed a wan smile. "I've told you everything that happened."

Ray just shook his head. "I don't believe in any of the paranormal nonsense. But—" He glanced at Jenna. "It's getting harder to ignore."

"Now that," Toni noted with a huge grin, "is a statement definitely worth putting on the record."

"I wouldn't." Ray locked eyes with her.

Before they both could stare each other down until the world threatened to end, or Hell froze over, whichever came first, Allison asked about the one lost soul that had seemed to fall off everyone's radar. "Do you think you'll be able to find out what happened to Helen?"

Ray sighed. "Honestly? I can't say. But we've dug up the old case file. We'll comb through it."

He got up to leave, and Toni was right behind him. "I'll walk out with you."

Nodding, Ray started for the door, then stopped, turned. "Allison?"

"Yes?"

"I can promise I'll damned well give it my best."

That, she thought as the door shut softly behind them, was good enough.

EPILOGUE

One Week Later

WITH HER BIG DOG CURLED up on his bed, quietly snoring over the soggy remnants of a rawhide bone, Allison settled into one of the wicker chairs on the back deck. The last of the late-afternoon sun's golden light shifted across the lawn in a narrow slant. She closed her eyes for a moment as a lazy breeze brushed over her face, remembering Steve's soft breath-of-a-whisper in her ear last night.

Her eyes had fluttered open to see him standing beside her bed. For Steve, dying had been like having his favorite song switched off, mid-tune. He'd had to get past the disappointment, the anger, before he could accept that he was exactly where he needed to be.

He'd told her not to worry.

I'm all right, Sis. Really.

Allison blinked back a tear. He'd faded away before she'd had the chance to tell him that with Jeff's help, Tammy was keeping the studio up and running, keeping Steve's dream alive. Later, when she'd thought about it for a while, she'd realized her brother must have known that.

There was a period afterward—she hadn't been able to get back to sleep—when she'd stood gazing out her bedroom window. It had dawned on her as the morning light slowly brought the world into focus—the quick jerk of Katie's head just before she had vanished with Josh and his little dog, Scooter, her gaze darting toward the darkness past Allison as she'd sensed the monster who had called himself Neil. *He's coming.*

She had known.

Psychic abilities tended to reach back through generations, often passed down from mother to daughter. Hadn't she read that somewhere?

But without the help of a living relative, the history would be impossible to trace.

She glanced up when Paul stepped out of the workshop. He gave her one of those easy smiles that made her heart stutter, and jotted something down on his notepad. Allison smiled back at him as he moved toward her, the low light casting a warm glow over his bronzed skin. It was good to see his healthy color back, his arm finally free of the sling.

He bent over, gave her a light kiss before settling into the chair next to her. "I'm assuming Toni's left for the airport."

Nodding, Allison checked her watch. "About twenty minutes ago." She couldn't help but grin at the memory of it. Jenna had booked an evening flight home, so they wouldn't have to rush. Just as they were walking out the door, Ray had shown up, off duty, relaxed in jeans and a snug T-shirt that made the most of his broad chest. Insisting that he drive them to the airport.

When Toni launched into a one-sided debate—her Mustang was perfectly capable of getting them to where they needed to go— he'd just smiled and nodded, then ushered them out to his Jeep.

The sheriff was totally gone over her.

Did she know?

Of course, she did.

A small alarm sounded inside her when a frown began inching its way over Paul's face. "What is it?"

His lips curved—a bit edgy, she thought. "Toni asked me if I'd be working the construction end on the development outside

337

of town. Told her I'd declined to bid, because of the impact to the local landowners." He paused, eyes narrowed. "Didn't take much to notice she was relieved to hear that. Whatever's going on there, could be that your dad's man—Trevor Wilcox—somehow ties into it."

The deep sigh that rushed from her left her feeling drained. She wasn't ready to deal with this. Not yet.

"I'm sorry." He brushed a stray curl away from her face. "Let's talk about something else. I've got an additional crew coming over in the morning. Your studio should be finished in a couple of weeks." Through the beat of silence, she could feel his gaze on her. "It'll be good for you to get back to work."

Allison nodded. Work was exactly what she needed. The Atlanta showing at Maison's had been postponed until October. By then the air would be crisp, the trees a blaze of orange and red and burnished gold. It would take the lion's share of the days between now and then to pour her spiritual self into the focal piece—a sculpted image of the Giant Oak she'd found at the creek's edge. Allison's face, together with her sister's—wide, sad eyes that held a spark of hope, the young face, innocence marred with scratches—would fill the oval spot in the center of the trunk.

Into the Light. A new theme. Because life, real, or imagined, shouldn't reflect a nightmarish existence through a landscape of darkness.

Life was about finding your place in the world. And resolution.

Eventually, Allison would have to send the diary to Bobbie Jean's son, wouldn't she? He deserved the chance to find his own truth and make peace with it.

She sat there with Paul in comfortable silence while the last of the day slipped into twilight. Out on the lawn, a cricket chirped, and in the shadows behind the window at the front of the workshop, a light winked on. Then vanished.

Allison glanced at Paul. He'd turned his face up to the first glittering pinpoints of starlight. Behind the window, the light winked again.

A weak spirit struggling to get her attention. She'd wondered if she would see it again.

Had her mother's spirit been that fragile?

Run... Maybe the energy it had taken to project that single, frantic thought into Katie's head was all that had been left of their mother.

A sigh shuddered out of her.

"Hey." Paul took her hand. "Are you all right?"

For a long while, Allison gazed into his deep blue eyes, saw the turns in her own path reflected there. Then smiled. "I will be."

FROM THE AUTHOR

Dear Readers,

Thank you so much for taking this paranormal journey with me! If you enjoyed reading Lost Girl, please consider leaving a review on Amazon. No need to get fancy with words, just a few short sentences will do. Reviews help authors more than you can imagine.

For new release updates, cover reveals, and more, please subscribe to my Newsletter: *http://newsletter.annefrancisscott.com*

Thanks so much for reading,
Anne

ALSO BY
ANNE FRANCIS SCOTT

Lost Souls
(Book Two of The Lost Trilogy)

ABOUT ANNE

Anne is a Readers' Favorite award finalist author in paranormal fiction. She has a fascination for haunted houses, ancient cemeteries, and ghostly mysteries. Those passions fuel her writing, giving her the chance to take readers to an otherworldly place and leave them there for a while. She hopes that journey is a good one...

If you'd like to know more about Anne, visit her website, where she talks (okay, maybe rambles a little) about her personal paranormal experiences.

http://www.annefrancisscott.com/about-anne.html

Made in the USA
Middletown, DE
04 August 2020